I0775124

IRRESISTIBLY
Wicked

THE WICKEDS: DARK KNIGHTS AT BAYSIDE

MELISSA FOSTER

This is a work of fiction. The events and characters described herein are imaginary and are not intended to refer to specific places or living persons. The opinions expressed in this manuscript are solely the opinions of the author and do not represent the opinions or thoughts of the publisher. The author has represented and warranted full ownership and/or legal right to publish all the materials in this book.

IRRESISTIBLY WICKED
All Rights Reserved.
Copyright © 2025 Melissa Foster
V1.0

MELISSA FOSTER® and WORLD LITERARY PRESS® are registered trademarks of Melissa Foster. All Rights Reserved.

This book may not be reproduced, transmitted, or stored in whole or in part by any means, including graphic, electronic, or mechanical without the express written consent of the publisher except in the case of brief quotations embodied in critical articles and reviews.

The author reserves all rights to license use of this work for generative AI training and development of machine learning language models. The author expressly prohibits any entity from using any part of this publication, including text and graphics, for purposes of training artificial intelligence (AI) technologies to generate text, graphics, or images, including without limitation, technologies that are capable of generating works in the same style, voice, or otherwise significantly similar tone and/or story as this publication.

Cover Design: Elizabeth Mackey Designs
Cover Photography: Michelle Lancaster, @lanefotograf

WORLD LITERARY PRESS

A Note to Readers

Get ready to fall for one of my absolute favorite playboys, Zander Wicked. He's been a salacious flirt since we first met him in *Bayside Desires*, and I wondered if he'd ever whisper in my ear to settle down. Zander lives a fast life, on his motorcycle, on the job, and with women. But one split second shatters his world and forces him to face the kind of truths he's spent a lifetime outrunning. Life-altering events often lead to revelations, and Zander's leads him down his own path, which is riddled with unexpected obstacles. I adore this story, and I hope you will, too.

If this is your first Melissa Foster book, while interconnected, all Love in Bloom stories are written to stand alone, so dive right in and enjoy the ride.

Be sure to check out my online bookstore for exclusive discounts on ebooks, print books, audiobooks, early releases, bundles, and more. Ebooks can be read on the e-reader of your choice, and audiobooks can be listened to on the free and easy-to-use BookFunnel app. Shop.MelissaFoster.com

Don't forget to sign up for my newsletter so you never miss a release. MelissaFoster.com/news

About the Love in Bloom Big-Family Romance Collection

Love in Bloom is the universe in which all of Melissa's series take place. Although many series interconnect, so you never miss an engagement, wedding, or birth, all Love in Bloom books are written to stand alone and may also be enjoyed as part of the larger series.

Where to Start

You can start with any book or series without feeling a step behind. If you are an avid reader and enjoy long series, you may enjoy starting with the very first Love in Bloom novel, *Sisters in Love*, and then reading through all the series in the collection in publication order. Melissa offers free downloadable series checklists, publication schedules, family trees, maps, and more on her website.

Save on Bundles in All Formats & Enjoy Early Releases
Only from Melissa's Online Bookstore
Shop.MelissaFoster.com

See the Entire Love in Bloom Collection
MelissaFoster.com/love-bloom-series

Download Series Checklists, Family Trees, and Publication Schedules
MelissaFoster.com/rg

Download Free First-in-Series eBooks
MelissaFoster.com/free-ebooks

Playlist

"Fix You" by Coldplay

"Rise Up" by Andra Day

"I'll Be There" by Jess Glynne

"Hold On" by Wilson Phillips

"Unsteady" by X Ambassadors

"Unstoppable" by Sia

"I Won't Give Up" by Christina Grimmie

"Believer" by Imagine Dragons

"Hold On (Change is Comin')" by Sounds of Blackness

"Keep Holding On" by Avril Lavigne

"Roots" by Grace Davies

"Manchild" by Sabrina Carpenter

"Pink Pony Club" by Chappell Roan

"Quarter to Midnight" by Jeremy Elliot

"Big Plans" by Why Don't We

"Your Love Is My Drug" by Kesha

"Rock and a Hard Place" by Bailey Zimmerman

"Soulmate" by Chanin

"Without You With Me" by Matt Hansen

"Thank Me for That" by Tyler Braden

"I Wanna Be the One You Call" by Benson Boone

"Never Stop (Wedding Version)" by SafetySuit

"Cooped Up / Return of the Mack" by Post Malone, Mark Morrison, Sidekick

"Worst Way" by Riley Green
"You Are in Love (Taylor's Version)" by Taylor Swift
"Kiss Me" by Dermot Kennedy
"Mystical Magical" by Benson Boone
"Sorry I'm Here for Someone Else" by Benson Boone
"Azizam" by Ed Sheeran
"Greedy" by Tate McRae
"Snap Yo Fingers" by Lil Jon, E-40, Sean Paul
"Something to Help" by Dean Lewis
"Life with You" by Kelsey Hart
"Heaven" by Niall Horan
"Haters" by Television Skies
"Lose Control" by Teddy Swims
"Apt." by Rosé and Bruno Mars
"Steal the Show" by Lauv
"Mess Me Up" by Gary Allan
"Beautiful Things" by Benson Boone
"First Time" by Matt Hansen
"Timeless (Taylor's Version)" by Taylor Swift
"The Weight" by The Band
"The Sound of Silence" by Disturbed
"Riders on the Storm" by The Doors
"Say Don't Go (Taylor's Version)" by Taylor Swift
"Love Someone" by Brett Eldredge
"Fall Into Me" by Forest Blakk
"Love You a Little Bit" by Tanner Adell
"Closer" by Nine Inch Nails
"Kiss the Girl" by Brent Morgan
"You Are the Right One" by Sports
"Hallelujah" by Jeff Buckley

"Water Under the Bridge" by Adele

"I Had Some Help" by Post Malone, featuring Morgan Wallen

"This Is Home" by Cavetown

"A Place We Knew" by Dean Lewis

"(Kissed You) Good Night" by Gloriana

"Yellow" by Coldplay

"The Scientist" by Coldplay

"Back to You" by Selena Gomez

"All I Ever Do" by Adrien Nunez

"Fallin' for You" by Colbie Caillat

"If You Want Love" by NF

"Walked Through Hell" by Anson Seabra

"I Guess I'm in Love" by Clinton Kane

"Pour Some Sugar on Me" by Def Leppard

"Anyone" by Justin Bieber

"Love Me Back" by Max McNown

"More Than Words" by Extreme

"Tennessee Orange" by Megan Moroney

"Feels Like This" by Ingrid Andress

"Latch" by Natalie Taylor

"Hurtless" by Dean Lewis

"Human" by Christina Perri

"We All Need Someone" by The Strumbellas

"Run to You" by Lea Michele

"Uptown Funk" by Mark Ronson, featuring Bruno Mars

Chapter One

ZANDER WICKED DRIFTED out of a dream, greeted by the scents of perfume and sex and the warmth of two soft womanly bodies draped over him. Just the way he liked it. He opened his eyes, trying to get his brain to focus on the unfamiliar room and remember the names of last night's playmates. *Katie and Miranda? Or was it Megan?* He'd gone out after church, which was what the Dark Knights motorcycle club called their Wednesday-night meetings. The evening came rushing back in a blur of tequila shots, dancing, and a hell of a good time with the buxom blonde and curvy redhead.

Blondie's hand slid down his stomach, and she murmured, *"Morning."*

"Let's make it a good one. Don't stop there," he coaxed, earning an appreciative sound as she kissed her way down his body. The redhead snuggled closer, and he palmed her ass, turning to kiss her as his cell phone rang somewhere beside the bed. *"Fuck."*

"I'm up for that," Red said as he leaned over her in search of his phone, her lips finding his chest.

"Let it ring," Blondie complained, trying to tug him back down to the mattress.

He snagged his phone from the nightstand, unsure how it got there, and saw his older brother Zeke's name on the screen right below the time, *7:20*. *"Shit."* He bolted off the bed. "I gotta go." Zander was known for fucking around in his personal life, but he worked for his family's business, Cape Renovations, and he took that work seriously.

"Wouldn't it be more fun to *come* and *then* go?" Red taunted.

"Yes, it would," he said as he tugged on his jeans. "But my alarm didn't go off, and I'm late for work."

Red rolled onto her back and stretched, thrusting her breasts out. "I turned it off."

"Why the hell did you do that?" he barked.

"It kept buzzing, and I was tired. It's New Year's Eve."

"Not yet, it's not." He uttered a curse, put on his socks, and shoved his feet into his boots, scanning the clothes strewn across the floor for his T-shirt, flannel, and cut—his leather vest with the club patches on the back.

"Let's exchange numbers and hook up tonight," Blondie suggested.

"Yeah. Call us when you're off work," Red chimed in as he pulled on his T-shirt. "We can ring in the New Year right."

Zander raked a hand through his hair, flashing the cocky grin that had gotten him more than his fair share of favors. "I could lie and say I'll call, but as I mentioned last night, that's not how I roll." He didn't want to get tangled up in any strings and never went home with the same woman twice. Three of his four siblings and all of his local cousins had gotten engaged or married over the last few years, and he was happy for them, but he wasn't built for that kind of life. He loved everything about women, from their supple bodies and creative brains to their femininity and sass, too much to settle for just one. He was happy to be the good-time guy they fucked around with before they committed to a ball and chain.

"Maybe I'll see ya around sometime. Happy New Year." He tossed them a wink, grabbing his flannel and cut on his way out the door.

Assaulted by the cold New England air, he put on his flannel and tossed his cut onto the passenger seat of his Challenger with his guitar as he climbed behind the wheel.

He called Zeke as he pulled out of the driveway. Zeke was a year older than him and was his only remaining single sibling. Like their oldest brother, Blaine, they shared their father's tall, broad stature, dark hair, and blue eyes. Their brother Justin, who went by the road name Maverick, was adopted, but he must have been destined to be a Wicked, because he looked a lot like the rest of them. Growing up in a biker family, they also shared their father's love of the club. Fierce loyalty and protectiveness were ingrained in their souls, but that's where their likenesses ended. Blaine could be a bossy asshole, Justin was artistic and good-natured, and while Zander was impetuous with a filter that left a lot to be desired by others, Zeke was level-headed and methodical, always thinking of ramifications to others before taking action. He'd saved Zander's ass more times than he could count, and he was the only reason Zander had graduated from high school—a fact Zander still carried guilt over.

"Dude, where the hell are you?" Zeke fumed before Zander could get a word out. "Tobias and I have been waiting on your ass for forty minutes to install the support beam." Tobias Riggs, their sister Madigan's fiancé, also worked for their family's business.

"Sorry, man. I'm not far," Zander said. "I met these chicks at Undercover last night, and I had no idea one of them turned off my alarm this morning."

"Jesus, Zander. I thought you were making it an early night after church."

"I did. We got back to their place before ten."

"Maybe you should save threesomes for the weekends."

Zander chuckled. "Sorry, bro, but when the ladies want to play, I'm *not* walking away. And don't give me shit. You know I never miss work unless I'm too sick to move." The few times that had happened, Zeke had been there to clean up his puke and make sure he didn't get dehydrated.

"Just get your ass here, will ya?" Zeke gritted out.

"On my way. Is Preacher there yet?" Preacher was their father's road name.

"What do you think?"

Shit. Their father was a tough, tattooed biker and renovations expert. He and his brother Conroy had founded the Bayside chapter of the Dark Knights decades ago, and all their sons were proud members. At six-plus feet tall, with slicked-back black-and-silver hair, pitch-black brows giving him an intimidating stare, and a trim beard, their father exuded an air of authority that few would defy. But like all the Wickeds, beneath that rough exterior was a heart of gold, doling out stern life lessons with compassion and teaching through actions, not anger. But no matter how much he loved his son, at thirty years old Zander had no business pulling shit like this, and he knew he'd have his ass handed to him for being late.

"We told Preach you were bringing doughnuts and coffee," Zeke said.

Zander grinned. Like their grandfather, their father had a

serious sweet tooth. A few Boston cream doughnuts, combined with Zander's ability to charm his way out of any situation, would help take the edge off their father's irritation. "Thanks for the save, man. See you soon."

He ended the call as he drove through an intersection, and never saw the silver pickup barreling through the red light until it was too late.

"WHERE'S THE FUCKING money, Shauna?" Brian hollered through the phone. "I can't show up empty-handed."

Shauna Flores bristled against the attack from her childhood-best-friend-turned-boyfriend-turned-roommate, gripping the steering wheel tighter despite being stopped at a traffic light. They had a long history of partying together to escape their volatile home lives, a pattern they'd carried forward for too many years, but they'd worked hard and had fought their way *out* of that mess. She'd thought for good. They'd both been sober for three and a half years, but Brian had fallen off the wagon a few weeks ago when shit had gone down at work and he lost his job. She knew what it took to fight addiction, and she was trying to be supportive rather than judgmental, but she was almost a year into her career as an EMT, and she was never going back to that destructive lifestyle.

"I told you I don't think you should go to that party. I don't care what John says. You know he's still using, and you shouldn't be around him. Especially no—" She gasped in horror as a silver pickup plowed into the side of a car in a horrifying collision of crushing metal and shattering glass in the middle of the intersection, sending the car careening on two wheels off the road and flipping as it rolled down the embankment.

As an EMT, instinct had her ending the call with Brian and calling 911 as she grabbed her seatbelt cutter from the glove pocket on the door and flew out of her car to get her first aid kit and crowbar from the trunk. Tires screeched as the truck fled the scene, and she sprinted across the debris-covered road toward the gully.

Thick, dark smoke billowed from the engine of the upside-down car, which was leaning toward the crushed passenger side, one tire spinning. Her heart thundered as she ran down the hill, scanning the surrounding area for bodies, but there was only debris.

She ran to the driver's side, needing to get the people out before the car caught fire. The window was shattered, the airbag blocking her view. She heard moaning coming from inside.

"Hello? Can you hear me?" she shouted, working fast to clear away the glass from the window with her winter gloves.

"Yes!" a panicked male voice answered as she tore off her gloves, catching sight of the lucky number four tattooed on her left hand between her thumb and index finger.

If ever she needed luck, it was now. She cut away the airbag using the seatbelt cutter, and the driver came into view, hanging upside down, trapped by the seatbelt, a piece of metal lodged in his side. She did a quick visual assessment. *Male, thirtyish, lacerations on his face, bleeding from his head and his left side.* She tore away the airbag and looked for passengers, but didn't see anyone else in the vehicle. "I'm Shauna. I'm an EMT, and I'm going to get you out of here. What's your name?"

"There's smoke!" Struggling against the seatbelt, his eyes wide with panic, he shouted, *"Get me out!"*

She was working on it. He was a big man, and it would be nearly impossible to get him out the window safely with that metal in his side. "Don't worry. I'm going to get you out. Can you tell me your name?" She'd have to pry the door open.

Fighting against the seatbelt, he yelled, *"I don't...help me!"*

She grabbed the crowbar and got to work, trying to pry the door open. "I need you to stay as still as you can while I get this door open. What's your name?"

"Zeke," he said as she fought with all her might to open the door.

She'd traded lifting bottles for lifting weights and, more recently, had added pole-dancing classes to mix things up. Both of which gave her killer upper-body strength.

Zeke flailed, panicking and rambling incoherently as she fought to get the door open. She urged him to stay calm, but he continued fighting, and just as the door gave way, he went limp. *Fuck.* The smoke thickened.

"Zeke, can you hear me?" She needed to get him talking, conscious, and out of the vehicle. *"Zeke!"*

His eyes fluttered open as she grabbed the cutting tool for the seatbelt.

"That's it. What's your last name?" His eyes closed again. *"Zeke,* stay with me. Can you tell me your last name?"

He opened his mouth, but no words came.

Between the shock and his head trauma, she wasn't surprised by his inability to speak, but she didn't like it. "I'm going to cut the seatbelt and get you out of here. I'm sorry, but it's probably going to hurt." Stabilizing his head and shoulders as best she could, she cut the seatbelt and used all her strength to drag him out of the car.

He cried out in pain as his body hit the ground, but getting him farther away from the vehicle was imperative. She dragged him a few feet, slipping under his weight, causing another anguished cry. Flames ignited from the hood of the car, and Shauna dug the heels of her boots into the dirt, dragging him a safe distance from the wreckage.

He was shivering as she laid him in the grass, that freaking metal sticking out of his left side. Worried about hypothermia, she shrugged off her coat and placed it over his right side, quickly checking for a medical alert bracelet or necklace. "I need to get my first aid kit. Try not to move."

She sprinted back to the mangled car and peered inside to make sure she hadn't missed any other passengers. It was empty, except for a shattered guitar and a leather vest. She snagged the vest to put over him.

Rushing back, she shook out the vest to rid it of glass and laid it over him, taking in the DARK KNIGHTS patch above a skull with dark eyes, sharp brows, and a mouth full of jagged fangs, with a BAYSIDE CHAPTER patch beneath it. She didn't know much about the Dark Knights, but she knew they were an important part of the community, and they held all types of charity events.

"You're lucky you weren't on your motorcycle," she said as she put on sterile gloves from the first aid kit and withdrew the scissors.

He mumbled incoherently as she cut his T-shirt away from the metal and opened a package of gauze. "Zeke, do you know what day it is?" she asked as she used the gauze to try to stop the bleeding and stabilize the metal in his side.

He slurred a response.

"Can you tell me who the president is?"

He said something that sounded like "Preach," and then his

eyes rolled back in his head and his body went slack again.

"Wake up, Zeke!"

He didn't respond.

"Come on, Zeke. *Open your eyes,*" she ordered, relieved to finally hear sirens in the distance.

He remained still and silent, but he was breathing.

Using her knuckles, she applied pressure to his sternum, and he cried out. Relief swamped her. "I need you to stay awake." She grabbed more gauze, trying desperately to stop the bleeding in his side. "Where were you headed this morning?"

He groaned, his eyes closing again.

"Tell me about your motorcycle. I bet it's cool, huh?" She had to keep him talking.

His eyes fluttered open and locked on hers, stealing her breath for a split second before those deep pools of blue brimmed with fear, pleading as he weakly panted out, *"Don't…let me…go."*

Her chest constricted, an unfamiliar choke of emotion stealing her voice. There was something familiar in his eyes, something tugging at her. She tried to break that chokehold but was unable. *What the hell? Get your shit together, Shauna.*

"You're not going anywhere, big guy. Not on my watch." She hoped to hell that was true, but she was worried about his blood loss. "We're going to get through this together. You hear me?"

He mumbled incoherently.

"I've got you, Zeke. Just stay awake. We music buffs have to stick together. What kind of music do you like?" He mumbled again as she grabbed more gauze. She began singing her go-to song when she needed strength, "Keep Holding On" by Avril Lavigne, hoping it would give him strength, too.

Moments later the first responders arrived, a different crew from her own since it wasn't her jurisdiction. As the firefighters headed for the wreckage, Shauna brought the medics up to speed, reluctantly stepping back as they stabilized Zeke. She felt uneasy, like she was breaking a promise. *Don't...let me...go.* She'd heard things like that plenty of times from people in crisis and had no idea why it hit differently this time.

She kept an eye on Zeke as she gave the police a description of the accident and the truck that had hit him. When the ambulance drove away, she couldn't shake the feeling that she should have gone with him.

She turned back to the scene. The flames were out, the police and firemen milling about, doing their jobs. She went to get her coat, which was lying beside a bloody patch of grass where Zeke had lain. That's when the gravity of what had happened hit her, and the breath rushed from her lungs. She hadn't even realized she'd been holding it. She'd handled dozens of emergencies that were worse than this one, but this was the first she'd handled on her own, without any time to mentally prepare or get into the headspace of anticipating a tragedy, as she usually did when she arrived at work.

She felt like she'd run a marathon and prayed Zeke would be okay as she picked up her coat and found his leather vest beneath it. A lump lodged in her throat, and she pressed the coat and vest to her chest, pride gripping her. She'd handled it, and she hadn't flinched or floundered. She'd always thought she had it in her, but until now she hadn't known for sure. Her phone rang, startling her. She pulled it from her pocket, seeing Brian's name on the screen, and didn't think as she put it to her ear. "Hey."

"I need that money..."

She closed her eyes, accepting a pang of guilt as she tuned him out, unable to deal with the selfishness of addiction when she'd just been knee-deep in a life-and-death situation.

Chapter Two

AFTER A GRUELING twenty-four-hour shift, Shauna was whipped. The guys weren't kidding about New Year's Eve taking its toll, only they didn't know the additional burden she carried. Every time they were dispatched, she worried it would be for Brian, and she hated that feeling. It made her resentful that after all their hard work, Brian was right back at square one, which wasn't fair to him. She knew addiction was a demon that could sink its claws into a person and lure them back to the dark side without warning. It could do the same to her at any time, and if the tables were turned, she had no doubt that Brian would never give up on her.

Even with all of that going on, she hadn't been able to stop thinking about the guy she'd helped on her way to work. Those pleading blue eyes and the desperation in his voice—*Don't...let me...go*—still had her in a chokehold. The strange feeling that she shouldn't have left him had stuck like glue, too, an urgent voice in the back of her mind refusing to be ignored. As if her promise carried more weight than it ever had before. She didn't like not having complete control over her emotions and needed to put whatever this was to rest.

"You did great today," her partner, Howie Glazer, a short,

stocky paramedic with military-shorn red hair and an affable personality, said as he closed his locker.

"Thanks."

He grabbed his bag and smirked. "But you might want to brush up on your cooking skills before our next shift."

The crew took turns with firehouse chores, including cooking. The guys were always giving her shit about her mediocre cooking skills, and she gave it right back to them, all in fun, of course. "The way you shoveled the food into your mouth, I doubt you tasted a thing."

He laughed and shook his head as he headed out the door. "See ya in a few days, Flores." They worked a schedule of twenty-four hours on, then forty-eight hours off before reporting back for their next shift.

She put her belongings in her duffel bag and grabbed her coat before heading downstairs. As she came around the corner, she nearly bumped into the firehouse captain, Rodney Chaney. "Whoa. Sorry, Cap."

Cap was a tall Black man with a trim gray goatee and the kind of face that could be stern as stone or warm as a summer day, depending on his mood. He was one of her favorite people and one of the biggest reasons she'd become an EMT.

"That's all right. I know you're anxious to get out of here." A broad smile stretched across his face. "Congratulations. You survived your first New Year's Eve with us. How did it feel?"

That was a loaded question for her, and he knew it. "Pretty freaking awesome. It made me even more grateful to be on the right side of things."

"This job will do that for you."

So do you and the rest of the crew. She would be forever grateful for all of them.

Shauna had never had a family that took care of each other the way Cap and the guys at the firehouse did. She didn't grow up with role models to help build her self-esteem or show her how to handle difficult situations. Her parents had been angry drunks who'd partied too often and had cared too little. Brian's parents had been just as bad. It had been her and Brian fending for themselves since they were little kids. They hadn't learned much from their parents, but they'd learned how to drink and smoke to escape their painful lives, which was probably one reason she and Brian had continued partying long after they'd left town the day they'd graduated from high school.

As anxious as they'd been to get away from their parents and carry out their big plans of making names for themselves doing God only knew what, they were still just scared kids, guarding their freedom and afraid to come out from under the familiar haze of too much alcohol and weed. Brian had gotten into heavier drugs on and off, but he didn't do them every day, and she had never done them at all. Somehow, in her young, convoluted mind, doing heavier drugs would make her exactly like her parents, as if she hadn't already fallen into that trap.

They'd continued living in that rebellious, scared-child state of mind, or what Shauna had later deemed their *escape state*, for a little more than two full years. Until the night of her twentieth birthday, July fourth, when she'd had nothing to show for those years but cottonmouth and a foggy mind. That night, when she was rip-roaring drunk, she'd told a stranger she didn't want to live that way anymore, and he'd said, *Then don't. Every minute of the day is a chance for change. Make this one yours.*

She'd taken his advice and had started partying less, trying to clean up her act so she could get started on her new life. It wasn't that hard for her to stop drinking or smoking, but Brian was still into partying, and his peer pressure made it more difficult. She'd been trying on her own for a while when she'd found Brian unresponsive in the dank bedroom they'd shared, in a house full of people with substance use issues and runaways. She'd called 911, frantic and sobbing on the inside but coherent and calm on the outside. It was all a blur after that, men rushing in, peppering her with questions, giving Brian Narcan as she pleaded with them to save him and not call the police. That was the night she'd met Captain Rodney Chaney. He'd spoken to her with compassion, not judgment, and had said, *We're here to help, not to give him a reason to do it again.*

She now knew that Cap said that to many people every year, hoping they'd find their way to a better life. She also knew he never saw most of those other people again. But she'd been so desperate for someone to see her and Brian as more than mirrored shadows of the only way of life they knew that his kindness, that olive branch, had been exactly what she'd needed to feel comfortable enough to seek him out and to try to find her way clear of her addiction.

That moment of kindness had also sparked the start of their friendship, which had led to his guiding hers and Brian's journeys to sobriety and his mentorship. As always happened when she thought about that time of her life, her emotions snuck up on her.

She cleared her throat and said, "I'd better get going."

"Give Brian my best. Is he feeling better?"

Guilt overshadowed those warmer emotions. Cap had invited her and Brian to Christmas dinner, but since Brian was drinking again, she'd said he had the flu. She hated lying to him. She just hadn't wanted him to worry, and she had faith that with her help Brian would come out from under the beast before it swallowed him whole.

"He's getting there. See you Sunday."

She headed out to her car, and as she climbed in behind the wheel, she saw Zeke's leather vest on the passenger seat. Her chest tightened. She should have taken it with her in the ambulance today and dropped it at the hospital during one of their calls, but she had been late to work and hadn't been thinking clearly.

Or maybe it was because whatever she'd felt when their eyes had connected was stronger than anything she'd ever felt before, and it had rattled her in the same way Brian's overdose had, which made no sense. She didn't know this Zeke guy, so why would she feel anything beyond the normal emotions she felt when she was helping anyone?

The question made it impossible to ignore what she'd been trying to deny since yesterday. She'd told him she wouldn't let him go, but what if he hadn't made it? Her stomach twisted. Maybe if she saw he was okay, she could finally get him out of her head. That leather vest was the perfect excuse to see him again.

She drove to the hospital and spoke with the emergency room desk clerk. The clerk couldn't find a patient named Zeke who had been brought in yesterday morning, but she tracked the time of admission to an Alexander Wicked, who was in the ICU.

Shauna headed up to the ICU. The waiting room was packed with dozens of solemn-faced women and men. Most of the men were wearing black leather vests with Dark Knights patches like Alexander's. She hoped that didn't mean he was holding on to life by a thread and made her way to speak with Teri, the unit coordinator at the desk.

Teri looked up from the computer and smiled. "Hi, Shauna."

"Hi. I was first on the scene for Alexander Wicked yesterday, and I came to drop off something that was left behind. He was in pretty bad shape. How's he doing?"

"Zander? He's got a fractured skull and a brain bleed. They've got him in a medically induced coma."

Shauna's chest constricted. "Oh, man. How bad is it?"

"They won't know until he's stable enough to bring him out of the coma. I heard he was totally out of it when they brought him in, combative and confused, didn't know where he was or what had happened."

"I guess that explains why he told me his name was Zeke."

"That's one of his brothers."

"What about internal injuries? He had a piece of metal lodged in his side."

"I heard about that. He got lucky. It wasn't deep enough to hit any vital organs, but he has a couple of broken ribs, one of which punctured a lung."

"He was lucky. I hope he's going to be okay."

"He'd better be. Did you see the waiting room?"

"*Yes.* It's packed. I thought visiting hours didn't start until ten."

"They don't. Most of them have been here since he came in yesterday morning."

Shauna couldn't imagine having that many people who cared about her. "He must be a special guy."

"He is. He's also a shameless flirt and a wicked charmer with a reputation for following through with every salacious comment he makes. Half the women around this town are crazy about him, but he *is* one of the good guys. All of the Dark

Knights are. My heart broke when I heard about Zander's accident."

The way Zander's pleading eyes had seared into Shauna's mind made it easy to believe that under different circumstances, they held more dangerous powers. "I'll throw a little extra luck out there for him. Is it okay if I put this in his room?" She held up his cut.

"Sure."

Teri gave her his room number, and Shauna headed down the hall.

When she stepped into Zander's room, a dull ache formed in her chest. He lay motionless beneath stark-white sheets. A ventilator tube protruded from his mouth, and another ran from his chest tube to a ventilator on the floor. An IV snaked up to a bag hanging beside the bed, and wires connected him to various monitors. The steady beeping of the monitors and the rhythmic knocks and whooshes of the ventilator underscored the severity of his situation.

She made her way closer, taking in his chiseled, scruff-covered jaw and angular nose. He had the kind of dark brows that drew attention to the blue eyes she couldn't see behind his closed lids, but she recalled them clear as day in her mind. His hair was longish on top, thick dark waves brushed away from the bandage on his bruised forehead, and the sides were closely shorn. When she was in work mode, things like looks didn't register, but she wasn't in work mode now. It was no wonder he was the town crush. Even banged up and bruised, he was incredibly handsome. She still couldn't shake the feeling that she knew him, but her mind must be playing tricks on her, because she couldn't remember the last time she'd noticed how handsome any man was with any sort of interest.

And I shouldn't be noticing it now.

She set his vest on the chair and glanced at the door, knowing she should leave, but her feet refused to move. That invisible pull drew her gaze back to him. His arms rested on top of the sheets, tattoos snaking out from beneath his hospital gown, over the backs of his hands, and around one of his middle fingers. She reached for his hand. It was big, rough, and calloused. She wondered what he did for a living.

She was suddenly nervous, unsure what to say, but she wanted to say something to comfort him. "Hi. It's me again. I'm glad you made it. You look a lot better than you did yesterday without all that blood and a piece of metal hanging out of your side. I was worried you'd lose your spleen." *God, shut up. If he can hear you, that's not going to help.* She tried to be more positive. "You've got a lot of people out there pulling for you, so stay strong. You've got this." *Now I sound like a freaking Hallmark card.*

She took a deep breath and laughed at herself. "I'm sorry. I don't even know why I'm here. I guess I needed to see you. I promised not to let you go, and you should know that you've been front and center in my mind this whole time. You have all sorts of secret powers, don't you, Mr. Wicked? I hear you're *quite* the playboy. It makes sense. I mean, even banged up, you're probably the best-looking guy in this hospital."

Ramble much?

She brushed her thumb over the tattooed skull on the back of his hand, recognizing it from the patches on his vest. "I brought your vest back. Is *that* why you've taken up residence in my head? I bet it is. Well, Zander, now that it's safely back in your possession, you can leave me be, right?" A pang of something akin to longing tiptoed through her. She held his hand a little tighter. "I guess this is it. Let me give you a piece of advice, *Not-Zeke.* You clean up real nice, but giving women the wrong name under any other circumstance is frowned upon, so how about using your special powers to heal that head of yours? Can you do that for me?"

Closing her eyes, she sent a silent prayer out to the universe that he'd pull through without complications or cognitive deficits. Gently placing his hand back on the sheet, she took one last look at him and had the strange feeling that she shouldn't leave, which meant she was losing her mind, so she said, "Don't let me down, big guy. Take care of yourself."

As she turned to leave, she pulled her keys out of her coat pocket and looked at her lucky key ring. She'd had the worn brass circular charm with a number four stamped into it since the day she decided to turn her life around. Seeing it had helped her stay strong when she'd needed it most. She glanced back at Zander, and a little voice told her he needed that luck more than she did.

Her pulse quickened as she took the brass charm off the key ring and tucked it into the pocket of his vest, then hurried out the door.

SHAUNA PARKED IN front of the two-bedroom cottage she and Brian rented. It was an older home with tiny rooms, no yard to speak of, warped front steps, and a rotting deck, but it was clean and safe inside, and they liked their landlord, Claire. She'd never forget how monumental it had felt to sign the lease on a place they could call home that wasn't in a crappy area and felt more permanent than the shared houses they'd been renting. The fact that they'd signed the lease on the fourth of the month two and a half years ago had seemed like a good omen.

But now Brian was drinking again.

She climbed out of her car with a heavy heart and made her way up to the door. The curtains were closed, painfully reminiscent of the old days, when they'd hide away with their joints and booze, only coming out from under them long enough to work at whatever meaningless job they had at the time. She opened the door, hoping he wasn't spiraling back into that darkness.

There was a blanket on the couch, Brian's sneakers discarded beside the coffee table. She glanced into the kitchen. A few dishes were in the sink, a bowl on the counter. Dishes never bothered her, but the beer bottle sticking out of the trash can made her stomach knot up.

Brian came out of the bathroom wearing jeans and a hoodie. His light brown hair was damp and finger-combed, his cheeks freshly shaved. "Hey," he said cheerily. "I thought I heard you come in."

"Hi. How was your night?" She studied him as he crossed the room to her, the warm smile she'd known from the time she was a child stretching across his face. That smile had comforted her in the worst of times and laughed with her in the best of them, which brought a rush of conflicting feelings.

"Good. Listen, Shauna, I'm sorry for yelling at you yesterday. You didn't deserve that, and I don't want you to worry. It's a new year, and I'm starting it right. I'll get control of this. I'm gonna get my shit together and go to a meeting today, and I'll find another job."

"I'm glad to hear that." She wanted to believe him and hoped he meant it, but she knew it wasn't that easy. "Do you want me to go with you to the meeting?"

"No. I'm sure you need to sleep."

Despite her fatigue, she said, "I don't mind. I can sleep later."

"No. I've got this," he assured her.

"Okay." Once again, she wanted to believe him, but addiction could turn the most reliable person into a liar. "Did you sleep on the couch last night?"

"Yeah, for a bit." He snagged the blanket off the couch and began folding it. "I got in pretty late."

"Did you go to John's?" she asked carefully. The flash of defensiveness in his eyes cut her to her core.

"*Yes*, I did, but I meant what I said. That was *it* for me. I'm done. I won't let you down again. *Anchors forever*, right? I go down, you go down, and I love you too much to do that to you."

Still waters or reckless tides, anchors forever, side by side. They were barely out of high school and high as kites sitting on some stranger's boat that they'd snuck onto in a Jersey Shore marina when they'd made that promise to each other, but that didn't undermine their vow. Their love and loyalty to each other were unbreakable. But she'd made the cardinal mistake for people in recovery. She'd gotten too comfortable, had taken his sobriety for granted. She knew better, and she could kick herself for missing the early signs that Brian was in trouble. If she'd only paid more attention, maybe she could've kept him from picking up the bottle again.

"Brian, you know this isn't about me. I'm here for you, and I'll support you in every way, but whatever you do or don't do has to be for *you*."

"I know. It *is* for me, but I know I let you down, and this is tearing you up. I can see it in your eyes."

"Addiction is a disease, not a character flaw," she reminded him *and* herself. "What you see are my feelings toward this fucking unfair disease."

"Yeah, well, we both know the disease and I are one and the same. I didn't just let you down. I let *myself* down, but I'm not some dumb kid anymore. I made mistakes, and I'm not minimizing them. I know this is bad, and I take full responsibility. You do *not* need to worry."

Exhausted, she could do little more than nod, because of course she'd worry. They might not be a couple anymore, but they'd always be joined at the hip, and she knew how promises could be made with confidence in times of clarity and just as quickly drowned in weaker moments.

"I need to sleep," she said.

As she headed for her bedroom, she realized that for the first time since she'd started working at the firehouse, he hadn't asked how her shift went.

Chapter Three

ZANDER TRIED TO open his eyes, but his eyelids were too heavy. He felt strange, like he was underwater, trying to get to the surface. Muffled voices and a steady *beep*, *beep*, *beep* had him trying harder. He managed to open them just enough to see through the fuzz of his lashes. Squinting against too-bright lights, he made out shadowy figures moving closer to him.

"He's *awake*. Honey, he's awake!" His mother's face appeared close to his, her smile warm, her eyes worried. "Zander. Hi, sweetheart. Dad and I are right here with you." She took Zander's hand as his father leaned down from the other side of the bed, Preacher's familiar blue eyes studying him.

"We're here, son." He placed his rough, warm hand on Zander's forearm. "How do you feel?"

"Tired." Zander didn't recognize his own scratchy voice. He tried to see beyond his parents, searching for the angel who'd been singing and talking to him, but he couldn't focus. "Where is she?"

"Who, baby?" his mother asked.

All Zander wanted to do was sleep. "Angel," he murmured groggily.

"Sounds like those pain meds are doing their job," his father said with amusement.

"She was…" He swallowed, but his throat felt rough. "Real."

"You probably heard the nurses talking, sweetheart. You're in the hospital. You were in a car accident last week," his mother explained.

They weren't making sense. Wouldn't he remember a car accident? The last thing he remembered was leaving some woman's house and talking to Zeke on the phone. "Accident?"

"Yes, honey. You were on your way to work, and a truck ran a red light and hit your car," his mother explained. "The guy who hit you took off, but they got him. Traffic cameras caught the whole thing, and Justice is handling it. You won't need to go to court. You can put all of your energy into getting better, and he'll take care of everything." Justice was an attorney and a Dark Knight.

"You got pretty banged up," his father said. "Broken ribs, a punctured lung. You fractured your skull, too. You've been in a medically induced coma for a week. They just brought you out of it this morning. We explained all of this to you earlier, but the doctor said between the pain meds and the sedation, it might be hard to process."

A *week*? That didn't seem possible. He reached up to feel his head and winced when he touched a large, tender bump.

"That's going to hurt for a while," his mother said.

"All those times your brothers teased you about being thickheaded, little did they know it would come in handy one day." His father's voice was laden with emotion.

"They here?" Zander asked hoarsely.

"They were earlier," his mother said. "You've been going in and out of sleep all afternoon."

"The whole family was camped out in the waiting room for days," his father said. "Aunt Ginger, Uncle Con, and all your cousins, including Baz. He and Emerson came home from Indonesia with little Brennan the minute they heard what happened. Your uncles and aunts from Colorado, New York, and Maryland are all praying for you, and Grandpa Mike has been here every day."

"Hitting on nurses?" Zander managed.

"You got that right." His mother smiled. "Mads got into an argument with one of the nurses because she wouldn't let her spend the night in your room, and your grandfather did his best to sweet-talk that nurse."

Zander smiled, imagining his sister giving some poor nurse hell, and his ornery grandfather, who was still madly in love with his late wife, doing his best to charm a nurse for Madigan.

His father gently squeezed his forearm. "You gave us quite a scare, Alexander, but the doctors have assured us that in time you're going to be just fine."

Zander apologized, or at least he thought he did as he gave in to the weight of his eyelids, whispering, *"Tired."*

"Get some rest, honey. We'll come see you tomorrow." His mother brushed his hair away from his forehead and kissed him there. "I love you, sweet boy."

"We all do," his father said.

"Love you, too," Zander managed, and finally surrendered to the lull of sleep.

ZANDER'S DREAMS WERE chaotic. One minute he was

cruising along the coast on his motorcycle, and in the next he was thrown back in time to his cousin Ashley's funeral. Just as the pain of that loss slayed him anew, he was catapulted forward again, infiltrating a dogfighting ring with the club, carrying one of the lifeless dogs out to his truck, and then everything disappeared, and he was standing in total darkness, calling out for his family, unable to find them. Her voice threaded into his dream like a melodic beacon in the darkness. He followed it, but the faster he ran, the farther away it seemed. *Wait. Don't leave me.* The singing stopped, and he stilled, breathing hard, listening intently.

Her voice slithered through the darkness. "I heard you don't have any major cognitive deficits. I'm glad you took my advice to heal."

Her voice faded into the darkness, and he felt like he was floating. Then he heard her again, a tender whisper calling out to him. "So many flowers, pictures, and gifts, and all I got you was this song by Andra Day. I heard it on my way to my pole class, and it reminded me of you." She started singing just above a whisper about being tired and broken down and standing by him, helping him rise up.

Her voice was soulful and real. He wanted to live in that melody, wrapped in the comfort of her voice. He was so caught up in the soft sounds of her singing, he felt like he was floating. As her voice faded, something brushed over his hand. He curled his fingers, trying to capture whatever had touched him, but there was nothing there. He forced his eyes to flutter open, catching a glimpse of a woman walking out the door, her dark hair pinned up in a ponytail.

"Come back," he said, his throat scratchy and raw, but she was already gone, and he was fading back into the darkness.

Chapter Four

ZANDER GRABBED THE drawings he'd just picked up from a local architect and climbed out of his truck at Cape Renovations. It had been three months since his accident, and he was glad to be back on his feet. But everyone was constantly checking on him, treating him like he was made of glass, and he couldn't take it anymore. To make matters worse, his father was still giving him menial jobs instead of letting him work on the major renovation project Zeke and Tobias were tackling.

He eyed his father's beloved black Trans Am, grinding his back teeth against the conflicting emotions gnawing at him. He had many fond childhood memories of watching his father tinker with that car, and later, of helping him fix it up. He had his old man to thank for his love of fast cars, but the accident had changed the way Zander looked at many things. He'd much rather see his old man driving a car that had airbags, which made no sense coming from a biker who would never give up his motorcycle. But he'd become acutely aware of how fragile life was, and when he thought about the people he loved, he wanted to protect them even more fiercely than before. Protecting them meant changing his ways. He hadn't been able to stop thinking about the accident. If he hadn't gone home with those women, he wouldn't have overslept or been at the intersection at the moment that truck had barreled through it. He'd been selfish, living life to the fullest, consequences be damned. But that time it had nearly ruined all their lives.

Pushing those worries away, he headed inside to set his father straight.

It would not be an easy conversation. His father had always been one of his heroes. Zander had severe dyslexia and ADHD, which they hadn't known enough about to test for when he was young. It had gone undiagnosed for years. From the time he was a little boy, written words were mixed up, letters danced across pages of books and menus, and his thoughts were too chaotic for him to be able to concentrate. He'd thought those dancing letters were normal and that he was just too stupid to figure out how to read. He'd never mentioned what he saw to anyone. He knew he was different than his smarter, more patient siblings, and he hated it. He'd learned to deflect attention from those differences by becoming the class clown in school, and a jokester outside of it, which admittedly carried over into his adult life. He was labeled a troublemaker, and his father had tried to help him find something to capture his attention and keep him on the right side of trouble.

His father had given him his own set of tools and projects and had worked with him to complete them. Even if they worked on them for only ten or twenty minutes at a time a few days a week, and they took months to complete, his old man never gave up trying. The praise his parents had given him along the way had given the kid who didn't want to be different a sense of pride for being able to do the things his father could do.

Over the years, his father taught him everything he knew

about contracting, instilling confidence and giving him a trade that he excelled at. But he couldn't take the bullshit jobs anymore.

He headed down the hall and saw his mother sitting behind her desk, smiling up at his father, who was sitting on the edge of her desk. His father reached for her hand, bringing her up to her feet. Her mahogany hair brushed her shoulders as he guided her between his legs, his arms circling her. His parents had always been openly affectionate, and the way they looked at each other was something to be revered.

Zander wasn't searching for that, but ever since his accident, when he saw his parents, or his siblings or cousins with their significant others, it tweaked something in his chest. He glanced away before it could settle in too deep and cleared his throat to let them know he was coming in.

"Hey, baby," his mother said, stepping away from his father.

"Hi, Mom. Sorry to interrupt your make-out session."

"Sure you are," his father teased. "Thanks for picking those up."

"No problem." Zander handed him the drawings. "What time are we meeting at the Martels' tomorrow?" The Martels owned the home they were renovating.

"I need you on another job tomorrow. Fascia repair and a few other things in Eastham. I'll text you the info."

"Seriously, Preach?" Zander asked incredulously.

His father's eyes narrowed. "*Yes*, seriously."

Zander glanced at his mother.

"Don't look at me. Your father makes the schedules." She arched a brow at Preacher, sending a silent message Zander couldn't read, as she sat down behind her desk.

"Come on, Preach. You've been making up menial shit for

me to do for two weeks, sending me to Hyannis to pick up drawings, organizing the workshop, painting."

"I'm not making anything up," he said sternly. "We got a call, and I need to handle it."

"Then give it to Zeke or Tobias," Zander challenged.

His father's jaw ticked, but when he spoke, his tone was softer. "Zan, we nearly lost you. You had a brain bleed."

"Yeah, three *months* ago. The doctor cleared me to go back to work, and I'm going to lose my damn mind if you don't give me some real work to do. Are you afraid I can't do the job anymore?"

"Of course not," his father said sharply. "I'm just trying to keep you safe. What if you're up on a ladder or using a power tool and you get dizzy and fall or hurt yourself? I don't want you landing back in the hospital."

"I haven't been dizzy in months. I'm recovered and clear-headed." Sometimes it took him a few extra seconds to remember the name of a tool or something else, but it wasn't often, and he didn't forget important things, like how to do his job. But he wasn't about to add that fuel to Preacher's fire. "This isn't about me not being fit to work, is it?" He gritted his teeth as Zeke and Tobias came into the office, eyeing them cautiously.

Zeke positioned himself closer to Zander than their father. He and Zander were near mirror images of each other, but Zeke had shorter, darker hair and less ink. Tobias, a former fighter with long light brown hair, dwarfed them both by a couple of inches and about thirty pounds of pure muscle, and stood at an equal distance between Zander and Preacher.

"Everything okay?" Zeke, always the mediator, asked.

"*No,*" Zander gritted out. "Preacher thinks I'm not ready to go back to real work."

"You're so damn stubborn," Preacher seethed.

"I wonder where I learned that from," Zander countered.

"Stop it." Zeke lifted his chin in Preacher's direction. "I've got Zan. I won't let anything happen to him."

"Jesus Christ," Zander fumed. "Dude, I don't need you watching out for me like a motherfucking hen."

"I'm not being a mother hen," Zeke insisted.

"You camped out at my place for three weeks after I got out of the hospital. That's more than Mom was there. I'm not injured anymore. I can take care of myself."

Zeke threw his shoulders back. "I never said you couldn't."

"You didn't have to say it—"

"There are worse things in life than being too loved," Tobias said evenly, his deep voice silencing them.

Zander gritted his teeth, Tobias's point giving him pause. Tobias had lost his mother when he was young, he'd had a falling-out with his father, and had accidentally killed his sister's fiancé, which severed his relationship with her at the same time he'd gone to prison. He and his family had since mended those broken fences, but he had a fucking point.

Before Zander could get a word out, his mother was on her feet, planting all five feet three inches of herself in the middle of them. She looked right at him and said, "Tobias is right. There's more than enough to be angry at in this world, and being cared for too much shouldn't be on that list." She turned to Preacher. "But my sweet, stubborn husband, Zander is right, too. Yes, we almost lost him, and Lord knows that affected all of us." Her attention shifted to Zeke as she said, "Deeply."

Zeke glanced at Zander with an expression that made Zander's chest constrict.

"But we *didn't* lose him," she said, her gaze softening as it moved over them. "I want to wrap each and every one of you in Bubble Wrap every time y'all walk out the door. That's what love is, but there's a fine line between protecting and suffocating. Preacher, you will push our son away if you try to cage him in. Haven't we suffered enough loss?"

All their expressions turned serious with the painful reminder. They'd lost their cousin Ashley years ago, and not a day passed that Zander didn't think about her. More recently, their cousin Tank's wife, Leah, had lost her brother, River. They hadn't known River, but through Leah, they'd come to know him, and since Tank and Leah were raising River's two young daughters, they'd grieved with them, too. All of which underscored the reason Zander wanted to change his ways. His family had grieved enough. He didn't need them worrying about him.

"You're absolutely right, darlin'." Preacher looked at Zander and said, "I need you on that job in Eastham, but after that, you'll join the guys at the Martels'. But you have to promise me, if you feel *off* in any way, you'll stop what you're doing immediately and tell one of us."

Zander gave a curt nod. "Understood." Preacher turned his attention to Zeke, and Zander said, "Don't even think about telling him to keep an eye on me."

Preacher held his hands up in surrender. "I was just going to ask what he and Tobias needed."

"We don't need anything," Zeke said. "Zan sounded angry, so we were seeing what was up."

"See? You *are* a mother hen," Zander said.

"Can you boys take your argument out of the office, please?" his mother said.

"I am *not* a mother hen," Zeke said as the three of them

walked out.

"He's a big-daddy cock," Tobias said.

They all laughed and headed out to the parking lot. Once outside, Zander said, "Sorry I blew up in there. That accident changed me, man. I don't want to be a burden or a problem anymore."

"You're not either of those things," Zeke said.

Zander scoffed and glanced at Tobias. "Dude, am I the wild one? The carouser, the boundary pusher, the one who crosses so many lines you can't see them anymore?"

The corner of Tobias's mouth quirked. "Mads calls you rascally."

"Nice try, but Mads says worse shit than that to my face," Zander said.

Zeke shrugged. "None of that makes you a burden."

"Bullshit. You've been saving my ass since we were kids."

"I have not," Zeke insisted.

"Bro, you didn't go away to college your first year so you could help me graduate from high school."

After Zander was diagnosed with dyslexia and ADHD, his parents had tried everything from medication and tutors to therapy and alternative teaching methods, but Zander had fought them tooth and nail. It didn't matter how supportive anyone was. He didn't want to be different. He refused to take the medication and made things difficult for teachers, tutors, and everyone else who had tried to help. Zeke, a natural-born teacher and the most patient person Zander knew, was the only one who figured out how to help Zander. He did it in private, somehow knowing that was what Zander needed. They spent hours in the woods claiming to be playing while secretly working on homework and hidden under blankets with flashlights and books after bedtime. In turn, Zeke was the only person Zander had ever allowed to yank his chain and rein him in when he got out of hand. Now it was time to stand on his own and regulate his own behavior without a safety net, but in order to do that, he had to get through to Zeke and break his hard-earned habit, too.

"And you're still doing it," Zander said. "You can't help yourself. It's in the fabric of your being, and I appreciate everything you've ever done for me. But I don't want to be a troublemaker anymore."

"From what I've seen, that's in the fabric of *your* being," Tobias said.

That's not far from the truth. "Yeah, well, not anymore. I'm done being that guy."

"Zan, there's nothing wrong with who you are," Zeke said.

It was no wonder he'd gone on to become a special education teacher, but his career had been cut short when he'd gotten into a physical altercation with an asshole who had made derogatory comments about the kids. Now, in addition to working with their family business, Zeke tutored middle schoolers and volunteered at the community center.

"Your filter's set a little low, and you don't think everything through, but that's okay," Zeke insisted.

That was putting it mildly, but Zander knew Zeke would never admit his biggest faults. They would all give their lives for anyone who was in trouble, but Zeke was a different type of savior. He had their mother's superpower of seeing right through people's strong facades, knowing who needed something extra and exactly what that *extra* was. Only Zeke's instincts were on steroids. He had some kind of sixth sense with nature *and* people.

"Look, I am glad you love me for who I am," Zander said. "Without you, and everyone else, who the hell knows how I'd've fucked up my life. But you're free, Zeke. Now you can use your superpowers to go out and get yourself a woman."

Zeke scoffed.

Tobias laughed and followed it up with, "I respect where you're coming from, man. Do you want me to ask Mads to stop checking up on you?"

Madigan had texted or called Zander nearly every day since the accident. "Nah. That would only hurt her feelings."

"What the hell?" Zeke said. "You don't want to hurt Madigan's feelings, but you're cool with telling me to fuck off?"

Zander clapped a hand on his shoulder. "Such a delicate little mother hen." He and Tobias laughed.

"Asshole," Zeke said.

"I've got to get out of here," Tobias said. "I'm going with Mads to her gig tonight."

"What is it this time? Puppeteering or musical storytelling?" Zander asked. Madigan was one hell of a businesswoman and believed in following all of her dreams. She was a musical storyteller, a freelance puppeteer, and she did puppet therapy at the Lower Cape Assisted Living Facility (LOCAL). She was also the founder and designer of the Mad Truth About Love greeting card line, which made light of the harder aspects of relationships.

"Storytelling, up in P-town," Tobias said. "I'll catch you guys later."

"See ya," they said in unison as Tobias walked away.

"You heading to the Salty Hog?" Zeke asked.

Their aunt Ginger and uncle Conroy owned the Salty Hog restaurant and bar, a Dark Knights hangout. Before the accident, Zander would head over to the Hog after a quick shower, where he'd either pick up a woman for the night or hang out with his buddies. But he'd been there a few nights ago, and instead of checking out women, he'd found himself listening for the voice he'd heard in the hospital. Just as he'd been doing everywhere he went. His parents were wrong. It wasn't a nurse's voice that had infiltrated his dreams and taken root someplace deep inside him. He'd thanked each of the nurses who had cared for him, and none of them had that sweet, strong voice that continued to call to him as loud as the open road.

"Not tonight. What about you?"

"Aria and I are heading over to the Stonybrook Gristmill to see the herring run. She's been acting funny again. Distant." Aria Bad was several years younger than Zeke and one of his closest friends. He had tutored her when she was in high school, and now she was a tattooist at their cousin Tank's tattoo shop. Aria suffered from social anxieties, and Zeke was super protective of her. Zander had a feeling he was also in love with her.

"Maybe she's seeing someone."

Zeke's face contorted like he'd said something ridiculous. "She's not."

"How do you know?"

"She'd tell me if she was seeing someone."

"Really? How many times has she called you up to brag about the hot guy she's hanging out with?"

Zeke's brows pinched. "She doesn't do that."

"Exactly."

"I'd know if she was seeing someone."

"Yeah? Remember how well Mads hid her booty calls with Tobias from us?"

Zeke's eyes narrowed.

"Think about it, dude. Aria is gorgeous, smart, and she just might be the sweetest woman we know. Sure, she has social anxieties, but plenty of guys are equipped to help her with that. And her job is literally touching guys all day."

Zeke's jaw clenched.

"It's not like she's gonna wait around forever for your ass."

"You know I can't go there," Zeke gritted out.

"Right, because you have too much in common and you have too much fun together," he said sarcastically.

"She's not into me like that, and we both know she probably shouldn't be."

His brother might be calm and restrained on the outside, but in the bedroom he had a darker side. One women sure as hell didn't write home to Mama about. "No, we don't. I think you shouldn't assume."

Zeke shook his head. "I'm her safety net. She's got enough anxieties to deal with. She doesn't need me fucking up our friendship."

"Thank God you're good-looking, because for a smart guy, you're really fucking clueless."

"See ya, Zan." Zeke walked away.

"If she pulls out her phone more than twice tonight, she's got a dude on the line," Zander called after him.

Zeke flipped him the bird.

ON THE WAY home, Zander filled his tank with gas and headed into Cumberland Farms, aka Cumby's, to grab something to eat. As he perused the snack aisle, he heard someone humming. He stilled, a tug of recognition stirring with him. He moved to the end of the aisle, searching for the source. There were a handful of people at the register and walking around the store.

He made his way through the store, checking each aisle; then he headed for the soda and coffee machines on the far wall. As he came around the last aisle, he heard the soft singing voice that had plagued his thoughts for the last three months. His heart beat faster, his gaze moving over the two teenage girls filling cups with soda to a curvy brunette adding several liquid creamer cups to her coffee. She wore black spandex workout shorts and a pink hoodie and looked to be in her early twenties. Her dark hair was pinned up in a ponytail, earbuds feeding the music that had her moving her full hips to a beat he couldn't hear. But that sweet, strong voice floated past with an intense familiarity, awakening something within him, drawing him forward like an invisible cable reeling him in.

She grabbed three more creamer cups and opened them, bobbing her head as she sang about a man-child running to her.

What the hell was she listening to?

"Fuck my freaking liiife," she sang, her hips rocking and her head bobbing.

He touched her arm. "Excuse me—"

She looked up with a broad smile that lit up her big brown eyes and brought out the cutest dimples he'd ever seen. But as he said, "Hi," her smile faltered and she stumbled backward, as if she'd seen a ghost, knocking her cup over and sending coffee spilling across the counter.

She gasped. "Shitshitshit."

"Sorry." They both reached for napkins at the same time,

their hands bumping. She pulled hers away, those beautiful eyes darting to him again as he began mopping up the mess. "I didn't mean to startle you."

"I...*um*...It's...I don't know what happened." She threw the cup away, her cheeks pinking up.

"I tend to have that effect on women." He finished cleaning up and threw out the napkins. "Let me buy you another coffee." He grabbed a cup and turned back to her. "Diesel or unleaded?"

"You know what? I don't need it. It's a sign. I'm over-caffeinated already. I need to..." She pointed behind her, walking backward toward the door. "Thanks!"

She turned and hurried out of the store, leaving him staring after her, empty cup in hand, unable to believe he'd found the woman behind the voice. *I knew you were real.*

Fuck. He didn't get her name.

He threw away the cup and flew out the door, looking for her. He scanned the cars parked out front and the ones at the pumps, but she was nowhere to be found. He ran to the side of the building in case she'd parked there, but the side lot was empty.

Cursing himself, he raked a hand through his hair and paced in front of the store. The one time he'd sell his soul for a woman's number, and he'd stood there, stunned as a schoolboy as she walked away. What the hell? Maybe the accident had messed up his brain after all. And why did she look like she'd seen a ghost?

I'll find you, Angel, if it's the last thing I do.

Chapter Five

SHAUNA FINISHED DRESSING for her pole class and sat on her bed to put on her sneakers Tuesday morning, when she heard Brian heading into the bathroom. She hated the feeling of dread settling into her chest, but the last few months had been a torturous roller coaster of broken promises and arguments, leaving her heartbroken and scared for her best friend and equally angry and resentful toward him. He no longer tried to hide the fact that he was drinking, and although he didn't do drugs around her, there was no missing the telltale signs that he was using again, like how angry and erratic he'd become, his shady disappearances and poorly delivered lies. She was constantly trying to come up with ways to convince him to get help, but she was running out of ideas. Lately she'd been taking on extra shifts at the firehouse, going to the gym more often, and taking more pole classes, just to keep from coming home, and she didn't know how much more of it she could take.

She finished tying her laces, pulled on her hoodie, and pushed to her feet to pin up her hair. As she reached for an elastic band on the dresser, her gaze caught on the certified letter she'd tucked into her underwear drawer. She'd received the letter a few weeks ago from her late grandfather's attorney.

More conflicting emotions swamped her. She'd loved her grandfather, and there had been a time when she'd thought he might want to save her from the nightmare of living with her parents. But when she'd finally gotten up the courage to ask, it was too late. He'd heard about her drinking and smoking weed, and he'd wanted no part of trying to help *another* troubled teen. He'd seen her as an extension of her father, and she'd validated it with every beer she drank and every joint she smoked. Her hopes had been shattered, and not long after that he'd disappeared from their lives.

Leave it to her grandfather to give her the means to help Brian wrapped in a mousetrap she'd *never* get caught in. He'd left her fifty thousand dollars with the caveat that she be alcohol and drug free for a year and happily married for two months. She'd seen too many marriages turn into nooses around people's necks to ever put herself in that situation. Not even for Brian. She'd find another way to help him.

She had to.

As she pinned up her hair, taking one last glance in the mirror, she remembered when she couldn't stand to see her reflection. Back then, she'd looked as defeated as she'd felt. Every feature had screamed of her unhappiness and substance abuse, from her bloodshot eyes and gray skin to her lifeless hair and drooped shoulders. Now she was proud of the confident, strong, clear-eyed woman in the mirror, with radiant skin and full, shiny hair, though her eyes were currently shadowed by worries about Brian.

Admiring herself wasn't an act of conceit or misplaced values. It was a measure of appreciation for how far she'd come and another reminder that she never wanted to go back to the person she'd been.

As *I'm proud of you* played in her mind, her thoughts traipsed back to Zander. She was anything *but* proud of the way she'd hightailed it away from him yesterday. After the accident, she'd secretly visited him in the hospital nearly every day while he was sedated, trying to figure out why she felt so connected to him. When she'd seen him breathing on his own, she'd forced herself to stop visiting and hadn't gone back. But she'd never stopped thinking about him. Lord knew she'd tried, but he'd plagued her thoughts like an unsolvable puzzle for the past few months. When she'd seen him at Cumberland Farms, standing right in front of her, as tall and strong as a towering oak instead of out cold in a hospital bed, she'd felt *caught,* and it had knocked her completely off-kilter.

"Hey, Shauna, you up?" Brian called through her bedroom door.

Closing her eyes for a second, she said, "Yeah. I'll be right out." She had no idea what shape he'd be in this morning. He'd come home last night after she'd already gone to bed, but she'd heard him stumbling around. Bracing for today's battle, she pocketed her phone and reminded herself to stay calm, which was getting increasingly difficult.

At least they'd been blessed with a sunny day. She headed out of the bedroom and opened the front windows on her way to the kitchen, where Brian was staring into the barren refrigerator. Without his help with the rent for the last couple of months, she'd had to tighten her belt where she could. "Good morning," she said cheerily, hoping for the best.

"Morning." His voice was rough. "You going shopping today?"

"Yes, but I really need you to find a job and start helping with the rent."

"This *again*? Can you please get off my ass?" He closed the refrigerator so hard, she startled.

"Trust me, the last thing I want to do is harass you, but I have bills to pay. Mine *and* yours. After paying for rent and utilities, my car payment, car insurance, groceries, gas, both of our cell phones, and the gym, there's nothing left."

"Give me a break," he sneered. "You make a boatload of money."

"I do not, and even if I did, that's *my* money. I work my ass off for it." She didn't mean to raise her voice and tried to take it down a notch. "Brian, I *know* you. You need help. Please let me help you."

"You *knew* me, but you don't know shit anymore." He stalked angrily toward her, breathing hard, his eyes blazing. "You think you're better than me."

"I do *not*, and you know it. I'm worried about you. I hate seeing you like this!"

"Then fucking leave. I don't need you, and you sure as fuck don't need me," he hollered, inches from her face, and for the first time in their lives, she was fearful of what her best friend had become.

Several hard knocks on the front door had them both turning toward the sound.

"This better not be one of your druggie friends," she said, heading for the door.

"Fuck off." He plowed past her and tugged the door open, blocking Shauna from seeing around him as he sneered, "Who the fuck are you?"

"I'm Zander Wicked. I'm with Cape Renovations."

What the...? She moved to see past Brian, and her heart nearly stopped. What was he doing there?

Zander's gaze shifted to her, moving assessingly over her with as much surprise as concern written all over his too-handsome face.

She realized he'd heard them arguing, and embarrassment washed over her.

Zander turned back to Brian, his jaw clenched, and said, "Claire Burrows said she spoke to Brian and let him know I was coming to fix a few things. Is that you?"

"Shit. I forgot." Brian grumbled, "She can handle it," and stormed out the door, knocking into Zander's shoulder.

Zander's hands fisted, his chest expanding with a deep inhalation as he watched Brian climb into his car and said, "Is he okay to drive?"

"*Yes.* He's just angry. It's no big deal." Lies came too easily when it came to covering for Brian, and she hated herself and resented him more with each one.

As Brian peeled away from the curb, Zander turned those blue eyes on her again with a serious expression, but he spoke with a softer tone. "It sure seemed like it was a big deal. Are you okay? I knocked a few times."

"Mm-hm. I'm fine," she said, lighter than she felt, trying to play it off like it really was no big deal. But now she felt awkward and embarrassed, because of yesterday and now this. "So, I guess you're here to fix the leaks?"

"Yeah. Listen, I'm sorry about startling you yesterday. I know this is going to sound crazy, but when I heard you singing, it sounded familiar. Do I know you from somewhere?"

Shit. Can today get any more difficult? She wasn't sure if she should tell him the truth. She didn't want him to know she'd visited him in the hospital, so she said, "Sort of. I'm the one who pulled you out of your burning car the day of your accident. I was at the intersection when it happened, and I stayed with you until the first responders got there."

He crossed his arms, studying her. "You pulled me out of a burning car? By yourself?" he asked with disbelief.

"I'm stronger than I look, and I'm an EMT, so I knew what to do."

"Damn. I thought you were an angel," he said more to himself than to her. "Did you sing to me?"

Briefly lowering her eyes in embarrassment, she said, "Maybe."

"You really are my angel." The smile taking over his face was unfairly captivating. "What did you sing?"

"You're asking a lot of questions. Do you really want to know?"

"Yes, absolutely."

He was so earnest, she almost laughed. "I sang 'Keep Holding On' by Avril Lavigne. It's kind of my go-to song when I need strength. You were in pretty bad shape, and I thought it might help you. I should have said something yesterday, but you caught me off guard. The last time I saw you, you were out of it, and suddenly you're standing there, full of life. I didn't know what to say."

"'Hello' is usually a good place to start," he said smoothly. "What's your name, Angel?"

The way he called her Angel felt as intimate as a touch. No wonder he was the town crush. He was disarmingly charming, and she was enjoying it. "Shauna."

"Shauna...?" He cocked a brow.

"Flores." As much as she was enjoying talking to him and still wanted to know why she felt like she knew him beyond the accident, she didn't want to miss her class since she'd already paid for it. "I don't want you to think I'm ditching you again, but do you need me to stick around to let you inside? Or to save you if you fall off a ladder? Because I'm late for a pole class."

"No. I'm good. Wouldn't want you to miss pole class." The glint in his eyes was pure trouble.

The kind of trouble that made her want to stay, which was exactly why she had to leave. "Great. Then I'm going to take off." She grabbed her keys from the foyer table and stepped outside, closing the door behind her. "Thanks for fixing the leaks."

"Thanks for saving my life," he said as they descended the steps.

She headed for her car. "Just doing my part to keep the single women around here happy."

He laughed. "Like I said, you're my angel."

As she climbed into her car, she was laughing, too, and it felt really good to have something to laugh about.

Chapter Six

THE TELEVISION PLAYED in the day room at the firehouse, though Shauna wasn't sure anyone was really watching it. The firefighters were all busy—Lance and Trey were playing cards, Mike was focused on his phone, as usual, and Paul was lying on a sofa, his feet propped up on the coffee table, reading a thriller and working his way through a bag of Doritos.

Shauna was sitting sideways in an armchair, her legs hanging over one arm, tapping her pen on the word search she was working on. It was early Wednesday evening, and they hadn't had a call since three. Downtime at the station had been the hardest part when she'd first become an EMT. She hadn't wanted to let her guard down, for fear she wouldn't be mentally ready when a call came in. Because of that, she'd stayed on high alert every waking hour, which she'd quickly learned could take a toll. Busy times like the beginning of today's shift, when they'd had one call after another, had taught her to treasure the moments they had to breathe and recharge. Still, there was that underlying feeling of the calm before the storm, but she didn't mind. Helping people who wanted to be helped was an easier storm to weather than wanting to help a best friend who wasn't ready yet.

As she circled a word, she said, "Hey, Mike, you're in my word search."

"Yeah?" He glanced at her, smirking. "You found 'sexy beast'?"

"No. 'Pompous,'" she said.

The guys laughed.

Mike smirked. "When you've got the biggest engine in the firehouse, you earn the right to be pompous."

"Then that would be me," Paul said, his eyes still trained on his book. "As your sister can attest to."

Lance snorted.

Howie sauntered in through the garage door. "Hey, Flores, you didn't tell us you were into bikers."

"What are you talking about? I'm not into bikers."

"You did help that toddler who fell off his tricycle a few weeks ago," Trey chimed in.

She rolled her eyes.

Howie hiked a thumb toward the garage door. "Well, there's a Dark Knight in shining armor out there looking for you."

Her eyes widened. *"What?"* She shoved her feet into her boots and bent to tie them.

"Who is it?" Trey asked.

"The guy she saved the morning of New Year's Eve. Zander Wicked," Howie answered. "Dude's got a hell of a rep—careful Flores."

No shit. What is Zander doing here?

Brian was home when Zander had finished working at their house yesterday afternoon, and Zander told him he'd be back today to finish the job. She hoped Brian hadn't caused a problem. She headed for the door, and the guys hurried after her. She turned and glowered at them. "Do you mind?"

"What do you mean? I'm just going to check the rig," Paul said.

"Me too," Trey said, and the others said the same.

"Way to go, Flores," Mike said. "Save a guy and pick him up. I need to try that."

"I did *not* pick him up, and *don't* follow me."

As she stalked toward the door, Mike said, "No way I'm missing this," and they all barreled out after her. Thankfully, the guys headed for the fire truck.

Shauna tried to play it cool despite her racing heart as Zander came into view. He was looking over his shoulder out the open bay door, holding a bag in one hand, his other hand casually tucked into the front pocket of his jeans. She slowed her stride, enjoying the view of him in his leather vest over a black T-shirt, his muscular legs wrapped in worn denim. Scuffed black leather boots made him that much hotter. *Maybe I am into bikers.*

Ugh. No.

It wasn't like she was even looking for a guy, and if she were, it wouldn't be a player. But there was no denying the flutter low in her belly.

Zander turned, an easy smile stretching across his face as he closed the distance between them. She realized she'd stopped walking and was staring at him. What was he doing to her? She'd always been more comfortable around guys than women. *Except around this guy, apparently.*

"There's my savior. How's it going, Angel?"

A soft laugh escaped before she could stop it. "Did you forget my name already?"

"No. You might be Shauna Flores to everyone else, but to

me you'll always be the angel who saved me."

"*Okay,*" she said, dragging out the word, unsure how else to respond. "What are you doing here?"

"I finished that work at your place today, and wanted to give you a thank-you gift, but you weren't home. So, I tracked you down."

"Damn. Dude's got game," Mike said loudly from across the bay by the fire truck.

She shot Mike an annoyed glance. He and the guys turned around like they weren't eavesdropping. "Sorry about him," she said, trying to wrap her head around the idea that Zander had brought her a gift *and* tracked her down.

"Don't be. He's right." He cocked a playful grin. "But that's not why I'm here. I felt bad for ruining your coffee the other day, so I got you this." He held out the bag he was holding.

Her pulse was going crazy, and she couldn't stop smiling. "You didn't have to get me anything."

"You didn't have to save me." He put the bag in her hand.

She peered into the bag and laughed when she saw a large box of her favorite French vanilla creamer cups. "Thank you."

"You're welcome. Feel free to shower me with eternal gratitude in the form of baked goods."

He was ridiculously smooth, and somehow, also sincere. "Trust me, you don't want to eat anything I bake."

"I wouldn't bet on that, but I'm happy knowing you now have a reason to think of me every morning."

She couldn't tell if he was teasing or flirting, but it didn't matter because he'd taken up residence in her mind three months ago without even trying.

"Do you have a few minutes to chat?" he asked.

"Um. *Sure.*" She glanced at the guys, who were still watching them. *Nosy bastards.*

Mike gave her a thumbs-up.

"Let's go outside," she suggested.

Once they were outside, Zander said, "Brian was in pretty bad shape when I was at your place earlier. Is he okay?"

The question took her by surprise. She hadn't talked to anyone about Brian's issues, and as much as it would be a relief to talk about it, she didn't know Zander well enough to breach her best friend's confidence. "Yeah. He's just going through a rough patch."

Zander nodded, but the muscles in his jaw flexed, like he wasn't buying it. "And you? How are you doing?"

"*Me?* I'm good." Hoping to change the subject, she said, "This guy brought me a whole box of my favorite creamer. It's like Christmas in April."

He chuckled. "I saw the way you were burning through them at Cumby's."

"Everyone's allowed a guilty pleasure, right?" That earned a devilish grin.

"Absolutely. I've got a list a mile long," he said, full of innuendo.

I bet you do.

He glanced at the firehouse. "So, how do you like being an EMT?"

"I love it. I really enjoy helping people."

"A hot woman with a savior complex. That's cool."

Did he call her hot? A flicker of heat hit her cheeks.

He raked a hand through his hair, eyeing her with confusion. "I'm sorry. I shouldn't have said that. I'm really not trying to pick you up."

"Wow. Way to insult a girl." She was only half teasing.

"That's not what I meant. You're gorgeous, but I'm not trying to take you home."

"I'm glad you cleared that up. For a guy with a reputation for being charming, you're falling a little short." *And for some reason, I find your honesty alluring.*

"Damn it," he gritted out. "I'm sorry. I just want to get to know you, and that's new for me."

"So, you don't usually get to know women? Given your reputation, I think that says a lot about the kind of guy you are."

"Yeah, that's the problem. If I were just trying to pick you up, that'd be easy, but that's not the reason I'm here. I feel this pull toward you, and I don't understand it. I mean, I'm attracted to you, so don't get all weird and think you're not hot. It's bigger than that. It's like I'm supposed to get to know you, but I'm totally screwing this up."

She couldn't believe he felt the magnetic pull, too. "It's kind of endearing, seeing Mr. Salacious get flustered."

"Great," he said sarcastically.

"Don't worry. I won't tell anyone you slipped off your player pedestal."

He laughed. "I don't give a shit about that. Can we start over?"

"Sure. Do you want to crash your truck now? Because I'll need to grab my crowbar and first aid kit."

He shook his head, laughing. "Can we walk and talk? I'm not good at standing still."

"A mover and shaker, huh? I can't go far in case we get a call, but we can walk around out here if you want."

He fell into step beside her as they walked along the grass beside the building. "So, are you from around here?"

It was kind of adorable that he asked such a simple question. "No. I'm from Jersey. What about you?"

"I'm a Cape boy, born and bred," he said proudly, like he'd never want to live anywhere else. "What brought you here?"

"I'm not sure I should tell you," she said, but she was only teasing. There was a time she'd been ashamed of her parents and how she'd grown up. As if she'd been the thing that had set them off course. After she'd started AA, she'd learned their addictions, lifestyle, and faults had nothing to do with her, and she was proud to have gotten away.

"Were you running from the law? I can see that. What'd you get caught doing? Stealing coffee creamer?"

"*No.* That's free at Cumby's. I was running from my parents," she admitted. "They weren't very nice, and they had substance abuse issues. Brian and I grew up together, and his parents were no better than mine, so we took off."

"I'm sorry to hear that. Sounds like you and Brian have been together a long time."

The way he said it made it sound like he thought they were a couple, so she clarified. "We have an unbreakable bond, but we're not a couple. We were, but we're not now."

"And you still live together?" he asked as they walked around the back of the firehouse.

"I know it's weird, but we left home when we were seventeen, and like I said, it's always been us against the world. I never saw my parents after that."

"You were just kids," he said incredulously. "My grandfather ran away at sixteen to escape his abusive father, but it was a different world back then. He worked construction, no questions asked, met my grandmother a year later, and married her at eighteen."

"Wow. Are they still together?"

"Unfortunately, my grandmother passed away several years ago, but they were together until the end. They raised their kids in a loving house, free from abuse, and given how hard it is to break those cycles, I think that's pretty damn amazing."

"It is. That says a lot about your grandfather."

"He's an ornery old bastard, but he's got a good heart, and we'll all be a mess when we lose him."

She loved how genuine his love for his grandfather was, flaws and all, and how easy he was to talk to. "Hopefully that won't happen for a long time."

"He's a strong dude, and stubborn. He's not going anywhere," he said as they walked around in the grass behind the building. "I'm curious about how you made it on your own at that age. It must have been hard."

"We weren't on our own. Brian and I had each other."

He seemed to think about that for a beat, his brows knitted and his eyes serious. "How old are you now?"

"Twenty-four. How old are you?"

"Thirty."

"Yikes," she teased. "You're an old man."

"Hey, don't knock it until you try it. I can…*Shit*. There I go again, sliding into the pickup lane."

She laughed. "Seems like that's a problem for you."

"Not for long." He said it like it was a challenge to himself. "How long have you been in this area?"

"Nice transition, pickup guy," she teased. "Just a couple of years. We lived in Wareham for a while before moving over the bridge to Bourne, and then we stayed in Falmouth, Mashpee, and a few other places befo—" She stepped in a hole and lost her balance, letting out a surprised *yelp*, but Zander caught her hand, pulled her upright, and steadied her with his other hand on her hip. He was *right there*, his blue eyes holding her captive.

"Thanks" came out too breathily.

He held her hand a little tighter. "Are you okay?"

"Yeah. Sorry." She motioned to the hole that had tripped her up. "My foot caught the side of that hole. You've got good reflexes."

"That comes from years of riding motorcycles." He looked down at her hand in his and brushed his thumb over her tattoo. When she tried to pull her hand away, he tightened his grip and lifted her hand, brushing his thumb over the ink again. "What's this?"

"That's a four. It comes right after three and before five," she teased.

He cocked a brow.

"It's my favorite number," she relented.

"If you want this hand back, I'm going to need to know the story behind that favorite number."

God, this guy. She laughed softly, loving his easygoing nature. "There's not much to tell."

"I doubt that. You put a permanent mark on your hand, which means a few things."

"Such as?"

"Well, it's upside down, which means it's there for *you*, not as a statement for others. Usually when people do that, it's a reminder about something. We shake with our right hands, and this tattoo is on your left. That's another indicator that you don't want people asking about it."

"And yet here you are, holding my hand hostage."

"That's right, and if you want this hand back, you'll explain why four is your favorite number."

She could make up anything, or refuse to tell him, but something about the way he was looking at her drew the truth. "I used to party a lot, and one Fourth of July I was at a beach party and drank way too much. All I remember is that I was so drunk, I could barely walk, and some guy put me in his car and drove me home. I was incredibly stupid. He could have been a psycho killer or a rapist, but I remember telling him I didn't want to live like that anymore, and he said—"

"*Then don't,*" they said in unison.

Her jaw dropped, and it was all she could do to stare at him in disbelief, which was mirrored in his expression as he said, "Every minute of the day is a chance for change. Make this one yours."

"It was *you*?" She was floored.

"Holy hell, Angel. You're that girl. I wondered what happened to you. The next day I went back to the house where I dropped you off to make sure you were okay, and a woman told me you were fine and that you and your boyfriend had moved on."

You checked on me? It took a minute for her to find her voice. "That night changed my life. No wonder we felt like we knew each other."

"It's pretty wild, isn't it? I'm guessing you're my secret charm bearer?" He fished a chain out from beneath his shirt, showing her the brass key-chain charm she'd put in his vest pocket in the hospital.

She couldn't believe he was wearing it, and she felt caught again. "Would you believe me if I said no?"

"Not a chance," he said with a laugh. "Why did you give it to me?"

"I don't know. I felt compelled to. I bought it the morning

after you drove me home, and I used it as a reminder to stay strong and turn my life around. I used that as my key chain, and it became my lucky charm. It helped a lot. Eventually I got the tattoo, so the reminder would always be right in front of me. When you had your accident, I was first on the scene, but the first responders were from a different firehouse. When they took you to the hospital, they left my coat on the ground, and I found your leather vest beneath it. I took it to the hospital after my shift ended the next morning, and I couldn't shake the feeling that we had some sort of a connection. At the time, the doctors didn't know whether you had any cognitive deficits, and when I saw you lying there, I thought you needed luck more than I did."

"Wow, Angel. Thank you. That's really something. I think it helped. Do you want it back?"

"No, thanks. I don't believe in taking back gifts."

"Good." He held her gaze. "Because four is my favorite number now, too."

His gaze was unwavering and intense, rooting her in place. The air between them thickened, pulsing with something alive and enticing, honing in on the moment. Heat sparked in her chest, climbing up her neck and cheeks. The breeze carried his leathery, spicy scent as it brushed over her skin, painting her with it. Her heart was pounding, as if trying to be heard, and she realized he was still holding her hand just as her radio sounded with a call for a motor vehicle accident, jerking her from the moment.

The air rushed from her lungs, kicking her work brain into gear.

She pulled her hand free, grateful for something familiar and steady to focus on, and responded to the call using the shoulder mic to the radio attached to her belt. "Medic one copies call." Turning to Zander, she said, "I'm sorry, I have to go."

She ran toward the front of the building, thankful for the escape.

Not because she wasn't attracted to him or curious about the unstoppable energy between them, but because she *was*.

Chapter Seven

ZANDER CRUISED INTO the parking lot of the old brick schoolhouse that had become the Dark Knights' clubhouse years ago and parked among the other bikes and vehicles. Climbing off his motorcycle, he scanned the groups of guys standing out front as he locked his helmet to the bike. He spotted Zeke and Maverick talking with their cousins Tank and Gunner and headed over. Belleau, one of Gunner's many rescue dogs, bounded toward him. Gunner and his wife, Sidney, both former marines, owned an animal rescue, and he often brought one of his dogs to church, like Preacher did.

Zander petted the old chocolate Lab. "How's it going, boy?"

"The bastard stole my beef jerky right out of my hand," Tank, his oldest cousin, said.

The Wickeds were a tough crew, but at six four, burly, and bearded, with dark hair, coal-black eyes, a body full of tattoos, and piercings in one nostril and both ears, Tank was the most intimidating of them all. Tank owned Wicked Ink, a tattoo parlor, and he was a loving husband and adoring father to two little girls and an adorable little boy.

"Don't make my dog out to be a villain. You asked Belleau if he wanted any," Gunner said, giving Tank a pointed stare.

Like his oldest brother, he had tattoos from neck to fingers, but his military-short hair was blond, like their father Conroy's had been before it turned silver. "Remind me to train *you* before you get a dog for the kids."

Tank ignored him.

"How's it going, Zan?" Maverick asked. "You doing okay?"

Zander tried not to let his brother's second question get to him, but before the accident there wouldn't have been that kind of second question, or the scrutinizing, worried look in his eyes. "Yeah, man. I'm good," he said, even though he wasn't. He was worried about Shauna. He'd been worried since he'd first heard her and Brian shouting at each other, but when he'd seen Brian earlier, the guy had been blitzed out of his mind and more belligerent than he'd been the day before. At least she wouldn't have to deal with Brian tonight since her shift didn't end until morning.

"Where have you been?" Zeke asked. "I thought you finished early today."

"I did. I stopped by the Brewster firehouse to give the woman who pulled me out of the wreck something, and I talked with her for a while." He'd told Zeke about Shauna when he'd seen him at the shop that morning.

"I thought you were brought in by the Eastham station," Tank said. As a former volunteer firefighter, he knew many local first responders. "They're all guys."

"I was, but when I was at Cumby's, I heard a woman singing and thought I recognized her voice, and—"

"You saw her at Cumby's, not the firehouse?" Maverick asked.

"No. I mean, at first, but we didn't talk. Then I went to her house—"

"So you stalked her?" Gunner asked, petting Belleau.

"*No.* I showed up for a job Preacher sent me on, and she lived there. That's when I told her I recognized her voice, and she said she pulled me out of the car."

"You said you went to the firehouse," Tank said. "How'd you know where she worked?"

What the hell was up with all the questions? "She told me she was an EMT, and I asked around."

"He totally stalked her," Gunner said, and the guys all cracked up.

"That's our Zander," Maverick said.

"Fuck you all," Zander fumed. "I did *not* stalk her."

"They're just giving you shit, Zan," Zeke said with a laugh. "I told them about Shauna before you got here."

Zander glowered at the others, gritting out, "Y'all are dicks," but he couldn't help laughing.

"What'd you bring her?" Tank asked.

"Creamer," he said as Belleau nudged him for more attention. He reached down and petted him.

"Dude, you went to the firehouse and creamed on her?" Gunner smirked, and the guys cracked up.

"No, you ass. I brought her coffee creamer."

"That some kind of new kink?" Tank asked.

"Shut the hell up," Zander said. "She saved my life, and I wanted to do something nice for her. Don't make it weird. And get this. Remember a few years ago when I drove that young girl who'd had too much to drink home from the Fourth of July beach bash, and I went back to check on her the next day, but she'd already moved on?" Their families had been hosting the Fourth of July beach bash for as long as Zander could remember.

"Yeah?" Zeke said.

"That was *her*."

"Seriously?" Tank asked.

"Crazy, right?" Zander said. "She was too out of it back then to recognize me now, and I didn't recognize her, either. She looks totally different, but she felt like she knew me, and I couldn't shake the feeling that I knew her. Check this out." He pulled out the necklace and showed them the charm. "I found this in my cut at the hospital. I had no idea how it got in my pocket, but I felt like it was important, so I kept it. It turns out she put it there after the accident. It was her good-luck charm. She bought it the morning after I drove her home that Fourth of July. She said I changed her life that night, and she's had it on her key chain all this time to remind her to stop drinking." He told them what he'd said to her back then. "She put it in my cut because she thought I needed luck more than she did."

"That's some kind of fate right there. Chloe would say there's a reason you were put back in each other's paths," Maverick said about his wife as the clubhouse door opened, and their cousin Baz peered out. Like Gunner, Baz was fair-haired, but with collar-length hair, Baz looked more like a surfer than a veterinarian.

"What're you all up to?" Baz asked.

Gunner clapped a hand on Zander's shoulder and said, "Zan was just telling us about his star-crossed connection with the woman who pulled him out of the burning car."

Baz pushed the door open all the way and said, "Tell me about it on the way in." Then he called to the other men standing out front. "Preacher's about ready to start the meeting."

Zander relayed the story to Baz while they headed inside,

blending into the sea of Dark Knights. Nearly every seat in the clubhouse was taken. Zander was greeted by several other members as he and the guys made their way to a table across the room, where Blaine was sitting.

"Hey, Blaine. How's it going?" Zander asked as he sat down.

"It'd be better if I could lock Lettie in the basement until she's thirty," Blaine said, thumbing out a text. Colette "Lettie" Wilder was his fiancée Reese's sixteen-year-old sister, who lived with them.

"Is she getting into trouble?" Zander asked.

"Not yet, but boys are texting her all the time," Blaine grumbled. "I fucking hate it."

"That's why I'm hoping we have another boy," Baz said. He and his fiancée, Emerson Lockhart, a single mother and a hell of a baker, were expecting another baby in late August.

"Remember when Ash and Mads were teenagers? Guys came out of the woodwork," Gunner reminded them as Belleau ambled over and lay at his feet.

"You have no idea what they put us through when they were Lettie's age," Tank said.

"Bullshit," Gunner argued. "We all had to keep an eye on them."

"Yeah, well, Tank and I had to watch all of you to make sure you didn't do anything stupid *and* keep an eye out for the horny little asshats who had their eyes on our sisters," Blaine said.

"I never did stupid shit," Zeke argued.

"Yeah, that was usually me and Zan," Gunner teased.

"Zeke might not have gotten into trouble often, but he had his moments," Blaine said. "When he was eleven or twelve, he snuck out, and I thought he was going to see a girl, so I followed him."

"Couldn't even get your own girls back then, huh?" Zander teased, and the guys laughed.

Blaine flicked him off. "He rode his bike nearly five miles to a beach and walked in the pitch-dark all the way down to where a dead whale had beached itself, and then he just sat there. I was watching him from the dunes, wondering what the hell he was doing, when three older kids showed up to steal a piece of whale bone, which is illegal. Doofus over here tried to stop them, so I had to kick their asses and haul his ass back home before Dad woke up."

"A'right, Zeke. Keeping life interesting." Zander high-fived Zeke as Preacher and Conroy headed up to their seats at the head of the table.

The din of conversations quieted. His father, the president of the club, and his uncle, the vice president, had earned that respect with thirty-plus years of helping the community and having the backs of every single member of the club and their families.

As they discussed club finances, old business, and prospects, Zander mentally replayed his conversation with Shauna, wishing he'd asked for her number. That was a strange thought for a guy who'd always done everything possible to keep from having attachments with women. He tried to stop thinking about her, but she stuck with him the same way her voice still played in his mind like an old favorite. *Only now I know the gorgeous face, curvy body, and spunky attitude that go with that voice.* But his thoughts weren't about her looks. That felt secondary. This was something else. Something he couldn't identify but was impossible to escape.

"We're happy to share that we've had eight middle schools sign on for the anti-drug program," Preacher announced, drawing Zander's attention. "If you're interested in volunteering, the forms are on our website."

Zander had already signed up to take part in the program in the fall, like he did every year. Preacher went over a few more items before handing the floor over to Conroy.

"Thanks, Preach," Conroy said. With wavy silver hair that brushed his collar, warm blue eyes, and a laid-back personality, women always said he seemed more like a movie star than the badass biker he was known to be. "The annual Bikes on the Beach event is taking place the second week of August. The club will have a table, and if you'd like to help run it, sign up online..."

Bikes on the Beach was always a wild time, drawing bikers, and women, from near and far. As Conroy talked about the suicide prevention ride and rally in the fall and other upcoming events, Zander's mind made a beeline back to Shauna.

When the meeting finally ended, Zander was *still* thinking about getting Shauna's phone number and trying to make sense of how badly he wanted it. She was beautiful, but she wasn't his usual type. He'd always gone for party girls with smoky eyes who tried to lure him in with fluttering lashes and sexual innuendos. Women who knew the score and were cool with having a good time, knowing full well he'd walk away after and probably forget their names. Shauna hadn't even tried to flirt with him. If anything, she'd called him on his shit.

And he freaking loved it.

He stuck around to talk with the guys for a while, then headed straight to the firehouse to get that number.

THE BAY DOORS were closed, so he went to the front door, but it was locked. Many fire stations on the Cape didn't have enough funding for staff to cover them when they were out on calls. Instead, they had emergency phones by the door with a direct line to dispatch.

He eyed the phone, thinking about trying to charm a dispatcher into giving him Shauna's number. But even the boundary pusher he'd been before the accident had too much respect for first responders to dick around with them like that. He thought about waiting for her to return, but the guys teasing him about being a stalker was too damn fresh in his mind.

Fuck it.

He climbed back on his bike and headed to the Salty Hog to try to get her off his mind.

Chapter Eight

THERE MUST HAVE been dark forces at play last night, because they'd had so many calls at the firehouse, Shauna was bleary-eyed by the time she got home. She stood in her living room Thursday morning, trying to make sense of the empty tabletop where the television was supposed to be. She blinked several times, wondering if her exhaustion was messing with her. *Nope.* The television still wasn't there. She looked around the living room and kitchen in case Brian had moved it. There were dirty dishes on the coffee table and the counter, but the television was nowhere in sight.

She glanced down the hall. Brian's bedroom door was ajar, his music spilling out. "Brian?" she called out, wondering if he'd moved the TV into his room.

He didn't respond.

Too tired to yell, she went to talk to him. "Brian, where's the TV?" she asked as she pushed the door open. The room was a wreck, the curtains closed, and Brian was bent over the nightstand snorting something. Her restraint snapped, and all the pent-up anger and frustration from the last few months came roaring out. "What the *hell* are you doing?"

He bolted upright and charged toward her, wild-eyed. "Get

the fuck outta here!"

"*No.* I'm paying the fucking rent." She stood her ground, the sight of the brown powder—*heroin*—on the mirror making her even more furious. "You can't do that shit here!"

"The hell I can't," he seethed.

"You don't get to make the rules when you're living off *my* money. Where'd you get the money for the drugs?"

"Leave me the fuck alone." He turned away, his movements jerky.

The answer hit her like a brick. "Where's the TV, Brian?"

"I don't fucking know. Maybe someone stole it."

"I'm not stupid," she fumed. "You sold it to buy heroin, didn't you?"

"*No.*"

"Yeah, right. I'm such an idiot. I kept telling myself you weren't that bad. That I could help you."

"Don't you get it? I don't want your fucking help!"

He spun around, his teeth clenched like a rabid animal, and grabbed her upper arms so tight, her knees buckled. He shoved her backward. Her back slammed into a picture hanging on the wall, the corner of the frame digging into her back. The impact knocked the wind from her lungs…and the ghosts of her past from their tethers. Images of her father hitting her mother flew at her, fueling her with fierce, unwavering strength. The picture crashed to the floor as she grabbed Brian by his shirt, yanking him down as her knee flew up, connecting with his gut. He cried out, and she threw him backward, sending him to his ass on the floor.

She stood over him, shaking with anger and so much heart-break at what her friend had become, it hurt more than the physical attack did. "Don't you *ever* put your hands on me again, or I *swear* I'll kill you."

He scrambled to his feet, a flicker of regret warring with the rage in his eyes. "I'm sorry—"

"*Don't.* I'm done watching you kill yourself. I can't even look at you right now. Get the fuck out of here." She stormed out of his room, heading for hers.

He ran after her. "Shauna, *wait*. I'm sor—"

His words were cut off as she slammed and locked her bedroom door. Shaking and gasping for breath, she lowered herself to the edge of the bed, giving in to the tears she'd been holding back for weeks.

Chapter Nine

HOURS PASSED WITH battering waves of anger, confusion, hurt, and a modicum of relief, though that was the one that hurt the most. Shauna was exhausted. Even after she'd heard Brian leave the house, she was too on edge to close her eyes. She didn't know if he'd come back even angrier or promising to get help. Either way she needed to be ready.

She couldn't fool herself anymore. She had to do something, but she didn't have any reasonable options. By late afternoon she was emotionally and physically depleted, and her back hurt. She felt like a zombie. Hoping a shower would clear her head, she locked the front door and headed for the bathroom. She hesitated in front of Brian's room, the chaotic state of it a mirror of what he'd become. The picture of them they'd taken this time last year lay on the floor among shattered glass and the broken frame, breaking her heart anew.

When she finally stepped beneath the shower spray, she tilted her face up, letting the water rain down over her. Memories tiptoed in. *Hitchhiking out of town with Brian the night they'd left home, getting high on the side of the highway. Climbing into cars with strangers.* At the time she'd told herself they were brave, and they had been to have gotten away from their parents, but they were also so damn young, and what they'd done was dangerously stupid.

As she washed her hair, she thought about the days after Brian had nearly died from an overdose. They'd both been so scared. But they'd been there for each other on their journey to sobriety, cheering each other on and dragging each other to meetings. They'd come so far. How had she let so much time go by without figuring something out so it wouldn't come to this?

She'd been to enough meetings to know better than to take the blame for his addiction, but that didn't make it any easier to face their current situation.

Fresh tears rolled down her cheeks. She told herself to get all her crying done now, because there was no way she'd let Brian see that weakness. Part of her hoped he wouldn't come back until he miraculously found a way to get out from under the drugs, but that thought brought a deluge of guilt.

She fought that guilt, and instead of shedding the rest of her tears, she did what she knew was best and forced herself to regain control. She was reaching for a towel when she heard a knock at the front door. Her stomach clenched. Brian had a key, but with the way things were going, he probably lost it. She wrapped the towel around herself and went to answer the door.

She peered out the sidelight window as she reached for the doorknob, and her heart nearly stopped. It wasn't Brian.

It was Zander.

He flashed her a cocky grin, sending her heart into a tailspin. *Shitshitshit.* She leaned out of his view, hiding behind the door. Why was he here? She looked down at her towel and cringed. She couldn't pretend she hadn't seen him.

What kind of crazy test of sanity is this?

She took a deep, calming breath and opened the door, hiding half of her body behind it. "Zander, hi. I wasn't expecting you."

"I wanted to come by and…" His brows slanted, his smile morphing to a clenched jaw, his eyes locked on her arm. "Who did that to you?"

She followed his gaze to an angry bruise on her arm and swallowed hard, averting her eyes. She'd been so upset, she hadn't even registered the tenderness in her arms where Brian had grabbed her, but now she remembered flinching in the shower as she'd washed them.

"No one. It must've happened when…" She heard herself lying, and stopped. That was how she'd ended up in this predicament. She couldn't, *shouldn't*, do it anymore.

"Shauna." He stepped closer. "*Who* hurt you?"

Emotions thickened her throat as she met his gaze, and she was hit with another wave of guilt as she said, "Brian."

His chest expanded with a deep inhalation, his nostrils flaring, his jaw tightening. "Where is he?"

She shrugged. "Not here."

"Go get dressed. You're coming home with me."

"What? *Why?*" Was he serious? This man she barely knew? *The guy who unknowingly changed my life once before?* That sobering thought gave her pause. She hadn't known him then, but had trusted him enough to get into his car, drunk, and tell him where she lived.

"Because no man should ever put their hands on you like that, and I'm not leaving you here for him to do it again." His tone carried no pity or judgment, only steady, caring insistence, and that, too, rattled her.

"Zander—"

"You're safe with me, Shauna." His voice was low and reassuring, but firm. "I have an extra bedroom. I promise I won't touch you. But if you don't trust me, then I'll take you to a hotel, or you can stay at the firehouse. Or if you want to stay here, I'll sit my ass down on your front porch and stand guard, but I am *not* leaving you here alone."

A lump lodged in her throat. The fighter in her who had made it this far wanted to say no, to prove she was strong and could handle whatever came her way. But as she stood there looking at Zander, she knew in her heart that she could trust him, and something about that made the tension she'd carried every minute of every day for as long as she could remember unfurl. She'd been strong for so long, fighting for survival, then for sobriety and to make something of herself, and more recently, she'd been fighting for her *and* Brian. She was wrung out, utterly and completely spent, and she knew she wouldn't sleep well there, whether or not Zander was standing guard out front. Just this once, she didn't want to be strong.

It took everything she had left to say "Okay" and step back, allowing him to come inside.

His gaze swept over her, moving from one arm to the other as she closed the door, fury rising in his eyes. *"Jesus,"* he whispered. His gaze dropped to an old bruise on her forearm.

"That one's from pole class," she managed.

"Shauna," he warned.

"I promise. I get them all the time on my arms and legs," she said shakily.

His arms circled her, embracing her so gently, she knew he was giving her a chance to step back. But she didn't. She pressed her cheek to his chest, soaking in his comfort, and the dam broke, tears flooding down her cheeks. He held her a little tighter, his hand moving soothingly up her back. She inhaled sharply when he touched the sore spot where she'd hit the picture frame.

He gently shifted them, keeping her tucked against him with one arm, and moved the towel a little lower on her back. His body went rigid, every muscle flexing. She closed her eyes, emotions swamping her anew, but then his arms were around her again, holding her more carefully.

"Never again," he said gruffly, and pressed a kiss to the top of her head, causing another deluge of tears.

Chapter Ten

ZANDER STOOD BY the stove in his partially renovated kitchen, stirring a pot of pasta. Meatballs bobbed in the sauce simmering on another burner, and the oven was preheating. He set the spoon down and began slathering garlic butter onto thick slices of French bread. He'd needed something to slow his spinning thoughts, and with Shauna sleeping, he couldn't very well work on his renovations.

When he'd seen her, puffy-eyed, wet hair sticking to her face and shoulders, and those damn bruises on her arm, his protective urges had ignited, hot, sharp, and biting. She hadn't shared the details of what went down with Brian yet, but there was plenty of time for that. When they'd gotten to his place, she'd looked like she barely had the energy to remain upright. He'd shown her the extra bedroom and had suggested she rest for a while. She'd said she was fine, which he'd expected to hear. She was so fucking strong, and with the little he knew about her, it was no wonder. It probably didn't help that the beach-front cottage he'd bought to flip looked like a construction zone. It was a work in progress, the two bedrooms and bath-room the only finished spaces. The living room and dining room were stripped to bare studs. Drywall was up in the kitchen, but it hadn't been painted, and there were no doors on the cabinets and no backsplash above the counters.

He'd given Shauna a gentle nudge toward resting, saying he had things to do. He didn't mention those things were not working on the cottage but trying to quell the urge to hunt Brian down and fuck him up for putting his hands on her.

She'd finally agreed to rest, and he'd seen a flicker of relief in her eyes, as if she'd desperately needed someone to give her permission to let her guard down. When she'd disappeared behind the bedroom door, he'd heard the turn of the lock and wondered if she ever had a chance to let down her defenses.

That was three hours ago. He'd spent that time bracing to tiptoe through an emotional minefield. He wasn't great at that. When his younger sister, Madigan, was upset, his blunt advice and suggestions weren't always appreciated, but when Gunner's wife, Sid, had been wrestling with her feelings for Gunner before they got together, she'd said Zander was a big help, so maybe he didn't totally suck at it.

As he put the tray of bread in the oven, Kitty, his fluffy gray cat, wound between his feet and meowed. She'd been wearing a path between Shauna's closed bedroom door and Zander since they got there, meowing like she was trying to tell him something. He lifted her into his arms and nuzzled against her fur. "I know, baby girl. You're not used to having other females in the house, but she's a special one, and she needs a safe place."

Kitty purred.

He heard the bedroom door open and turned as Shauna padded into the living room, her pretty dark eyes taking in the unfinished space. Her hair was pinned up in a ponytail now, and she wore a baby-blue sweatshirt with a dandelion on it, the seeds blowing in the wind, as if caught midwish. He wondered if she'd had many wishes come true in her life, and he had the strange desire to know what they were. Her faded jeans were torn on one knee, soft pink socks peeking out from beneath the long, frayed hems. It was those socks that tugged at him, out of place beneath the frayed denim and her guarded eyes, revealing another side to the hard edges she showed the world.

She lifted those troubled eyes to his before they drifted down to Kitty, and she smiled a little sheepishly, looking more rested and absolutely adorable. That tightness in his chest and the urge to protect her no matter the cost returned, and he knew in that moment that if she needed him to tiptoe through any minefield, he'd damn well become the best fucking tiptoer in the country.

"Did you sleep okay?" he asked, turning off the stove and oven as she came into the kitchen.

"Yeah, thank you. That bed is super comfy, and I opened the window. The sound of the ocean lulled me right to sleep." Her brows furrowed, and she glanced around the kitchen. "Is it too weird having me here? Maybe I should go."

"What do you think?" he asked Kitty in a hushed voice. "Is she trying to say she's already tired of us?"

"No, I'm not," Shauna said sharply. "How could I be? I walked into your house and immediately fell asleep. It looks like you just moved in and you've got a lot going on. I don't want to be in the way."

"You're not in the way. I've lived here for a few years, but I haven't gotten around to finishing the renovations. Besides, I figured you might be hungry. I made spaghetti." He tucked Kitty in one arm and took the garlic bread out of the oven.

"It smells incredible, but you didn't have to do that. Are you sure you don't mind?"

"Angel, if there's one thing I'm not, it's shy about saying what I feel. If I didn't want you here, I wouldn't have invited you. Okay?"

She nodded, and this time her smile was slightly less unsure, but he could tell she wasn't used to being taken care of and still felt funny, so he went for levity.

"Good, now relax and tell me how cute my furry girl is." He scratched the back of Kitty's neck, and she purred.

"She *is* awfully cute. I love animals. Is she friendly? Can I hold her?"

"Only if you promise to give her more love than you think she needs. She's kind of spoiled that way."

"I didn't know there was a limit to the love animals needed."

"I think you just earned a spot at the top of our favorite people list," he said as he handed Kitty over.

"Hi, cutie pie," she said, petting the cat. "What's her name?"

"Kitty."

She gave him an incredulous look. "You love your cat so much that I had to promise to love her before I could hold her, and you gave her a generic name?"

"It's not generic." He drained the spaghetti and began filling their plates.

"That's like naming your kids Girl or Boy."

"First of all, I'm not a marriage and kids kind of guy, so nobody is in danger of growing up with those names because of me. Second of all, she chose her name. She showed up out front a few weeks after I got home from the hospital. She bolted out of the bushes and scared the hell out of me. She was all skin and bones."

"Poor thing."

"I put out food and water for her and sat out there every day trying to get her to eat, but she wouldn't come near me." He put garlic bread on their plates and set them on the island. "One day I said, *Here, Kitty, Kitty,* about a dozen times, and that was the day she came to me."

She stifled a laugh. "That makes total sense. It couldn't be because she was used to your voice by then."

He was glad she was getting comfortable enough to give him a hard time. "It doesn't matter if she was. The fact is, she didn't come when I called her 'sweetie' or 'baby' or anything else, and if I've learned one thing about the female species, it's not to question things that make them happy." He put silverware, napkins, and Parmesan cheese on the island, then opened the fridge and nearly reached for a couple of beers. Thinking better of it, he said, "What would you like to drink? Water, Red Bull, soda, iced tea?"

"Iced tea is great. I can get it."

"It's okay. I've got it." He poured two glasses and set them on the island.

"Why is one chair higher than the others?"

"I'll show you." He sat in the chair beside the higher one and made quick kissing sounds.

Kitty wriggled out of Shauna's arms to the floor, then jumped onto the higher chair and faced Zander, staring at him. He scratched behind her ears, and she purred, tipping her face up. He kissed her chin.

"You bought her a high chair so you could pet her? That's pretty freaking cute."

"I didn't buy it. I made it. I couldn't find one that was the right height when I sat beside her." He gave Kitty one last pet and got up to feed her. "She keeps me company while I eat." He filled Kitty's bowls with fresh water and food and placed them on her mat on the floor.

"Shall we?" He pulled out a chair for Shauna.

As she sat down, he sat beside her, and she got quiet again. She pushed the food around on her plate with her fork, stealing glances at him. He knew from the awkward silence that she was waiting for him to ask about what happened, but he knew better than to push.

He wanted her to feel safe, and he'd wait as long as she needed him to, without any expectations or demands, so she'd never feel alone again.

WITHOUT THE DISTRACTION of the cat, awkwardness trickled in for Shauna as they ate. She knew Zander must have a million questions, and he deserved answers. She just didn't know where to start, so she tried to break the tension. "This is delicious."

"Thanks. I can't take credit for more than the garlic bread. My mother keeps my freezer stocked with food. All I had to do was cook the spaghetti and heat up the sauce."

God, was he one of those guys who expected women to do all the things he considered to be beneath him? "You're thirty and your mother still cooks your meals?"

"I don't ask her to." He took a drink and said, "She does it for everyone. I think it's a mom thing."

"You're lucky," she said, and immediately regretted it. She didn't want him to feel sorry for her.

"I am, for many more reasons than that." He held her gaze, compassion brimming in his eyes. "I have great parents, and I'm really sorry you didn't."

"I don't want your pity."

"That's not pity. It's truth," he said emphatically. "Pity implies that I feel superior, and I definitely don't. We don't have any say in who our parents are. It's the luck of the draw. What I feel is sad that you weren't loved the way every child deserves to be loved. That you didn't get the gentleness you should have gotten from them before you were set free in a world that can be too damn rough."

Unexpected emotions bubbled up inside her.

"I don't know what the situation was with your parents, but it was bad enough for you to take off at seventeen, which tells me a lot." He stabbed a piece of meatball with his fork. "You got the short end of the stick, and that fucking sucks."

Something about his vehemence and understanding made it easier for her to talk about it. "It does suck. I used to think it was my fault that they were like that, but I've learned that their addictions, their fights, and my father's abuse had nothing to do with me."

His fork stopped halfway to his mouth, his eyes narrowing.

She realized how much she'd revealed and quickly added, "Sorry. I don't mean to dump this on you. I don't usually talk about it."

"You're not dumping," he said evenly. "Did your father ever hurt you?"

She didn't answer right away, pushing spaghetti around on her plate, but she wasn't going to go backward and hide in shame over the shit her parents did.

"Only once physically," she finally said. "And I'm not rationalizing for him, but it wasn't like he hit me or anything. He and my mother fought a lot, and they'd get physical with each other, but they just yelled at me. That's why I stayed out of the house as much as I could. Well, that and the fact that they were usually drunk or high. The one time I tried to get between them, they both pushed me out of the way. Until then, I think I'd hoped that my mother would clean up her act, but that's when I knew I was really on my own."

"How old were you?" He ate the meatball he'd speared.

"Seventeen. It was about two weeks before graduation, before we ran away. I know it looks like I went from an abusive family to being with an abusive guy, but it wasn't always like this with Brian."

"I don't think you did that." He tapped her leg with the side of his. "And just so you know, I'm the last guy you need to worry about judging you."

The honesty in his eyes was underscored by his reassuring tone, allowing relief to whisper in. "Okay."

"Tell me about Brian. You said you grew up together?"

"Yeah. I've known him forever. He lived around the corner from me, and we rode the bus to school together every year. Neither of us has any brothers or sisters, so we'd hang out together after school. When other kids were playing at the park, we were knocking around down by the creek or in the junkyard around the corner. We bonded over our horrible home lives and commiserated about how much we hated our parents and their fighting. We snuck out at night to get away from their yelling, and we'd bang on each other's bedroom windows. I can't tell you how many times I cried on his shoulder, cursing them. Every week I'd swear I was going to run away, but every time I said it, Brian said I had to wait until I graduated from high school or they'd put me in a foster home and arrest my parents."

"A foster home might not have been too bad," Zander said. "My brother Justin, who goes by the road name Maverick, was fostered by my parents before they adopted him. He came to us when he was eleven, and he'll tell you it was the best thing that ever happened to him. Well, before he fell in love with his wife, Chloe, and they had their daughter, Marybelle. But there are plenty of people who haven't had that kind of experience, so who knows what would've happened."

"I didn't know what being in the system even meant back then," she admitted. "It was this undefinable thing that could happen to kids, and we thought it was bad." She ate a forkful of spaghetti, remembering how the idea of a bad foster family had stopped her from leaving. "Was it hard for you to have another kid in the house?"

"No, there are a lot of us. I have three brothers and one sister. Blaine is the oldest, then there's Maverick. The two of them had a rough start, but now they co-own Cape Stone, a stone masonry and distribution company. Then there's Zeke. He works with me at our family's renovation company, and my sister, Madigan. Mads is a jack-of-all-trades. She's a puppeteer and a musical storyteller, and she makes greeting cards."

"Wow. Are you all close?"

"Yeah, very. We're close to my cousins, too. Tank, who looks like his name and owns a tattoo shop, and Baz—he's a vet—and Gunner. Gunner and his wife, Sid, own an animal rescue. But I grew up with the Dark Knights' families. I was used to being around lots of kids. I thought it was cool when Mav came to stay with us, but I was just a little kid. I know it was tougher for Blaine. As the oldest, he was used to being the big dog, and Maverick is only a year younger, and he wasn't used to answering to anyone. It took Maverick a solid year to let his guard down, and that was probably the only time in my life when I wasn't the biggest troublemaker in the family."

She laughed softly. "You were a troublemaker, huh?"

"Some would say I still am, but that's enough about me. I'd like to hear the rest of your story, if you don't mind. You said you and Brian have been best buds since you were kids. When did you start partying?"

"I don't remember exactly how or when, but by the time we were fourteen, drinking and getting high were part of our daily routine. While other kids were out at community fairs with their families and amusement parks with friends, we were planning our escape for after graduation. We thought that was enough, you know? Like that piece of paper and leaving our parents behind would change our lives."

"It did change your lives," Zander said.

"Eventually," she admitted. "But leaving didn't really solve anything. It just brought different fears. We were scared *all* the time. Scared our parents would drag us back home, scared of the world around us, living in awful situations with other runaways and druggies. We kept partying to escape those fears, and we did it for way too long. Brian got into snorting heroin a few times a week toward the end, when he could afford it, but I never did."

He took a drink, and as he set the glass down, he said, "Why didn't you?"

"I was too afraid. For some reason, in my stupid mind, alcohol and weed weren't as bad."

"Your mind is far from stupid. Even when you were under the influence, you kept yourself from getting in deeper."

She smiled, appreciating that more than he could know. "I

guess you're right. That Fourth of July when you drove me home, I had stumbled by some kids my age, and one of them said something to the others about never wanting to turn into a waste case like *that girl*, and she was referring to *me*." She twirled spaghetti around her fork. "That was the first time I really saw myself through someone else's eyes, and I didn't like what I saw. I felt so lost and alone, but I didn't know how to become someone else. Then you gave me the answer I needed."

She ate the spaghetti. "You made it seem easy, like it was within my reach. Within my *control*. The trouble with being an addict is that the substance has the control. It's like the carrot ahead of the horse. But I held on to your words like a lifeline. They became my carrot, and I focused on cleaning up my act and partying less. But Brian had a harder time, and eventually he overdosed." Her voice cracked. It hurt to admit that aloud. "Thankfully, I found him in time, and the first responders were able to revive him. That was his turning point."

"That must have been terrifying."

"It was," she said softly, remembering the fear that had consumed her. "I don't know what I would have done if I'd lost him. I would have been completely alone."

Zander covered her hand with his and squeezed it reassuringly. "I've got news for you, darlin'. You've entered the Wicked zone, and once you're in it, you're pretty much stuck with another best friend for life."

"You are *not* stuck with me for life," she said with a laugh, and then ate another bite of pasta.

"I never said *I* was stuck. I said you're stuck, because that's how Wickeds roll. I, on the other hand, am in need of another best friend. Gunner was my wingman, but now he's married, and Zeke and I are like this." He crossed his index and second finger. "But he's a mother hen, not a great wingman."

"You expect me to find you women?"

"Hell no. They flock to me on their own. You just need to tell them how great I am."

She crossed her arms, amused by his arrogance. "And what if I don't think you're great?"

"You will. You won't find a cooler friend than me. You're not getting out of it, and I'm a great listener, so go ahead and finish your story. What happened after Brian overdosed?"

She couldn't believe how easily he made her smile. "There must have been someone watching over us that night, because the fire captain gave me pamphlets about NA and AA. I remember thanking him so many times for saving Brian and begging him not to turn Brian in to the police. He told me he was there to help, not to give Brian a reason to do it again."

"Sounds like a good man. You're lucky they were able to save him. I lost my cousin Ashley to an accidental overdose several years ago. That's the kind of loss you never get over."

Her stomach sank. "I'm sorry. That's horrible."

"Yeah. It was. She was Madigan's best friend, and not a day goes by that I don't think about her. But it was a long time ago, and I know she's still hanging around, watching over us, laughing at the stupid shit we do." He shook his head, and his tender smile told her how much he loved his cousin. "How did Brian stop using back then?"

"It wasn't easy. He didn't trust anyone, and I was desperate to help him, but I didn't know how. The captain who had been so nice that night is the captain at the firehouse where I work. Back then Cap made me feel like someone finally saw us as people worthy of something better, not just as boils on the ass of society. So I went to the firehouse, and I asked him what I needed to know to help Brian detox. Cap explained the risks of detoxing without medical supervision, and he was *not* cool with the idea of us trying to do it alone."

"I don't blame him."

"I get it, and I would never do it again, but we had no money, no insurance, and not a lot of faith in strangers. We felt like it was a big risk just asking for help. But Cap told me what to do and what to expect, and I scoured the internet, reading everything I could. Then Brian and I powered through together. It was hell for him. It was so painful, and he was so sick, he just wanted to die. It was hell watching him suffer. I begged him to let me take him to the hospital, but he refused. But honestly, as awful as it was, it was the best motivation for me to stay sober. I can't imagine what it would have been like if he'd been using every day."

"Jesus, Angel. It really was you two against the world."

"Mm-hm. Cap checked in with me a lot, and once Brian was past the worst of it, we went to meetings *every* day, together every step of the way. What most people don't realize is that even when you think you're past the worst of it, you're really not. It was months of struggling not to fall back into the addiction. Downtime was the hardest, being alone with our thoughts. We became gym rats, working out two, sometimes three times a day. Eventually I started volunteering at the firehouse, and we both found jobs and actually went to them every day. I went through a year of therapy. Brian didn't, but that didn't worry me. Not everyone recovers the same way. After a couple of years, we were both doing so well, I felt like we'd made it. Brian loved his job as a delivery driver, and I loved my time at the firehouse. The guys there became like family, and Cap was a great mentor. He helped me become more confident, and I got up the courage to ask him if I could work there if I went through EMT training. Since he knew about my past with alcohol and weed, I was afraid I wouldn't be allowed, but here I am."

"You've really turned your life around."

"I have, and I'm proud of that. Brian had turned his around, too. The thing is, addiction never goes away. It's like a vulture on your shoulder waiting for the right moment to dig its claws into you, and I let my guard down with Brian. Something happened at his work, and I missed all the signs. We were living our lives, and we didn't talk as much. He was irritated a lot, which I wrote off as regular work stress." Guilt crept in, and she twisted spaghetti around her fork, fighting those feelings. "He didn't tell me he lost his job until a few weeks after it happened, and by then he was drinking again. He promised to stop, and he hid it from me, but over the next several weeks, he got back into drugs, and that sparked an endless cycle of promises and heartbreak."

"Why did he get physical with you?"

She finished her bite of spaghetti before answering. "Because when I came home, our television was missing. I went to confront him and walked in on him snorting what I'm pretty sure was heroin, and I lost it. I knew better than to fuel that fire. I learned a lot in those substance abuse meetings and heard so many stories from people in recovery and from their families. I know all about how loved ones feel like they've been disrespected when people with substance abuse issues use drugs in their houses or behind their backs. I used to think it was selfish of them not to understand their loved ones' addictions. But there I was, thinking, *How could you do this to us. To me?* I understand where they were coming from now, but I also know his addiction has nothing to do with me. Unfortunately, that doesn't help as much as it should."

"I'm glad you know that, because it really doesn't, but I'm sure that doesn't make it any easier. You love the guy, and lies hurt, no matter what the driving force behind them is. Why haven't you asked him to move out, or moved out yourself?"

"It's complicated." She took a bite of garlic bread. "I thought about moving out, but he can't afford rent, and I'm not going to leave him homeless. I'm living in this cloud of guilt with all these bad feelings about what he's doing, but I also love him, and I have faith that this isn't who he will always be. This is addiction trying to swallow him up, and I will *never* give up on him."

"He needs rehab, darlin'," Zander said gently.

"I *know*, but there's only one way he's getting that, and I can't do it."

He lifted his chin, his eyes narrowing. "What do you mean? You can't do what?"

"My grandfather, who I haven't seen since he told me he wanted nothing to do with me when I was a teenager, passed away a couple of months ago and left me fifty thousand dollars. Sounds great, right? I mean, not that he died, but it's the answer to my problems. Except it's not. He left it inaccessible unless I can prove I've been sober and drug free for two years, which I can, no problem. But I also have to be married for two months."

"Oh, *man*." Zander turned on the chair, facing her.

"Right?" She finished her garlic bread. "Who does that?"

"Someone who wants to ruin his granddaughter's life?"

She smiled, remembering what he'd said about not being the kind of guy to get married or have kids. "I love that you're not a fan of marriage, either. Most of the guys I work with think I'm nuts for not wanting to get hitched. I want to help Brian, but I'm never getting married. I'm not about to be a noose around someone else's neck."

"Why would you be a noose?"

"*Hello?* I drank and smoked weed for years instead of growing up. I don't know if I was chemically addicted like Brian was or not. Once he stopped and that peer pressure was off, it wasn't hard for me to stop drinking or smoking. I never had withdrawals, and when I see other people drinking, it doesn't make me want to drink. But maybe that's because I was the sober one when he was detoxing, and those memories are etched into my mind. All I know is, addictions are never cured, and how I feel today could change with the wind. I don't want to fall off the wagon and ruin someone else's life."

"I see your point, but I don't think addiction makes you a noose." He broke one of his pieces of garlic bread in half and handed her one half. "When someone loves you, they should support your sobriety every way they can, and if you fall off the wagon, it's that love that should pick you back up." He cocked a brow. "But *marriage*? That's the noose."

"You're not wrong." Reaching for her drink, she said, "I can count on one hand the number of happily married couples I know."

"That's why we should get married."

She choked on her drink and started coughing and laughing. *"What?"*

"I'm serious. You saved my life. Let me do this to help save your friend's life."

"No way! You're crazy."

"Maybe so, but I'm good at it. Think about it. Neither of us is the marrying type, so it's not like we'll want to stay married. We fake a whirlwind love affair for two months, plus another few weeks to cover your ass, and then you get the money to help Brian."

"You're a nut. I'm not getting married to you or anyone else."

He shook his head. "Then let me give you the money."

"Zander, *stop*." Holy crap. He really was nuts. "I'm not marrying you, and I'm not taking your money."

"Fine. I'll lend it to you. Then if you ever fall in love and get married, you can pay me back when you collect your inheritance."

"What part of *not getting married* didn't you understand? I think your head injury might have had lasting effects after all."

"Come on, Shauna. I've been working since I was a teenager. I have plenty of money sitting in the bank gathering dust. That doesn't even include the insurance money that'll come in from the accident in the next few weeks, and I've got nothing to spend it on besides Kitty, and she doesn't cost much."

Shauna glanced at the enormous basket of cat toys in the dining room and the handful of toys littering the floor between the living room and the kitchen. "All those toys and your half-finished house say otherwise. I appreciate your offer, but I will find another way to help Brian."

She didn't know how, but one way or another she was going to figure it out.

Chapter Eleven

AFTER DINNER, SHAUNA insisted on helping Zander with the dishes. She stood beside him by the sink humming softly as he washed and she dried. She'd been through so much, Zander hadn't been sure if having her crash at his place would be uncomfortable for her or make him edgy, but this was nice and enjoyable, and she was clearly more relaxed. He was glad to hear her humming, but he'd heard the guilt in her voice when she'd told him about the inheritance, and he knew she was struggling over the situation with Brian.

She was loyal to the point of putting herself in danger, and if there was one thing Zander respected above all else, it was loyalty. He didn't think she had a chance in hell of coming up with enough money for rehab, and there was no way he'd let her sit by Brian's side again as he tried to detox. Not after he'd put his hands on her. She might believe in Brian, but Zander had worked with enough people in recovery through the club to know how drugs could turn a normally mild-mannered person into a monster.

He wouldn't be standing there right now if it weren't for Shauna's selfless act of bravery. He wanted to help in return, and he wanted her to know she was not alone in this.

As he handed her a plate, he said, "Hey, Flores, can I ask you something personal?"

"You say that like I haven't been spilling my guts to you all evening."

"I'm just wondering, with everything going on, are you going to AA meetings, or should you be going to them? I'm not trying to say you should. It's just…if you need someone to go with you, that's what friends are for. I'd be happy to tag along."

She looked at him for a long moment as she finished drying the plate. "That's really nice of you to offer, but even with all the stress, I haven't had the urge to drink or smoke."

"Fair enough." He began washing a glass. "If that changes, I'm here to help."

"I appreciate that, and trust me, if I felt even a little bit like I might falter, I'd go to meetings and contact my sponsor." She set the plate on the counter with the other dishes and flashed those killer dimples. "You know, for a bachelor, you're not bad at this domestic stuff."

"I'm a man of many talents." He handed her the last glass.

"Oh yeah?" she said as she dried it. "Such as?"

"Most of them aren't appropriate for a new best friend."

"That's weird," she said sarcastically. "I heard you only use your talents on *new* friends, which makes sense." She glanced around the unfinished kitchen and said, "Clearly you're not very good at finishing what you start." She lowered her voice. "Women aren't big on that kind of repeat performance."

He laughed and shook his head. "Trust me, they beg for more."

"Exactly," she said snarkily, as if he'd proven her point. "But I don't want to know about your dirty deeds. I want to know what's going on with your cottage. You said you've lived here for a while?"

"Yeah. I bought this place to flip it, but I was having too much fun living my life to give it up and spend my free time renovating. But that changed after the accident. A lot of things changed, actually. I wanted to take control of my life, and this was as good a place to start as any."

"Life-threatening accidents tend to have that effect on people. But the accident wasn't your fault. Was your life that out of control?"

"Not out of control in the sense of drinking too much or anything like that, but I definitely like to have a good time. It's just that my drug of choice is women. I might not have caused that accident, but the accident caused my family, my club brothers, and my friends a shitload of worry, and if I hadn't gone home with a couple of girls the night before, I wouldn't have been late for work or been at that intersection for the accident to happen. That's on me. It was *my* choice to go home with them. I've always been the good-time guy who acts when an impulse hits and worries about it later." He realized that was what he was doing now. "Shit. *Sorry.* You're going through hell, and I'm doing it again, putting myself first and laying my crap on you."

"I don't mind. I like getting to know you. It makes me feel less like I'm the only one juggling excess baggage."

"Are you taking pleasure in my heartache, Flores?" he teased.

"I didn't mean it that way." She laughed softly. "But kind of, yeah."

"Well, you wouldn't be alone in that, and you're not alone in carrying that excess baggage, either. Every person on this earth is struggling with something, and if they tell you otherwise, they're lying. The bottom line is, I don't want to be the guy who causes my family and friends to worry anymore. You know what I just realized?"

"That you're done trying to change your ways and want to get the heck out of here and pick up a woman or two?"

He laughed. "Why would I do that when I'm having such a great time with you?"

"Because I won't sleep with you, obviously."

"I didn't offer for you to crash at my place so I could sleep with you." He couldn't resist teasing her back and said, "I mean, you'll probably want to sleep with me after a while, and normally I'd be into that, but I'm changing my ways."

Now she was laughing. "That's *not* going to happen."

"I'm just sayin', it wouldn't surprise me." He schooled his expression. "Seriously, though. I'm not going to be that guy anymore. Not that I was ever an asshole. I never pretended to want more than a good time, and I have nothing but respect for the women I spend time with. That said, random hookups were fun." He smacked against his chest. "But it's time to treat the old bod like a castle instead of a nightclub, and hanging out with you inspires me to stay on track."

"Why? Because I don't want to sleep with you?" she said with attitude.

He took the towel from her and dried his hands. "No. Like I said, that'll change."

She rolled her eyes.

"I'm only kidding." He draped the towel over the edge of the sink. "You inspire me because you made the effort to grow up at twenty, and you thought you'd been living off the rails for too long. Meanwhile, here I am at thirty, just starting to find my way onto the right track."

"Then I'm even happier that I gave you my good-luck

charm, because from what I hear, you're going to disappoint a lot of women. Not that I know anything about being a playboy, but I imagine that'll bring some of that begging you mentioned, and you may need to stay strong and ward it off." She punctuated *stay strong* with a punch to the air.

"You know what? That's another good reason we should get married."

"No, it's not!" she said with a laugh.

"Hear me out, because it'll help me as much as it'll help you. If you were my wife, it would get women off my back, which would make it easier for me to change my ways. Then you'd let me lend you the money, knowing you'd be able to pay it back in a couple of months."

She pointed at him. "You're insane, and the last thing I need is a crazy-ass fake husband."

"I can't fix my crazy, but I'd be your real husband during that time, legal and everything, and you'd totally have bragging rights to the hottest guy in Bayside."

"Ohmygod." She leveled Zander with a serious stare. "I think you mean the hottest *player*, and what makes you think I'd want half the town's sloppy seconds?"

"Ouch." He put his hand over his heart. "That stung."

"You just got done telling me that you're a player who goes home with more than one woman at a time."

He cocked a grin. "That wasn't the part that hurt. You called me *sloppy*."

Laughter burst from her lungs, which made him crack up, too.

"Has anyone ever told you that you're the coolest chick around?"

She waved her hand dismissively. "Only everyone."

"A'right, bestie. I can't stand around letting you harass me all night. I need to get to work on the backsplash."

"Yeah, you do," she teased. "That thing's an eyesore."

"Is that right, smart-ass? Now you have to help me with it."

She looked at him like he'd lost his mind. "I don't know how to put up a backsplash."

"Then it's about time you learned."

SHAUNA SET ANOTHER tile in place. They'd been at it for a while, working side by side, applying thinset, measuring, leveling, cutting, and placing tiles. She was perched on the counter, and Zander was standing in front of it. Music played through a Bluetooth speaker, the two of them singing as they created a beautiful backsplash of white vintage subway tiles with distressed hints of grays and blues, giving them a rustic beachy vibe.

Zander glanced over as she reached for another tile. "Looking good over there, Flores."

"Thanks." He clearly meant the tiles and not her. While he had only a smidgen of dust on his cheek, she was a mess. She had dust on her clothes and thinset in her hair. She was glad she'd changed into shorts, since she'd only brought one pair of jeans, and Zander had lent her one of his T-shirts to wear so she wouldn't get the one she brought dirty. "I didn't expect to enjoy this as much as I am."

"You like the power of wielding a..." He looked at the trowel, and his brows knitted. "A handheld weapon?"

She laughed.

He placed another tile. "Have you done any kind of home projects?"

"Yes, plenty of them, but not like this. Mine were out of necessity. If a sink was clogged or a toilet lever broke, Brian or I would fix it instead of bothering our landlord. But this is different. It's messy and physical, but it's also transforming. It's like we're giving your kitchen a whole new beginning."

She liked working with Zander, too. He was patient, appreciative, and funny. They teased each other about songs they liked and songs they didn't, and they fell into an easy rhythm, like they were a team and had worked together a hundred times before.

She set the tile in place, and he reached over to push the left side of it up higher. Their fingers brushed, and something warm fluttered in her chest. He smiled as he pulled his hand back. It wasn't a cocky or flirty smile. It was the kind of smile friends shared, which made her feel silly for that flutter of warmth she'd felt. But hey, she was only human. They were working so closely, it was hard not to notice his rugged scent and the way his arms flexed and his jaw muscles bunched when he was concentrating on setting a tile in place.

She picked up another tile and said, "You're very trusting. I could mess up your whole design."

"If you were my wife, I'd *let* you mess up the design."

And there it was, the playfulness that drew a light laugh. "Zander, you do not need or want a wife, and I will not drag you through my mess." She climbed off the counter to stretch her legs, and Kitty bounded into the kitchen carrying something black in her mouth.

"What have you got?" Shauna crouched to see what she was holding.

"That's her cut."

"You're kidding." She held up the tiny black leather vest with Dark Knights patches on the back and eyed Zander with amusement. Kitty tapped Shauna with her paw, and Shauna petted her.

"Don't give me shit about it," Zander said. "I get enough of that from the guys."

"I just think it's funny that the big, badass biker dresses his kitty-cat."

"I told you she was skin and bones when I got her. My cousin Baz is a vet, and when he was checking her out for me, she was trembling, and he suggested I get her a sweater."

"That makes sense." She held up the vest. "But this is a funny-looking sweater."

He chuckled. "I know, but every time I took off her sweater, she'd drag it back to me. Then Mads bought her a few dresses, and I was like, no way. My cat's got to be cool, so I had the vest made for her. And as you can see by the way she's tapping you, she likes wearing it."

"Is *that* why she's tapping me? I don't know how to dress a cat."

"I'll show you." He snagged the vest, lowered his big body to the floor, and put Kitty in his lap. The cat sat right there, letting him put her front legs through the armholes and button it up her chest.

Shauna took out her phone to take a picture and saw another text from Brian. Her stomach knotted up. He'd texted earlier, and she hadn't responded. She didn't have the energy to fight with him or to hear endless apologies and empty promises. Not tonight. Tonight was *hers*. She was allowing herself one night to breathe in this happier, safer place, with a guy who didn't need a damn thing from her and wasn't screwing up her life. Was that too much to ask? One frigging night to pretend she was a typical young woman with a new friend and her life wasn't complicated and Brian wasn't a fucking mess.

She swiped past the text and took an insanely cute picture of Zander dressing Kitty. "You are unbelievable."

"Thanks for noticing," he said with a cocky grin.

"I meant dressing your cat."

"I said don't give me shit." He picked up Kitty and rubbed noses with her. "Who knows what she's been through all alone out there in the wild. If my baby girl wants to wear clothes, I'll buy her a whole frigging closetful."

Why did she find that so endearing? "I wasn't giving you a hard time. I think it's adorable." She looked at the picture. He really was annoyingly attractive, and his love for Kitty only amped that up.

"Like what you see?"

"The cat? Yes."

He appeared amused. "You can admit you're checking me out, assessing me as temporary husband material."

"You're in the picture?" she teased.

"Best friends are supposed to build each other up," he said to Kitty as he petted her. "First she calls me sloppy, and now this?" He glanced at Shauna with a mischievous twinkle in his eyes. "I might have to rethink this friendship."

She could get used to this. Their friendship might be new, but their easy camaraderie and teasing made it feel like they were old friends who had history together and had earned the right to give each other a hard time.

"Although," he said in Kitty's ear, "she's pretty good at tiling. Maybe we should keep her around. Think about how much work we could get out of her. What's that?" He put Kitty up to his ear, pretending to listen. "She could be your temporary stepmom if she'd only let me help her with her friend?"

God, he was too much. She laughed. "Don't bring your cat into this."

The last thing a happy-go-lucky guy like Zander needed was her and Brian's drama, but as they continued teasing each other and she took pictures of Kitty in her cut and Zander loving her up like she was the most precious cat that had ever lived, she kind of wished he did.

Chapter Twelve

ZANDER LAY IN bed staring up at the ceiling, one arm bent over his head, his other around Kitty, who was curled up beside him. For the first time in forever, Kitty hadn't followed him into the bedroom when he'd turned in for the night. She'd sat outside Shauna's closed door and had finally come to bed about an hour ago. It was nearly two in the morning, and he couldn't stop thinking about Shauna. The more he got to know her, the more he dug her. She was cool and smart and unafraid to give him shit. He loved being around her, and talking with her was like talking to someone he'd known forever. Only, when Shauna spoke, he wanted to hear every word she said.

How many times had he given his brothers and cousins shit about being so into a woman she was first and foremost in their minds at all times? And here he was spending hours trying to figure out what to do about Shauna's situation with Brian.

He told himself that's what friends did and went back to trying to figure out how to help her. She loved Brian too much to walk away and let him fend for himself. Not that Zander wanted her to. Zander lived by a code of honor, which included helping those who couldn't help themselves. Before she'd turned in for the night, he'd tried again to lend her the money for Brian's rehab, but she was too proud to take him up on it. He'd have to find another way.

The sound of a car approaching too fast on the dead-end gravel street jerked him from his thoughts, propelling him to his feet and sending Kitty scampering off the bed. He got to the window as the car fishtailed, headlights slicing through the darkness, tires screeching, sending gravel flying against the front of the house as the car crashed into the bushes.

What the hell?

Zander pulled on jeans, snagged his phone, and hauled ass out of his bedroom.

Shauna rushed out of her room in her sleeping shorts and a tank top, her eyes wide. "What was that?"

"A car crashed into the bushes. Stay here."

As he headed for the front door, someone pounded on it and shouted, *"Shauuuna! I know you're in there!"*

Shauna froze. Zander's blood boiled as more pounding shattered the silence.

"Shaun…Talk to me!" Brian slurred. *"Please!"*

"How does he know you're here?" Zander asked through gritted teeth.

"I don't know," she said anxiously. "I didn't answer any of his texts."

"I'll take care of it." He reached for the doorknob.

"No!" She tried to push past him. "This is my mess. I'll handle it."

"The last time you saw him, he put his hands on you." His gaze dropped briefly to the bruises on her arms. "That's *never* happening again."

"I *need* to talk to him, Zander," she insisted.

"Then you can do it from behind me." He opened the door,

hulking over Brian, who was swaying unsteadily on the front porch in a ripped T-shirt and jeans. His light brown hair stood on end, his eyes were wild and bloodshot, and he reeked of alcohol.

Zander set a dark stare on him. "Back the fuck off my porch."

"*Shaun…*" Brian bobbed and swayed, trying to see around Zander. "*Shauna.*"

"I said back the fuck up." Zander stepped onto the porch and kept going, forcing Brian to stumble down the steps.

"Shauna!" Brian hollered.

"Brian, *stop it.* I'm really worried about you." Shauna's voice was thick with restraint. "You could have killed yourself or someone else, and that scares me."

Zander knew what she was doing, turning her anger into compassion, trying not to fuel his intoxicated demise with judgment, accusations, or blame, and he respected the hell out of her for it. He knew it must be killing her, and he wouldn't have been so kind.

"I *had* to see you. You're not answering my texts," Brian whined.

"There's a reason for that," she snapped. "How did you find me?"

"That stupid tracking app you put on our phones. *'Member* how I hated it?" Brian laugh-slurred, but his humor faded fast. "You can't just disappear, Shauna. I *need* you. I can't do this without you. Just…come home. *Please.*" He stumbled forward.

Zander blocked his way. "She's not going anywhere with you."

"Who are *you?*" Brian yelled, looking confused, like he hadn't seen Zander standing there the whole time. "Is this who you're with now, Shauna? He doesn't know you! Not like I do, baby—"

"I'm *not* your baby," Shauna seethed, but there was a thread of sadness woven in that twisted Zander up inside. "And I'm not with Zander, but I'm not safe with you anymore, and I *am* safe here."

Zander stole a glance at her, the sadness in her eyes cutting him to his core.

"I'm sorry. I know I messed up, but..." Brian's shoulders slumped, anger draining from his features. "You can't erase yourself from my life. *Still waters or reckless tides*, Shauna. You're my anchor. Remember?" He held shaky hands out, palms up, as if showing her something tangible. "This is a reckless tide. I'll drown without you. I don't know how to be *me* without you."

Zander clenched his teeth against the urge to tell him he'd done this to himself, and he wasn't allowed to use mental manipulation on Shauna. But the heartache emanating from Brian had Zander biting his tongue, giving Shauna a chance to respond.

Silence stretched between them.

"I know you can't do this alone." Her voice was laden with sadness. "I want to help you, but I will not stand by and watch you ruin everything you worked so hard to become," she said clearly, evenly, and with finality.

It was that finality that had Zander looking at her, checking on the cost of those words, and seeing a pillar of strength holding herself together during an earthquake that was rocking her to her core. Her hands were fisted, her eyes glassy, and her mouth tight.

"I'll stop. I promise," Brian pleaded, stepping toward her, but Zander stood his ground, an immovable wall between them.

Brian shouted over Zander's shoulder. "I love you, Shauna. Just give me a chance. Tell him…tell him you don't need him! We've got this, Shauna. You and me against the world."

"That's enough," Zander demanded. "*Look* at her arms." He stepped to the side only far enough to clear Brian's view of Shauna. "See those bruises? *You* did that to her. That's not love, man. That's abuse. The only reason you're still standing is that Shauna loves you." He paused, letting it sink in. Regret rose in Brian's eyes. "And the rest of this shit? Driving drunk and putting innocent lives in danger? Crashing into my bushes and trying to blame *her*—the woman who has stood by you and has been trying to help you turn your life around for months—for your sorry ass? That's not right, man, and I don't think that's who you want to be."

"I didn't mean…" Brian looked pleadingly at Shauna. "I'm sorry."

"You want it to be you and Shauna against the world again?" Zander said, bringing Brian's eyes back to him. "Then get help. I'll even help you get that help, but I'll be damned if I'll *ever* let you near her again until you do." He held out his hand. "Give me your keys."

"I'm not giving you my keys!"

Zander stepped closer. "Either you give me your keys, or I will call the cops right now and put your ass in jail."

"You gonna let him do this, Shauna? Is this what you want? Me in jail?" Brian spat.

"This isn't about what *she* wants. This is about what has to happen to keep her safe." Zander reached for his phone.

"*Fine.* Don't call the fucking police," Brian snapped. "My keys are in the car."

Zander grabbed his arm and turned to Shauna.

"Get the hell off me!" Brian tried to yank his arm free.

Zander tightened his grip, glowering at him. "Shut your mouth. I'm driving you home so you can sleep off whatever shit is in your system." He glanced at Shauna. "My keys are on the kitchen counter. Take my truck. We'll meet you at your place."

He didn't wait for a response as he dragged Brian over to his car and put him in the passenger seat. The floor was littered with empty liquor bottles and beer cans. "Put your fucking seat belt on."

Zander locked the door, and as he went around the driver's side, he saw Shauna watching them. He climbed behind the wheel and cranked the engine. Thankfully, the car still ran, though the bumper was crunched.

He glanced in the rearview as he drove away and saw Shauna heading inside.

"You think she needs you," Brian sneered, his words sharp with fury. "But you don't even know her."

Zander didn't respond until he stopped at a red light. Then he looked at him and said, "That's the difference between you and me. I know that strong woman back there doesn't need anyone. She's saved her own ass more times than anyone should ever have to. You're damn lucky she wants to save yours."

Brian's face crumpled, the fire in his eyes doused by tears. "I know," trembled out. "I love her, man. You have to believe me. She's all I have."

That was the problem. Zander believed him on both accounts.

Brian was a weepy mess the whole way to his and Shauna's house. Zander hauled his ass inside and into his bedroom, taking in empty bottles on the bed and dresser, shattered glass and a broken picture frame on the floor, and on the nightstand, a mirror, filthy with fingerprints and drug dust, the smudged remnants of lines still evident beneath the snorter straw.

It made him sick to think Shauna had to deal with that.

He got Brian to lie down, and as he began picking up the mess, Brian mumbled apologies meant for Shauna. Zander was about to toss the mirror and straw into the trash can, when he thought better of it. If Brian was using daily, he'd be out-of-control needing a hit when he woke up. Zander would have to deal with that later. Right now he wanted to get this place cleaned up before Shauna got there.

He gathered the empty cans and fished a picture of Shauna and Brian out from under the shattered glass on the floor. Their arms were slung around each other's shoulders. A dainty gold bracelet with a dangling triangular charm shimmered on Shauna's wrist. It was hard to believe the clean-cut, clear-eyed guy in the photo was the same unshaven, wasted man on the bed.

Every ounce of Zander wanted to judge him, to find him unworthy of Shauna. But he knew better, and the light in Shauna's eyes in that photo told him he was doing the right thing.

AS SHAUNA DROVE Zander's truck to her house, she was sick with embarrassment and too many conflicting emotions to wrap her head around. She had been ready to give Brian a piece of her mind when she'd heard him yelling through the door, but when she'd seen him looking like he'd crawled out of the gutter, her heart had broken. In that moment, she was glad

Zander was standing between them, because she'd been fighting the urge to go to Brian and make sure he was okay, and that would have made him think what he'd done was acceptable.

She tried to push all of that aside and pull herself together as she parked in front of her house and hurried inside. The living room was a pigsty, with bags of chips and other crap on the floor and dirty clothes strewn about. The armchair was turned the wrong way, and one of the kitchen chairs was knocked over. What the hell had Brian done in there?

It was a harsh reminder of the way they used to live.

She headed down the hall and found Zander kneeling on Brian's bedroom floor, thumbing out a text. Most of the shattered glass had been picked up, and the picture of her and Brian and the broken frame were on top of the dresser.

Zander looked up and put a finger over his lips, shushing her as he rose to his feet and lifted his chin toward the hallway.

"Shauuuna," Brian pleaded groggily.

"I'm right here." She glanced at Zander and whispered, "I'm sorry about all this. You don't have to stay."

"I'm not going anywhere, and you're not going in that room alone with him."

As much as she wanted to tell him she'd be fine, she no longer fully trusted that she would. She didn't recognize this version of Brian. The guy who sold their television, physically hurt her, and showed up at Zander's house acting irrationally wasn't the same kid she'd partied with years ago. As much as it broke her heart, it also scared her. She appreciated Zander's insistence.

"Shaun, *please*," Brian croaked out. *"I'm sorry."*

Zander put a hand on her back. "Sit with him. Tell him whatever he needs to hear so he'll sleep, and then we'll talk."

She nodded, trying to ignore her rattling nerves, and went to sit on the edge of the bed beside Brian. Zander went back to cleaning the floor, but he watched them intently. The air buzzed with tension so thick, it sparked, like every iota of his being was on high alert. He reminded her of a snake, coiled and ready to strike, and she knew if Brian touched her, Zander would strike.

"Shauna?" Brian's thin, hoarse voice drew her attention.

His eyes fluttered open, the lost look in them tugging at her heartstrings. He reached for her, struggling to sit up. As their arms came around each other, Zander's jaw tightened, his chest puffing up with a deeper inhalation.

It was all too much, part of her breaking over Brian and part of her undeniably drawn to Zander, though she knew she shouldn't be. He was just being kind and protective because that's who he was. She closed her eyes against all of those feelings and whispered, "I'm here, Brian. I'm right here."

She sat with him for a long time, and with every word she whispered and every slurred apology and tormented plea Brian eked out, there was no escaping the unbearably sad web they were caught in.

When he finally fell asleep, she and Zander quietly left the room, leaving the door ajar. Zander put his hand on her back again, giving her the support she hadn't realized she needed as he led her into the living room. Her thoughts were reeling. She was angry that Brian had put her in this position and was guilt-ridden over having that thought. She was on the verge of tears, and at the same time, she wanted to punch something. Apparently her ability to stay calm in any situation didn't carry over to this one.

Zander set down the trash he must have carried out of Brian's room and stepped closer. "You okay, Angel?"

She wrung her hands, knowing what she had to do, but when she looked into Zander's caring eyes, her throat clogged with emotion. He must have sensed how overwhelmed she was, because he embraced her, and *God*, she wanted that comfort, but she put a hand on his chest, pushing free for fear she wouldn't be able to follow through with what had to be done if she didn't do it right then.

Steeling herself against all the emotions swamping her, she said, "I've never felt unsafe around Brian before. When we were younger, getting wasted turned him into a marshmallow. But now…" She lowered her eyes, feeling like a traitor for admitting it.

Zander pressed his big, rough hands to her cheeks, tilting her face up so she had no choice but to look at him. "It's scary seeing someone you love become someone you don't recognize."

He brushed his thumb over her cheek, gazing deeply into her eyes for so long that fluttery warmth spread through her chest again, and that brought another wave of guilt. Her best friend was in the process of killing himself, and she was getting lost in Mr. Blue Eyes. She wrote that off to exhaustion and the overwhelming emotions of the last twenty-four hours, but then he lowered his hands and looked away, as if he'd felt whatever that was, too.

He cleared his throat before facing her again and said, "After we lost Ashley, her best friend, Bethany, got mixed up in drugs. We all tried to help her, but no matter how hard we tried, or what we did, our hands were tied until she was ready."

"I know that's how it works," she said too sharply, annoyed with herself for being attracted to him. She needed Zander's help in a much bigger way than tucking Brian in. "I think

Brian's hit rock bottom. At least I hope so, because I can't do this anymore. I'm terrified he's going to kill himself or accidentally hurt someone else. Is your offer still good?"

"Absolutely. A couple of my brothers are on their way over to stay with Brian. Once they get here, we'll go back to my place. You can stay as long as you need to while we figure this out and get Brian taken care of." He started picking up empty bottles and cans from the floor.

Shocked that he'd made arrangements for his brothers to stay with Brian, her misinterpreted question took a back seat. "Why did you drag your family into this? They don't even know me or Brian." Too frustrated to stand still, she began picking up, too. "I don't need them. *I* can stay with Brian."

He stopped cleaning up and gave her his full attention. "You've barely slept in two days, and if Brian is using daily, he's not going to be as apologetic when he wakes up as he was tonight. He's going to need a hit, and he's going to be furious and take it out on anyone standing in his way of getting high, and that is *not* going to be you. I assume he's got drugs on him, or hidden somewhere. My brothers will make sure he only takes enough to be able to make it through the day until we get this figured out. This is about safety for you and Brian. If he doesn't have drugs hidden somewhere, he's going to be a raving nightmare, and my brothers are far better equipped to handle that than you are."

"They'll get him high?"

"I know it sounds counterintuitive to give him drugs so he can think clearly, but with addicts, it's the only way. They'll give him just enough to take the edge off. Remember what his withdrawals were like when he wasn't using every day? The agony of withdrawing after daily use will be ten times worse, and so will his desperation. If we have any hope of convincing him to get help, he needs to be able to think past the obsession of getting that next hit."

Thank God one of them was thinking clearly. "You're right. I wasn't thinking about how fast the withdrawals would hit, and I definitely don't want to go through that again. But can't *you* stay with him instead of bringing your brothers into this? I can stay at your place. I'm not afraid to be alone."

"I don't think you're afraid." He closed the distance between them and said, "I don't know who Brian associates with, who he owes money to, or who he told where he was going tonight. There's no way in hell I'm going to leave you alone."

She hadn't thought about that, either. "You think someone might come looking for money?"

"I don't put anything past anyone. Blaine's fiancée Reese's mother was into drugs, and she owed her dealer a lot of money before she went into rehab. Reese was taking care of her teenage sister, Lettie, and Lettie was abducted by the asshole their mother owed money to."

"Holy crap. Did Reese get her back? Did he hurt her? Is she okay?"

"We got her back, but not without bloodshed. Mostly inflicted by us on the asshole's crew, but Blaine took a bullet."

"Oh my God. He was *shot*?"

"Yeah. We do what we have to do to protect our own. Look, I'm not trying to scare you, but I'm sure as hell not letting anything happen to you."

The roar of motorcycles interrupted them, and her nerves kicked up even more.

"That's them." He held her gaze and said, "I promise you'll feel safer knowing they've got your back, too."

Floored by how quickly he'd thought this all through, she watched him go to the door and pull it open. He didn't step outside to greet his brothers. He stood in the doorway, his arms crossed, his piercing blue eyes darting back to her, then to the hallway. She didn't know about his brothers, but she couldn't imagine anyone making her feel safer than Zander did.

As he and his brothers talked in hushed voices, she quickly tried to pick up the rest of the mess and hoped Brian hadn't gotten himself tangled up with people who were *that* dangerous. But she knew she had to get him help before it was too late. No matter what the cost.

She was doing dishes when she heard Zander and his brothers come inside.

"Hey, Angel," Zander said.

She closed her eyes briefly against the nickname. She'd gotten used to it. She even liked it, but she worried his brothers might think it meant something other than the girl who had saved his life. But that was insignificant compared to what they were up against. She shut off the faucet and tried to calm her racing heart as she turned to greet them. Zander stood between two big, ridiculously handsome, dark-haired men wearing black leather vests over T-shirts and jeans.

"Hi," she said, hoping they couldn't hear how nervous she was.

"Shauna, this is Blaine." Zander hiked a thumb at the guy to his right, who looked like a tough version of James Marsden.

Blaine nodded curtly. "Nice to meet you."

He was the one who'd been shot. He looked like he wasn't afraid of anything. "You, too."

"And this is Zeke." Zander motioned to the other guy.

The *mother hen* could have been Zander's twin, but with

shorter, darker hair and more-serious eyes. Zeke smiled, and that was different, too. It was a nice, friendly smile, but it lacked the edginess of Zander's. "It's nice to finally meet the woman who saved our brother." He glanced at Zander for only a few seconds, but the affection lingered in his voice as he turned back to her and said, "Thank you for helping him."

"I'm glad I was there to help."

"And we're glad to have a chance to return the favor," Zeke said. "We'll take good care of your friend."

"Thank you. I'm sorry Zander roped you into this, and I'm sorry I brought trouble to his doorstep."

"He didn't have to rope us in. That's what family is for," Blaine said.

Zeke nodded in agreement and clapped a hand on Zander's shoulder. "It's a refreshing change from this guy bringing the trouble."

Zander shrugged him off and said, "You didn't bring trouble, darlin'. That's not your burden to carry."

He and his brothers asked about the people she and Brian used to hang out with, none of whom lived nearby, and the places Brian used to go for drugs. It seemed like a lifetime had passed since then. His brothers were kind and concerned and, thankfully, not judgmental.

Afterward, Zander said, "Why don't you grab enough clothes for a few days so we have time to figure this out, and then we'll take off."

She didn't argue. They obviously had a plan, and she was grateful as she headed into her bedroom to pack. She grabbed her uniforms, workout clothes, and a few other outfits. When she grabbed a handful of underwear out of her dresser drawer, she uncovered the certified letter. Her stomach twisted. She didn't want to bring Zander further into her mess, but she felt like she was standing on the edge of a cliff with Brian, and if she didn't do something fast, she was going to lose him. She stuffed the letter into her bag and finished packing.

On the way back to Zander's cottage, he stopped and bought a big bottle of her favorite French vanilla creamer, while she struggled with the decision she thought she'd already made. Their friendship felt like a miracle, a *gift* that was almost too good to be true. She didn't want to jeopardize it by asking for more, but if ever there was a time to ask for help, it was now.

"How are you holding up?" he asked as they drove away from the convenience store.

"I don't know. I'm overwhelmed, confused about what to do, and relieved that you and your brothers are willing to help, but I'm sorry for interrupting your lives."

"You didn't interrupt our lives. You're a welcome addition to them."

"Yeah, right," she said sarcastically. "It's okay to say I'm a pain in the ass. I feel like a freeloader."

"You're not a pain in the ass. You're going through some shit, and we're happy to help. Besides, there's not going to be any freeloading going on at my place. If you think you're just going to walk around looking pretty, you've got another thing coming."

"What does that mean? I told you I'm not having sex with you," she said flatly.

"Who said anything about sex? I've seen what you can do with tiles. I'm going to put your sexy ass to work."

Sexy ass? Nobody had ever called her sexy. She tried to ignore the flutter that flattery caused. They were quiet the rest of the way to his place. When he turned onto his gravel road, she was hit with an unexpected wave of relief. The kind of relief she'd once found coming home to her and Brian's rental cottage, when it had been the one place she could let down her guard and relax.

As they neared the house, a man came into view leaning against a post on the porch, and she gasped.

"It's okay," Zander said. "That's my brother Maverick, and that mountainous man coming around the side of the cottage is my cousin Tank. They go by their road names. They were keeping an eye on the place."

She exhaled with relief as he parked. "When did you have time to coordinate all of this?"

"I was texting Zeke when you got to Brian's. I told him what was up, and then he put the word out. We're used to this. It's what we do."

"Like the Mafia?" She'd never seen anything like this.

"No, darlin'. We're better than the Mafia." He grinned. "We're Dark Knights." He threw his door open. "Come on. I'll introduce you to two of the greatest men you'll ever meet."

As they climbed out of the truck, she saw two motorcycles parked by the trees on the other side of the house. Zander put a hand on her back as his brother and cousin met them halfway to the front door. They were rougher-looking than Blaine and Zeke. Maverick had a mop of dark hair, a trim beard, and ice-blue eyes. He could definitely pass as a blood relative of Zander's, while Tank had Shauna's nerves pinging. She thought Zander and his brothers were big, but Tank was enormous, with coal-black eyes and matching hair and beard. Every visible inch of him was tattooed, and he had piercings in his nostril and his ears.

"Hey, Mav," Zander said, and they gave each other a quick

one-armed embrace. Then he and Tank did the same. "Thanks for watching out for the place."

"No problem," Maverick said, tossing a smile and a nod to Shauna.

"Gunner and Colonel are set to relieve Zeke and Blaine tomorrow afternoon if you need them," Tank said in a deep, gruff voice.

"Thanks, man." Zander turned to Shauna and pressed his hand to her lower back, settling her nerves a little as she processed how much they were doing for them. "Guys, this is Shauna."

"Hi. I'm sorry for all of the trouble tonight," she said.

"It's no trouble, sweetheart," Tank said. "Keeping you and your friend safe is all that matters."

"It's in our blood. Hang around Zan enough, and you'll realize he shows up for us and anyone else who needs it, too," Maverick said. "In any case, it's nice to meet you, Shauna. Thanks for dragging this guy's ugly ass out of his burning car. We'd've been lost without him."

"No truer words," Tank said.

It was nice to see they admired Zander as much as he did them.

"You guys can take off," Zander said. "I've got it from here."

"You sure?" Tank asked. "You want to get some rest? We can take shifts out here, and I can cover you tomorrow, too, if you have to work."

"I appreciate it, but we're good. Go home to your wives and babies."

"You don't have to tell me twice." Maverick glanced at Shauna and said, "Let me give you a reason to smile. I'll show you my little girl." He whipped out his phone so fast, she didn't have time to respond.

As Maverick showed her pictures, gushing about Marybelle, his adorable chubby-cheeked, blue-eyed, almost-two-year-old daughter with wispy brown hair and a smile that melted Shauna's heart, Zander said, "Dude, Shauna's had a rough night. Give her a break."

"Let's go, braggy daddy." Tank grabbed Maverick's sleeve, dragging him away, and Maverick tried to get Tank to look at the pictures.

"Sorry about that," Zander said.

"It's okay. He's obviously proud of her, and it was nice to see something happy tonight. I still can't believe all of those guys showed up just because you asked them to."

"Really? From what I've seen, you've been doing the same for Brian forever," he said as they headed inside.

"I guess I do." Gathering her courage like a cloak, she said, "I'm scared for him. I'm afraid he's going to end up lying in a ditch somewhere or overdosing again."

He closed and locked the door behind them and said, "I know you are, darlin'."

"Earlier, when I asked if your offer still stood, I didn't mean your offer for me to stay with you. I meant, are you still willing to lend me the money for Brian's rehab and marry me so I can pay you back?"

"*Oh,*" he said, his brow furrowing.

"If you'd rather not, I understand," she added quickly. "I know it's a crazy idea, and you've done so much already." Now she felt stupid for thinking he meant it. "Don't worry about it. I'll find another way." She headed for the guest room.

"It's not a crazy idea," he said.

She turned around to see if he was kidding, but he looked dead serious. "It kind of is."

"Not to me," he said as he closed the distance between them. "I've been racking my brain trying to figure out how to convince you to let me help, and I keep coming back to the same damn answer. If you won't let me lend you the money, then the only hope Brian has is if we get hitched."

"Really?" She could barely breathe. "What about your family? They'll think you're nuts."

"They already think I'm nuts."

"But after everything they did to help us tonight, you'd risk upsetting them to help me?"

"This isn't about them. I *want* to help you, and I want to do this. I think it's what I was meant to do. I could've died in that accident. What are the chances that you'd pull me, the guy who drove you home and said something that changed your life *years* earlier, out of a burning car?" He took her hand, lifting it between them, his gaze lingering on the tattoo. He brushed his thumb over the number four, and then his eyes found hers, and he said, "Think about it. My accident was on the thirty-first. Three plus one is four. I don't believe in fate, or at least I didn't, but do you know what today is?"

"Thursday?"

"It's Friday morning, Angel. April *fourth*."

"And April is the fourth month of the year," she said incredulously. "You'd really do this for me?"

"Without a second's hesitation."

"Thank you." Overflowing with gratitude, she threw her arms around him, tears stinging her eyes.

His arms circled her carefully, holding her below the spot where she'd hit that frame on the wall. "I told you I'd always have your back, bestie."

She smiled as she stepped out of his arms. "You're one hundred percent sure? Because I think we need to move fast. I don't know how long it will take to find a rehab center to take him, and I want to pay you back as quickly as possible, so we probably need to tie the knot quickly, too."

"We'll figure it out. If we can't find one on our own, we've got some connections through the club I can reach out to."

"Hopefully it won't come to that. Your family has done enough. But you have to promise that if you wake up tomorrow and change your mind, you'll tell me. I won't blame you or be mad. I'll figure something else out."

"I'm not changing my mind." He cocked a grin. "I've got no problem being your sugar daddy."

She smiled. "You are *not* going to be my sugar daddy."

"Is that offensive? Sorry. You can call me your trophy husband."

She crossed her arms, staring him down, but it was hard to keep a straight face when he was flashing that coy smile. "More like a temporary pretend husband I'm hiring to help me out of a bind."

He cocked a brow. "Are we talking silk bindings?"

"*Zander*, I'm being serious." A laugh slipped out despite herself.

"So am I. If I'm going to be your husband, I want to make sure I fulfill *all* of my husbandly duties."

She planted a hand on her hip. "We're not having sex, so get that thought out of your head."

"Okay, but if you change your mind—"

"I *won't*."

"Hey, I'm just giving you a hard time. I'm happy to help,

and I don't expect you to sleep with me."

She sighed. "I know you don't."

"But I've got to be honest. I knew what you meant when you asked if my offer was still good back at your place."

"You *did?* Why didn't you say so?"

He cocked a grin. "I wanted to hear you ask me to marry you."

"*Zander.*" She smacked his chest, but she had to laugh, because she'd already learned that *that* was Zander. He had a way of making the heaviest times feel lighter. "Do you have any idea how hard that was for me to ask you?"

"Yes, but now you're smiling, so it was worth it." He narrowed his eyes. "Even if your smile is a little diabolical, like you're considering hitting me for real."

"I *should* hit you."

"You're a feisty one." He waggled his brows. "I like it."

"Good *night*, Zander." She headed for the guest room.

"Nighty-night, almost wife."

She glowered over her shoulder, and he blew her a kiss.

What have I gotten myself into?

Chapter Thirteen

ZANDER STOOD SHIRTLESS and barefoot on the beach behind his house, coffee mug in hand, watching the morning waves roll in as an app on his phone read him information from a website. He heard the patio door open, and something inside him lit up. *Shauna.* He was worried she'd change her mind about getting married, and he'd be right back to square one, trying to figure out how to convince her to let him help with Brian. His inclination was to turn around and ask if she had changed her mind, but he fought that urge, which was no easy feat for a guy who acted first and worried about repercussions later. But things were different with Shauna. She'd been through so much, he was determined to let her breathe this morning and ease her into that conversation.

"Good morning," she said as he turned around. Her eyes widened, and she lowered her voice. "*Sorry.* I didn't know you were on the phone."

"I'm not." He ended the text-to-speech narration, drinking her in. *Damn.* His future wife looked hot in the morning. Her messy dark hair tumbled over the shoulders of her lavender sweatshirt, which covered all but the hem of her shorts. "I was just listening to something."

"Oh, good." Those dimples came out to play as she wrapped her arms around herself, shivering. "*Brr.* Aren't you cold?"

"Not anymore. Have you seen yourself in those shorts? I might have to buy you some baggy sweatpants…and a mask."

"You're into thunder thighs and *masks*? Okay, weirdo."

"I'm the king of causing thunder between thighs," he said arrogantly, chuckling at the eyeroll it earned. "And the mask is to cover that gorgeous smile of yours and those insane dimples. They're too fucking cute, and don't knock my future wife's thick, juicy thighs. They saved my life."

"Your future wife?" she asked carefully. "Does that mean you haven't changed your mind?"

"Wickeds never back out of a deal." He draped an arm over her shoulder, pulling her against his side. "You're stuck with me, Flores, and you're stuck with this." He handed her the coffee mug. "I tried your recipe of twelve parts creamer to one part coffee. I don't know how you drink that shit."

"Easy. I hate the taste of coffee, and I love everything French vanilla."

"Guess that makes sense. Hold the mug between both hands. It'll warm you up."

"I'm already getting warmer. You're like an oven."

"You calling me hot, darlin'? Because I'm not sleeping with you no matter how much you compliment me. That's not what this arrangement is about."

"Oh, *darn*," she said sarcastically.

"I knew you'd regret it."

"Shut up." She nudged him with her arm. "Do you have coffee out here every morning?"

"I never did until after the accident. I used to take a lot of shit for granted."

She sipped the coffee. "Mm. Your taste buds must be broken. This is perfect."

"Good. Let me know when you've had enough caffeine to talk about Brian."

She went rigid against him. "Did something happen?"

"No. I talked to Zeke a little while ago, and Brian was still out cold."

"Good. I feel horrible about bringing your brothers and cousins into this. I'd better get ready. I should be there when Brian wakes up."

"I don't think you should. It's best if we let the guys handle him while we take care of all the things we need to do. Like finding him a rehab center. If we can find one that'll take him, then we'll need to talk him into going."

"I've been thinking about that." She gazed out at the water, then down at the mug in her hands, worry riddling her features. "What if he won't go? I mean, I hope he will. He was so happy when he got out from under his addiction before, and I know in my heart he'll want that again. But he may not hear what's in his heart when he's this lost. What if he's pissed, like you were worried about? Or if he takes off and we can't find him?"

"He can't take off with the guys there, and there's nothing my brothers can't handle. Blaine can be a bulldozer, but in this circumstance, that's not a bad thing, and Zeke will keep him in line. If anyone can find a way to calm Brian down, it'll be Zeke. He's the most intuitive person I know. He was one of the best special ed teachers on the Cape."

"If he was such a good teacher, why did he stop?"

"Because some asshole made derogatory comments about the kids and took it too far. Zeke put him in his place, and lost his job because of it."

Her eyes widened. "He beat the guy up?"

"Zeke gave him what he deserved. He has the patience of a saint, which should tell you how far that guy pushed him. But Zeke still helps kids. In addition to working with us, he tutors middle schoolers and volunteers at the community center. Like I said, you won't find better guys to watch over Brian."

"They won't hurt him, will they?"

"No. Even if he comes at them, they know how to handle it without hurting him. Through the club, we're pretty well versed in handling the complexities of addiction, and they'll keep us up to date throughout the day while we look for a rehab center for Brian."

"Okay. I'm still worried about convincing him to go."

"I know he has to want it for himself, but he was in bad shape last night. I don't think you're wrong to worry that he'll end up hurting himself or someone else. You'll need to use all the tools in your toolbox. If he won't do it for himself, maybe he'll do it for you, which isn't the best tactic, but if it gets him in the door, it might be enough to save him."

"That's what I was thinking, too. He doesn't know about the letter from the attorney, so please don't tell him."

"That's not my story to tell. Do you want me to keep it from my family?"

"As much as I'd like to say yes because it's embarrassing and makes me look like a taker, I'd never ask you to do that. Plus, I just saw your back. You have a huge tattoo that says FAMILY with intricate roots snaking through the letters. That tells me how important they are to you."

"They absolutely are, and I appreciate you not asking me to lie to them. That said, it shouldn't be embarrassing that you'll go to any length to help a friend, and a taker would've taken the money the first time I offered. I'll deal with my family when the time is right. But first, let's get things in order. Do you have a copy of your birth certificate?"

"I have the original. It's at my house. Brian made me take it when we ran away. Why?"

Brian really had watched out for her. "You need it to get married."

"Okay," she said a little shakily. "I hate to be pushy, but like I said, we should do it fast so I can pay you back as quickly as possible."

"I've already checked into it. Once we apply for the marriage license, it takes a few days for it to come through. I figured we'd apply today and schedule a date for the wedding with the justice of the peace. If you tell me where your birth certificate is, I'll have Blaine meet us at the end of the road with it on our way out."

"And you're sure I shouldn't see Brian first?"

"You can if you really want to, but I think it'll be harder to convince him to go anywhere if you're talking in hypotheticals rather than having a plan in place. I know you're strong, but if he starts making promises and begging you to trust him, it's going to be harder for you if you don't have a next step readily available. If we're lucky enough to find a place to take him quickly, that's a fire in your belly, too."

Her brow knitted. "You're right. I just feel guilty leaving him to deal with strangers."

"That's because you love him, but you're doing the right thing."

"I don't have any doubt about that. He needs help."

"That's today's goal." He tried to lighten the mood. "Well,

that and starting the process for that ball and chain linking you to the hottest guy in Bayside." That earned a smile. "You should write a prenup to protect yourself. I don't want you worrying about me going after any of your stuff."

She looked at him like he was nuts. "You have a beach house, a truck, a motorcycle, and who knows what else, and you're worried about protecting *me?*"

"You're going to be my wife. My top priority is protecting you." He opened the patio door and said, "Let's go, Angel. Time to fuel up and figure our shit out."

ZANDER WASN'T KIDDING about fueling up. He made a feast of eggs, pancakes, and sausage, and when Shauna said she wasn't a big breakfast eater, he lectured her about the importance of eating protein in the morning.

"I work out every day and I'm doing just fine, thank you." She snuggled Kitty as Zander set two plates, piled high with food, on the island.

"You work out every day?" He pulled out a chair for her.

She put Kitty on the floor by her food dish and sat beside Zander. "Yes."

"Cool. What gym are we going to?"

"Excuse me?"

"I don't know how trusts or inheritances work, but I'd imagine they're not okay with a fake relationship. Do you know if there are home visits, or do they talk to friends and family? Or your boss?"

"I don't know. I wasn't planning on getting married, so I

never called the attorney."

"You should probably do that today. If I'm going to be your husband, it has to look real. I assume you'll need to move in here, and we'll need to be seen together. Working out together makes that easy."

Wow, he'd really put some thought into this. "Okay. I guess we can work out together when I'm not at the firehouse or taking a pole class, assuming you're not at work. I guess that means evenings or maybe weekends."

"We'll figure it out." He ate a bite of sausage. "How do you like pole class?"

"I love it. I wanted something different and fun. It's a great workout. I had no idea how hard it would be when I first started." She lifted the edge of her shorts, showing him a bruise on her thigh. "Hard-earned bruises."

"Better than the other kind," he said. "I can't wait to watch you work that pole."

"I don't *work* the pole. I'm not a stripper. And you're *not* coming to my pole class."

"What's wrong with wanting to see my wife do what she loves?"

"Zander," she warned.

"We can talk about it later. I know you've got a lot on your mind right now." He nodded to her fork. "Eat up so we can get started."

"You're going to be my husband, *not* my boss, so please don't tell me what to do."

"Sorry for trying to look after you." He dunked a piece of pancake into a pool of syrup, and the sight of it was so tempting, her mouth watered. "I've never had to answer to anyone, and the last thing I want to be is someone else's boss."

"Good." She doused her pancakes with syrup and cut off a piece. As she lifted her fork to her mouth, Zander's lips quirked in amusement. "I'm not eating this because you told me to."

"I didn't say anything." He ate another bite.

"You said plenty. Just not out loud."

"Listen to you, sounding like my wifey already."

Chapter Fourteen

IT TURNED OUT that even applying for a marriage license made them both break out in a cold sweat. At least Shauna wasn't alone in her fear of holy *nooserimony*. The rest of the day passed in a flurry of phone calls and difficult conversations. They must have called a dozen rehab facilities. Every conversation carried the weight of hope, guilt—because even though she was doing this to help Brian, doing it behind his back felt like a betrayal—and eventually disappointment. Shauna had lost hope with each rejection.

They finally got lucky and found a rehab facility that was willing to admit Brian tonight. It was two hours away, but she'd drive for a whole frigging day if that was what it took to help him. Zander had spoken to Zeke, and as he'd expected, Brian had drugs in his pocket and had tried to do a hit when he'd woken up. He'd been furious when Zeke and Blaine had intervened, making sure he only did enough to get him through the next several hours, and he was even angrier that Shauna wasn't there and the guys weren't letting him out of their sight. She had no idea how his brothers handled *that*, but she was grateful they had. Zander was right. If she'd been there, she would never have been able to focus on finding a rehab center.

Now they were on their way to talk to Brian, and she was a nervous wreck, fidgeting with a rip in her jeans. Unable to focus past her worries, her gaze darted between the world speeding by and Zander behind the wheel. "I don't want Brian to know you're lending me the money for rehab."

"Then he won't," he said with a small smile.

She gazed out the window again, worrying for the millionth time that she was asking too much of Zander. He'd been incredibly supportive, making calls, reassuring her that they wouldn't give up, and telling her she was doing the right thing when the guilt pressed in. They'd gone over a hundred different ways the conversation could go with Brian, and he'd even made her lunch when she said she didn't want anything. How he'd known she needed sustenance was beyond her, because she hadn't even realized she was hungry until he'd asked her to take a bite for him, and then she couldn't stop.

He turned down her street and reached across the cab of his truck to take her hand, drawing her eyes to him as he pulled over at the end of the street. "Are you sure you're up for this?"

"Yeah. I'm good," she lied as convincingly as she could.

"You were humming your strength song just now. Do you want to talk some more about what you're going to say or how he might respond? Or take a few minutes before we see him?"

She hadn't realized she was humming and was surprised he'd remembered what she'd said about that song. "I'd like to skip this part altogether and have him miraculously be sober and off drugs and past the hard parts, but that's not going to happen."

"I can talk to him so you don't have to," Zander offered for the dozenth time.

"Thanks, but you know it has to be me. Let's get it over with."

He kept hold of her hand as they drove the rest of the way down the road to the cottage. When he cut the engine, he said, "I don't want you alone with him. I don't trust him not to get violent again."

She didn't either, but she knew if Zander was in the room, she'd never get through to Brian. "He's not going to open up to me with you or your brothers in the room."

"My brothers are taking off after we get there, but I'm not leaving you alone with him."

"Then he won't talk to me," she said, frustrated. "I know you're worried, and I appreciate that more than you can imagine, but can't you wait on the porch or something?"

His jaw clenched. "Fine, but only if the door stays open so I can hear if there's trouble."

A thread of relief wound through her, but hell if it wasn't chased by guilt. "Okay."

He tightened his grip on her hand, leaning closer. "This is going to suck. It'll probably be one of the hardest things you've ever done, but you're doing the right thing by helping him. That said, if it gets to be too much or you feel unsafe, you get the fuck out of there or just say my name, and I'll be inside before you take your next breath. Got it?"

A lump formed in her throat. She didn't even want to think about that happening, but she knew she had to, and she nodded.

He climbed out of the truck and was opening her door to help her out before she could do it herself. As they headed up the walk, the front door flew open and Brian charged out hollering, "Finally! Where the hell have you been?"

Zeke and Blaine were on his heels, and as they grabbed his arms, Zander stepped in front of Shauna, an immovable barrier, shoulders back, chest out. As Brian shouted and cursed, Zander said, "Let 'im go."

Blaine and Zeke shot Zander dark looks that said, *Are you fucking crazy?* Shauna was wondering the same thing.

Zander nodded curtly, staring down Brian as they released him. Brian hollered at them about never touching him again, and Zander spoke over him in a voice so lethally calm, it gave Shauna shivers. "If you want to speak to Shauna, you'll shut your mouth and listen to what I have to say."

"The fuck I—"

Zander's hand flew out like a snake striking, snagging the front of Brian's shirt and lifting him off his feet. "If I have to tell you to listen one more time, Shauna leaves. Got it?"

Shauna held her breath.

Brian looked at her. The desperation in his eyes was palpable, bringing rise to more strangulating guilt. But she and Zander had talked about this. She knew the only way to get Brian to agree to go to rehab was if he believed he'd lose the thing he cared about most. *Her.*

"I *will* leave," she said, fighting the urge to add, *I'm sorry.*

"Here's how this is going to work," Zander said as he lowered Brian to his feet, still clutching his shirt. "You two are going to talk—"

"*Alone,*" Brian demanded.

"That's up to Shauna. If she feels like she can trust you, you'll have a chance to talk with her alone." Zander hauled him forward, speaking through gritted teeth. "If you lay one finger on her, it will be the last thing you ever do. Do you understand?"

"Whatever, man," Brian sneered.

"That's not good enough. I want your word that you will

not touch her, so if you do, she'll know never to trust you again."

"I won't fucking touch her," Brian barked.

Zander glanced at Shauna. "Do you trust his word on that?"

"Yes. I know he doesn't want to hurt me," she said, hoping it was true.

"Don't disappoint her," Zander warned. "She's all you've got left."

When he released Brian, Brian didn't give him a second glance. Instead, his pleading eyes locked on Shauna, tugging at the heartstrings that formed from years of being each other's lifeline. She struggled to keep from running over and hugging him, telling him everything would be okay if he'd just go to rehab. She had to be stronger than the urge to comfort him. Not only because he needed to *believe* he'd lose her, but because he truly would if he didn't agree to get help. Brian's future, and their friendship, hung in the balance of their next conversation.

That reality filled her with determination and courage. Acutely aware of Zander and his brothers watching Brian's every move, she said, "Do you want to talk inside?"

"Yeah," Brian grumbled.

She ushered him into the cottage, leaving the door open. When Brian reached for it, she stopped him. "Leave it open. I don't feel safe with you."

"Shauna, I'm not going to—"

She held up her hand, silencing him. "I'm not taking any chances."

"What the hell," he said under his breath, skulking into the living room. "You don't trust me anymore, but you trust a stranger?" He paced like a caged tiger.

She wanted to tell him that Zander was less of a stranger

than *he* was at this point, but she knew better than to say anything inflammatory. "This isn't about him. This is about *us*, Brian. You and me."

"Then why is he even here? Why are you staying at his house and not here with me?"

"Because I let my guard down, and I let *you* down. I should've been there in a bigger way when you were complaining about work and when you stopped going to the gym and stopped going to meetings—"

His nostrils flared. "Don't start this again. Don't get on my ass about shit. Can't you just come back home, and we'll figure this out?"

"No, I can't. I love you, Brian, but I can't watch you kill yourself. I almost lost you once, remember?" She saw it then, a slight lowering of his shoulders, the memory taking form behind his bloodshot eyes. "I don't want to lose you. I *can't* go through that again."

"That's not going to happen. I'm *fine*."

His insistence was rough, but she heard a fissure in it and softened her tone. "We both know you're not fine, and I know it's the drugs speaking."

"Then why are you giving me shit?" He continued pacing.

"Because I want to help you, but if you won't let me, then I can't be around you anymore."

He stilled, breathing harder as he turned and met her gaze. "What are you saying?"

"I'm saying this is the last time you'll see me if you don't get help."

"Then *help* me," he pleaded. "Move back in, and we'll do it together, like before."

Her throat thickened painfully as she shook her head. "I

can't. This isn't like before. You're using all the time. I can't live like this. I'm terrified that you owe people money, and they're going to come looking for you—"

"I don't owe anyone money. I'm not fucking stupid. I'd never put you in danger like that!"

"That's a relief, but I'm still in danger from *you*, Brian. You physically hurt me. Whether you meant to or not, it happened. We promised we'd never turn into our parents, and I'm trying to help you help yourself. I found a rehab center—"

"I don't want to go to fucking rehab," he hollered. "I'm not some goddamn junkie."

She caught sight of Zander watching them from the doorway but didn't let it slow her down. "You're right. You're not. You're my best friend, my anchor, but right now you're pulling me into the worst kind of storm. I don't want to drown, Brian, and I sure as hell don't want you to." Tears threatened, but she managed to keep them at bay as she said, "I'm only going to ask you one more time, and if you tell me no, then I'm going to take my stuff and walk out of your life for good."

"*Shauna*—" His voice cracked.

"Don't," she said firmly. "I found a rehab center that will take you right now, and if you care at all about yourself and all those promises we made to each other, you'll let me take you there so you can heal. And when you get out, I'll be there to help you get back on your feet. We'll go to meetings together just like before. But if you won't go, then you're choosing to ride this reckless tide alone, and I won't go down with your ship."

His gaze darted frantically around the room, and he paced again. "You'd walk out on me?"

"If you choose drugs over your well-being, *yes*. I have to.

You know that deep down in your heart. If you didn't have drugs in your system, you would want me to walk away for my own safety."

He stopped pacing again, staring down at the floor, opening and closing his hands.

"Please look at me." She waited until he did. "You're not alone in this. I'm right here, ready to help."

His shoulders dropped, the tension around his jaw and eyes draining like she'd pulled a plug. "I can't do this without you."

"You don't have to," she said softly, hope rising inside her. "Just say you'll go to rehab, and we'll pack your things and leave right now."

He blinked several times, his eyes glassy. "I don't want you to see me in there. Not like that."

She wanted to tell him that she loved him and he didn't need to feel ashamed, that seeing her might help ground him while he was going through rehab. But he was on the verge of agreeing to get help, so she gave in. "Then I won't visit you. Just *please* let me help you."

The fear and reluctance on his face were palpable. "You'll be here when I get out?"

"Yes. I promise. Every step of the way. Just like before."

He was quiet for so long, she feared she was losing ground.

"Okay," he relented, full of defeat. "I'll go."

Tears spilled from her eyes. "Thank you." She wrapped her arms around him. "I love you."

Over Brian's shoulder, she saw Zander watching them, his jaw clenched so tight, it had to hurt, but he was nodding, as if to say she'd done good. She held on to that encouragement like a brass ring, needing it as much as she needed Brian's embrace.

Chapter Fifteen

SHAUNA WAS COMPLETELY drained as she drove down her street Sunday morning after her shift at the firehouse. She pulled into the driveway and cut the engine. As she looked up at the rental cottage, her stomach sank, and she realized her mistake.

That wasn't where she lived anymore.

At least not for the next few months.

She sank back in the driver's seat, thinking about Friday night. Brian hadn't been happy about Zander driving them to the rehab center. She'd reminded him that she didn't feel safe alone with him, and eventually he'd stopped arguing. When they arrived at the center, Brian had been so scared, he'd begged her again to let him detox at home with her. It was agonizing. He'd gotten mean after that, accusing her of abandoning him and saying he didn't need her. His words had cut like knives despite knowing it was the addiction talking. She was thankful Zander was there to help convince him that detoxing at home wasn't a good idea for Brian or for her.

Zander had been incredible every step of the way. They'd moved most of her things into his house Friday night, and even though she'd spent the last twenty-four hours working, he'd been texting and checking in with her throughout her shift, making sure she was okay.

Clearly she wasn't okay. She'd driven to the wrong house.

Work was a good distraction, but in the downtime between calls, she thought about Brian and felt guilty for letting Zander help her. *And for thinking about Zander in ways I shouldn't.* Yesterday morning came rushing back, heating her cheeks. She'd run into the bathroom to brush her teeth before work and had nearly barreled into Zander, naked, all his glorious muscles still dripping from the shower and a freaking python dangling between his muscular thighs. He'd just cocked a grin and said, *Mornin', Angel,* and had casually reached for a towel, while she acted like it was her first day with a new tongue, stumbling over an apology. *Don't you know how to lock a door?* He'd been amused, and as he'd taken his time drying off before wrapping the towel around his hips and covering up the monster that had been peppering her thoughts ever since, he'd said, *Kitty doesn't usually open the door and barge in.*

It wasn't only his appearance that got to her. It was the way he was with her, fun-loving, caring, and unfiltered. Why did she have to like that so much? And that smirk that said more taunting things than words ever could? Then there were those mesmerizing eyes that always held playful innuendos. Everything about him made her body come alive.

But that was *not* what their relationship was, and she had to wrap her head around that immediately, because she needed this fake relationship to work for Brian's sake.

And that's exactly what it was. *Fake.*

Determined to pack those misguided feelings away, she restarted the car and gave herself a pep talk as she headed to Zander's house. She reminded herself she was a woman who knew how to handle men without falling all over them. She could totally do this, and anything else life demanded of her.

By the time she reached Zander's place, she felt more in control.

She headed inside, greeted by the heavenly smell of bacon and the sound of Zander playing guitar. She spotted him in the kitchen, leaning against the counter as he played, and her traitorous body threw a little party at the sight of his naked chest, jeans hanging low on his hips, feet bare. He looked up, catching her staring, and a smile lit up his handsome face. Arrogant bastard.

"Welcome home, Angel," he said as she headed into the kitchen, and leaned his guitar against the wall.

"Did you buy a new guitar? I saw a shattered one in your car when you had the accident."

"No. I have a few of them. How was work?"

Why couldn't he be less attractive and more of an asshole? Was this some kind of test or punishment? "It was okay. Busy. How was your morning?"

"Pretty chill. You're just in time for breakfast." He turned off the stove and began piling bacon and eggs onto plates.

"Thanks, but you didn't have to make enough for me. I'm not much of a breakfast eater, remember?"

"The way you fought me on eating breakfast the other day and then licked your plate clean? I know better." He set two plates on the counter. "What do you drink after your shifts? I assume you're tired and probably don't want coffee, so you can rest for a while before we go out."

"Water's fine, thanks, but...we're going *out*?"

"Yeah, after you get some sleep." He filled a glass with ice water. "I'm taking you shopping for a wedding dress."

What? "Zander, this isn't real. It's not a forever marriage, and I don't even wear dresses."

He came around the counter. "I don't care if it's forever or not. I'm taking you shopping for an outfit for our wedding."

"Why is that so important?"

"Because neither of us wants to ever get married for real, so if we're doing this, I want to do right by you. Every bride deserves to wear something special for their wedding."

That was quite possibly the sweetest thing she'd ever heard. "You're lending me money *and* marrying me. That's enough—"

He sank down on one knee.

She looked at him like he'd lost his mind. "What do you think you're doing?"

"What does it look like I'm doing?" He held up a gorgeous diamond ring.

Her jaw dropped, disbelief and shock spreading like pins and needles inside her. "Where did you get *that?*"

"I bought it while you were at work yesterday."

"Please tell me those aren't real diamonds."

"What kind of cheap bastard do you think I am? I wouldn't buy my queen fake shit. Now, can you please stop talking long enough for me to do this?"

"*No.* Get up! I'm not taking that ring. What is wrong with you?"

He rose to his full height. "There's nothing wrong with me. I live by a code, and I don't care if our marriage is temporary. You're still going to be my queen, and that means something to me." He cocked a grin. "I've got a reputation to uphold, you know."

"Your reputation is not going to suffer if you don't give me a freaking ring."

"This has to look real, remember? A ring and a dress are basic necessities for a bride. If you don't like dresses, well, I've seen your legs, and that's a damn shame, but we'll find you something else to wear."

"We're getting married in a courthouse next Friday. *Nobody* is going to see us."

"I'll see you. This is my only wedding, too, and I assume we'll have to take pictures for the attorney. It has to look like you're wildly in love and can't live without me, so let's do it right. Look at this ring. It's perfect for you." He held it up again, as if the first time didn't send her emotions into enough of a flurry, and said, "Four diamonds, and see how they're inset flush with the sides of the band? They won't rip your latex gloves at work like a fancier setting would."

Her heart squeezed at his thoughtfulness. "Zander…?" She took a step back, overwhelmed. "I can't take it. It's too much."

"Sure you can." He flashed that heart-melting smile. "I know you're used to taking care of yourself, and I understand that being in control is as much a part of you as living life on a whim is a part of me. But we're getting married, and if you never get married again, I want to feel like you didn't miss out. I'm not trying to throw you a fancy wedding, but for once in your life, let someone spoil you. Let *me* spoil you."

Emotions bubbled up inside her. "You already *are*. You don't need to do more."

"I *want* to do it. This is my wedding, too. Let me feel good about it. Come on, Angel. Let's have some fun. If we're going to sell the world on this, we need to let go of our reservations and get swept away in the idea of holy matrimony." He took her left hand in his and said, "What do you say, Shauna? Will you marry me and show the world we're not just great looking, but we're also the best damn actors around?"

He was too persuasive for his own good. "You're not going to let me say no, are you?"

"Nope." He slipped the ring onto her finger. "It fits. That's got to be some sort of sign."

"Zander," she pleaded.

"I believe you mean, *Yes, Zander, I'll marry you.*"

She laughed. "You're getting this ring back after we end the marriage."

"Is that a *yes*? Because I didn't hear it."

"*Yes*, you pain. Yes, I'll marry you and wear your beautiful, too-expensive ring."

"Attagirl." He laughed and pulled her into a hug. "See how easy that was?"

"As easy as swallowing nails."

Chapter Sixteen

ZANDER WATCHED SHAUNA with amusement as she wandered through another clothing shop at the Hyannis mall, eyeing dressy outfits as if each one was more offensive than the last. She was a funny girl, so tough and stubborn, she'd snubbed the first two clothing stores as being too fancy. She'd tried about a dozen times to give the ring back, but he'd stood his ground and had caught her admiring it at least as many times. She didn't *need* fancy clothes. She was cute as hell in an oversized green crop top that showed a tempting path of golden-brown skin just above the waist of her hip-hugging jeans. But he was determined to find an outfit that she'd feel comfortable wearing. One she'd admire herself in with the same sparkle in her eyes as when she looked at the ring. And he was going to make sure she had fun finding it.

"Hey, Angel, when was the last time you bought something fancy?"

"I don't *do* fancy. I wear a uniform at work, workout clothes, or jeans."

He cocked a grin. "And sexy little outfits when you're working the pole?"

She glowered at him.

He laughed. "I'll make you a deal. You try on a few dresses and anything else you want, and even if you don't find something you love, I'll take you to dinner."

"You're resorting to bribery?" She sifted through a rack half-heartedly. "I could be into that. What's on the menu?"

He couldn't resist riling her up and waggled his brows, lowering his voice seductively. "*Anything* you want."

She rolled her eyes. "Make it shrimp tacos and you've got a deal."

"It's your loss."

She laughed and plucked a simple peach dress off the rack. "Is this what you had in mind?"

"That dress does *not* deserve you." He took it from her and put it back on the rack. "You're strong and snarky. You need something sexy and flirty that demands attention but doesn't beg it."

"I don't even know what that means."

He sifted through the rack and pulled out a sexy little floral number. "Like this."

"Flowers? Really?" She crossed her arms. "That's…a lot."

"So are you, Angel. You're trying it on."

She sighed. "They'd better be good tacos." She reached for the hanger, but he pulled it away. "Zander, I need to check the size."

He looked at the tag. "It's an eight."

"That won't fit. I need a ten or twelve, depending on the cut."

"I'll never understand why women's sizes aren't universal between brands, like guys' sizes are." He exchanged the eight for a ten *and* a twelve. When she reached for them, he pulled them away.

"I thought you wanted me to try them on," she said.

"I have a feeling it'll be like pulling teeth getting you back into that dressing room, which is why we're going to choose a few more first."

"Damn it," she grumbled. "That was the point."

"See? I know my future wife well. You can't trick me." He pulled a little black dress off a rack and held it up. "Now, this is hot."

"I'm not going to a nightclub."

"Yeah, but you'll look drop-dead gorgeous in it."

"If you love dresses so much, why don't you wear one?" she challenged.

"And show off my legs? Not after the way you ogled me when I stepped out of the shower."

"I didn't *ogle* you," she snapped, but she was laughing.

"Well, you sure didn't hightail it out of the bathroom."

"Because I was late for work—"

"And I was naked," he tossed out, egging her on.

"That wasn't *my* fault! I had to brush my teeth."

"And ogle me." He lowered his voice to a whisper. "Don't worry. I won't tell anyone." Then, louder, he said, "I'll make you a deal. If you try on the black dress, after dinner I'll leave the bathroom door wide open from now on."

She deadpanned.

He laughed. "I'm kidding. If you try it on, I'll take you out for dessert at that great French bakery in Wellfleet. They have the best pastries stuffed with chocolate or cream, with powdered sugar on top."

"No thanks. I'm not into fancy desserts."

No fancy clothes. No fancy desserts. He was noticing a pattern. He wasn't into fancy things either, but he wanted to do nice things for her, to show her she was worth the extra effort. He chose not to push it now, since she'd agreed to try on a few dresses, which was clearly a sore spot for her. "How about ice cream?"

That earned a genuine smile. "How many scoops?"

"However many you'd like."

Their banter continued as they picked out slacks and tops and other outfits.

"If I hate everything I try on, I'm getting married in my workout clothes," she said as they headed for the dressing room.

"I knew you were only in this for the tacos."

She flashed a cheesy smile and disappeared behind a curtain.

Zander was too anxious to sit still. He'd never taken a woman shopping before, and he was having fun. "Need some help in there?"

"No," she said with a laugh.

"Are you sure? I'm good at taking women's clothes off."

"You're such a *guy*."

"A wildly charming guy," he tossed out. "It's a curse."

"I'll stock up on sage," she said from behind the curtain.

A minute later she opened the curtain, her eyes downcast as she took a tentative step forward, absolutely stunning in the little black dress, all legs and luscious curves.

Zander whistled long and low. "Damn, girl."

She crossed and uncrossed her arms. "It's too tight."

"Tight is *good*, darlin'." He held her gaze. "You're on *fire*."

The air vibrated with unspoken attraction, her eyes shimmering with heat. *Fuck*, that was sexy. But in the next breath, she planted a hand on her hip, trying to stifle a smile as she said, "I don't care if I'm burning down the whole damn store. I'm *not* wearing this."

"Why not? You look amazing."

"I look like I'm trying to get attention, and that's *not* me."

"And yet, you're smiling," he pointed out, knowing she was right. She wasn't an attention seeker, but *damn*. The world was missing out.

"Because it's absurd that I even have to say it." She turned on her heel and stalked back into the dressing area, pulling the curtain shut, speaking from behind it. "I'm not trying on any more dresses."

"Naked works for me."

He heard her laugh and pictured her dark eyes glittering, her dimples coming out to play. *Man*, he liked that. He liked *her*, and he was having way too much fun with a woman who was too easy to pretend to love.

He paced and was mulling over that dangerous thought when a text rolled in from Madigan.

Mads: *I heard you were helping the girl who pulled you out of the wreck and drove her friend to rehab. If she needs an ear from someone who won't try to get in her pants, I'm around.*

A laughing emoji popped up.

He wasn't surprised she'd heard about that. His brothers and cousins had checked in with him last night to make sure everything had gone smoothly, but he hadn't told them about the whole marriage thing yet. He wanted to talk to his parents first, but Madigan's comment irked him. Maybe it shouldn't, given his reputation, but it did.

Zander: *Thanks. I'll let her know.*

Zander: *And I'm not trying to get in her pants.*

Madigan sent an eyeroll emoji.

As he pocketed his phone, the curtain opened again and Shauna stepped out, all lean shoulders and rounded hips in a cream halter-top jumpsuit with a plunging neckline, a cinched waist, and wide-legged slacks. He couldn't take his eyes off her. But it wasn't just her looks that held his rapt attention. It was the dark-haired beauty beaming at him as she said, "What do you think?" and spun around with the flair and grace of the strong, confident woman he already knew her to be.

Holy hell. The jumpsuit was backless, and it fit snugly around her gorgeous ass, which he couldn't help but notice was made for holding on to, and his hands itched to prove it. But as she finished her spin, his eyes were drawn to those fucking bruises on her arms, and his every muscle seized up.

He fought to keep his expression in check, not wanting to dim the light in her eyes. "You're going to make the justice of the peace wish *he* were marrying you. Maybe you should wear sweats to the courthouse. Baggie ones."

Her deepening dimples hit him square in the center of his chest as she said, "You're ridiculous."

"And you're marrying me. I'd say that makes me ridiculously lucky."

"I'M LEAVING THE tags on so you can return it after the wedding," Shauna said as they left the store with the cream jumpsuit. Zander had coerced her into trying on all the other outfits, including the dresses, with his flirty comments and that all-too wicked smile. He made it fun, and after seeing his reaction to the jumpsuit, which she loved, she wasn't as opposed to trying on more. She couldn't remember the last time anyone had looked at her like she was the prettiest thing he'd ever seen, but the jumpsuit was definitely the winner.

"That's not happening," Zander said. "You can't return gifts."

"It's not a gift," she challenged. "According to you, it's a necessity to pull off this ruse."

"The hell it is. It's a gift to my future wife. Come on." He grabbed her hand and headed to the other side of the corridor.

"Where are we going?"

"To get wedding rings." He nodded to a jewelry store up ahead.

"Don't waste your money." She stopped walking. "You don't have to wear a ring, and I already have one." She tugged her hand free and held it up, wiggling her fingers to show him the ring.

"That's an engagement ring. When we say our vows, we have to exchange wedding rings."

She looked at him like he'd lost his mind again. That was becoming a habit. "We won't have *vows*. We're signing papers and saying I do."

"Everyone has vows."

"Not us," she insisted.

"Whether we write them or they're written for us, we're promising to love and respect each other in sickness and in health. I intend to honor that bond, and unless you're cool with women hitting on me, we need rings."

"Like a ring would stop them?" She laughed. "Look at you. You're one of those guys who's blessed from head to toe."

A devilish spark glimmered in his eyes. "I knew you were checking me out after my shower."

"I'm not talking about *that*." She motioned to his face and body, trying to ignore the flutter in her chest as she cataloged his deliciousness in a gray T-shirt and his leather cut, low-slung jeans, and those biker boots that gave him an edge. "You give off this energy. People can't help but be drawn to you. Practically every woman we've walked past has checked you out." *Oh God. Did I really say that last part out loud?*

"A ring could help stop that."

She shook her head, wondering why he wanted a ring so badly.

"Guess you're not the jealous type, huh?" he coaxed.

"It's a fake relationship, Zan. What do you want me to say?"

His brows knitted. "Aren't you a *little* proud to be marrying me? I mean, I'm a pretty great guy."

"You're an amazing guy, but it's hard to be proud when I feel like I'm taking advantage of you," she said quietly. "You're doing everything to help me, and I'm reaping all the benefits."

"That's not true. You've made it clear that there will be no taking advantage, so you're not reaping *all* the benefits."

She laughed. "I'm serious."

"I'm just pointing out the obvious. I, on the other hand, have a fun new roommate who's easy on the eyes, snarky enough to keep me from getting bored, and isn't afraid to break a fingernail helping me fix up my cottage. I'd say I'm reaping some kick-ass benefits, too."

"Do you spin everything positively?"

"Fuck yeah. Life is too short to live in the muck, and I can tell you right now, I will not stand for guys hitting on you while you're wearing that ring. I take this role very seriously, and now that you're my fiancée, every other guy on this planet is out of luck."

Fake or not, it felt good to be looked after. The next thought hit like an *aha* moment. If it felt good to hear him say that, then didn't he deserve to feel that way, too? She was about to say as much, when a thought gave her pause, and she had to ask, "Why would you want to stop women from hitting on you?"

"Because I'm just going to turn them down."

"But this isn't real. You don't have to do that."

"You keep saying that, but a vow is a vow, and I told you I live by a code. I'd never disrespect you by being with someone else when people think we're married."

As she tried to process his commitment, he said, "You're putting way too much thought into this. Let's pick out our rings." He slung an arm over her shoulder and headed into the jewelry store, speaking low as he walked up to the counter. "Time to test your acting skills, gorgeous."

The tall brunette behind the display smiled as they approached. "Hi. Are you looking for something special today?"

"As a matter of fact, we are." Zander held Shauna a little tighter and said, "My fiancée and I are shopping for wedding rings."

"How exciting," the brunette exclaimed. "When is the big day?"

"Friday," Zander answered.

"*Oh,*" the woman said with surprise. "Nothing like waiting till the last minute, but don't worry. That's not a problem. We have a large stock of wedding bands."

"I had planned on a long engagement," Zander said, eyeing Shauna mischievously. "But when I got down on one knee this morning, I couldn't wait to call this sweet darlin' my *wife*."

Shauna's cheeks burned. Why was he laying it on so thick?

"Love is like that," the woman said. "It's been known to upend all sorts of plans. How long have you been together?"

"It seems like forever, doesn't it, Angel?" Zander said without missing a beat, and then he kissed her temple.

The kiss took her by surprise, and it wasn't a quick peck. It was a warm, intimate press of his lips that lasted so long, she found herself leaning closer. She had to put her hand on his chest to steady herself, imagining how good those soft, warm lips would feel on hers. When he finally drew back, her skin tingled.

He smirked victoriously, jerking her from her reverie.

Shitshitshit. What was she doing? She should *not* be thinking about how good that felt when the saleswoman was looking at her expectantly.

Zander's eyes danced with amusement.

Her competitive side reared its head. He wasn't the only one who was going to ace his role. Remembering what Zander said about it seeming like they'd been together forever, Shauna said, "It sure does. I barely remember the night we first met. It seems like a lifetime ago. Then he crashed into my life again, and sparks flew—"

"More like flames, darlin'." Zander glanced at the saleswoman and said, "Marriage wasn't even on her bucket list, but she couldn't resist me."

We're going there, are we? Shauna slipped her arm around his waist and gazed up at him, letting the attraction she'd worked hard to tamp down show through. "How could I, when you swooped in like a knight in leather armor and knocked me off my feet?"

"You did spill your coffee," he reminded her.

She smiled, remembering how shocked she'd been seeing him standing there. That felt like a lifetime ago, too. "Yes, I did, and then you showed up everywhere I was, like a sexy stalker, and suddenly everything in my life made sense."

Zander's eye warmed. "Mine too, darlin'." The way he said it made her want to believe him as he pulled her into a hug and kissed the top of her head.

"Now, that's a love story," the saleswoman said with awe.

As Shauna stepped out of Zander's embrace, he said, "It's one for the record books. The sooner that ring is on her finger, the better." He tossed Shauna a gratified wink, as if to say, *We did it, Flores.*

And the Oscar goes to Zander Wicked, for getting me swept up in the idea of marrying him after all.

Chapter Seventeen

LATER THAT EVENING, they left the Shrimp Shack laughing at another of their horrible jokes, just as they'd been doing while they'd stuffed their faces with shrimp tacos. Zander couldn't remember the last time he'd had such a good time.

As they headed down the street to the local ice cream shop, he bumped Shauna with his shoulder and said, "Do you think it's possible to become emotionally attached to a shrimp taco? Because that last one was shrimply perfect."

She laughed. "There you go again, being *shellfish*, making me listen to your horrible jokes."

"Now, *that* was bad."

They both laughed.

"Admit it," he said. "You dig my horrible jokes. You're just bummed you didn't take me up on sharing the last taco."

"You put enough hot sauce on it to burn a hole in your gut. You'll pay for it later, and I'm not coming to your rescue."

"I've got a gut of steel, but on the off chance I keel over tonight, tell Zeke I said he has to marry you so you get your money."

"Look at you, already passing me off on someone else. Speaking of your brother, does he know we're getting married?

Have you broken the news to the rest of your family yet?"

"Not yet. Who are you going to let in on this secret? I don't think we should tell too many people the truth, in case the attorney sends a PI to check out our story."

"I should tell Cap, but I'm not going to tell the guys I work with. Howie might tell his wife, and Mike's got loose lips."

"Then it's probably best not to mention it. I'm planning on telling my family when I see them at work this week. We need a witness for the wedding, and I'm sure my parents will offer."

"I forgot about a witness."

"I'll see what they say, and while I'm at it, maybe I'll inform Zeke that he's my replacement if I keel over, so you don't have to tell him."

She gave him a disbelieving look. "You're not dying, and I am *not* marrying your brother."

Good. The last thing he wanted was for her to hook up with his brother...*or anyone else*. But now he was committed to the ruse. "Why not? Zeke's a great guy."

"How can I marry anyone else when I'll be in mourning for lack of bad jokes?"

He grinned. "Then wear black and fake cry when you say your vows."

"I'm not saying vows," she insisted.

"*I do* is a vow." He pulled open the door to the ice cream shop, and bells chimed above them. "Hear that? That's the universe agreeing with me."

"You need to get your hearing checked. All I heard was *This guy's a nut. Run!*"

He laughed and followed her inside.

As they stood in line, she glanced around them at the colorful booths with cups of crayons on wide tables and gigantic murals of ice cream cones and sundaes on yellow walls. She lifted her gaze to the pink ceiling, painted to look like it was covered in rainbow sprinkles, and said, "This place is awesome."

"Wait until you taste the ice cream."

She leaned against him and said, "I hope you meant what you said about no limit on scoops, because ice cream is my guilty pleasure. How about you?"

"Ice cream's a fun treat." He lowered his voice for her ears only and said, "But my guilty pleasure involves licking other things."

Her eyes widened in surprise, but there was no missing the heat rising in them.

"What do you say we make this a scandalous Sunday?" he asked.

She blinked several times, disbelief replacing the heat in those pretty eyes. "I'm not…We're not…"

"Relax, Angel. I'm talking about sharing the Scandalous Sundae." He pointed to the chalkboard. "Five scoops and five toppings. If you're not up to it, we can go for the four-scoop Sweet Surrender. There's no shame if you need something smaller. Not everyone can handle that much *pleasure* all at once."

She boldly held his gaze. "I can handle more pleasure than you can imagine."

Damn, he liked that confidence. "Watch yourself, Flores. I've got an insatiable imagination for pleasure."

"So I've heard," she shot back. "Are we doing this, or are you one of those guys who are all talk?"

Before he could answer, she stepped up to the counter. He'd been so caught up in their banter, he hadn't even realized the other customers had finished ordering.

A few minutes later they were sitting side by side in a booth with their Scandalous Sundae between them, spoons in hand. He eyed a heap of whipped cream on a mountain of chocolate-chip ice cream, covered in chocolate sauce and all the toppings. "I don't know, Flores. You might not survive this."

With a challenging expression, she plunged her spoon into the sundae, scooping up a pile of chocolate-chip ice cream with a hefty amount of whipped cream, chocolate syrup, nuts, and chocolate sprinkles, topped with the biggest cherry he'd ever seen. As she lifted it toward her mouth, it wobbled, and she dove forward to catch it, a few sprinkles landing on her shirt.

He laughed, and her hand flew over her mouth, her eyes dancing with laughter.

"I can't believe you stole the best bite as fast as you could."

"*Oh*, did you want that bite?" she asked innocently.

"I literally made eye contact with it."

"That's a little concerning." She filled her spoon with whipped cream and chocolate sauce. "Maybe you should consult a therapist."

"I'll give you a therapist." He glanced at the sundae. "At least you left me a cherry."

As he reached for it, she snagged the stem with her fingers and popped the cherry into her mouth, her dimples deepening as she ate it.

"What the hell?" He laughed. "You broke the cardinal rules of sundae sharing."

She pointed her spoon at him. "It's not my fault you're blabbing instead of eating."

"I see how you are." He dipped his spoon into the peppermint ice cream, then tapped it to the tip of her nose.

"Hey!" She wiped it with a napkin, grinning from ear to ear.

"Don't waste the goods."

"You're lucky it only ended up on your nose."

"Is that a threat?" She dipped her finger in the chocolate sauce and sucked it off.

She was killing him. Those plump lips wrapped around her finger and her gorgeous eyes, glimmering tauntingly, were trouble waiting to happen. Gritting his teeth against their mounting attraction, he stabbed the sundae with his spoon, and she scooped the chocolate sauce from the top of it. As he lifted his eyes to hers, she dipped her finger in the chocolate again, and her hand shot out, painting his cheek with it as she howled with laughter.

"I can't believe you did that. I should make you lick it off." He grabbed a napkin.

"Dream on, Casanova."

He hauled her across the bench, and she squealed as he locked his arm around her. "Get that tongue ready, Flores."

"I'm *not* licking you!" She buried her face in his neck, cracking up.

"You assaulted me with chocolate. You gotta pay the price."

She tried to wriggle out of his grip as he stuck his finger in the ice cream.

"Don't you dare!" she warned.

"That sounds like a challenge to me."

He painted a Z on her cheek, and she squealed. She was too fucking cute, laughing and trying to get free as he tugged her closer, said, "I marked you like Zorro," and then dragged his tongue up her cheek, licking the sweetness from her skin.

"Zander!"

She tried to push out of his arms, but he kept her close. They were both cracking up as their eyes connected with the impact of a thunderclap, commanding attention as everything else faded away. Silence stretched between them, hot and hesitant. She scraped her teeth over her bottom lip, restraint and desire battling in her eyes.

Fuck. What am I doing?

She wasn't some chick looking for a good time, and she didn't need the likes of him mucking this up for her. She needed a friend who would do right by her, and damn it, he was going to be that guy.

Letting go of her was harder than it should have been, and for a split second he thought he saw a flicker of something similar in her eyes. But in the next breath, she was snagging a napkin like nothing had happened. Either he needed to get a fucking grip, or she was as good at switching gears as he was. He was starting to think it was the latter.

"Don't mess with a Wicked, darlin'. We always win."

"We'll see about that." As she wiped his cheek, she said, "You're a mess."

He grabbed a napkin to wipe his face. "At least my shirt's clean. You dropped some sprinkles in your feeding frenzy."

She looked down at her chest. "Were you checking out my boobs?"

"No." He laughed.

"*Mm-hm.* Careful, Wicked. We don't want to blur those fake-relationship lines." She lifted the top of her shirt and lowered her chin, licking the sprinkles off it.

Yeah, definitely the latter. "Now you're just trying to make me jealous."

She rolled her eyes and ate another bite of ice cream. "This is the best decision we've made since we met."

"Better than helping Brian?" he asked.

"No, but it's a close second."

"Hey," he said gently. "How are you feeling about the whole Brian thing? You haven't talked much about him tonight."

She pushed her spoon around a scoop of chocolate ice cream. "I'm worried about him, but I know we did the right thing. He's where he needs to be, and now it's up to him to follow through. I kind of hate that he won't let me visit, but if that's what it takes for him to get better, then I'm okay with it." She set a warm gaze on Zander. "I can't thank you enough for helping me with all of this."

"I'm glad you let me." As she lifted a spoonful of ice cream dripping in chocolate sauce toward her mouth, he said, "Little did I know I was engaged to a dessert thief. I think I need to add a clause to our prenup."

"We don't have a prenup." She ate the spoonful of ice cream.

"We do now." He pushed a clean napkin in front of her and grabbed a crayon from the cup, putting it on the napkin. "Write this down." He tapped the napkin. "Zander shall get the first bite of every sundae from this date forward."

She laughed. "And I thought the last taco made you *shell-fish*."

"This is self-preservation. Go on." He tapped his index finger on the napkin again. "We've got to knock it out anyway. Might as well do it now."

"We don't need a prenup."

"If this is what marriage looks like, I definitely need legal protection."

She looked at him like he was being ridiculous as she scooped chocolate syrup onto her spoon and then nudged whipped cream on top of it.

"See? Dessert hoarder." He bumped her with his shoulder. "Seriously, though, you're inheriting a lot of money. You need to protect yourself with a prenup."

"If you think I need one so badly, then you write it up." She pushed the napkin toward him.

"You won't be able to read my handwriting." He pushed it back to her.

"Has anyone ever told you that you're a pushy pain in the butt?" She picked up the crayon. "How do we do this?"

"I don't know. Just write that you'll keep your shit and I'll keep mine."

She deadpanned. "I don't think it works that way. I think you have to list what you have."

"Go ahead then, and write that I have no claim over what-ever's on your list."

As she touched the crayon to the paper, she said, "This feels wrong. I'm borrowing *your* money. I'm not afraid you're going to try to rip me off."

"That's why I have to protect you. What if I'm an asshole?"

"If you were, you wouldn't be helping me."

He pulled the sundae bowl in front of himself and put his arms around it. "You never know."

"Yes, I *do*."

IF THERE WAS one thing she knew for certain about Zander, it was that he was not someone she had to worry about trying to rip her off. To prove her point, she reached her spoon over his arm to get some ice cream, and he slid the bowl back toward her.

"See?" she said.

"Stop delaying and start writing. Make sure you cover everything."

"If you're going to make me do this, then let's do it right." She grabbed her phone and googled how to write a prenup. "Here's a list." She held it out to him. "You read. I'll write."

"You read it. I need ice cream." He picked up his spoon and dug into the ice cream.

She rolled her eyes. "It says to identify financial and personal property, but I don't want to know how much money you have."

"That's good because I have no idea. Write down your inheritance."

"That's going to you."

"I want it listed as yours. I trust you to pay me back."

She wrote it down to appease him.

"What else do you have?" he asked.

"Not much. My car and the gold bracelet Cap gave me to commemorate my first year of sobriety."

"Write that down. It sounds special."

"It is. It's really pretty, too. It has a triangular charm with a lotus flower on the front to symbolize new beginnings. But what makes it so special is that Cap had *I believe in you* engraved on the back. That may not seem like much, but I worked really hard to better myself, and no one ever told me they were proud of me like that before. I doubt it's worth much. Maybe it shouldn't go on the list."

"I saw that bracelet in a picture of you and Brian in his room. A gift like that is priceless regardless of what it cost."

Zander glanced at her wrist. "Why aren't you wearing it?"

"I don't wear it to work, and with everything that's happened, I forgot to put it back on."

"You should wear it when we get married, so you have it in the pictures."

She liked that he'd thought of that. "I left it at the cottage."

"We'll stop by and get it on the way home. You should have it with you, since there's nobody staying at your place."

"Good point. I need my jewelry box anyway to put this ring in until I figure out how to tell the guys at work what's going on."

"Just flash the ring and say you're tying the knot. What's next on the list? Personal property, right? I've got Kitty—"

"Kitty is *not* personal property."

"She's the most valuable thing I have," he argued. "If something happens to me, as my wife, you'll have to take care of her." He pointed to the napkin. "Write that down."

"Nothing is going to happen to you."

"I've got scars that prove anything is possible. Promise me you'll take care of her, or I'll need to rethink this marriage."

"*Of course* I'll take care of her." She tapped the crayon on the napkin, an uncomfortable thought rolling through her mind. "What if something happens to me while Brian's in rehab? I know this is a lot to ask, but will you make sure he gets through it okay? You don't have to stick around afterward, but—"

"Yes," he said without hesitation, shocking her.

"You'd really do that?"

"I said I would, didn't I? The guy's got nobody but you. If ever he needed help, it'd be then. I wouldn't leave him hanging, either. That's not how I roll. I'd make sure he got to meetings and whatever he needed."

Part of her felt like all of this was too good to be true and she should expect a shoe to drop. She looked down at the tattoo on her hand. He'd come out of nowhere before, and he'd helped to change her life. She thought about Cap and how he'd done the same. Maybe there was something to fate. Zander had shown her who he was back then, and now. Brian was finally getting the help he needed. Help she could not have gotten him on her own, so she pushed the whispers of doubt away and counted herself lucky.

"I told you you're not an asshole." She ate a spoonful of ice cream.

"Don't count your chickens." He tapped the napkin again. "Write down Kitty."

She rolled her eyes, and as she wrote it, she said, "What other personal property do you have? And please don't say another living creature, or I'm going to have to report you to the authorities."

"No more living creatures. Just my truck, my bike, my speedboat, and my house. One day I'll get another sports car, but until then, that's it."

"You have a *speedboat*, and you're worried about *me* having a prenup?"

"I already told you. As my future wife, protecting you comes first. Do you like speedboats?"

"I've never been on one."

"We'll fix that as soon as it gets a little warmer out."

She studied him for a minute. "Aren't you a contractor? How do you have any money left over with all that stuff?"

"Are you knocking contractors? We work hard, and we earn good livings."

"I didn't mean it like that. I just…You've done well for yourself. I was doing okay financially before Brian lost his job. I earn a good living and saved where I could, but I can't imagine having my own place, much less everything that you do. How did you manage it?"

"It wasn't planned, that's for sure. Planning isn't my thing."

"For a pantser, you sure ended up in a good place. That can't just happen."

He sat back and said, "I don't know what to tell ya, Angel. I never went to college, so I've got no school debt, and I've been working my ass off since I was a teenager. When I first started working, my parents taught me to put half of what I earned into a savings account that I don't touch, and that's worked out well for me. My truck and bike are several years old and paid off, and I bought the boat from a buddy and traded renovation work for most of the cost. I've got a mortgage, but I bought the place right before it went into foreclosure, and I got a good deal. If I were smarter, or if I'd listened to my family's advice, I'd've done the renovations sooner and sold it instead of carrying it for years and paying all that interest. But I was having too much fun dicking around and picking up women to slow down."

She waved her hand. "I don't need details, but just so you know, that whole thing about dicking around instead of working on your house? It sounds like you were happy living that way. That doesn't mean you weren't smart. It means you chose to live life on your terms, which isn't a negative. But we don't need to go there."

"I appreciate that, but there's no place to go. I'm just telling you how I got here. But you've seen how I live. I'm a simple guy. I live at the beach, so every day is like a vacation. It's not like I spend money on travel. I've got my family, friends, the brotherhood, and now I've got an ice-cream-hoarding almost wife." He cocked a grin. "What else do I need?"

"You make it seem easy and attainable."

"You're only twenty-four, darlin'. I've got a lot of years on you, and I didn't have to battle the things you have. To be honest, I don't know how I would've handled being in your shoes, but I know it wouldn't have been as well as you have."

She set her spoon down and said, "I think you would've handled it better."

"Then you think wrong. I'm just blessed with a great family that has given me good direction and kept me in line as best they could." He sat back. "Don't you see how impressive you are? You got yourself out of a shitty situation at seventeen. At that age I was nothing but a cocky mess of hormones. If not for my family, I could've easily ended up much worse off than you. I'm just now stepping out of that dick-around zone. You took it upon yourself to create the life you wanted, and now you've got a great job, a cute place, and a solid car."

"I am proud of that."

"And you should be. Life is not about material shit. It's about how we feel and how we make others feel, and thanks to that sweet heart of yours, you'll have your other best friend back on track in no time."

She looked down at the ring shimmering on her finger and felt a little guilty hoping the time didn't pass too quickly, because she had a feeling these were going to be the best months of her life.

THEY STOPPED AT Shauna's cottage after leaving the ice cream shop so she could pick up her jewelry box. "It feels weird being back here knowing I don't have to worry about what's waiting for me inside," she said as she unlocked her front door.

Zander put his hand on her back. "I'm sorry that you had to deal with all of that."

"That's life, right?" She stepped inside, confused by a lemony scent, and halted in her tracks at the sight before her. For a minute, she thought she'd walked into the wrong house. The place was spotless. There was no clutter, no dirt on the floor, no discarded clothes or misplaced furniture.

"I cleaned up while you were at work yesterday. I didn't want you to come back to a mess in case you came here before you came back to my place."

Astonished, she turned to him. "You did this? How did you get in?"

"I snagged Brian's keys the other night. I knew if I asked to borrow yours so I could clean, you'd say no."

"Zander…? I don't even know what to say. I feel like I'm always thanking you. I could've cleaned up." But the truth was, she'd been so thrown off when she'd driven there this morning, cleaning up hadn't even crossed her mind.

"You've been cleaning up messes your whole life, Angel. It's not a big deal, and don't worry." He held his hands up. "I didn't go into your room and snoop around, or rifle through your lingerie drawer. I didn't want you to feel violated."

An incredulous laugh bubbled out.

His brows furrowed. "Why is that funny?"

"Don't take this wrong, because I truly appreciate what you did, but you *snuck* into my house, and you don't want me to feel violated?" She laughed again. "I'm sorry. It's just funny."

He smiled. "Yeah. I guess it is. Sorry. I should've asked permission. I'm still new at this responsible-adult thing."

"It's okay, and for what it's worth, I don't feel violated, and you're doing a great job of adulting. This place has never looked this good. If you ever get tired of contracting, you could be a houseboy. I bet you'd earn good tips if you wore booty shorts and went shirtless."

"Now who's blurring those fake fiancée lines?" He touched her back again. "Let's get your bracelet and jewelry box, and anything else you need."

"I want to get my pillow," she said as they headed down the hall.

"What's wrong with the pillow at my place? It's brand-new."

"Nothing. I shared it with Kitty this morning, and I thought she might like her own." She'd heard Kitty scratching on the bedroom door when she was getting into bed after work that morning, and Kitty had jumped right onto the bed and curled up with her.

"I think you just got a little hotter, Flores." He leaned against her doorframe and crossed his arms, watching her as she went around to the dresser.

"Because I want to spoil your cat?"

"Exactly."

"I've never had a pet. It was nice to have something to cuddle with." She opened the wooden jewelry box where she kept the bracelet, but it was empty. She closed it and scanned the top of the dresser.

"What's wrong?"

"My bracelet isn't in it." She opened the top dresser drawer, but that was empty, too. "I probably left it in the bathroom."

He pushed off the doorframe as she walked past him. "I didn't see it when I was cleaning, but I didn't look in the vanity drawers."

She rummaged through the vanity drawers and started to panic, trying not to think the worst. But she wasn't naive. A gold bracelet doesn't just go missing. "It's not here."

"Is there anywhere else you would've put it? In your nightstand, maybe?"

"No." She took a deep breath, her heart breaking. "I think Brian took it. I should've checked after the TV went missing, but I never would've thought…" Hurt burned deep in her chest. "How could he do this to me? He knows how important that bracelet is."

Zander pulled her into his arms. "He wasn't thinking straight," he gritted out.

"I hate this." She squeezed her eyes shut against the sting of tears.

"I do, too." He held her tighter. "I think this calls for a *John Wick* marathon. What do you say, darlin'?"

Every time he called her that, it made her smile, but this time it was more than the endearment that had her lips curving against his chest. He somehow always knew what she needed, and that was astonishing to her. "I like the way you think, Wicked." *And the way you feel.* Which was why she stepped out of his arms and said, "Let me grab my pillow."

He followed her into the bedroom, and as she went to get her pillow, he grabbed her jewelry box. It was a good thing he did, because she would've forgotten to bring it. He motioned to the pillow and said, "You can scream into that if you want to."

"I bet you'd love that, you perv," she teased, and swatted him with the pillow.

He laughed. "You sure you don't want to take anything else?"

She looked around the sparse bedroom, feeling a strange sense of emptiness. But when she met his gaze, she didn't feel quite so empty. "No. I'm good. But I think when you were listing all the good things in my life, like my job and my car, you forgot to mention my kick-ass fiancé."

He slung his arm over her shoulder, and as they left the bedroom, he said, "It's about time you noticed."

Chapter Eighteen

MONDAY WAS A bitch. It seemed like everything that could go wrong on the job did, and on top of that, Zeke was in a pissy mood, and Tobias, the guy who rarely smiled, was whistling like one of Snow White's happiest dwarves all fucking day. Zander considered waiting to talk to his parents about Shauna until tomorrow, but Shauna had brought it up again that morning. She was a lot more anxious about it than he was, and he wanted to put her mind at ease. But he'd only seen Preacher for a few minutes, when his father had stopped at the job site and said he'd heard about what had gone down over the weekend with Brian. Zander had been in the middle of handling a cabinetry issue, so he'd quickly filled Preacher in about Brian and had said he'd swing by his parents' house after work to talk to them.

He wasn't worried about telling them he was helping Shauna. For as far back as Zander could remember, his parents had ingrained helping others into him and his siblings by raising them with foster kids and helping families in the community. As he climbed out of his truck in front of his parents' house, the rambling two-story, with its wide front porch, gabled roof, and breezeway that led to a multicar garage, brought a sense of comfort.

He headed up to the house, and memories rolled in of running around the yard wreaking havoc with his siblings and cousins, wrestling in the grass, playing football and other games, while their parents barbecued or hung out on the patio. He had many memories of waking up in the middle of the night to the roar of motorcycles and hearing his father's hushed, deep voice as he held court in their living room when something had gone down in the community. He had even fonder memories of sneaking out in the middle of the night looking for trouble, and finding it.

He thought about Shauna sneaking out to get away from her parents. He fucking hated that she'd needed to get away from the people who should have done everything they could to protect her. And her fucking grandfather turning his back on her? That made Zander even angrier. Zander had often been a little jerk when he was young, treating everything like a joke, but he'd never once doubted that his parents would go to the ends of the earth for him. Not when he was getting in trouble at school or when he was a mouthy teenager and said horrible shit to them. He'd had a safety net his whole fucking life. He still did, and it infuriated him, and broke his heart, that Shauna had never had one.

Until now.

He pulled open the kitchen door, and their parents' dogs, Milo, a fluffy brown mutt, and Buster, a golden retriever mix, bounded over to greet him, their tails wagging.

"Hey, guys." Zander crouched to pet them, happily accepting their slobbery kisses as his grandfather walked into the room.

"Well, well, look what the cat dragged in. And here I was enjoying the peace and quiet."

His grandfather's craggy voice brought a smile. Zander still remembered the burlier grandfather of his youth, whose authoritative presence captured everyone's attention, the way Preacher's did. Neither had demanded that power, nor did they abuse it. Their confidence drew respect, and the way they treated everyone like family kept it. His grandfather was leaner now, his once-thick dark hair wispy and gray, his square jaw and strong features softened with wrinkles, but his blue-gray eyes were just as keen, always searching beneath the surface.

"How's it going, old man? You here mooching dinner again? They ought to start charging you rent."

"Let 'em try," he grumbled, and embraced Zander, giving him a hard clap on the back. "Good to see you, boy. I heard you helped put a guy on the right path this weekend."

"Hopefully it'll do some good. Where are Mom and Preach?"

"They're in the den, on the phone with Uncle Biggs and Aunt Red." Biggs Whiskey was one of Zander's uncles on his mother's side. He'd founded and ran the Peaceful Harbor, Maryland, chapter of the Dark Knights.

"Everything okay?" Zander asked as they headed out of the kitchen with the dogs in tow.

"Yes, sir. Bear and Crystal are having another baby." Bear was one of Zander's cousins from Maryland. He and his wife already had an adorable little boy they named after their late uncle, Axel.

"Yeah? Good for them," Zander said as his parents walked out of the den.

"Hi, sweetheart," his mother said. "Did Grandpa tell you the good news about Bear and Crystal?"

"Yes, he did. I'm happy for them. That'll be one lucky kid.

They're great parents."

"You're thinking better them than you, aren't ya?" his father asked.

Zander grinned. "I wasn't going to say it out loud."

"You didn't have to," his grandfather said. "After what you said when you heard Baz and Emerson were expecting another baby, we know where you stand."

"What are you talking about? I said I was happy for them, too," Zander insisted.

"That was right after Zan's accident. He was still in the hospital when Baz told him," his mother said in his defense. "You probably forgot, honey, but I believe you said something to the effect of, *Better you than me. I'm allergic to diapers and commitment.*"

Zander laughed. He was about to say that was accurate, but he held it back, remembering why he was there. Apparently he wasn't quite as allergic to commitment as he'd thought.

"You did offer to teach Baz how to keep that from happening," his father said with a chuckle. "You sticking around for dinner, son? Zeke's joining us."

Normally he would stick around, but Shauna had to work tomorrow, and he wanted to ease her worries before she went. "No, thanks. I just came by to tell y'all that I'm getting married."

"Not with those allergies, you're not," his mother said, and the three of them laughed.

"Yeah. You're getting married, and I'm giving away my Trans Am," his father joked, earning more laughter.

"I'm serious," Zander said. "I'm getting married on Friday."

His parents' smiles faded.

"This ought to be good," his grandfather said, rubbing his

hands together as he lowered himself to the couch.

His father lifted his chin, his eyes narrowing. "Come again, son?"

"You heard me. I'm getting married on Friday."

"I think we'd all better sit down," his mother suggested, and she sat beside his grandfather.

Zander and his father remained standing, his father's stern expression throwing him off. "Why're you looking at me like that? I'm helping Shauna, the girl who pulled me out of the burning car. You know, the one who *saved my life*. She needs money for Brian's rehab, and she's got an inheritance from her grandfather, but she can't get it unless she's married for a couple of months. I'm stepping in to help her out. We'll be married for two months plus a few weeks so it looks real. Three months max. What's the big deal?"

"Here we go," his grandfather said, like he was watching the start of a race.

"What's the big *deal*?" his father shot back. "Didn't we teach you anything? Wickeds don't half-ass things. Especially not an institution as sacred as marriage. That's not something you jump into with a predetermined end date."

"It's really *not* that big of a deal. You know I've got no plans of walking down an aisle for real, and neither does she."

His mother popped to her feet. "Then why do it, honey?"

"Because it's the only way she can afford to help her friend. I offered to lend her the money, but she's afraid she'll never be able to pay it back since she never wants to get married. I also offered to give her the money—"

"*Zander*, have you lost your mind?" his father fumed. "What do you even know about this girl?"

"I know she saved my life. That's enough for me, and it

should be enough for you, too," Zander implored.

"You're not thinking this through," his father gritted out.

"That's nothing new," his grandfather said under his breath.

"*Jesus Christ.*" Zander paced. "Don't you get it? For once in my life I *am* thinking something through. This is a fake marriage for a few months to help out the woman who saved my life. How can the three of you, of all people, find fault in that?"

"Do I need to make you a list?" his father barked. "You're being reckless. I'm sure this inheritance comes with all sorts of caveats to protect the money from being handed out to a scammer. How are you going to make everyone believe you're suddenly so in love you're getting married, when you've flaunted your affinity for one-night stands for the last decade?"

Zander drew his shoulders back, holding his father's stare. "There's *nothing* I can't do."

"Honey." His mother touched his arm, speaking more softly. "It's commendable that you want to help Shauna. Your heart is in the right place, but marriage is not just a big deal. It's the *biggest* deal there is. You two might not think you'll ever want to get married, but look at your brothers and cousins. We know they weren't saints, but when they met the right person, everything changed. A marriage is something you can't take back. You can divorce or get an annulment, but it still happened. You might fall in love with someone in a few years and wish you'd never said *I do* to someone else first."

"That's not happening for me, Mom, and I don't think Shauna's worried about that, either."

"Boy, you have no idea what you're talking about," his grandfather said gruffly. "When the right woman snags your heart, you've got no say in the matter. You'll be down for the count before you know what's happening, and most of us never want to get back up again."

"That's you and the rest of them, Gramps. It's not me. I'm not built for that forever shit," Zander insisted.

"Does she know *who* you are?" His father stalked closer, staring him down. "The real you? The guy who goes home with different women every week? The one who woke up with *two* women the morning of the accident?"

"*Zander*, is that true?" his mother snapped.

Zander gritted his teeth and didn't bother answering his mother. He didn't have to. She knew who he was. "Shauna knows exactly who I used to be."

His parents exchanged a glance that was sharp and loaded with doubt, pissing him off even more.

"Zander, I know right now the accident is still fresh in your mind, and you think you want to change," his mother said carefully but firmly. "But change is not that easy, sweetheart. You have to stop and think about Shauna. Three months is a long time, and your father is right. For you two to pull this off, people have to believe you're in love, and I'm sorry, honey, but while you know about loving family and friends, being in love is a subject you know nothing about. You can't be flirting with other women or even checking them out—"

"No shit," Zander barked. "You think I'm a fucking idiot?"

"Watch your mouth," his father warned. "Your mother is right. You're going to hurt this girl, Zander, and you'll never forgive yourself."

His father's words landed like spears, sparking fury and disillusionment. He looked between his parents and his grandfather. "Thanks for having faith in me," he gritted out sarcastically. "All this time I thought you stood behind the lessons you taught us about putting others first. This marriage is happening with or without your support, and if you care about me at all, you won't screw this up for her by telling anyone outside the family the *reason* we're getting married."

He turned and stalked out the door, storming past Zeke in the driveway.

"Whoa, dude." Zeke grabbed his arm. "What happened? You look like you want to kill someone."

"Ask your parents," he fumed.

"I'm asking *you*."

In no mood to repeat the whole fucking story, he said, "Shauna's got an inheritance and needs the money for Brian's rehab, but she's got to be married for a few months to get it. I told Mom and Dad I'm marrying her on Friday, and they're up my ass about it."

"You're getting *married?*" he said incredulously. "Bro, what's the rush? Brian's already in rehab."

"Yeah, because I paid for it. She wants to pay me back, which means getting the marriage clock ticking so she can get her money." He headed to his truck, but Zeke followed.

"Slow down, Zan. Can we just sit down, have a beer, and talk about this? There's got to be another way."

"Are you fucking kidding me? I thought if anyone had my back, it would be you."

"I'm trying to have your back, but come on. You and marriage? Those two things do not go together, and you know it."

"Like I said, way to have my back, bro. I'm out of here." Ignoring Zeke's pleas to chill the fuck out, he climbed into his truck and sped away.

If ever there was a time when Zander wished he had his motorcycle, it was now. He could use some wind therapy to cool off before going home. Instead, he hit the highway, cranked the tunes, and ground his back teeth. He felt blind-sided. Not just by his parents and grandfather, but by Zeke. He was the one person who had always had his back, no matter what kind of shit he got himself into, and this wasn't even for himself.

He was still on edge when he got home.

As he headed up to the front door, he saw Shauna through the window. She was vacuuming in her workout shorts and a crop top, her head bobbing and her ass swinging to some beat he couldn't hear. He laughed to himself, the tension draining out of him. How could coming home to someone he barely knew make him so happy? He never imagined he'd go against his family for anything, but as he made his way inside, there wasn't even a question. He refused to be just another person who let Shauna down.

She was shaking her ass, belting out something about moonbeam ice cream and taking off jeans—*his kind of song*—and the living room looked like it had been hit by a hurricane. Cat treats and glitter littered the floor and furniture, along with what appeared to be pieces of balloons and feathers.

Shauna looked up and startled. She quickly turned off the vacuum, and as she took out her earbuds, she said, "You scared the crap out of me. How long have you been standing there?"

"Long enough to see this." He turned around and shook his ass.

She covered her face with her hand, laughing, but her smile faded fast, and she wrinkled her nose adorably. "I'm sorry about the mess, but don't worry. I'll clean up everything."

"I don't care about the mess. What happened?"

"Ask her." She pointed to Kitty, lounging on the couch like

a queen. As if on cue, Kitty rolled onto her back and stretched, looking insanely cute.

He cocked a brow and picked Kitty up.

"Don't fall for that cuteness. This is all her doing."

"This sweet little girl?" he teased, snuggling Kitty. "No way."

"I'm telling you, she's got a little devil in her. I stopped by the craft store after my pole class to get stuff to make a glitter bomb birthday card for Mike, one of the guys I work with, and I thought it might be fun to get Kitty a new toy. But they didn't sell cat toys, and I had ordered takeout to pick up on the way home to surprise you since you're doing so much for me. Rather than take the time to go to the pet store, I thought I'd make her toys. I bought helium balloons and feathers to tie to the strings, thinking that when the balloons floated up to the ceiling, she'd chase the feathers around."

He freaking loved that she'd thought about making something for his cat, but he loved that she wanted to surprise him with dinner even more.

"Little did I know devil cat would launch herself off the couch, trying to get the balloons instead of the feathers, and knock over my glitter jar. I tried to catch it, and missed, but I managed to knock over the bag of Kitty's treats I found in the cabinet. Meanwhile, she was freaking out about the glitter jar crashing to the floor."

He laughed.

She planted a hand on her hip. "You laugh, but I swear she's possessed, because that's when she noticed the feathers tied to the strings on the balloons. I kid you not, she leapt onto the back of the couch and turned into a flying squirrel right before my eyes, launching herself onto one of the balloons and puncturing it with her claws. As she's going down with the loudest meow you've ever heard, I dive across the room to catch her, and my foot slips on glitter."

"Oh, man." He winced.

"You're telling me? I'm stumbling forward, arms flailing, and manage to catch her on my way down."

"Did you get hurt?" he asked through his laughter.

"Just my ego."

And there they were. The dimples that had him pulling her into his arms for a quick hug with Kitty as he said, "You're my hero for saving my girl."

"Your girl is a demon." She scratched Kitty's back, and Kitty purred. "Oh my gosh, I have been a nervous wreck all day about how things would go with your parents, and I got so caught up in this mess, I almost forgot to ask how it went."

He kissed Kitty's head and put her on the couch. "It didn't go great, but fuck 'em. We're doing this."

"What? *No.* I don't want to cause a rift between you and your family. I'll find another way to pay you back."

"You're not causing a rift."

"Yes, I am. I'm the one you're marrying."

"This was my idea, remember? You didn't tie me down and force me to say I'll marry you. I *want* to do this for you, and you're not going to change my mind, so you might as well save your energy."

Her brow furrowed, her eyes narrowing. "I appreciate that, but will you at least tell me what happened?"

He shook his head. "I don't want you worrying about it."

"Too late." She crossed her arms. "I've been worried about it since you convinced me this was a good idea."

"It *is* a good idea. Brian is where he needs to be, and you're not in danger of getting physically or emotionally battered."

She uncrossed her arms, her expression softening. "I appreciate it, but if we're doing this, then we have to be honest with each other. I know you're tough, but this is your *family*. I know how much you love them, and to be honest, I can't blame them for thinking this is crazy. I haven't told Cap yet, for that very reason. You're not just helping me, Zan. You're changing your life, even if only temporarily, for a recovering alcoholic. You moved me in, and you're putting a ring on your finger—"

"I never told them about your background. We never got that far, and I wouldn't have anyway. It's up to you to decide who you want to share that with."

"*Oh,*" she said with surprise. "Thank you, but you could have told them. I wouldn't have minded. I understand why they're upset, but still, I wish you'd talk to me about it. It has to hurt that they're not supportive when you were so sure they would be."

"What do you want me to say?" he snapped. "That I'm bummed? You're damn right I am." He paced. "I thought I'd have their support without question. I was raised to believe nobody rides alone, and it's always been that way. It's not like I don't understand their worries about the sanctity of marriage. I get it. They think we'll spin around in a few years and find our soul mates, and regret having already been married once."

"Well, *that's* not going to happen. At least not for me."

"Me either, and I told them that." He didn't want to admit the next part, but she deserved to hear it, because even though he'd do everything within his power not to fuck this up, this was new territory for him, and honesty had to be paramount. "They're also worried that I'm the same guy I was before the accident, and I'll embarrass you or hurt your feelings by flirting with other women when we're married."

"*Oh*…um…? Do they know it's not like that between us?"

"That doesn't matter. It still has to look real, but as I said before, I'm *not* that guy anymore, and I sure as hell wouldn't do that to you."

"I believe you," she said without hesitation.

She couldn't know how much her trust meant to him. "Good. Now can we stop talking about them and have some of that takeout you mentioned?"

"Yes," she relented. "But I need to finish cleaning up first, and—"

"The mess can wait." He hooked an arm around her neck, pulling her against his side as they headed into the kitchen. "You've had a hard day of making up stories about my cat when we both know you had a wild party with your pole-class friends while I was gone. Thank you for getting them out before I got home."

"It was the least I could do," she said without missing a beat.

Coolest woman on the planet. "Just so you know, I'm getting a nanny cam." He reached for the bag of Chinese food on the counter.

"Hey, Zan?"

The change in her tone from playful to softer had him glancing over as he opened the bag. "Yeah?"

"Thanks for sticking by me. I know it's not the same, but you don't have to ride alone. You've still got me. I've never ridden on a motorcycle, but I'm loyal, and you know I can save your life."

"I'll be proud to have you as my ride or die, Flores. It's you and me against the world."

"You, me, and Kitty," she said, picking up Kitty to cuddle her.

That sounds pretty damn good to me. "Do you think they'll accept a paw print as the witness signature at the courthouse?"

"You've taken care of everything else. Leave finding a witness to me."

Chapter Nineteen

EARLY WEDNESDAY MORNING, before the end of her shift, Shauna tried to work up the courage to talk to Cap about what was going on with Brian and Zander. She'd tried yesterday, but every time she talked herself into it, they either got a call or she chickened out. She never should have lied to him about Brian's relapse. It wasn't lost on her that she thought of Cap like a father figure, but she'd never felt bad about lying to her own father. Luckily, Cap wasn't one to poke around in her personal business. The day Zander had come by the firehouse, Cap had mentioned knowing the Wickeds and attending fundraisers hosted by the Dark Knights. He'd said they were good people, but she hadn't asked for more information, and he hadn't offered. She hoped that when she told him what was going on, he wouldn't fire her for lying or completely lose trust in her.

On top of that, when she and Zander had texted yesterday, his texts didn't have the same fun, flirty vibe as they had in the days prior. She could tell something was wrong. They'd talked on the phone late last night after the rest of the crew was asleep, and she'd heard the strain in his voice. It was like pulling teeth getting him to open up to her, but he finally told her that his cousins and brothers had been giving him shit all day, trying to talk him out of going through with their plan. She'd said they should forget the whole thing, but Zander wasn't having it. *You're not getting rid of me that easily.*

It was his determination that fueled her confidence now, as she finished restocking the rig and headed inside to find Cap. She caught herself absently stroking the underside of her left ring finger with her thumb and made herself stop. She didn't know how it had happened so fast, but she'd gotten used to playing with the bottom of her engagement ring and had been brushing that empty spot all day.

She found Cap coming out of the kitchen as she came down the hall. "Cap? Can I talk to you for a sec?"

"Sure. What's up?"

"Would you mind if we talk in your office?"

"Fuck!" Mike hollered from upstairs, as Trey and Howie howled with laughter. *"Flores!"*

Shauna stifled a laugh. Zander had helped her make a spring-loaded glitter bomb that looked like a birthday gift for Mike instead of a card. She'd put it in his locker about half an hour ago.

Cap cocked his head. "You need to handle that first?"

"Nope. Sounds like he found the birthday present I left him."

As she hurried toward his office, Cap said, "What'd you give him?"

"A glitter bomb."

"Brave girl." Cap shut the door behind them. "Take a seat."

"Thanks." She sat on the chair across from his desk, and he took the seat beside her, which wasn't unusual, but for some reason, today it made her even more nervous.

"What's on your mind?"

"A couple of things." She wrung her hands. "What I'm about to tell you might make you lose all trust in me, and I would understand that, but I also hope you'll try to see it from my side and give me a chance to earn that trust back."

His expression turned serious. "Are you drinking again, Shauna?"

"*No.* I promise," she said quickly. "I never want to go back to that, and if I ever did, I'd tell you right away. I wouldn't jeopardize other people's lives by being less than one hundred percent on the job."

"That's good to know. Then what's got you so worried?"

"Remember over the holidays when you invited me and Brian to Christmas dinner, and I said Brian was sick?"

"Yes."

"He wasn't sick. He relapsed. He lost his job, and at first he was just drinking, and I didn't want to say anything, because I thought I could get him back on track. But then things got worse, and I wanted to get him into rehab, but I couldn't afford it. I was afraid to say anything because I had already lied to you, and I wanted to help him so badly. I just kept trying, but..." She shook her head. "Last week I caught him snorting heroin, and he grabbed me—"

"Where is Brian now?" Cap leaned forward.

"He's in rehab, and I'm okay."

"How bad was it? All those bruises you said were from pole class, did he do that to you? Should you press charges?"

"No. It wasn't like that. The random bruises really *are* from pole class. I promise. That was the first time he's ever grabbed me, and thanks to Zander Wicked, now Brian is where he needs to be to get help. But, Cap, before I tell you the rest, I'm really sorry I lied to you."

"Me too," he said with disappointment and compassion. "I wish you'd come to me. I could've helped before it got that far."

"I know. I just…I was scared that you might tell me I have to move out of there in order to keep my job, and he couldn't afford the rent without me. I was stupid to try to help on my own for so long, and I promise, I learned my lesson. I'll *never* allow myself to be in that position again. Not even for a day."

"I'm holding you to that. How does Zander play into this?"

She sat up straighter and said, "He is helping me pay for Brian's rehab. I haven't told anyone this, and I need your word that you won't tell anyone what I'm about to tell you."

"That's a big ask for someone who just admitted lying to me."

"I realize that, but I want to be honest with you. It's nothing horrible. It's just not something to be proud of."

"Now I'm worried," he said with a wrinkled brow. "But you have my word."

"Thank you. That means a lot to me. Especially now." She told him about the inheritance, and that she'd been staying with Zander, and about Brian showing up in the middle of the night. Then she told him about Zander's brothers and cousins stepping in to help, and finally, she told him about their plans to get married. "With how bad off Brian had gotten, marrying Zander is the only way I can think of to get Brian into rehab right away."

"Married?" Cap sat back and whistled. "When you make an entrance, you don't mess around."

"I know it sounds crazy, but it's just for a few months, and Zander has been amazingly supportive and a good friend." She looked down at the tattoo on her hand and warmed with the memory of when she realized Zander had been the one whose words had set her on the path to change her life. When she lifted her gaze, Cap was watching her intently. "He's the one who drove me home that Fourth of July when I decided I wanted to change my life. We didn't realize it until that day he showed up here and we got to talking. It's the weirdest thing, Cap. With the accident, and his showing up at our cottage to do the work for our landlord, and everything that's happened since, it feels like we've known each other longer."

"They say people come into our lives for a reason."

"Like you came into mine," she said fondly. "I'm grateful he's willing to help, but his family isn't thrilled about it."

"I can't say I blame them. This is something you see in movies. Are you sure about this? I can lend you the money to pay Zander back, and then you can take your time reimbursing me."

"That's really nice of you, but it would take me a lifetime, and borrowing money from my boss wouldn't be right."

"Can you get into legal trouble over this?"

"Probably if they find out," she admitted. "But I'm willing to take that chance for Brian to get help."

"You must really love him," Cap said compassionately.

"Always have, always will."

He steepled his hands beneath his chin, studying her. "I didn't even know you and Zander were dating."

"We're not. I mean, technically we're engaged now, but it's not real."

He glanced at her left hand. "Guess there's no need for a ring."

She caught herself brushing the underside of her ring finger with her thumb and flattened her hand on her leg. "That's what

I said." She lowered her voice, as if sharing a secret. "But he got me the most beautiful ring I've ever seen in my entire life."

"Really?" he asked with shock. "Are you *sure* there's nothing between you two?"

"Yes. It's not like that."

He arched a brow. "Does *he* know that?"

She smiled. "Yes, and trust me, Cap, he's not the marrying type any more than I am. He's been honest with me about how he's been a player his whole life, and now he's trying to change, but not for me. For himself. He had a revelation after the accident."

"A lot of people do, but going from a player to a husband is like going from zero to one fifty in three seconds flat. Are you sure this is what you want to do?"

"Yes. I want to help Brian, and Zander has never made me feel uncomfortable in any way. He's…" *Charming? Kind? Generous? Sexy?* She definitely shouldn't mention sexy. "He's so real, I can't imagine him making any woman uncomfortable."

"I'm sure he knows better. The Wickeds have deep roots in the community and a reputation for being trustworthy."

"How well do you know his family?"

He crossed his ankle over his knee. "Well enough to have a conversation if you need me to."

"No, I don't. He can handle them however he sees fit. But I don't want to ruin his relationship with them over this."

"I doubt anyone could ruin their relationship with any of their kids. They're a tight-knit, loyal group."

"That makes me feel a little better."

"Haven't you met them yet?"

She shook her head. "No. I met his brothers and his cousin, but it all happened so fast, and we had to get all our ducks in a row with Brian and the bank and the courthouse. We're picking up the marriage license tomorrow and getting married Friday morning before work."

"That *is* fast. I know you're both adults and you don't need anyone's approval, but it would seem to me that meeting his family before marrying into *their* family might go a long way," he suggested. "Let them see who you are. Maybe that'll ease their minds."

"That makes sense, but to be honest, I was kind of relieved that he didn't ask me to meet them. I didn't want to bring his family into it at all, because the marriage isn't real, you know? It's a blip in our lives, a few months that'll fly by and then be over." A pang of disappointment caught her off guard, but she dismissed it, knowing she and Zander would still be friends after they ended the fake marriage.

"I meant to ease their minds, and yours," he said.

"Maybe you're right. I'll bring it up to Zander, but I have a big favor to ask you. Actually, I have two."

He waved a hand. "Fire away, Flores."

"The first is, I know you promised to keep our conversation to yourself, but I want to be sure you won't mention it to the guys. I need to figure out how to tell them I'm getting married, but Zander and I think it's best if only you and his family know the truth, since it has to look real."

"I won't say a word."

She exhaled with relief. "Thank you. The second favor is a bigger one. Would you be willing to come to the courthouse with us Friday morning to be our witness? We have the first appointment at seven thirty, and the clerk said we'd be out of there in twenty minutes. Thirty minutes, tops."

A wide smile appeared, and he said, "I've got to be honest

with you. I had hoped that if you ever got married, you'd ask me to walk you down the aisle."

"You *did?*" That warmed her all over.

"Yes, indeed. You're the closest thing I'll ever have to a daughter. I realize this isn't the white wedding I'd anticipated, but I'd be honored to be there for you."

She got choked up. "Really? Does that mean you forgive me for lying to you?"

"Yes, I forgive you."

"Thank you!" She jumped up, and as he rose to his feet, she threw her arms around him, but quickly stepped back. "Sorry. You're my boss. I shouldn't hug you."

"It's okay, but, Flores?" He waggled a finger at her. "Just so we're clear, after Friday I'll have blackmail to hold over your head, so don't even think about lying to me again, or you will find out just how much trouble you can get into for this sham of a marriage."

She couldn't stop smiling. "Yes, sir. I promise I won't." She drew an X over her heart, and couldn't wait to tell Zander they had a witness.

Chapter Twenty

ZANDER WALKED INTO the clubhouse Wednesday night like he was heading into battle, his shoulders back, his chin up, and tension straining every muscle. The room was alive with conversation, heckling, and laughter, but Zander couldn't even fake a smile. The last two days had been riddled with too many questions and opinions he had no interest in hearing. At least his parents and Zeke had kept the news of his and Shauna's plans in the family as he'd asked, but *fuck*. He couldn't believe none of them had his back, and now Shauna wanted to meet them. When they'd spoken earlier, she'd been excited that Cap had agreed to be their witness and relieved that he'd forgiven her about Brian. She'd been through enough emotional roller coasters. There was no way he'd put her in his family's crosshairs when they were acting like people he didn't recognize.

He wondered if they'd act that way if he were one of his siblings, and gritted his teeth, knowing the answer. They all had opinions *aside* from their concerns about his history of a revolving bedroom door, and they all boiled down to the same thing. They thought he was too impulsive and short-sighted to get married, even as a temporary favor. It didn't seem to matter that he didn't shirk his responsibilities at work or with the club, or that he'd always been there for the family, no matter what else he had going on. The only one who gave him an inch of slack was Baz, who said he'd gone through life-altering changes when he'd met his fiancée, Emerson, and he knew if Zander wanted to change, he would succeed. But Baz had still given him a laundry list of reasons he should consider options other than marriage because he agreed with Zander's parents about the sanctity of marriage.

It was infuriating that the rest of them couldn't see him as anything other than that impulsive guy. But Shauna did, and that was what mattered.

He stepped out of the way as a couple of guys came through the door and saw his brothers and cousins sitting in their usual spot on the far side of the room. Gunner and Blaine looked over. Gunner lifted his chin in a silent hello, the tension in Blaine's jaw mirroring Zander's.

In no mood to get more shit, Zander headed for a table on his side of the room, where Rubin "Justice" Galant, the sharp-witted attorney who had handled Zander's case for the accident and a single father to an adorable little girl named Patience, was thumbing out a text.

"Hey, man, how's it going?" Zander pulled out a chair and sat down.

"Not bad. Just scheduling a playdate for Patience and Gracie."

"Gracie? Starr's little girl?" Their friend Starr was a single mom who waitressed at the Salty Hog.

"Yeah. Patience and Gracie have been taking dance classes together, and we've had a few playdates for them." Justice pocketed his phone. "You should've seen the girls last weekend. One minute they were playing with their dolls on the patio, and the next they're making brownies out of mudpies. It was hours of unstoppable giggles and messy chaos."

"Sounds like they had a great time."

"They did. They've been begging for a sleepover. That's what we're working on setting up."

Zander sat back, picking up on Justice's use of *we've* and *we're* referencing him and Starr. Justice was not only a loving father, but he was also a handsome man with rich brown skin and an affable demeanor that could put anyone at ease. Zander could see him with the attractive, snarky, tattooed blonde. "So, will this sleepover be for Patience *and* Daddy?"

Justice grinned and shook his head. "No, man. I'm taking it slow. We've got little kids. It's not the same as freewheelers like you."

"My freewheelin' days are coming to an end," he said, testing it out. It felt good to say it with the excitement he felt about helping Shauna instead of hiding it like it was a big, bad secret. But his timing was lousy, because his brothers and cousins were heading their way, and Blaine and Tank looked like they were ready to give him hell. He'd warned them not to tell anyone the marriage wasn't real, and if they blurted it out and fucked it up for Shauna, he was going to lose his shit.

"Really?" Justice asked, drawing him back to their conversation. "Did you meet someone worthy of a second date?"

The comment grated on his nerves despite the fact that his father was right. He'd not only earned that reputation—he'd fucking flaunted it. But he was going to make damn sure that Shauna and their temporary marriage were treated with respect.

"I met someone worthy of marrying," Zander said as Blaine, Maverick, and Tank blew past the table, making a beeline for Preacher and Conroy, who had just walked into the clubhouse.

Zeke, Baz, and Gunner stood a few feet away from Zander. Gunner held his hands up and said, "Is it safe to come over there, or are you going to chew us out again?"

"That depends. Are you all here to give me more shit?"

"Not me, man," Gunner said. "I value my life."

"We know you're a stubborn bastard, and you're going to marry her no matter what we say," Baz added.

"Damn right, I am. Take a seat, assholes." As they sat down, Zander eyed Zeke, still standing a few feet away. "You got something to say?"

"Yeah," Zeke said tightly. "I don't have to think it's a good idea for you to marry a woman you've only known for a week in order to have your back. You bleed, I bleed, bro."

Zander nodded in acknowledgment. "I appreciate that." He held out a fist, and Zeke bumped it with his own.

As Zeke sat down, Zander stole a glance at Preacher, Conroy, and the others, huddled by the front door. His brothers' and Tank's backs were to him. Preacher's gaze shifted in Zander's direction, as serious as ever. Zander looked away, sure they were talking about him.

"Dude, you've known this woman for only a *week* and you're marrying her?" Justice asked. "That's not even enough time for you to have knocked her up. Did you sign up for some kind of reality show or something?"

"*No.* She's the EMT who pulled me out of the wreck. We were meant to be, and we just don't want to wait. We're tying the knot Friday morning. I got her a ring, took her shopping for a wedding outfit, and her boss is going to be our witness."

"Damn." Justice shook his head. "I never thought you'd settle down. She must be something special. What's she like?"

It didn't go unnoticed that neither Zeke nor their cousins

offered to attend the wedding, much less be their witness. Zander tried to push that irritation away enough to focus on describing Shauna. Smart and strong were too easy. Shauna was anything *but* easy. Beautiful was an understatement, and not because of her curves or her gorgeous face, but because her heart bubbled over into everything else about her, and that made her shine like nothing he'd ever seen.

Finally, he said, "She's like a midnight ride on your favorite bike, and I don't mean that sexually. She's bold and unstoppable, roaring on the straightaways, grounded and stable on the curves, and able to handle whatever life throws at her without losing traction."

"Damn, bro," Zeke said. "I didn't know you were that deep."

Zander held his gaze. "Maybe you should stop underestimating me." He glanced at Justice and cocked a grin. "Shauna is all *that*, with killer dimples, thick thighs, and a great ass."

"There he is!" Gunner cheered, and they all cracked up.

Zander's laughter faded as Preacher announced the start of the meeting, and Blaine, Maverick, and Tank headed back to their usual table without as much as a glance in his direction.

The next hour and a half were a living hell. Zander stewed over the huddle and the cold shoulder he was given. By the time the meeting ended, he was ready to bolt.

"You hitting the Hog with us tonight?" Gunner asked. "Sid's meeting us there."

Zander pushed to his feet and said, "Not tonight. I'm taking off." He headed for the door, excited to go home and see the one person who wouldn't be judging him.

"*Zander.*" Preacher's deep voice cut through the din of the other members.

He looked over, and his jaw snapped tight as he spotted Blaine, Maverick, and Tank standing behind Preacher, their arms crossed. *What the hell is this?* He threw his shoulders back, meeting their steely stares as he stalked toward them.

"What?" he gritted out.

"I know you're going through with your plan on Friday no matter what any of us think," Preacher said. "At least do the right thing and bring this woman by the house to meet your mother and the rest of the family tomorrow night."

Zander narrowed his eyes, searching their faces. There wasn't a fissure among them. "She has a name. *Shauna.* Are you all going to treat her right? Because if you make her feel anything less than welcome, we're going to have problems."

Preacher nodded curtly. "Understood."

Zander pointed at the others. "That goes for each of you, too."

They lifted their chins in acknowledgment.

"Fair enough." Zander headed for the door, weaving around the other members, and came face-to-face with his uncle Conroy.

"Hey, Zan. I heard your news, man. Want to talk?"

His aunt and uncle were the only two who hadn't reached out to him, which told him everything he needed to know. If they'd supported his decision, he'd have heard from them.

"Not even a little." Zander stepped around him, blazing a path through the tension, and disappeared into the night.

Chapter Twenty-One

SHAUNA GAZED OUT the truck window feeling like she was going to throw up.

It was Thursday evening, and she and Zander were on their way to his parents' house to meet the rest of his family. She'd changed her clothes three times, finally settling on mustard-yellow low-riding, wide-legged jeans with a cropped black tank top, a white cardigan, and sneakers. She hadn't planned on wearing the engagement ring. It felt wrong to wear something so expensive when his family was already upset. But Zander had said he hadn't given it to her to have it sit in a box and encouraged her to wear it. It seemed important to him, and he reminded her that they were trying to make everyone else believe their relationship was real, and she shouldn't let his family's opinions change how they acted.

That was part of the problem. This was all an act, and yet when it was just the two of them, it didn't feel like an act at all. It felt like they'd become close friends, confidants. But she was so nervous, meeting his parents would take one hell of an act if she had any hope of it going well. *An act of God, that is.*

Zander's hand covered hers and squeezed, drawing her attention. A conspiratorial gleam shone in his eyes. "What do you say, Angel? Should we blow them off and go for tacos instead?"

How did he always know how to make her smile? "As tempting as that sounds, we're already late, and it would just give them another reason to dislike me." Blaine had texted Zander as they were on their way out the door, asking him to swing by his place to let his dog out because Blaine and Reese had to pick up Lettie at a friend's house and wouldn't have time to do both.

"They don't dislike you," Zander said. "They're worried about me. I told you I'm the guy who does dumb shit."

"You say that, but I don't see it. You've done all the right things by me. You protected me before you even knew me, and you helped Brian without hesitation. So either you're a really good actor, or I must be missing something."

He glanced at her. "I'm not acting. Just changing. I have a chance to do the right thing and pay a favor back. It feels good, and don't worry, nobody's going to change my mind."

He turned down a residential street and held her hand a little tighter, the muscles in his jaw working overtime. "Looks like they meant for you to meet the whole family. My aunt and uncle and cousins are here, too," he said as he pulled over behind a line of other vehicles.

She took a deep breath. "How many more people are here?"

"My aunt Ginger and uncle Conroy, and their family. You've already met Tank. His wife, Leah, and their three kids, Junie, Rosie, and Leo, will be here, along with Baz and his fiancée, Emerson, and their little boy, Brennan, and Gunner, and his wife, Sid. I'm sure my grandfather is here, too."

"Great." The knot in her stomach twisted.

He cocked a brow. "Reconsidering my taco offer?"

"Yes," she said honestly, and he laughed. "I'm not really.

You think they're protecting me, but I think they're protecting you. They love you, and as hard as this is, take it from someone who didn't have a family that cared enough to make sure I had lunch money, much less didn't sign three months of my life away. As hard as this is, that protection is something to be valued."

"I value them, Angel, but you're going to be my wife. So we're going to walk in there with our heads held high, and if anyone makes you uncomfortable, we'll turn around and walk out."

"We can't just *leave*."

"The hell we can't. I'm not going to stand for anyone making my girl feel uncomfortable."

As good as it felt knowing he'd protect her feelings at all costs, Shauna was used to being thrown into new situations without knowing what she was walking into, and she knew meeting the family who didn't want her there was going to be anything *but* comfortable. Zander had mentioned that Zeke, Baz, and Gunner were coming around, and he thought they'd have his back tonight. She really hoped that was true, because the worst part of all of this wasn't the embarrassment of having to borrow money or marrying a guy she barely knew, no matter how much it felt like she knew him. It was knowing she was causing a fissure between this incredible man and his generous family.

That was why she had to remind him, "I'm your *fake* girl, Zan, and they're your *real* family."

"After tomorrow morning, you'll be my real family, too." He held her gaze as he lifted her hand and pressed a kiss to the back of it, setting off those flutters in her chest. "Let's go, darlin'."

Her nerves were on fire as they headed up the walk. Zander took her hand on their way up the porch steps. "It's you and me against the world, Angel. Ready to let me show you off?"

Show me off? She knew he was trying to make her smile, but she was too nervous to muster one. "As ready as I'll ever be."

He opened the front door and put his hand on her lower back as they walked in. As reassuring as that familiar touch was, she longed for his hand. Holding it had made her feel safer, more grounded.

There were boots and shoes by the door, jackets hanging on hooks, and a narrow table with a candle and a framed photograph of what could only be a young Zander. She'd know his mischievous smile anywhere. He was holding hands with a little blond girl who was sticking her tongue out at the camera, just like Zander was, and a little mahogany-haired girl who was gazing up at him with wonderous eyes.

She pointed to the photo and whispered, "Is that adorable boy you?"

"Yeah. That's Ashley with the blond hair, and Madigan."

Shauna's heart squeezed for their loss.

Zander's hand pressed on her back, guiding her toward the living room as he called out, "Mom? Preach?"

"Out back," someone yelled from outside, though Shauna didn't see anyone through the screen door as they entered the living room.

Family photos decorated the living room walls, telling a story of kids growing up with parents who loved them. She recognized Zander and his brothers and Tank, and Madigan's wondrous eyes were easy to spot, even in the pictures of her as an adult. Ashley was in so many pictures, Shauna could see they kept her spirit alive. No wonder Zander said he thought about her every day. She assumed the other people in the pictures were also his family.

Theirs was a warm, loving home, with a family who clearly treasured one another, so different from the home she'd grown up in. She shouldn't be tearing this family apart.

"Zander," she said just as a strikingly handsome man appeared on the other side of the screen door. He was big, broad, and bearded, with slicked-back salt-and-pepper hair and a stern facial expression that had her holding her breath. He wore jeans and a black leather vest over a white dress shirt, which was rolled up to his elbows, exposing colorful tattoos on his forearms and his hands.

Zander tensed beside her as he and the man locked eyes. His hand slid across Shauna's back, his fingers curling around her waist, holding her closer, as if protecting her.

That had to be his father. Shauna's heart raced as a petite woman hurried up the steps onto the deck, her mahogany hair brushing the shoulders of her red dress as she came to the man's side and glanced through the screen door. Her face brightened, but there was a hint of tension in her eyes as she said, "Hi, honey."

"Hi, Mom," Zander said tightly.

Holding Shauna against his side, he guided her out the door with him, as if they were parts of the same being. The yard spilled out around them, and Shauna felt like she was seeing it in slow motion. The sun hung low in the sky, shimmering over a small pond, colorful gardens, and the lush lawn where dozens of chairs with pretty flowers and white bows tied to the backs were set up in front of a gazebo. Glass lanterns glimmered on either side of an aisle between the chairs, and more lanterns sparkled on the gazebo steps. Twinkling lights were wound through branches of tall trees and around the frame of the gazebo, illuminating gorgeous greenery and flowers decorating the entrance. Women in pretty dresses and men wearing jeans, white shirts, and leather vests just like Zander's father were milling about, watching Zander and Shauna, as little girls in frilly dresses darted around them, chased by a dark-skinned little boy. Shauna tried to make sense of what she was seeing, but couldn't.

"What is all this?" Zander demanded, his grip tightening around her.

"Hopefully, if you and Shauna will allow it, it's for your wedding," Preacher said.

The shock in Zander's eyes was as sharp as the astonishment consuming Shauna.

"You caught us off guard the other evening, honey," his mother said. "Of course we're concerned about you two getting married. You might be a grown man, but you're still our child, and we haven't even had a chance to get to know Shauna." She smiled warmly at Shauna.

Shauna tried to smile in return, managing a shaky one as she tried to process what was happening.

"But you were right, son," Preacher said firmly, and turned a serious gaze on Shauna. "This brave young woman saved your life, and that should've been enough for us to support your decision to help her in whatever way you deem appropriate."

Her throat thickened.

"About damn time you came around," Zander said. He looked at Shauna, and the relief in his eyes was palpable. "What do you think, Angel? Should we forgive them, or head out for those tacos?"

"*Um.*" She was still in shock, her heart racing as the magnitude of the love his parents had for him hit her full force, and she choked out, "Can I talk to you alone for a second?"

"Of course." He turned their backs to his parents and stepped toward the slider.

"Are they leavin', or are we gettin' married?" a little girl hollered.

"Rosie, hush!" another little girl yelled, and then there was a burst of giggles.

"We can't do this," Shauna whispered quickly. "This is like a real wedding, and we're not real. It's not fair to your family."

"Remember when I said you entered the Wicked zone? This is what I was talking about. It took them a while to come around, but *this* is who my family is. And trust me, they wouldn't have done it if they didn't support it."

"He's right, honey," his mother said from behind them, drawing her attention. "You might not be getting married forever, but you're still marrying into our family, and that means something to us."

"Darlin', it would be my honor to officiate your wedding," Preacher said with a smile that softened those granite edges. He glanced at Zander, adding, "Lord knows this is probably the only chance I'll get to marry this guy off."

A nervous laugh slipped out, and Zander took her hand. "What do you say, Flores?"

"I think they might be as crazy as you are. This is so much more than I ever imagined, and that makes me one lucky girl."

"You're marrying me. *That's* what makes you lucky," Zander said, and they all laughed as he pulled her into a hug.

"They're laughin'! Uncle Zannie, are we getting married?" a little girl with light brown skin and a mass of golden-brown ringlets shouted as she ran toward the deck in a frilly pink dress.

Sprinting behind her was a fair-skinned, freckle-faced young girl with red ringlets, wearing a pale green dress and a look of determination, hollering, "*Rosie!* Papa Tank said no deck yet!" as Rosie scrambled onto the deck.

"Are you gonna be my auntie?" Rosie shouted as she ran past Shauna, giggling up a storm, and launched herself at Zander. "Uncle Zannie, save me!"

Shauna and his parents laughed as he hoisted Rosie into his arms, and Preacher scooped up the other girl, her ringlets springing around her shoulders. The girls' giggles filled the air, and holy cow, seeing Zander grinning from ear to ear with that little girl in his arms was the sweetest, sexiest thing she'd ever seen, bringing all those flutters rushing back.

Zander tickled Rosie's belly and said, "Shauna, these are Tank's girls, Rosie and Junie."

"Is Shauna gonna be our auntie?" Rosie asked.

Zander locked eyes with Shauna. Happiness radiated off him, so real, it felt electric and binding, as he said, "Shauna's not only going to be your auntie. She's going to be your *coolest* auntie *ever*."

"Yay!" Rosie and Junie cheered.

Whoops and cheers rang out, and as the rest of Zander's family headed in their direction, his mother sidled up to Shauna and said, "In all the chaos, we didn't formally meet. I'm Reba, and I'm sorry for the rough start. Preacher and I look forward to getting to know you."

"Me too. Thank you so much."

Reba embraced her and said, "Brace yourself, sweetheart. Here come the troops, led by my daughter. She can be a lot."

"I've got her, Mom," Zander said, setting Rosie on her feet and putting a hand on Shauna's back as they headed off the deck.

Shauna barely had time to brace herself before his family converged on them, with dogs and toddlers in tow. "Hi. I'm Madigan," his sister exclaimed. She was a petite bundle of energy and, holding the hand of a big, broody-looking guy with longish hair and linebacker shoulders, said, "And this is my fiancé, Tobias. We're *so* happy to meet you."

Tobias smiled and nodded as Madigan pulled Shauna into a hug.

Madigan leaned back, her gaze zeroing in on Shauna's left hand. "Oh my God! Look at that rock!" She held Shauna's hand up for everyone to see, like she'd uncovered a secret.

Shauna's stomach dipped, but Zander was already sliding an arm around her waist, flashing that easy grin as he said, "Gotta protect my rep. Nothing less than the best for the only fiancée I'll ever have." He winked, and laughter rang out around them.

"Age before beauty. Out of my way," an older man with a craggy voice said as he pushed through the crowd and studied her with keen eyes. "So, you're the filly who got Zander to stand up to his old man."

Chuckles rang out behind him.

Zander scoffed. "Shauna, this is my grandfather Mike."

"Hi," she said. "I've heard nice things about you."

"All lies," his grandfather said with a wink. "I've got some advice for ya." He leaned closer and lowered his voice. "You've got to fake it till the check clears, so when he pisses you off, which he will, you come see me. I'll tell you stories that'll make you appreciate him for his good looks and sense of humor."

She laughed.

"Get out of here, old man," Zander teased. "I won't piss her off because I don't want her subjected to the likes of you."

"He's jealous," Preacher called out, earning more laughter.

"A'right, let's get the introductions over with," Zander said, and with a hand on Shauna's back, he pointed to a curvy blonde who appeared to be not much older than Shauna and a teenager with long brown hair. "This is Blaine's fiancée, Reese, and her sister, Lettie."

"Hi," Reese and Lettie said in unison.

"Thanks for letting Woody out," Lettie said.

"He was as ornery as ever," Zander said about their dachshund, and then he motioned to a tall, elegant blonde hoisting an adorable toddler into her arms. "And this is Maverick's wife, Chloe, and their daughter, Marybelle—"

"And this is my baby brother, Leo!" Rosie shouted, tugging the giggling dark-skinned toddler behind her. "He's gonna be the ring boy, and we're gonna be flower girls, and that's our mama and Papa Tank." She pointed to a petite woman with a mass of reddish-brown curls and a pretty, freckled face tucked beneath Tank's thick arm.

Tank nodded, and the woman waved and said, in a Southern drawl, "Hi. I'm Leah."

More introductions rolled out like a steady tide. Shauna accepted hugs and nods and said, "Nice to meet you," more times than she could count as she met Zander's aunt and uncle, Ginger, a strawberry-blonde with tortoiseshell glasses and a warm embrace, and Conroy, a handsome man with collar-length wavy silver hair and bright blue eyes as playful as Zander's. She met Zander's other cousins, Gunner, a fully tatted, fair-haired Marine veteran and his cute brunette wife, Sidney, who was also a Marine veteran, and Baz, an easygoing veterinarian with longish blond hair, his fiancée, Emerson, a sweet, pregnant golden-brown haired beauty, and their precious little boy, Brennan, whose dark hair stood straight up.

When she'd met everyone, including Buster and Milo, Preacher and Reba's dogs, Zander slid his arm around her and said, "How're you holding up, darlin'? Do you need CliffsNotes?"

"Nametags would be better."

"That can be arranged," Madigan said.

"We should have thought of that when we planned this," Reba said.

"When *did* you plan this?" Zander asked, glancing at his father. "Last night at church you and your henchmen looked like you were ready to throttle me."

Preached cocked a grin, a surprising glint of a tease rising in his eyes. "You shocked the hell out of us the other night, son. I thought you could use a little payback."

Holy shit.

"Are you freaking kidding me? You let me leave church thinking y'all had abandoned me?" Zander glowered at Blaine, Maverick, and Tank, and they all cracked up.

"You should've seen your face," Blaine said, and high-fived Maverick and Tank.

"Better watch your backs," Zander warned, which only made them laugh harder.

"You boys can work that out while we get Shauna ready for your wedding," Madigan said, and linked her arm with Shauna's, dragging her toward the house with Reba, Ginger, Reese, Lettie, Chloe, Leah, Sid, and Emerson on their heels.

Chapter Twenty-Two

"WHAT DO YOU mean, get ready?" Shauna asked as they ushered her into the house and down the hall.

"You know that text Zander got from Blaine about letting Woody out?" Reese asked.

"Yeah," Shauna said.

"It was a ruse to give us time to sneak into Zan's house and pick up your wedding outfit," Madigan explained as they entered the master bedroom, where Shauna's jumpsuit was hanging on the closet door.

Stunned, Shauna said, "How did you even know I had something to wear?"

"Zander mentioned it to Zeke at church last night. I didn't see any heels in your closet, but I found cute sandals and I figured that's what you planned on wearing." Madigan pulled out a chair in front of a makeup desk and mirror and said, "Sit down. We'll do your hair."

"This is going to be so much fun," Chloe said. "I'll help you with your makeup."

Shauna's stomach dipped. She'd never spent time with women. She saw her friends at pole class, but they didn't socialize outside of class, and they certainly never did her hair.

She didn't know how to act around them or what to say.

"Girls, Shauna's just met our very loud, very pushy family," Reba said. "How about we let her breathe for a second?"

"You're right," Madigan said. "Sorry."

"It's okay," Shauna said.

"When I met the Wickeds, I'm sure I was like a deer in the headlights," Reese said.

"You should've seen me when I first met everyone," Sidney said. "I've known Gunner and his family forever, but I'm an only child and I was raised by my dad, who's ex-military. I was used to hanging out with military guys. Becoming part of the girl squad was like culture shock."

"Do you have any brothers or sisters?" Leah asked.

"No." Shauna shook her head.

"That's not such a bad thing, trust me," Madigan said, earning laughs from the others.

"I wish I could have invited your parents," Reba said. "Preacher tried to track them down, but we weren't able to find them."

Oh God. How was she going to explain this? "It's better that you didn't. I haven't been in contact with them since I was seventeen. They weren't...like your family."

"My mother wasn't either," Chloe said.

"Same," Reese added.

"Yeah, our mom sucks," Lettie said.

"Not many families are like this one," Emerson said sweetly.

"You can say that again," Leah said. "When I lost my younger brother, River, the Wickeds barely knew me, and they were right there for me and the girls every minute of the day. If not for them, I don't know how we would've survived."

"You would've survived, sweetheart. You're stronger than

you know." Ginger put her arm around Leah, hugging her against her side.

Seeing the woman who had lost her daughter comforting Leah for the loss of her brother made Shauna's heart hurt. "I'm sorry you lost your brother, Leah, and Ginger, Zander told me about Ashley. I'm sorry you lost your daughter. I'm sorry all of you lost her."

"Thank you," Ginger said. "River and Ashley will always live on in our hearts."

"Shauna," Reba said gently. "I'm sorry for whatever happened with your parents, but if you ever want to talk about it, maybe over a glass of wine sometime, we're here for you."

"Definitely," Madigan added.

Even though she was nervous about dumping all her baggage on them at once, she had a feeling this supportive group of women wouldn't be too quick to judge. "Actually, I'm sober, but maybe we could talk over coffee?"

"I'd like that very much," Reba said.

"Me too!" Madigan said.

As the other girls chimed in, eagerly offering to be there for her, Ginger suggested they all meet at the Salty Hog for lunch one day soon. Everyone talked at once, and Shauna learned that Ginger and Conroy owned the Salty Hog and that Leah occasionally helped out as a waitress.

"Shauna, give me your phone number, and I'll set up a group text so we can coordinate." Madigan pulled out her phone.

Shauna rattled off her number, and a minute later, her phone chimed with a text. "That was fast."

"That wasn't from me. I'm still adding everyone to the group," Madigan said. "I'm adding our friends Marly and Evie, too. They're in the book club. You'll love them."

Shauna pulled out her phone, and her pulse quickened as she opened a text from Zander.

Zander: *You okay in there? Are they interrogating you? Need me to rescue you?*

"Is it from my brother, or is some other guy making you smile like that?" Madigan asked.

Shauna tried to quell her smile. "It's Zander. He's just checking on me," she said as she thumbed out a reply. *I'm fine. Everyone's really nice. They picked up my outfit. I just have to change.*

"That's thoughtful of him," Leah said.

"Unless he's begging her not to bolt," Sidney said.

"Or telling her he's got cold feet," Emerson added.

"The way he stood up to me and Preacher, I don't think that's happening," Reba reassured her.

"I hate clingy guys who text all the time," Lettie said.

"Zander doesn't know the meaning of the word *clingy*," Reese said, and they all laughed.

Shauna's phone chimed with another text, and the girls raised their eyebrows.

"*Clingy,*" Lettie said in a singsong voice.

"He's not clingy," Shauna said. "We text all the time. It's just a friendship thing."

"Careful," Chloe said. "Texting is innocent until it starts to include devil emojis and eggplants."

They all laughed.

"He does *not* send me eggplants," Shauna said, laughing as she opened and read the text.

Zander: *Don't change. I like you just the way you are.*

Her heart stumbled, and as she read it again, her phone

chimed, and a flame emoji popped up.

Madigan leaned in, scanning the text before Shauna could think to close it. Her eyes lit up and she read it aloud. *"Don't change? I like you just the way you are?"*

Shauna's cheeks burned as the girls exchanged curious looks.

"That doesn't sound fake," Sidney said.

"That doesn't sound like Zander," Reese said.

"Are you sure there's not something real going on between you two?" Emerson asked.

"*Yes.* He's just being sweet," Shauna said to herself as much as to them, and pocketed her phone.

"Well, you'd better tell him to stop, or I'll start rooting for you two to be a real couple," Madigan said.

"That's not going to happen," Shauna said with a hint of discomfort that she needed to squash. "This is already the weirdest day of my life. I'm getting married for real to a fake husband. Can we not make it any weirder, please?"

"Yes, girls, give Shauna a break," Reba said. "We have a wedding to prepare for."

"Time to work our magic," Madigan said excitedly, guiding Shauna into the chair.

There was a flurry of activity as Madigan began brushing Shauna's hair, and the girls chatted about hairstyles and makeup. "Do you know how you want to wear your hair?" Madigan asked.

Shauna shrugged. "I never style my hair. I usually wear it up."

"Then leave it to us," Madigan reassured her. "You're going to knock Zander's socks off."

As they primped and curled and applied her makeup, they asked Shauna about her work and told her about theirs. Shauna was fascinated to hear that Reese was a forensic scientist. She also learned that Chloe was the administrator for the assisted living facility where Zander's grandfather lived and that Emerson was a part-time editor and an extraordinary baker who sold her cookies at the Salty Hog and other places around Bayside.

"I can't cook worth beans," Shauna said.

"We can teach you," Reba offered. "The girls and I love getting together to cook."

"And gossip," Sidney added.

"*Lots* of gossip." Lettie rolled her eyes. "They gossip more than my friends."

"Nobody gossips more than high schoolers," Reese argued.

"Wanna bet?" Lettie said, laden with teenage attitude.

"How else would we know what was happening in our kids' lives if we didn't gossip?" Ginger said lightly. "Everyone needs some girl talk, right, Shauna?"

"Honestly, I've never really had girlfriends to talk with," she admitted. "I mean, I have friends at pole class, but we don't socialize outside of class."

"I never did either before these girls swept me into their nest," Sid said.

"Wait a minute. Can we back up? Shauna, you take *pole* classes? Like pole dancing?" Chloe asked.

"More like exercise, not dancing. It's great for upper-body strength." Shauna turned to look at her, but Madigan tugged her head back.

"Hold still or you're going to have rogue curls," Madigan chided. She was standing in front of the mirror, holding a lock of Shauna's hair. "I'm almost done."

"Sorry," Shauna said. "I could've just kept my ponytail in.

You didn't have to go to all this trouble."

Madigan waved the curling iron. "If you say that one more time, I'm going to put this where the sun don't shine."

"She'll do it," Sidney warned.

Shauna pressed her lips together in mock fear, which made everyone laugh. They asked a dozen questions about her pole classes, and she told them they should come try one.

"I'll definitely take a class with you," Madigan said. "Tobias will *love* it!"

"Can I take a class?" Lettie asked Reese.

"Sure, if you want Blaine to lock you in the basement," Reese teased, and Lettie rolled her eyes.

"Okay. Done!" Madigan set the curling iron down and stepped aside.

As the girls gathered around, *ooh*ing and *aah*ing, Shauna stared with wonder at her reflection. She didn't recognize the person with silky waves and slightly smoky eyes looking back at her. Her hair was shiny and full, her makeup soft and subtle, transforming her from an on-the-go girl to a beautiful young woman.

"Oh, sweetheart, you are radiant," Reba said with awe.

"Gorgeous," Chloe said.

"She looks *hot*," Lettie clarified with teenage enthusiasm.

"You are truly lovely," Ginger said, touching Shauna's shoulder. "What do you think, honey?"

"I'm blown away. This feels like a dream. Is that really *me*?" She laughed nervously.

"It better be, or Zander will kill us," Sidney said.

A knock sounded at the door, and Shauna popped to her feet, her nerves catching fire.

"Just a minute!" Reba called out as the girls ushered Shauna into the bathroom to change her clothes.

The bathroom was quiet, amplifying Shauna's thundering heart, and the soft hum of conversation on the other side of the door as she changed into her jumpsuit and put on her sandals.

She stood in front of the mirror, adjusting the halter top on the jumpsuit. It was as soft as butter and fit even more perfectly than she remembered. The expression on Zander's face when she'd walked out of the dressing room flashed before her, and heat slithered down her chest. That was a look she'd never forget, and one of the main reasons she'd chosen the jumpsuit. It felt like her, simple, comfortable, and dressy enough to show Zander how much she appreciated his help.

She swallowed hard and pressed her fingertips to the sink for stability against the nerves weakening her knees. She drew in a few deep breaths, trying to match the woman in the mirror to the one who had signed up for this. A courthouse wedding felt more contractual, easier to deal with. Some paperwork, a few signatures, and empty words. A means to an inheritance. But the woman staring back at her didn't look transactional. With her makeup done and her hair cascading in gentle waves over her bare shoulders, she no longer looked simple or casually dressy. She looked like a bride.

Her chest constricted.

This is really happening.

It wasn't just the ceremony and legal vows. Zander's family and friends rallied around not only him, but *her*. Madigan was definitely a Wicked, bossy and take-charge, but sweet and endearing, and his mom…*God.* Reba had said the nicest things, and she sounded like she meant every single one of them. Shauna would have done anything to have a mom like that when she was growing up. And the others? None of them treated her like she was a temporary visitor in their world. They treated her like family. Like Cap treated her.

Oh no. Cap.

She grabbed her phone, feeling awful that he was going to miss the wedding, and thumbed out a text.

Hey, thank you again for being willing to show up for me tomorrow at the courthouse. That means the world to me, but it turns out we won't be having a courthouse wedding after all. Zander's family surprised us with a backyard wedding tonight, so I don't need a witness anymore, but I wish you were here. I know you wanted to walk me down the aisle, and that means more to me than you can possibly know, but the wedding is happening now. I'm sorry.

As she sent it off, a soft knock sounded at the bathroom door. "Sweetheart?" Reba said. "Do you need any help?"

"No, thank you. I'm coming." Shauna slipped her phone into the pocket of her jumpsuit and took one last look in the mirror and a deep, calming breath. As she opened the door and stepped out of the bathroom, she had the strange sense that she was walking toward something more real than anything she'd ever known.

Reba gasped, her hand flying up to cover her heart. "Shauna, honey, you are absolutely breathtaking."

Shauna felt a blush rushing up her chest to her cheeks as the girls gathered around, raving about how pretty she looked. "You guys," she pleaded. "I appreciate your compliments more than you can imagine, but you're making me even more nervous."

"It's your wedding day. You're supposed to be nervous."

Goose bumps chased up her arms at the familiar deep voice. She whipped her head to the side, and her heart leapt. Cap stood before her, wearing slacks and a crisp white dress shirt and that comforting smile she knew so well. She blinked several times, her emotions sneaking up on her. "*Cap?* What are you doing here?"

"I got a call from Preacher after you and I talked yesterday. He wanted to see what kind of gal his son was marrying."

"I guess you lied well, huh?" she teased.

"You know it," he said warmly. "You clean up nice, Flores."

"Thank you. So do you. I'm so happy you're here."

"Me too," he said. "Are you ready?"

"Wait!" Madigan exclaimed. "She needs the bridal things. Something old?"

"She's got me," Cap said, holding out his arm.

As Shauna took it, Madigan said, "Something new?"

"My ring!" Shauna held up her left hand.

"Damn," Cap said. "You're sure Zander knows this is temporary?"

"*Yes.* He said he has a reputation to uphold," Shauna said.

"Oh, *Zander*," Reba said with a shake of her head, and the girls laughed.

"Shauna needs something borrowed and something blue," Madigan said, looking around.

"I've got her covered. She can borrow my necklace." As Reba took it off, she said, "It's blue topaz, Zander's birthstone."

"Are you sure you don't mind?" Shauna asked.

"Honey, you're marrying my son. You're one of us now. What's mine is yours." As Reba put the necklace on her, she said, "Except Preacher. He's all mine."

"Except when he's a pain," Ginger chimed in. "Then she'll gladly kick him to the curb."

"There is some truth to that." Reba looked thoughtfully at Shauna and said, "Okay, honey. We're going to get out of your hair, but we'll be right there with you, cheering you on."

She felt so much gratitude, she bubbled over with it. "Thank you."

One by one they hugged her, wishing her luck as she thanked each of them. Then it was just her and Cap. She held his arm tight.

"You sure you want to do this?" he asked.

"*Yes*, but you could have warned me about the Wickeds."

"Preacher would have kicked my ass if I had ruined his surprise."

She wasn't talking about the wedding. She had a feeling they were going to be hard to walk away from, but she kept that to herself as they headed outside.

As Shauna stepped off the deck, she was even more grateful for Cap's presence. Madigan played the guitar, and Conroy was taking pictures of Shauna and Rodney as they crossed the yard toward Junie, Rosie, and Leo, who were standing with Leah and Tank at the head of the aisle. The kids were beaming at Shauna, each of them holding a basket. Tank and Leah were blocking her view of the gazebo, but the chairs were full, and everyone was looking their way.

"Here she comes!" Rosie bounced on her toes, waving wildly. "We're ready!"

"She knows, Rosie!" Junie chided, then waved just as energetically.

"Give her the flowers, Papa Tank!" Rosie hollered.

Shauna was so nervous as Tank stepped forward, she had to remind herself to breathe.

"Welcome to the family, sweetheart," Tank handed her a bouquet of white lilies.

"Thank you," she said shakily.

With a nod, Tank moved to the side, and then, finally, she saw Zander. He was standing in the gazebo with Preacher and his brothers, looking like a dream she'd never imagined, and she was hit with a sense of comfort and belonging that breathed air into her lungs and courage into her heart. He was wearing a white dress shirt, sleeves rolled up like the other men, his leather cut, and jeans, but unlike the others, with their perfect hair and practiced gazes, Zander's hair was tousled, his smile crooked, and he was looking at her like she wasn't just his temporary bride. But in that look she saw, and felt, something else, something *more*. An underlying disbelief, like this wasn't part of the plan.

Was that possible? Could he feel it, too?

Her heart cracked open, soft and stunned, still tender from her time with the girls, and for one wild, heart-thundering moment, she wanted to believe it.

Chapter Twenty-Three

ZANDER COULDN'T TAKE his eyes off Shauna, standing at the end of the aisle with Cap. He'd never seen her like this, with her hair down, lustrous waves framing her gorgeous face, a wayward strand blowing across her shoulder with the breeze. She looked elegant and defiant at once, and it knocked the air right out of his lungs. Junie, Rosie, and Leo began making their way down the aisle, throwing rose petals and waving to everyone, briefly capturing Zander's attention. They were cute as hell, but as Leo toddled up to give Zeke the wedding rings, Madigan began playing the "Wedding March." Shauna stepped into the aisle, and everything else faded away.

Shauna moved with the confident strength of a lioness as she made her way toward him, her back straight and chin lifted, pretending she wasn't nervous. She was so damn strong, refusing to let anything stop her from doing what she needed to. But Zander knew her well enough to see the flicker of insecurity in her eyes, the tightness of her jaw, and the way she was gripping Cap's arm like a lifeline.

A flood of feelings locked into place, heat behind his ribs, a pulsing ache in his chest, and the unrelenting *"Mine"* growling through his head. It wasn't the greedy, shallow desire Zander was familiar with. No, this wasn't just a *want*. It was a *need*, driven by deep admiration and primal protectiveness.

She and Cap stopped in front of the gazebo. Cap leaned in, whispering something that made her smile, and then he kissed her cheek and went to sit down.

As Shauna climbed the steps, her and Zander's eyes connected with a silent ferocity that was so fucking real, it felt dangerous. It scared the hell out of him and made him want her even more. Not just for a night, and not just in his bed.

Preacher cleared his throat, jerking Zander from his thoughts. He must have been staring, because his brothers chuckled.

"If I've learned one thing from raising five stubborn children, it's that life rarely follows expected paths," Preacher said, earning murmurs of agreement. "But without the unexpected trials and tribulations that life throws at us, we wouldn't have met the incredible people who have since become family. We're gathered here today to welcome another new member into our family and to witness a promise between Shauna and Zander. A promise that didn't start as a fairy tale and wasn't born from unrelenting love, but comes from the vital stepping-stones on which love grows. A promise born from trust and friendship."

Shauna gripped the bouquet she was holding tighter. Zander fought the urge to reach for her hand.

Preacher looked between them and said, "Today is about honoring your choices. Alexander, do you promise to stand with and support Shauna as her partner, her protector, and her friend, in sickness and in health, with honesty and respect, from this moment forward?"

His father's use of his given name made the moment feel even more momentous.

Shauna mouthed, *Alexander?*

She was so damn cute. He opened his mouth to say his *I do*, expecting it to be easy. It was just two simple words pledging a temporary commitment, but as her eyes brimmed with trust, the gravity of what they were doing hit him full-on. He didn't feel panic or regret, only a deep-seated surety that this was bigger than anything he'd ever felt before and the determination to do it right. He held Shauna's gaze as the words clawed their way up from his heart, and he said, "I do."

His father turned to Shauna and said, "Before you do this, it's only fair that I warn you. My son is a hell of a good man, but he can be a handful."

Laughter rumbled around them.

"His charm alone makes him a handful. But charm and all *that*?" She smiled so big, her dimples popped as she held her hand out, as if presenting Zander to Preacher, and said, "I think he's more like an armload, but I can handle him."

More laughter rang out, and Zeke said, "She's got your number, Zan."

Yes, she does, and I fucking love it.

"Sounds like this young lady can hold her own," Preacher said. "Shauna, do you promise to stand with and support Zander as his partner and his friend, in sickness and in health, with honesty and respect, from this moment forward?"

"I do," she said.

The mix of trust, worry, and unmistakable hope in her eyes nearly did Zander in.

Zeke handed him the rings.

Zander took Shauna's left hand, feeling it tremble as he slid the ring on her finger and whispered, "I can't believe you're my wife."

She laughed so softly, he was sure he was the only one who heard it as she took his ring from him and slid it onto his finger.

He wrapped his fingers around hers, unable to look away as his father said, "With an open heart and prayers you both survive, I now pronounce you husband and wife."

As cheers rang out, Preacher said, "Are we sealing the deal? Because, son, this is when you'd kiss your bride."

Shauna's eyes widened with surprise.

"What do you say, Angel?" Zander asked. "I know you're dying to kiss me."

"I am *not* dying to kiss you." She laughed, and so did everyone else.

Zander stepped closer, lowering his voice. "Then I guess I'm in this alone, because I'm dying to kiss you."

She blushed a red streak, and he thought she might look away, but her eyes didn't shift. They locked in. He barely had time to register the flicker of heat in them as she grabbed his shirt, hauling him into a kiss like she owned him. *Oh yeah, Angel, you were dying to kiss me, too.* He took control, wrapping one arm around her as her arms snaked over his shoulders and he threaded his other hand into her hair, taking the kiss deeper, earning the sexiest sound he'd ever heard. His tongue slid savoringly over hers, tasting, taking, *possessing*, in an unhurried claiming, when what he really wanted was to ravage her until the sun came up, but he was all too aware of their audience cheering and whistling.

Fuck.

Forcing himself to break the kiss, he kept her close, taking in her flushed cheeks and the intoxicated haze in those gorgeous eyes. She blinked several times, as if she was having trouble getting ahold of herself. Then all at once, her eyes sharpened, and her lips twitched into a nervous smile that said, *Holy shit. Did I really do that?*

He grinned and took her hand, turning to their family and friends, and said, "And to think I almost asked for a handshake."

AS THE NIGHT wore on, someone kicked off a playlist with a mix of country music, classic rock, and pop. There were toasts with champagne and sparkling cider, enough food and cake for an army, and countless lingering glances between Zander and Shauna. They weren't the *hey, want to hook up* glances he usually gave women who caught his attention. These were deeper, checking in on her, making sure she was okay, and yeah, he couldn't stop thinking about that scorching-hot kiss, which his mind naturally took to the next level, wondering how the rest of her would taste. He had a feeling that kiss was taunting Shauna, too, because she'd kept a polite distance and had been looking at him a little differently. Her eyes carried a charge he hadn't seen before. Curiosity shaded by desire and tempered by restraint. As much as he wanted to push past it and convince her to explore, that wasn't part of the agreement, and he respected her too much to push.

The sun had set long ago, the lights in the trees casting a soft glow over their evening. Zander stood by the dessert table, untouched drink in hand, alone for the first time tonight, which meant he was free to watch the woman who had captivated his attention before he even knew she wasn't just a figment of his imagination. Madigan and the other girls had absconded with his wife a little while ago, and he couldn't be happier for her. He'd hoped the girls would welcome her as warmly into their group as they had the other women.

He spotted his angel sitting on the deck steps with Emerson and Chloe. Marybelle toddled over in her pretty pink dress and patted Shauna's knee. A momentary flash of unsurety shone in Shauna's eyes. Zander had the strange desire to rescue her from that unease, but Chloe said something that made her smile, and his glossy-haired wife—*Holy shit. I have a wife*—lifted Marybelle onto her lap. Marybelle put her chubby little hands on Shauna's cheeks and leaned in. Zander knew she wanted to rub noses. That was Marybelle's newest thing, but Shauna's gaze flickered between awe and uncertainty. She turned to Chloe, her brows pinched. Chloe must have clued her in, because Shauna turned bright eyes back to the happy toddler and rubbed noses with her. Marybelle bounced excitedly, and Shauna rubbed noses with her again.

"Rethinking this whole marriage thing?" Blaine asked as he sauntered over with Maverick and Zeke.

Zander scoffed. "No, man. It's the least I can do."

"Because she saved your life?" Maverick asked.

Nah, because it's her was on the tip of his tongue, but he held it back because he wasn't supposed to feel like that, and went with "What do you think?"

"I think you might be crazy," Blaine said, and took a swig of his beer.

Zander ground his back teeth to keep from arguing that point.

"But aren't we all?" Blaine added. "I get it, man. I mean, I was all in helping Reese with her situation when she thought I was nothing but a pushy asshole."

"You are a pushy asshole," Zander said, breathing a little easier with his support.

"There's a reason everyone calls you a bulldozer." Maverick tossed out the barb with a grin.

"No shit," Blaine bit out. Then a slow grin slid into place. "But I still got my girl, and it didn't take me a *year* to get her."

Zander chuckled. Maverick had spent a year trying to get Chloe to go out with him.

"That just goes to show that I've got staying power in *and* out of the bedroom," Maverick said.

As they argued, "Pink Pony Club" came on, and Madigan squealed, drawing Zander's attention as she grabbed Lettie and Reese and dragged them into the middle of the lawn to dance. They called out for the other girls to join them.

Zander stepped away from his brothers to get a better view of Shauna, and Rosie darted past, snagged two cookies off the table, and hollered, *"Grandpa Mike! I got you a cookie!"* as she ran off.

Shauna pushed to her feet with Marybelle in her arms, laughing about something with Chloe and Emerson. They headed for Madigan but detoured over to Sid and Leah, coaxing them into joining the others. Shauna was a sight to behold, swinging those gorgeous hips with his niece in her arms, earning sweet smiles and probably a few giggles.

Zander saw Cap heading his way. He had congratulated Zander and Shauna earlier, but they'd been caught up in the chaos of the moment. *And that unforgettable kiss.*

"How are you doing, Cap?" he asked as Cap sidled up to him.

"I'm good. This is some celebration. If Shauna hadn't clued me in, I would think this was a reception for two people in love."

"I've got to be honest. I was shocked when I found out my parents planned this, but I'm glad they did. Shauna said she never wants to get married for real, so I'm glad she'll always have this."

"I am, too. I haven't seen her this happy in a long time."

"Well, we're both glad you could make it tonight."

"Shauna is like a daughter to me," Cap said with a serious lilt in his voice. "I'm embarrassed to have missed the signs that things were going awry at home. I won't make that mistake again, and I want to say thank you. What you're doing for her and Brian is above and beyond what most people would do."

"I wouldn't be here if not for her. I'm just glad she finally agreed to let me help. It was like pulling teeth to convince her this was a good idea."

"Yeah. Shauna doesn't trust easily."

"I don't blame her. She's been through a lot, and I don't exactly have the type of reputation to back up my claim to do right by her."

"I'm glad you're honest about that, because I did some checking up of my own," Cap said. "I hope you won't take her trust for granted. I have nothing but respect for your family and for the work you do through the club to support the community, but don't think for a minute I won't come after you if you hurt her."

Zander held Cap's gaze. "I give you my word I will do everything in my power to make her life better, not worse."

"I'm holding you to that," Cap said. "If you'll excuse me, Gunner said he wanted to talk with me before I take off."

"Five bucks says he's going to try to talk you into getting a pet," Zander said.

"He can try."

As Cap walked away, Zander looked across the lawn at Shauna, no longer holding Marybelle and dancing with the girls. Her smile lit up the whole damn night. He thought about what Cap had said, and his heart physically ached at the idea of ever causing Shauna pain.

Preacher and Conroy stepped into his line of vision with shit-eating grins on their faces.

"You keep looking at her like that, and people are going to start talking," Preacher said.

Conroy grabbed a cookie from the dessert table. "I'm pretty sure that kiss lit the rumor mill on fire. Platonic, my ass."

"Hey, don't go starting rumors. She grabbed *me*. You saw it."

"Yes, but we also saw the way you've been looking at her all night," Preacher said.

Shit. He hadn't even thought to hide it. "It's not like that. I'm just glad she's having a good time and she's got the girls in her corner. She doesn't have many people to lean on."

"Well, son, now she's got all of us, and she'll never have to worry about that again." Preacher clapped a hand on Zander's back. "Even after she dumps your ass."

Zander half laughed, half scoffed. "On that note, I think I'll go dance with my bride."

"Hey, Con, did you notice he didn't say *temporary* bride?" Preacher asked as Zander stepped away.

"Yes, I did, Preach," Conroy said.

Zander turned back to set the record straight. "This may be a temporary arrangement, but I made a promise, and she's going to ride on the back of my bike. That makes her my queen, and she'll never feel like anything less."

He headed over to Shauna, dancing with Madigan and a few of the girls, and *damn*, his wife had moves. She looked lost in the moment, throwing her head back with a laugh as she and the girls shimmied. She danced with a carefree energy that was effortlessly alluring, too natural to be purposefully sexy or performative. He had a feeling she rarely had a chance to let her guard down like this and didn't want to steal it from her, so he hung back, enjoying the show.

As the song came to an end, he sauntered over and slid his arm around Shauna, drawing her against him. "Mind if I take this gorgeous girl for a spin before I take her home and tuck her in?"

Madigan grabbed Shauna's arm. "No, we're not going to let you corrupt her. She's the sister we never knew we needed."

"Yeah, I love these girls, but it's nice to meet someone who isn't all about pink toenails and dresses," Sid said.

"And she's joining our book club," Chloe added. "You're going to have to pencil our time with her into your schedule."

Shauna beamed, but he couldn't resist teasing the others. "You expect me to walk away and let *you* corrupt her?"

"No, you can have your dance." Madigan pointed at him. "But she's one of us now and we're keeping her after the divorce, so don't screw things up and make her not want to hang around once your deal is over."

"That's never been a problem before," he said arrogantly. "Women always want more of me, not less."

"He's totally going to screw this up," Madigan said frustratedly. She pointed to her eyes with two fingers, then pointed them at Zander, mouthing, *I'm watching you.*

He chuckled and put a hand on Shauna's back, guiding her away from the girls.

"You should've quit while you were ahead," Shauna said as he drew her into his arms.

"I did. You're dancing with me, aren't you?" He loved the slightly bashful smile that earned, and hell if it didn't make him want to kiss her again. She felt incredible in his arms, their bodies moving as one to the beat of a slow country song. "In case I haven't told you enough tonight, you look beautiful."

The blush on her cheeks deepened. "Thank you, but you've told me enough."

"What can I say? You're the most beautiful woman I've ever married."

She laughed softly. "I can't believe we actually did it."

"Believe it, Angel. How does it feel knowing I'm all yours?"

"Like I must be the crazy one."

"Then I'm in good company." The song "Never Stop" by SafetySuit came on. "Hear that? They're playing our song."

"We have a song?"

"Hell yeah, we do." He went for levity, singing, *"This is my fake love song for you. You've got limited time to brag that I'm yours, send other women home crying at night. You'll be sleeping like a baby, knowing you've got the best guy around."*

She laughed. "That's quite a song."

"Only the best for my queen." Their gazes lingered as they swayed to the music. He could get lost in those gorgeous eyes, soaking in the feel of her soft curves, the quiet intensity of her gaze, and the heat and curiosity hovering between them. One song bled into the next, the temperature between them rising. They didn't speak, but their bodies sure as hell did, their grips tightening, their hips swaying in perfect sync, and lust seeping between them, binding them together in a silent dance of desire. Then there was that look she was giving him that said *I want more, but…*

The song "Worst Way" came on, bringing lyrics about not romancing a woman, but letting his hands and mouth do the talking. As if the fucking playlist had heard his thoughts.

He needed to get himself back on track, but there was no way that was happening with her in his arms. "Are you having a good time, or are you overwhelmed and ready to head out?"

"A little of both," she said carefully. "Your family is amazing, and everyone has been wonderful, but being close like *this* is kind of…"

Dangerous. "You're thinking about that kiss, aren't you?" came out before he could stop it.

"No," she said too fast. "I don't want to talk about that kiss."

"That makes me *want* to talk about it," he said honestly.

"Zander," she whispered harshly, but she was smiling, and she was too fun to tease for him to want to stop.

"What? You've got to admit, it was a hell of a kiss."

"So?"

Time to test the waters. "So maybe we should try it again. See if it really was that good."

She stared at him for a beat, heat and hesitation warring in her eyes, but in her next breath she said, "That's not what this is."

"I know it's not. I'm just trying to be a good husband, leaving the door open. I'd hate for you to be fantasizing all night about kissing me again and then leave you hanging. And hey, if lips are too intimate, I'm happy to let you kiss me elsewhere."

"Ohmygod." She laughed. "Would you stop? I feel like everyone's watching us."

"That's just me, darlin'. I can't take my eyes off you." *Ap-*

parently I can't shut my fucking mouth, either.

"I'm serious, Zan," she said quietly.

He casually glanced around. *Damn.* His parents and a handful of others were watching them. His father arched a brow, as if to say, *You're not looking at her like that, huh?*

That doused the flames.

Time to rein it in, asshole. She's right. That's not what this is.

"Want to get out of here before it gets any weirder?" he asked.

"Yes."

THE RIDE HOME was quiet, save for the sexual tension humming between them. Zander tried to focus on the road, telling himself to get a grip before things went further. The last thing either of them needed was more complications.

He helped her out of the truck, and in an effort to get them back on track, he slung an arm over her shoulder as they headed up the walk, falling back to the comfort and familiarity of friendship and joking around, the way things were before that kiss. "So, what're you going to call me? Your old man? Your hubby? Your ride or die?"

"I was thinking...*Zander.*"

"Everyone calls me that. You'll come up with something special. Remember, we've got to convince everyone you couldn't live without me." He unlocked the door and threw it open. She started to walk past, and he lifted her into his arms.

"Zander!" She laughed, which was exactly the reaction he'd hoped for. "What are you doing?"

"Carrying my bride over the threshold," he said as he carried her inside.

"You know this isn't legally required, right?"

He kicked the door closed behind him. "Yeah, but it gave me a reason to have you in my arms again."

As he lowered her feet to the floor, her hands slid down his chest. She was *right there*, those beautiful brown eyes gazing up at him so intensely, the air crackled around them, but it wasn't his body aching to be heard this time. It was that organ in his chest that had gone unnoticed for so long speaking too loudly to ignore. He put his hand over hers, keeping it on his chest, wanting to be sure she heard what he said next. "All kidding aside, thank you for trusting me. I'll try my best to be the kind of husband you deserve."

"You don't—"

He put two fingers over her lips, shushing her. "I *want* to. Let's leave it at that."

She reached up to move his fingers away from her lips but kept hold of his hand and ran her thumb over the barbed wire tattoo on his middle finger. Her brows knitted, and she studied the tattoo closer. The tangled barbed wire ran from the tip of his finger to his knuckle. In between the tangles, along the inside of his finger, was the musical abbreviation *sfz*.

Her eyes flicked up to his. "When did you get that?"

"When I was eighteen. Why?"

She looked at it again, her brow riddled with confusion.

"What's the matter?"

"My middle name is Zoe," she said just above a whisper, as if they were the only two people in the world who should hear it.

Now it was his turn to be confused. He tried to make sense

of it, but there was no making sense of this. He and Shauna were like a custom home whose unique elements had been forged years before the architect had even conceptualized them.

"Why do you have that tattoo?" she asked.

"It's a musical abbreviation." He curled his fingers around hers. "Or maybe it's another sign that we were meant to be in each other's lives."

She held his gaze, her eyes wide and searching, as if he'd become someone new she was seeing for the first time. Only he knew it wasn't just him who was evolving. Their electrical charge echoing in the silence was inescapable.

"I'm gonna..." She stumbled backward, pointing behind her toward her bedroom. "Yeah. I'm...I've got to work in the morning, so..."

He knew whatever this was, was so big and so real, it scared her. It scared him, too, but it intrigued him even more, and he wanted to explore it. Hell, he wanted to dive in headfirst and get lost in it. He gritted his teeth to keep those thoughts from coming out as she took another step backward.

"This was fun...Thanks...for the...*Yeah*. I'm, um, I'm going to bed." She turned around, nearly tripping over Kitty, and hurried into her bedroom. Kitty darted in behind her, slipping in before she closed the door.

You can run from this, my sweet bride, but I have a feeling it's already a part of us.

Chapter Twenty-Four

SHAUNA TRIED TO convince herself she wasn't tired as she got ready for work Friday morning, though she'd only slept a few hours thanks to her *now husband*, Mr. Wicked Kisser. Every time she'd closed her eyes she'd seen flashes of him. She looked down at her beautiful rings, still shocked they'd gone through with the wedding. She might have thought she'd dreamed up the whole incredible evening if Conroy hadn't sent them the pictures shortly after they'd gotten home last night. She'd never seen herself so happy or so pretty, and Zander? Her pulse quickened just thinking about the way he'd looked at her when she'd walked down the aisle, but seeing it in pictures had cemented the image into her memory. She'd forever remember their heart-thundering glances that had stoked the desire brewing between them nearly to the point of combustion. And she'd definitely never forget that toe-curling, soul-rocking kiss. *God, that kiss…*

The kiss I initiated in front of his entire family.

She still couldn't believe she'd done that, but it had felt like a now-or-never moment, and she hadn't wanted there to be a never. The trouble was, she hadn't known kisses like that existed. How could a single kiss make her knees weaken and her entire body tingle and burn? How could one kiss, a *first* kiss, leave her loneliest parts begging for more? It wasn't just the way he looked at her or that smoldering kiss that was turning her into a hot mess. It was everything about him, from the way he made her feel safe enough to let her guard down to how he held nothing back, making her laugh by swooping her off her feet one second and sending her up in flames the next with those piercing blue eyes and a soft-spoken promise. *All kidding aside, thank you for trusting me. I'll try my best to be the kind of husband you deserve.*

Zander Wicked possessed the rare and innate ability to ruin a girl for all others with an intimacy that didn't require physical touch. He needed a neon blinking light on his forehead that read WARNING! THIS MAN WILL RUIN YOU FOR LIFE.

And leave you wanting more.

So much more.

She finished dressing, and as she put on her boots, she thought about the moment she'd seen her initials tattooed on his finger. The sight had stolen her breath, but it was their connection, that buzz of electricity and the bone-deep ache to kiss him again, that had sent her world spinning. She cringed with the memory of being unable to string a sentence together before escaping into her bedroom. Maybe Zander didn't notice her foray into Flusterville.

Yeah, right.

The man didn't miss a thing.

She needed to get over it. What's done was done, and there was no undoing it. She would write off that embarrassing escape as a blip on their radar screen and write off their kiss—*the best kiss I've ever had*—as temporary madness, and move on. At least she'd have the next twenty-four hours to figure out how to do that before she'd see him again.

She slid the rings off her finger and tucked them into her jewelry box, surprised to miss the feel of them. Trying to ignore that sensation, she grabbed her keys and pocketed her phone, thinking about the tattoo on his finger. Last night, when she couldn't sleep, she'd googled *sfz*, just to be sure it really was a musical abbreviation. It was, but it still looked like a monogram made just for her. After that revelation, she'd downloaded the book Madigan and the girls were reading for their book club and had begun reading it in hopes of turning her brain off. It hadn't helped her sleep. The story was steeped with sexual tension…and she couldn't wait to get back to it.

As she opened her bedroom door, she was surprised to hear the sound of Zander's guitar. Her pulse spiked. She thought he'd be at work by now.

She followed the scent of something delicious down the hall and found a visual feast. Zander was sitting on the couch in the living room, shirtless, with his broad, muscular back to her, playing the guitar. Her eyes locked on the FAMILY tattoo on his back, with all those roots snaking through the letters, and Madigan's words came back to her. *She's one of us now, and we're keeping her after the divorce.* Shauna had been so overwhelmed after the way Zander's family stepped up for him and how they'd accepted her with open arms, even if some were cautious, she hadn't allowed herself to think Madigan had meant what she'd said. But maybe if she and Zander made it through these next few months unscathed, she *could* remain friends with him and Madigan and the girls.

"Good morning," she said. "I thought you'd be at work by now."

He turned, a warm smile stretching across his face like he

was genuinely happy to see her, and boy did that feel good. "Morning, Angel." He set his guitar on the couch. "I told them I'd be a little late. I wanted to start our new life right and see my gorgeous wife off to work."

Her thoughts stumbled over what he'd said, and she got even more distracted as he pushed to his feet. His worn jeans hung low on his hips, bringing back the image of him naked, and her traitorous body forgot all about her fatigue, getting wired and restless all over again.

Nonono.

She tried to will those thoughts out of her head. She needed to think of him like one of the guys at the firehouse. How many times had she seen them walking around half-dressed? *But they don't have rock-hard abs I could wash my clothes on, and I've never wanted to kiss any of them so badly, I got hot and bothered just thinking about it.* As the thought hit, her mind tiptoed back to what he'd said about going into work late for her.

"You didn't have to do that," she said. "I can get myself off."

His smile turned salacious. "Well, I can help with that, too."

A rush of heat washed through her, and for a brief, tantalizing moment, she allowed herself to toy with the idea. But as her body screamed *yes*, her rational brain took hold. She had too much riding on this to screw it up. "I'm good, thanks. I need to go to work."

"Just trying to be a good husband." He picked up a small paper bag and a to-go cup from the coffee table and carried them over to her. "I made you a breakfast…" His brows knitted, and his jaw clenched. He held up the bag, staring at it for a beat before saying, "*Burrito*. It's got eggs, cheese, sausage, and a few veggies thrown in for good measure. It should still be warm, and coffee just the way you like it, with enough creamer to drown in."

She sighed inwardly. How was her heart supposed to survive this man? Nobody had ever taken care of her like this before. "Thanks, but you didn't have to do all of this," she said as he handed them to her. "I could've grabbed coffee at Cumby's or the firehouse."

"I stopped by Cumby's on the way home the other day. You can't go there anymore."

"Why not?"

"There's a wanted poster with your picture on it for creamer hoarding. It would be embarrassing if I had to bail my new wife out of jail."

There was no suppressing her smile.

"Damn, darlin'. Seeing those dimples is the best way to start a morning."

She laughed softly. "You don't have to be a superhero husband. You're already the best one I've ever had."

"And I aim to keep it that way."

Their gazes held for a beat longer than usual, awareness skimming through her entire body. "I'd better get to work. Please tell your family how much I appreciate everything they did for us."

He opened the door and said, "I'll walk you out."

She was about to say he didn't need to when his hand landed on her lower back, and he said, "They're your family now, too, darlin'."

That hit so deeply, she almost let herself believe it.

SHAUNA SAT ON the ambulance bumper reading on her phone, trying to sneak in a few more chapters before she had to cook dinner for the crew. Madigan had sent a group text earlier, trying to schedule a time she and the girls could get together for lunch, and Shauna had mentioned that she'd started the book. Everyone had commented about different parts of the story, being careful not to give away spoilers, which whetted her whistle for upcoming chapters. Coordinating so many people's schedules wasn't easy, and they still hadn't confirmed a date to get together, but she was having fun texting and looking forward to seeing them again.

She tried to tune out the guys as she read. It had been quiet until they'd rolled out of the firehouse giving each other a hard time and trying to rope her into their banter. She'd been keeping her distance, figuring out how to tell them about her new marital status. Earlier, when Lance had said she looked tired, he'd asked what she'd been up to last night and had immediately started teasing her about having gone on a date. Not that they had any reason to believe that, but they'd been in prime heckling form all day. When she and Zander were swapping silly cat videos and funny marriage videos earlier, the guys had accused her of sexting because they said she'd looked *too* happy. She wasn't about to follow that up with a marriage reveal.

And then there was Cap. He'd been giving her knowing looks all day, but she knew he'd keep her secret until she was ready to share it. Even if it took a couple of weeks.

"She hasn't blinked in five minutes," Mike said, inching closer to her.

"Is she breathing?" Trey asked.

"She's in a book coma," Paul said. "I recognize the signs."

They closed in on her, taunting her with gossip about a male nurse and a female doctor who were supposedly hooking up at the hospital, and when that didn't get her attention, they moved on to what she could only assume was fake gossip about other members of the firehouse getting caught having sex in the fire truck. She gave them a cursory glance and went back to reading.

"Maybe she's not reading. Maybe she's looking at porn," Howie called from the other side of the bay.

"Do you really think I'd look at porn right here, out in the open?" She *had* just gotten to a steamy scene, but they didn't need to know that.

"Is there a rule against that?" Trey asked. "Asking for a friend."

The guys laughed.

She pushed to her feet, ready to escape their nonsense, but Mike snagged her phone out of her hand and ran across the bay, laughing. She went after him, but he was faster.

"'Does my sexy scientist want to do a little hands-on research?'" Mike read aloud as he ran.

"Yeah, baby. I could get into a sexy scientist," Paul said.

"I swear, Mike, if you don't give me my phone, I'll end you!" Shauna threatened as she sprinted around the ambulance after him.

He continued reading, practically shouting, *"She licks her lips as she wraps her fingers around my cock—"*

Just as Shauna snagged the back of Mike's shirt, "Hey, guys, is my wife around?" rang out from behind her in a familiar deep voice. *Zander.* Panic flared in her chest, but her stupid heart did a somersault at the ease with which he'd said it, as if they'd been married forever.

Mike whipped his head around. "Wife?"

Shauna yanked her phone from his hand and turned around without responding. Zander was holding three large pizza boxes, his hair was damp, and boy did he look good in a white T-shirt under his leather cut, worn jeans, and an amused smile. "Hey," she said as casually as she could while her mind raced through explanations to give the guys. "I wasn't expecting to see you."

"I thought I'd surprise you and your friends with dinner. But I've got to admit, I didn't expect to catch you chasing another guy around so soon after we tied the knot." His eyes shimmered with the tease.

She felt the guys watching them, and though her insides were twisting and she had no idea how she was going to explain this to them, she couldn't help but smile at Zander's easy humor. "The asshole stole my phone."

Zander feigned anger. "Want me to take him out?"

She shook her head as she stepped closer and lowered her voice to just above a whisper. "I haven't told them we're married yet."

"Shit. Sorry, darlin'," he whispered. "Guess we'd better ham it up."

He swept one arm around her, balancing the pizzas in the other, and kissed the ever-loving hell out of her. Why did he have to be such a good kisser? *Fuck it.* If this was happening, she might as well enjoy it. She kissed him back, but quickly discovered her mistake. She enjoyed it too much and didn't want to stop.

As their lips parted, it took her a minute to clear her lust-addled brain. A devilish glint shimmered in Zander's eyes as he reached for her hand, giving it a reassuring squeeze, and said, "Damn, I missed you."

He was a hell of an actor. She needed the guys to buy it, and they sure as hell better after that kiss. Just in case, she flashed her most adoring smile and said, "If you're going to bring me pizza every time you miss me, I might just keep you around."

"Wait a second," Lance said. "You guys aren't really married, right? Tell me you were kidding."

"We're really married," she said.

The guys exchanged concerned glances.

"No offense to either of you," Howie said, "but haven't you only known each other a week or two?"

"Sort of," Shauna said. "We actually met a few years ago, and reconnected with his accident." It was a stretch, but it was the best she had.

"Why'd you tell us you were just friends?" Mike asked. "And why go from friends or more to *married* so fast?"

Now it was her turn to lay it on thick. "I never thought I was the kind of person who could get swept off my feet, but then Zander crashed into my life, and I found out how wrong I was." There was a little too much truth in that sentence, so she added more to temper it, even if only as a reminder to herself. "It was like an outside force was driving us together."

"Look, we know it's fast. As Shauna said, it took us by surprise, too." Zander gazed into her eyes and said, "When we reconnected, it was like we'd stumbled into an unfinished story someone else had written for us. We kept finding points where our lives had crossed, like everything in our lives had led us to that moment."

She was stunned. That was exactly what it felt like. Was this just an act? Or did he really feel that way?

"And you all know how great Shauna is," he said to the guys. "She's not just gorgeous and smart with a wild sense of humor. She's as careful as she is badass. She can handle anything that comes her way, and trust me, I'm a lot to handle."

"You can say that again," she said more to herself than to him.

"See? She's no wallflower." He looked at her again, only this time it was as penetrating as it was at the wedding, stirring all the emotions she'd been trying to bury. "But beneath all that snark, armor, and beauty beats the sweetest of hearts, and I'm the lucky bastard who gets to call it mine. I look forward to a lifetime of showing her just how special she is." He lifted their joined hands and kissed the back of hers. "So yeah, it's fast and maybe even reckless. But life's short, and we aren't going to waste a second of it. Right, Angel?"

"Mm-hm," she managed, holding on to her runaway emotions by a thread.

"So, what do you say, guys?" Zander asked. "Do you want to congratulate us and eat some pizza, or shall we let my beautiful wife showcase her cooking skills?"

They all spoke at once, joking about wanting to live for another day, warning Zander not to let Shauna near a stove, and finally—*thankfully*—congratulating them on their nuptials.

As the guys took the pizzas inside, Zander said, "I think they bought it."

"*I* bought it." She laughed. "A little warning before kissing the hell out of me would've been nice."

"I thought you wanted it to look real."

"I *did*, but that was a bit *too* real. Especially in front of the guys."

"Hey, don't pretend you didn't kiss me back."

"Yeah, because—"

"You like kissing me," he said with a smirk.

She couldn't even try to deny it. "Next time, keep those lethal lips to yourself."

Flashing an arrogant grin, he draped his arm over her shoulder in the way that already felt familiar and said, "Afraid you'll get carried away in front of your friends and want to jump my bones?"

"I don't even want to *kiss* you in front of them."

"Could've fooled me."

"*Zander,*" she warned.

"Save the making out for when we're home alone. Got it."

Her traitorous body revved up at the thought, but she managed a snarky "Dream on, Wicked."

Chapter Twenty-Five

THE CAR IDLED at a red light, the music low, and as happened often at crossroads, Shauna's thoughts took her back to the morning of that dreadful crash. For the millionth time, she pondered why she'd been so drawn to Zander, she kept going back to see him at the hospital. Even then, it had felt like there was something bigger at play. Something unavoidable and important.

It had only been a week since they had gotten married, but somewhere along the line, real life had started to blur with the fake one they were playing up when they were in public. They'd gone to the Salty Hog last weekend for lunch, and what had started as simple hand-holding had turned into an arm around her shoulder, cheek kisses, and whispered inside jokes. All of which were in plain sight of Ginger, Conroy, and Zander's friend Starr, a sassy blond waitress who, Shauna learned, was also a member of the book club. Shauna didn't hate this game she and Zander were playing, but it was dangerous. They'd gone for a walk on the beach the other night, and she'd caught herself reaching for his hand when they passed a group of people, as if he was *hers.* They'd also done such a good job of convincing the guys at work that their relationship was real, they tossed around

Zander's name as often and as casually as they talked about Howie's wife.

And it wasn't just happening in public. Their home lives no longer felt separate. The changes happened quietly, nestled between work shifts, shared meals, inside jokes, and texts that had gone from funny videos to messages that arrived at just the right moment after a rough call or when she was thinking about him. *Missing him.*

She told herself the anticipation of seeing him in the mornings, the comfort she took in the scent of his bodywash in the shower and the feel of his hand on her back or the sound of his guitar, and the thrill when he came home after work, dirty and tired, and lit up when he saw her, were normal for roommates. But she knew they weren't. She'd never felt those kinds of thrills when she and Brian were together. That was the other thing that was rocking her to her core. It had only been a week, and she wasn't stressing over Brian. She felt a little guilty about that, but at the same time, she was realizing how much energy she'd put into worrying about him. She'd carried the weight of his addiction for both of them, and it was nice not to be the one worrying for a change. She didn't need to be taken care of, but she liked when Zander made her coffee or asked after her. He'd even left flowers tucked beneath her windshield wiper one day when she was at work. She was no expert on romance, but the things he did and said felt like the most romantic things in the world.

Then there were those electrically charged moments between them when the air was so thick with desire, she could taste it. Sometimes that happened when they were just being lazy on the couch, not touching or talking, but watching a movie or when she was doing a word search and he was trying to distract her in that adorably charming way he had. Their eyes would lock, and they'd both fall silent.

She'd had to force herself to stop looking at the pictures from the wedding, because she couldn't stop staring at them, scrutinizing them for real emotions versus simply being swept up in the moment.

Someone honked, jerking her out from her reverie, and she swore for the millionth time she was turning off those feelings before things became any more complicated.

By the time she reached Zander's house, she'd pushed them down deep and chained them under lock and key for good measure. She grabbed her bag, and as she headed up to the walk, Zander came out carrying a duffel bag and a big suitcase, looking hot as sin in his usual jeans, T-shirt, and leather cut.

"Hey, darlin'. Perfect timing."

"Are you going away?"

"Sure am."

The pit of her stomach sank as he put the luggage in the backseat of his truck. *So much for chaining down those feelings.* She was naive to think he was feeling the same thing she was. He was just better at the game than she was. It made sense. He was a player, even if she'd let herself forget it for a little while. He was probably going away to find someone to hook up with where nobody would think he was cheating on his fake wife.

Trying to hide her disappointment as he headed inside with her, she said, "How long will you be gone?"

"Just the weekend," he said, walking past her and heading down the hallway.

Kitty wound around Shauna's feet. She set down her backpack and picked her up. "Guess it's just you and me this weekend."

"Mads is picking up Kitty in an hour," he called out.

She held Kitty a little tighter. "You don't trust me to watch her?"

"Sure I do." He came out of the hall carrying her pillow.

"Hey, that's *my* pillow."

"Yup," he said on his way outside.

She hurried after him. "You can't take my pillow. I need it." Ignoring her, he tossed it in the truck. "*Zander*, I'm too tired for games. Take your own pillow."

"It's already in the truck." He smiled coyly. "You're adorable when you scowl."

"Don't try to charm me. Why are you stealing my pillow?"

"I thought you might want it on our honeymoon. I know you're tired, but we've got a long drive, and you can sleep on the way. I've got your pillow, a blanket, snacks, your word search books, and I picked up a paperback of the book you're reading for the book club. Why don't you put Kitty back inside and make sure I didn't forget anything you want to bring."

"Our *honeymoon*?" Her lips twitched, wanting to join her overzealous heart, but the truth held it back. "You know this isn't that kind of marriage."

"Sure." His tone was casual, but as he took her left hand in his and slid her rings onto her finger, he said, "But that doesn't mean you don't deserve one," like he meant every word.

He was making their marriage of convenience feel hauntingly real.

"Besides, it'll make us more believable," he said, and swatted her ass. "Now, *go* do your thing so we can get out of here."

Chapter Twenty-Six

SHAUNA THOUGHT SHE'D be too nervous to sleep on the drive, but the motion of the truck and Zander's singing had lulled her into a deep sleep. She'd woken a few hours later, feeling refreshed and immediately had gotten nervous again about going on a honeymoon with Zander. A honeymoon implied romance and intimacy. But he wasn't acting any different than he had last week, so she tried not to, either. With the windows down and music blaring, they sang too loud, making up lyrics they'd forgotten, and teased each other between eating handfuls of gummy bears and bags of chips, and her anxiety had been short-lived.

Until now.

Zander didn't just plan a little getaway. They were on their way into their suite in a fancy hotel with marble floors and crystal chandeliers in Niagara Falls, New York. *Niagara Falls!*

He opened the door and stepped back, allowing her to walk in first. With her heart hammering, she stepped into the suite, and her breath caught at the sheer size of it. She'd expected to see a room with a king-sized bed, but they were standing in the living room of a two-bedroom suite, with a couch, a large wall-mounted television, a desk by balcony doors, and a kitchenette with a small table that had a pretty wicker welcome basket filled with snacks and what looked like a bottle of champagne in it.

As relief and gratitude bubbled up inside her, a pang of disappointment snuck in. She'd been so nervous about what the honeymoon might mean, she hadn't considered her feelings about it. Even if she wasn't looking for love or forever, they'd gotten so close, she hadn't realized how much she'd *wanted* this to be more, or how much she'd hoped he'd wanted *her*. But those two bedrooms were a gentle reminder that this wasn't a real honeymoon. Zander was just doing exactly what he'd promised, being a great husband without any expectations of more.

He carried their luggage in, like this was perfectly normal, and her stomach hadn't knotted up with disappointment she had no right to feel.

Tucking *that* away, she headed over to the balcony doors. "Wow, we can see the falls from here. I might have to leave you a five-star review on Husbands R Us."

"Don't bother. One marriage is all I need. Which bedroom would you like?"

"Whichever one you don't."

"I'd give you the one with the best view, but I don't think you want to sleep next to me all night, so I'll give you the one with a view of the falls."

"Ha ha," she said, as if she weren't wishing for that invitation.

He carried her suitcase into one bedroom and tossed his bag into the other. "But if you get lonely..." He waggled his brows.

One more mixed signal and she was going to need a translator.

THEY SHOWERED AND dressed for dinner, making it to a cool restaurant with mismatched chairs, record albums on the walls, and flower boxes spilling over the railings just in time for the reservations Zander had made. They sat at a cozy candlelit table on the patio, serenaded by the soft, familiar beat of country-acoustic covers, the chatter of other diners, and the clink of silverware against plates. Zander was playing up the part of the adoring husband, telling the hostess and then their server that they were on their honeymoon. When he pulled his chair beside hers instead of sitting across the table, his grin both devilish and charming, the waiter nodded knowingly.

They were halfway through a delicious meal of steak and shrimp, crisp roasted potatoes, and vegetables sautéed so perfectly they melted on her tongue. Shauna lifted her glass, condensation cooling her fingertips as she sipped her iced tea. Zander had ordered the same. She hadn't asked him not to drink, but she was learning his thoughtfulness seeped into every part of his life.

"On a scale of one to ten, how was your first week of marriage?" he asked smugly.

She swirled the ice in her glass. "Not bad. My husband's a little cocky, but he's easy on the eyes and he's got a cute cat, so I'd say it's about an eight."

"Eight, huh?" His eyes narrowed. "What's missing?"

That was a loaded question. "He hasn't shared any of his deep dark secrets with me yet."

"Ah, you want to know my dirty secrets?"

She took a sip and set her glass down. "I said dark, not dirty."

"Dark and dirty go together," he said seductively.

She realized he might be just unfiltered enough to share something dark and dirty with her, and she didn't want to hear about his sexual escapades with other women. "I was thinking more like teenage drama or a tattoo you regret getting."

"I don't believe in regrets. They're a waste of energy. Life happens fast, and you can't change the past, so why bother overthinking it or beating yourself up over it?"

"Must be nice." She couldn't imagine what a life without regrets would even feel like.

"Sounds like you have a few." He leaned in, the candlelight reflecting in his eyes. "Want to share them with me?"

"I don't want to bore you."

"You haven't bored me yet, and you're my wife. I want to know more about you."

When he looked at her like that, like he was genuinely hoping she'd share, it made it hard not to believe there was something more between them. "You can probably guess what they are. I wish I'd handled things with my parents differently, stood up for myself, asked my grandfather to raise me before I started drinking and smoking. I wish I'd gotten help for myself, and help for Brian, sooner."

"I understand why you feel that way, but maybe you should cut yourself a little slack. Kids learn from their parents. You were afraid you might go into the foster system if you had tried to help yourself, and you'd been told that was a bad thing. You can't blame fourteen-year-old you for any of that. And as far as Brian goes, you've beaten yourself up long enough about that. You've given him the opportunity to regain control of his life. If you'd tried sooner, it might not have worked."

"Somehow, hearing it from you makes it easier to believe."

"Good, because like I said, you've spent enough time worrying about what could've been. Don't second-guess yourself, darlin'. You had good reasons for everything you've done, and you ended up with a fantastic husband."

"And he's not at all cocky."

"You've seen me naked. You know that's not true."

She laughed and shook her head, trying to clear that scorching visual. "Time for a subject change."

He chuckled and took a drink. As he set down his glass, he said, "I've got a wholesome secret I can share."

"Somehow I doubt that."

"I was *nine*," he offered in explanation. "The cutest girl in class wouldn't give me the time of day."

"The nerve of her," Shauna said.

"Right?" He grinned. "She was a goody-two-shoes, and she was friends with the well-behaved boys."

"You were too wild for her?"

"Too wild, too funny, too cute." He winked. "Anyway, I brought a grasshopper to school, and I walked by her table at lunch and casually dropped it beside her. It jumped onto her arm, and she gasped and made that sound girls make when they're scared—"

"What sound? I'm picturing her saying, *Zander, what the heck?* and swatting it away."

"She wasn't as tough as you. She kind of squealed, so I swooped in to save the day. I picked that sucker up and ate it."

"You *ate* it?"

"What can I say? I've always been willing to commit."

She arched a brow. "That's not what you told me."

"I mean commit to *getting* the girl, not keeping her. But it didn't matter, because she yelled, '*Ew! Zander ate a grasshopper!*' and then I became known as the kid who ate bugs."

"Aw, you poor thing. That must've hurt your little ego."

"Hardly. I used it to my advantage and told everyone I was practicing to be a Green Beret, which made me the toughest boy in class."

"Only you would come up with that." It was easy to imagine him as a little smart-mouthed charmer.

"Like I said, no regrets. Now it's your turn."

"I don't have any bug-eating stories, but I did moon over firefighters for about a year and tell everyone who would listen that I was going to marry one."

"All women think firemen have big hoses, but that's a myth. You should've said biker. We've got big pipes, our engines run hot, and we can ride *all* night long."

Now, that's a theory I'd like to test.

This new lustful side of herself was as pushy as he was. *Settle down, Flores. There will be* no *testing.*

"I was eight at the time," she said. "Definitely not thinking about their hoses. They were brave and they were nice to me when my mother nearly burned down our kitchen and blamed me for it."

His brows slanted. "Seriously?"

"Mm-hm. I thought a firefighter could save me from anything."

"No, I get that," he said sharply. "I mean, your mother really blamed you for the fire?"

"*Oh.* Yeah." She shrugged. "It's not a big deal. I got blamed for everything."

"It's a huge deal. *You're* a huge deal." He held her gaze, his leg pressing against hers beneath the table, stirring that ever-present current that had taken up residence between them.

She wanted to lean in to whatever this was, but she forced herself to sit back and jokingly change the subject, her escape whenever things heated up. Only this time, neither laughed it off, and as they finished dinner, that hum was more like a live wire, crackling and popping between them.

When they left the restaurant, Zander said, "Come here, wife," and took her hand, pulling her closer on their way to the truck. "I have one more surprise for you tonight."

"Only one? I might have to downgrade your review."

He slid his arm around her, tugging her against his side. "Trying to get me to up my game, Flores?"

"That depends. Does upping your game include dessert? I've never had room service."

They came to his truck, and he looked at her, standing so close, she could kiss those tempting lips if she went up on her toes. "Darlin', it includes anything your sweet heart desires."

Her heart wasn't acting very sweet at the moment. It was begging her to throw caution to the wind and say she desired *him.* She tried to push that urge away with a smirk but couldn't manage it and rolled her eyes instead, breaking their connection before she gave in to it.

"Careful, Wicked. You're getting a little too good at making fake feel real."

His lips curved into a tantalizing smile caught somewhere between enticingly sinful and charmingly playful, seriously hindering her ability to think clearly. He still hadn't moved, just stood there looking at her like he was waiting for something to happen. For her to make a choice? For permission? An act of God? Or maybe she was misreading him again, and he was just being the flirtatious guy everyone seemed to know him to be. Between her racing heart and that look, she was too confused to figure it out.

Get a grip, Flores. Don't make things weirder.

"Are we having a staring contest, or do I get to see the surprise?" *Way to go, Weirdo.*

His lips quirked ever so slightly before breaking into his naturally warm smile, taking down the tension a notch. He opened the truck door and stepped aside, offering his hand. "Your chariot awaits, my queen. Your surprise is an up-close-and-personal view of the falls."

"Are you planning on tossing me over them in a barrel?" she teased as she settled into her seat.

"Something like that."

They drove to Niagara Falls State Park and took an elevator from the observation tower down to a dock at the base of the gorge, where they were given ponchos to wear before boarding the *Maid of the Mist*, a massive boat that provided tours of the falls.

They stood on the upper deck among throngs of other people wearing matching ponchos as the boat moved away from the dock. Zander kept Shauna close with a tight hold on her hand. A loud horn startled her, and he pulled her against him with a chuckle.

A voice boomed through speakers as they glided past the American Falls, crashing down in a thunderous curtain illuminated by a spectacular blend of vibrant blue and purple lights, and beside them, Bridal Veil Falls, which was smaller but every bit as gorgeous. Spray drifted in the breeze, wetting their faces and hair. Zander took out his phone, but instead of taking pictures of the falls, he leaned in and took one of them. Then he pulled her hood over her ponytail and snapped a picture of her before it flew off.

As he started to pocket his phone, she said, "Wait. I want to take one of you," and snagged it from him. He tried to grab it, but she turned away, glancing at the screen to hit the camera icon, but it was locked. She was shocked to see a picture of them kissing at the wedding as his lockscreen. They didn't look like a fake couple. He had one arm belted around her, his other hand in her hair, and her arms weren't just draped over his shoulders. They were crossed behind his neck like they'd not only kissed a million times before, but they were celebrating their coupledom in front of everyone.

That rattled her as much as seeing the picture of them on his phone did.

Her pulse raced as she turned back to him. He looked like he was standing on a tightrope, afraid to speak or move for fear of tripping up something tenuous between them. Or more likely, she was imagining it. She wasn't exactly thinking straight right now.

Of course she was imagining it. "When did you make us your lockscreen?"

"The other day. I figured it would help sell our relationship to everyone. Does it bother you?"

"No. It just took me by surprise. It's just a picture."

His gaze didn't waver from hers. "A pretty great picture." He held out his hand. "I'll unlock it so you can take a picture." He unlocked it and handed it back.

She tried to play it off like she hadn't gotten so rattled she'd forgotten she wanted to take a picture, and said, "Give me that Wicked smile." And boy did he ever.

He pocketed his phone, finding her hand under their ponchos again. Between that picture, their closeness, this incredibly romantic trip he'd planned, and the enormity of the river stretching out before them like a surging path drawing them into something wild and untamable, her emotions were all over the place.

Rock walls loomed on either side of the river, greenery clinging to the cliffs. The observation tower and other buildings, though visible, felt a world away as the boat moved deeper into the river. The wind picked up, and the temperature dropped as they neared the most powerful waterfall. The roar of the falls amplified with the strengthening current, and their ponchos whipped and billowed around them, soaking their clothes. The mist was now a cold blast in her face. She huddled into Zander's chest, the boat rocking with the pounding of the falls. He put a hand on the back of her head, his other arm snaking around her, protective, strong, *safe*.

The roar of the falls was almost as deafening as the pounding of her heart as she looked up and found Zander watching her. They squinted against the stinging mist, droplets clinging to their lashes. His hand slid from her head across her jaw, cupping her cheek, and the world around them silenced. He gently tilted her chin up, his thumb brushing over her cheek, his piercing blue eyes searching hers, giving her a moment to pull away. They had an end date, and getting too close would complicate things, but pulling away was the last thing she wanted. He must have sensed it, because his mouth came down over hers, fierce and possessive, taking her in a merciless kiss.

Her fingers fisted in his poncho, steadying her not against the wind and rain whipping around them, but against the damn breaking inside her and the surge of white-hot desire overtaking her.

Chapter Twenty-Seven

THE DRIVE BACK to the hotel was a blur of passionate kisses at every stoplight and wishing he could magically transport them there. Never in his life had Zander wanted anyone as badly as he wanted the woman kissing him like she never wanted to stop as they stumbled into their suite. Their clothes were drenched from the falls, and his mind was three steps ahead as he kicked the door closed behind them. He wanted to strip her naked, taste every inch of her, feel her writhe and whimper as she came on his mouth, hands, and cock. But as they made out like they'd never get another chance, something else tugged at him. He hadn't been with a woman in months, and he hadn't *wanted* to be with, or even look at, another woman since he'd met Shauna.

That was new and a little fucking scary.

Fighting against those feelings as much as he wanted to give in to them, he tried to chase them away, taking the kiss deeper. Her mouth was sweet and hot and she was so fucking eager, he grabbed her ass, grinding against her so she could feel what she did to him, earning a needy moan. He did it again, seeking more. She gifted him the most lustful sound he'd ever heard, spurring him on. He needed to feel her skin against his and started to take her shirt off, but she put her hands on his chest and said, "*Wait.* You've been with a lot of women. Do I have to worry about diseases?"

"*No.* I wouldn't be kissing you if you did. I'd never put you at risk, and I have condoms."

"Okay, but promise me this won't change anything between us. I like what we have, and we both know this isn't forever."

And there it was, the answer to his quandary. Knowing she wasn't wrestling with bigger feelings stung and confused him, but he was a prideful bastard, and it made it easier for him to tuck his own emotions away. "Don't worry about me, Angel. I might not want to be a player anymore, but that doesn't mean I'm capable of catching feelings. The question is…" He threaded his fingers into her hair, tugging her closer, and slicked his tongue around the shell of her ear. "Can you handle this without catching feelings for *me*?" He nipped her earlobe, earning a sharp inhalation.

Her eyes brimmed with desire, but there was no missing the challenge rising in them. "I'm in this for the pleasure, not more baggage. But it's been a while for me, so I'm hoping you live up to your reputation and won't disappoint."

Loving that sexy snark, he gave her hair a tug, tipping her face up, and lowered his lips a whisper away from hers. "Darlin', with my mouth and your body, there's no room for disappointment."

Their mouths collided in a feast of rough, demanding kisses as they made their way toward the bedrooms. "Your room or mine?" he gritted out.

"Don't care." She pulled his mouth back to hers.

They stumbled into her bedroom, tugging off their shoes and stripping off their clothes between ravenous kisses. His cut and their shirts sailed to the floor, laughter ringing out as they struggled to tug off their wet jeans. Soft black cotton cradled her breasts and rode high on her rounded hips. There was no lace, no silk, no frills, just the rawest, truest beauty he'd ever seen.

"Jesus, darlin', you are dangerously sexy." He took her in a deep, passionate kiss, and then he stripped off that cotton, drinking in her full breasts, the tantalizing dip at her waist, those rounded hips, and her sweet, bare pussy. He took out her ponytail holder, tossing it to the floor with their clothes. Her damp hair tumbled around her face, reminding him of their wedding, tweaking something deep in his chest. "*Mm-mm.* You're dangerous, all right. Painfully beautiful."

As he took off his boxer briefs, her eyes locked on his cock.

"Talk about dangerous," she said. "I'm going to start calling you Loch Ness."

He laughed and hauled her in for a kiss.

They fell to the bed in a tangle of greedy gropes, lustful moans, and smiles against each other's lips. Zander shifted her onto her back, loving the feel of her supple curves against his heated, hard body. Her dark hair fanned out over the pillow, her cheeks flushed, dimples deepening as she reached for him, trying to pull him into a kiss, but he drew back, mesmerized by the beauty beneath him. The trust in her eyes got him all twisted up inside. *Fuck.* That was new, too. The *noticing.* He needed to chase those feelings away, but he wanted to run toward them.

"Why are you looking at me like that?" she asked, snapping him from his thoughts.

What the hell was wrong with him? He cocked a grin, falling back into the man she expected. The man she needed him to be. "I want to remember what you looked like before I set the bar so high no one will ever come close."

Needing to stay in that safety zone, he didn't give her time to dole out snark. He lowered his lips to hers in a slow, penetrating kiss that had her rocking against his cock, whimpering for more. She grabbed his ass with both hands, gyrating beneath him.

"That's it, darlin'," he gritted out. "Show me how much you want me."

He punctuated the demand with a brutal kiss, leaving her breathless as he nipped and kissed a path along her jaw and down her neck, earning sharp, sexy gasps, each one amping up his arousal. He slid his tongue along the pulse at the base of her neck, loving the quickening he caused. He wanted to memorize every little sound she made, the way she held her breath as he trailed kisses along her collarbone and breathed faster as he tasted his way down to her breasts.

She boldly held his gaze as he nudged her legs open wider with his knee, resting the base of his cock against her pussy. When he palmed her breast for the first time, it felt like her body was made for his hands. "I've been dying to get my mouth on these gorgeous tits."

Her eyes flamed.

He rained kisses over the swell of her breasts, and she inhaled a ragged breath. She was killing him with those needy sounds. He grazed his teeth over one taut nipple, and she moaned, her arousal wetting the base of his cock. "*Mm.* My Angel likes my teeth." Her cheeks pinked up, and he rocked his hips, dragging the length of his cock along her slickness. She pressed her lips together, but it did nothing to hide the lust in her eyes. "Don't hold back, sexy girl. I want you wild for me." He grazed his teeth over her nipple again and again, rocking against her pussy, earning more sharp gasps and sinful sounds as she writhed and clawed at him.

"*I can't take it,*" she pleaded.

"I can stop," he teased.

Her eyes narrowed. "Not if you value your life."

He laughed and lowered his mouth over one taut peak, sucking *hard*. A loud, pleasure-drenched sound sailed from her lips…straight to his cock. He wanted to pound into her, to feel her pussy wrapped around his dick and hear her scream his name in the throes of passion. But he loved pleasuring her. Seeing her so unguarded and free was too intoxicating to rush. His time would come, and so would she. The possessive bastard in him was determined to do more than set a standard. He was going to pleasure her so thoroughly, she wouldn't be able to look at another man without thinking of him.

He continued teasing and taunting with his hands and mouth and angled his hips, giving her friction where she needed it most. "*Feels so good,*" she panted out. She grabbed his hips, holding him tight against her, moving with him. "*Don't stop,*" she pleaded as he teased one nipple with his teeth and tongue, rolling her other between his finger and thumb. He bit down at the same time as he squeezed her other nipple, just hard enough to send her over the edge.

"*Zan—*" shot from her lips.

Music to his fucking ears. She rocked and arched, drenching the length of his cock, her body trembling, her breath hitching, as she rode out her climax. As she came down from the high, eyes at half-mast, "*More*" slipped from her lips like a plea. He lowered his mouth over her nipple again, giving her what she craved, earning more of those addicting sounds as he shifted beside her, and moved his other hand between her legs, teasing her slick, silken flesh. He pushed two fingers into her tight heat, using his thumb on her clit and his mouth on her breast.

"*Yes—*"

She was so fucking beautiful, giving herself over to him. He curled his fingers, seeking that magical spot that would make her lose control, and knew just when he'd found it. Her hips shot up, and she gasped, her fingers digging into his flesh. He quickened his efforts, using teeth and tongue, learning her body like his new favorite song. Her breathing came in fast, hard bursts, and he knew she was close. Working her faster, he squeezed her nipple and applied pressure to her clit, and she detonated, screaming his name as her hips bucked, her inner muscles pulsing tight and hot around his fingers.

She moaned and writhed as she came down from the peak, and he sent her soaring again. This time he didn't wait for the orgasm to ease. He moved between her legs, spread her thighs with his hands, and buried his mouth between them. Her hips rose, but he held them down as he feasted and teased, taking her higher and keeping her there. He reveled in her pleasure, heightening his own. She made sounds he'd never heard before, a symphony so full of ecstasy, he knew he'd hear it in his sleep.

When she finally sank back down to the mattress, panting for air, he took his time kissing his way up her body, tasting all the places he'd missed on the way down. The slight swell beneath her belly button, those delicious hips, the curve of her waist, her ribs, the underside of her breasts, and finally, those slightly parted lips.

Her eyes fluttered open, her sated smile simmering in them. "Your lips really are lethal."

"Don't die on me, Flores. We're just getting started." He kissed her softly. "That is, unless you've changed your mind."

She held his gaze, so blissful and beautiful, as she whispered, "You're not getting away that easily." His heart took an unexpected hit. He lowered his lips to hers, kissing her tenderly, before getting up for a condom. She watched him sheath his length and dragged her teeth along her lower lip, which made her look innocent and seductive at once.

She reached for him as he came down over her, and he was painfully aware of everything about her, her softness, her sweet scent and trembling hands, and the vulnerability in her eyes, giving him pause. Sex usually took no thought. He'd have a few drinks, pick up a willing woman, and go for it. *This* was different. Whether he was alone in his feelings or not, Shauna was special.

She was his *wife*, and he already knew that once they came together, he'd never be the same again.

THIS DOESN'T HAVE to mean anything, Shauna told herself for the dozenth time.

Zander had already unraveled her more times than anyone ever had. She'd never felt anything like the waves of pleasure he brought, and now, as she reveled in the weight of him, the feel of his thick thighs pressing down on her, his formidable cock resting against her entrance, and his piercing blue eyes looking at her like she was *more* than just a moment, she tried to believe her lie. She had to. There was too much at stake not to.

As he laced their fingers together, pressing her hands into the mattress beside her head, the number four key chain charm she'd given him dangled between them, brushing the valley between her breasts, making their coupling feel even bigger, which she didn't think was possible. He lowered his lips to hers in a deep kiss, pulling her under, sinking into her slowly. She felt every blessed inch of his thick length stretching her deliciously, sending sparks skittering through her. When he was buried to the hilt, her breath rushed from her lungs, and he gritted out, *"Fuck, Angel."*

His eyes were volcanic and so full of emotions, they couldn't be real. *"Kiss me,"* she said to keep her own misguided emotions from pouring out. He did, and their bodies took over, urgently finding their rhythm. Their kisses were feverish and possessive, every thrust of his hips sending pleasure radiating through her.

"Need *more*," he growled against her lips, and then reclaimed her mouth more demandingly. He pushed his hands beneath her ass, angling her hips, driving deeper into her as he guided her legs around him. He felt impossibly bigger with every powerful thrust.

Oh, how she loved the way he took control. She felt like she was fully awake and alive for the first time in her entire life. She clung to him, wanted the scintillating sensations searing through her veins and billowing beneath her skin to last forever. Her hands roamed over his body, groping and clawing at his shoulders, back, and ass, but she couldn't get enough of him.

He quickened his efforts, her thoughts fragmenting. Lust coiled deep inside her, tightening with every thrust, until she felt like a top wound too tight. He pushed his hands into her hair and fisted them, sending an explosion of pain and pleasure crashing over her. She cried out, and the world spun away. She was lost in a surge of ecstasy and Zander, so wild and vast she could barely breathe.

Just when she started floating down from the crest, he

crushed his mouth to hers, pistoning his hips, hurling her right back up to the peak, and kept her there. When the intensity finally eased, she thought she must be dreaming. This much pleasure wasn't possible, but she wasn't dreaming. Zander was still kissing her, gyrating his hips, making her feel like she was going to burst again.

He tore his mouth away, his eyes blazing into her. "Sorry, darlin', but you feel too good. I'm not going to last."

Did he really think he was disappointing her? "So much for your review."

His head dipped beside hers, and his chest rocked with his silent laughter. He nipped at her shoulder and said, "It's your fault. It's never felt like this before."

Her thoughts stumbled with that confession. Just as she reminded herself that they were only words and didn't have to mean anything, he sealed his mouth over hers, and their bodies took over again. He pushed his arms beneath her, holding her so tight, they felt like one being. Electricity scorched through her, and with the next hard thrust, she was lost to another powerful climax, and *"Shauna—"* flew from his lungs like a curse. Every inch of her answered him, even as she whispered lies to her own heart.

When they finally collapsed to the mattress, breathless and sated, their bodies intertwined, he buried his face in her neck, whispering, "Sweet Shauna, you *destroy* me," and it felt like the truest thing on earth.

Chapter Twenty-Eight

ZANDER WATCHED THE soft morning light sneak in through the curtains, snaking over Shauna's waist as she slept. He was usually on his back patio by this time, coffee in hand, admiring the view of the ocean he'd disregarded for too long. He'd never make the mistake of overlooking what he was blessed to have again.

Shauna sighed in her sleep, cuddling closer, as if she knew he was thinking about her. Her breath was warm against his chest, and man, she'd been beautiful last night, with no walls, no sharp edges. Just her sassy, sweet self, unguarded, and so fucking real, she'd gotten deeper under his skin. He'd been awake for quite a while trying to puzzle out his emotions. But as he lay with her in his arms, her body curved into his like she belonged there, the urge to give in to them was so strong, he wondered if the accident had rattled his brain so much that it had fundamentally changed who he was.

He might lose words every now and again, but he knew it wasn't the accident bringing those emotions out in him. It was *her*.

They'd lost themselves in each other three times last night. That wasn't his intent with the honeymoon. Sure, part of him had hoped they'd eventually get together, but he wouldn't have pushed it. He would've been cool sleeping in separate rooms. He'd just wanted to give her everything she deserved, and all the things she'd never allow herself to want. A honeymoon was at the top of that list. But when they'd kissed on the boat and when he'd given her a chance to change her mind, he'd wanted to give her that, too. The power to decide and the safety to let go and allow herself to be cherished. He wondered if she knew that every touch, every kiss, and every breath had meant something.

She shifted again, snuggling in, her hand sliding up his chest. Her fingers brushed the number-four charm she'd given him, and she stilled.

His hand drifted up her back, and he kissed her head. "Morning, darlin'."

She tilted her face up, her brown eyes sleepy and a little guarded again. "Hi." She pulled the sheet up, moving her head from his chest to his arm. Her cheeks flushed, and she looked up at the ceiling.

He wasn't going to let her regret what they'd done. They could do this without screwing things up. He'd get ahold of his emotions. They'd never done him in before. "You okay, Flores?"

"Uh-huh. I'm good."

She was anything *but* good.

He rolled onto his side and brushed a lock of hair from her forehead. "Are you going to freak out on me?"

She scoffed. *"No."*

"Sure about that?" He cocked a brow. "It's okay to feel a little overwhelmed waking up naked with me for the first time. I am…*blessed.*"

She rolled her eyes, but she was smiling.

"Talk to me, darlin'."

"It's just weird."

"What is?"

"*This.* You and me. Naked. Waking up together. We weren't supposed to be this way, and now we are."

Fuck. His knee-jerk reaction was to make a joke, get out of bed, and go for a run. Anything to escape a truth he knew would cut him to his core. But he stopped himself. Not only because he needed to know if she regretted it, but because he would never disregard her like that. If she did regret being close to him, he'd find a way to make it up to her. To make it right, even if it killed him. "Do you regret last night?"

"*No.* That's the problem. It was too good to regret." Her pretty eyes narrowed, and a smile played on her lips. "*Don't* let that go to your head."

"Too late, darlin', it already did." High on her admission, he hooked a hand around her waist, pulling her closer. "You know, if you can get over the weirdness, it doesn't have to change things between us."

"Why isn't it weird for you? Because you have so much practice?"

"Don't knock the practice when you reap the benefits."

She rolled her eyes. "Forget I asked."

"Hey," he said softly, and pressed his hand to her cheek, drawing her eyes back to his. "I've been up for hours weeding through the weirdness."

"You have?" she asked disbelievingly.

"*Yes.* I didn't plan on sleeping with you, but I'm glad we ended up here. I enjoyed the hell out of pleasuring my wife and watching her take off like a rocket."

"*Ohmygod.*" Her cheeks reddened and she tried to turn

away, but his hand was still on her cheek, holding her there, so she had no choice but to look at him.

"We're great together, Angel, in and out of bed, and we're legally married, so unless you're worried that you're going to fall madly in love with me, which I'd understand—"

She cut him off with an incredulous stare.

"I'm just putting all the cards on the table. Short of that, there's no reason not to continue enjoying each other. It doesn't mean we have to ride off into the sunset for eternity. I know you're not looking for more, and I'm still figuring out who I am after nearly dying."

Her gaze softened. "I'm glad you didn't die."

"Yeah?"

"*Mm-hm.* I didn't realize how badly I needed to get laid."

Laughter burst from his lungs. "Is that so?"

Now she was laughing, too. "I told you it's been a while."

"Well, don't worry, Flores. I'm not going anywhere."

"That's a shame," she said casually. "I was hoping you'd be *coming* over here."

Jesus. They were fucking perfect together. He hauled her beneath him, earning the sweetest laughter, and pinned her hands to the mattress. "You want me to come, do you?"

"Mm-hm. *After* I do," she said sassily.

Damn, he loved that. "How does my greedy wife want to come first?" He wanted to explore her boundaries. "Do you want my mouth on your tits?" He kissed her deeply, earning a wanton moan. "Or do you want me to lick your pussy until you're so wet and needy, you beg me to fuck you."

"Yes—"

He tangled his fingers in her hair, tugging her head, earning a sexy gasp as he dragged his tongue along the column of her neck, and growled, "After you come on my mouth, I'm going to bend you over and fuck you so thoroughly, you'll feel me in your throat."

"God, yes—"

He crushed his mouth to hers in a brutal kiss. She was right there with him, opening her mouth wider, allowing his tongue to plunge deeper, to fuck her perfect mouth, the way he hoped one day soon she'd beg him to do it with his cock.

MUCH LATER THAT morning, after satiating their carnal needs, they headed out for breakfast. Zander had thought about leaving their plans up to chance, but he'd wanted to give Shauna a honeymoon that made her feel as special as she was becoming to him. He'd spent his lunch hours googling places in Niagara that he thought she would enjoy seeing. Zeke and Tobias had teased him relentlessly about texting with Shauna all week and about the trip, saying he was *mooning* over her. He'd shrugged them off, saying he had a reputation to uphold and that it would be easier to sell their relationship if he took her on a honeymoon.

He parked in front of the café and said, "Give me one sec." He reached across the cab of the truck and opened the glove compartment. Several individual creamer cups tumbled out. "Shit. Sorry."

Shauna laughed as they picked them up from the floor, their heads nearly touching. "You brought my creamer?" Her voice was laden with disbelief, but it was the appreciation in her eyes that had his gut twisting up again.

"I can't have my wife getting arrested for creamer hoarding on our honeymoon." He winked and climbed out of the truck.

The café had a warm blend of small-town charm and industrial chic, with open ceilings, exposed metal beams, and a chalkboard menu on a red accent wall behind the counter boasting a breakfast menu of omelets, bagels, a plethora of baked goods, and a few mile-high sandwiches. Shauna ordered a chocolate croissant, insisting she wasn't that hungry, but Zander knew better. He ordered a massive pastrami, egg, and cheese sandwich on a bagel, with a side of hashbrowns and sausage.

They found a booth and sat side by side, falling into easy conversation as they ate. They talked about the falls, the boat ride, and what they'd seen of the town, carefully avoiding any more conversation about what was or wasn't going on between them.

Zander found himself noticing little things about Shauna again. Like how when their legs brushed under the table, she got this cute little smile, and how she tore off pieces of her chocolate croissant, eating it bit by bit, then licking the chocolate off her fingers and thumb, and stealing forkfuls of his hashbrowns and sausage between conversations. Why did he find that so fucking adorable?

"What a perfect morning." He draped an arm around her. "This is how we should start every day."

"At a café?" She licked chocolate off her thumb. "That would get expensive."

"I meant waking up together, sharing a few"—he waggled his brows—"and *then* having a hearty breakfast. But don't worry, I'm cool with eating in…after I eat you out."

"Shh." She put her hand over his mouth, her gaze darting around their booth, at the customers sitting nearby.

He covered her hand with his and licked slow circles on her palm.

Her eyes took on that heady look she'd had last night, but it was gone as quickly as it had come, as if she caught herself enjoying that secret touch, and she tugged her hand away. She focused on the croissant, tearing off another piece. He snagged that tasty treat from her fingers with his teeth.

"Hey!"

He laughed and tugged her into a kiss.

"You're so greedy." She speared a piece of sausage with her fork and pointed it at him. "What'd I tell you about keeping those lethal lips to yourself?"

"I can't recall. I did just get over a head injury." He hooked the crook of his arm around her neck, drawing her closer, and said, "Kiss me again, and maybe I'll remember."

"Now you're just pushing it."

Yeah, he was, and he had no intention of stopping. "What can I say? I want to nail the role."

"I've got your number, Wicked." She lowered her voice. "You want to nail *me*."

"You don't have to lower your voice. That's not exactly a secret."

THEIR BANTER CONTINUED as Zander took her to a nearby small town he'd found online, and they spent the morning exploring cool shops and interesting galleries. He'd never had the urge to hold women's hands or buy them things, but whenever he was near Shauna, he wanted to be closer. He liked snagging her hand and stealing kisses, for which he gladly accepted her snark, and he wanted to buy her everything she liked. She wouldn't let him, of course. His temporary wife was too prideful and careful for that. But he convinced her to let him buy her lavender, chamomile, and peppermint essential oils from a local apothecary—*for when you've worked your muscles too hard and need your hubby to massage your pain away.* He looked forward to using them with her, and from the look in her eyes, so did she.

They hit a bookstore, where Shauna checked out the romance titles, and Zander skillfully avoided putting his nose in any books. He went to pick out a few cute bookmarks and a booklight for her, admiring her from afar as she read back covers and the first pages of several books. When he asked which books she wanted, she said she didn't want any of them and put the three she'd been holding back on the shelves. Then she went to use the ladies' room, and Zander bought those three books, along with the other goodies.

She eyed the bag as she came out of the bathroom. "What did you buy?"

"Just a few of the…" *Fuck.* The word escaped him. *Not now. Not fucking now.* "*Things* you didn't want," he said to cover his ass, and then it hit him. *Books.* Fucking *books.* He hated his fucked-up head.

"Zan, I have a book to read, remember? You bought me the paperback of the one I'm reading for the book club."

"Yes, but when we were moving your stuff into my house, we moved two boxes of books, and you said a girl can never have too many books or too much ice cream."

"I can't believe you remember that, but that doesn't mean you have to spend all of your money on me."

"Thanks for clarifying." He draped his arm around her, heading for the exit.

"You're a pain."

"Tell me something I don't know."

As they made their way through gift shops and more art galleries, he loved learning about the things she liked and the things she didn't, but the morning passed too quickly. It was already after twelve. He wanted to spend all day taking her places where he could learn more about her, but he also wanted to share more of himself with her and bring her further into his world.

Soon enough he'd do just that.

They checked out the rest of the shops in town, and when they left the last one, a pet store, where they bought Kitty a pink outfit that had DADDY'S GIRL written in black across the back, he said, "Think we can find one of these in your size that says BIKER DADDY'S RIDE OR DIE?"

Shauna looked at him like he'd lost his mind. "Thinking about selling me to your father?"

"Hell no. Why would you say that?"

"Because if you think I'm calling you *Daddy*, I'm going to have to annul this marriage right now."

"How about your *king*?" he teased, taking her hand as they headed to the truck.

"I wonder if that estate attorney handles annulments."

Backing her up against the truck, he said, "You're *not* annulling us."

"Why shouldn't I?"

"Because you like what we have."

"The legal agreement? That's kind of a necessity at this point, since I've already borrowed the money. But I *could* work the pole to pay you back. That might be easier than dealing with a greedy biker with enough big-dick energy for ten guys."

He probably shouldn't enjoy her snark as much as he did, but hell if it didn't make him like her even more. "As long as you're my wife, the only pole you're *working* is mine."

"That's a lot of possessiveness for a guy I'm contractually obligated to tolerate."

He slid his hands down her waist and grabbed hold of her hips, pressing his body into hers. "You didn't seem obligated this morning, when you begged me to fuck you."

"I did *not* beg you." Her smile glittered in her eyes. "I invited you because you looked lonely."

"I looked lonely, huh?" He rocked against her, enjoying the heat rising in her eyes.

"Terribly," she said, a little breathless, her fingers curling around his waist. "I felt bad for you, all alone on the other side of the bed."

"It sure didn't feel like a pity fuck when I was balls deep inside you and you were screaming my name loud enough for the people in Canada to hear you." He nipped at her neck, earning a ragged inhalation. "But it's good to know pity comes with tongue."

He squeezed her hips, grinding against her as he brushed his lips over hers again. She went up on her toes, trying to kiss him, but he shifted just out of reach and said, "Next time you feel obligated to kiss me, try not to beg."

He stepped back and dug his keys out of his pocket, leaving her stunned, her jaw gaping and her lust-filled eyes blinking.

"Ready for our next adventure?" He unlocked the truck, and after she climbed in, he said, "Just so we're clear, we may be contractually obligated to the marriage, but I don't spend time I don't want to give. I was kind of hoping you didn't, either."

He closed the door and headed around to the driver's side. As he settled behind the wheel, she said, "You're not an obligation. I was *kidding*."

The grin he'd been holding back broke free. "I know. I was just fucking with you."

"You jerk." She swatted him.

He caught her hand, hauling her into a kiss. "I like you, Flores, and I like fucking with you. Literally *and* figuratively." He let go of her hand and nodded to her side of the truck. "Now, plant that sexy little ass in your seat so I can show you a good time."

She smirked. "Wouldn't that be easier if I stayed over here with you?"

He knew she was trying to take the upper hand, but just the idea of her riding him in his truck made his body flame. "Climb on, darlin'." He called her bluff, pushed his seat all the way back, and reached for the button on his jeans.

"I don't think so," she said too damn innocently, and planted her hot little ass in her seat. "You see, I like fucking with you, too, Wicked."

Chapter Twenty-Nine

LITTLE DID SHE know how much he loved that.

An hour later, with their stomachs full and smiles on their faces, Zander drove to Silver-Stone Cycles, the manufacturer of the most sought-after custom motorcycles in the country. As he pulled into the parking lot, Shauna said, "Buying me a book is one thing, but you're *not* buying me a motorcycle."

"Before I can buy you a bike, I need to teach you to drive one. But one day you'll learn that when you tell me not to do something, it only makes me want to do it more." He climbed out of the truck and went around to help her out.

"You aren't *really* going to teach me to drive a motorcycle today, are you?" she asked as she took his hand and climbed down.

"What if I say yes?"

"Then you're definitely in need of a psychiatric evaluation."

"I know several people who might agree with you, but that's not why we're here. We're picking up my bike to go for a ride."

"You bought a new bike? *Here?*"

"No. This isn't a dealership. It's one of their manufacturing plants. My cousin Dixie's husband, Jace Stone, is one of the owners of this company. I had my bike transported here so I could take you for a ride on our honeymoon." He put a hand on her back, heading for the building, but she stopped cold.

"That must have cost a fortune. Why would you do that, when we can just go for a ride when we get back home?" She sounded seriously annoyed.

"Angel, you're married to a biker. I get that you don't really know what that means yet, but it's more than riding motorcycles. It's a state of mind. It's as much a part of me as the blood in my veins, and it comes before everything else except you and the rest of my family. I see stretches of highway and winding mountain roads, and I see freedom waiting to be chased. We're surrounded by gorgeous countryside, and I want to share that with you. I want to show you how it feels to leave your worries and everything else behind, and give yourself over to the wind and the open road."

Her brow furrowed, but her eyes took on that dreamy look she got when she first saw Kitty, and her tone softened. "Couldn't you have just rented a bike? I don't like you spending so much money because of me."

She said it so sweetly, the urge to gather her in his arms was overwhelming, but he was skating a dangerous line, having already revealed too much of the truth. He needed to put a little space between what he felt and their reality. "Well, then, darlin', you've got the wrong impression. Bringing my bike here is a purely selfish act. In my world, a man's bike is like his wife. There's no substitute, and no self-respecting biker puts his wife on the back of another man's bike for her first ride. If anyone's going to believe we're madly in love, you've got to get to the point where you'd be shocked if I *didn't* have my bike shipped here."

"I guess I didn't realize it was that important to you."

"Now you know. Are you cool with going for a ride?" He'd researched the area, and with the help of his cousins in Upstate New York, he'd figured out the best places to ride.

"Yes, but I've got to be honest. I'm nervous about it. I've seen some pretty gruesome motorcycle accidents."

Fuck. He'd been so excited to share this part of himself with her, he hadn't thought about that. He gave himself hell for acting like the old Zander, putting himself first and not slowing down enough to realize how scary this might be for her. "I'm sorry, Angel. I didn't think this through. We don't have to go."

"I want to," she said quickly. "I'm just nervous, but I know you'll drive safely, and you're right. If we're going to sell this relationship, I need to be your badass biker babe."

He grinned, relieved. "Are you sure? I don't want you to feel pressured into it."

"I'm no wallflower, remember? I speak my mind."

"You sure do. Thank you for trusting me. I got you something." He climbed into the back of his truck and opened the crossover tool box.

"Do I get my own power tools?" she asked as he snagged a bag from inside the box.

"Maybe someday if you play your cards right." He jumped out of the truck and closed the tailgate. "I wanted to surprise you with the ride, so I hid these back there in case you wanted to lie down in the backseat on the trip up." He pulled the black helmet he'd bought her out of the bag and handed it to her.

"It's so shiny and pretty." She turned it around, a flicker of surprise rising in her eyes as she brushed her fingers over ANGEL written in pink script on the back of her helmet. When she lifted her eyes to his, they were soft and alluring. "I love it. Thank you."

"Good. Hopefully you'll like this, too." He took the helmet from her and handed her the black leather jacket.

"Zan, this is too much," she said as she admired it.

"You need it for protection."

She wrinkled her nose. "I don't want to think about that, but I'm glad you did."

He watched as she turned the jacket around and saw ZAN'S ANGEL embroidered in the same pink script as her helmet, with four white-and-pink flowers beneath it. It wasn't just practical or thoughtful like the helmet. It was possessive. He was telling the world she was *his*. Her eyes brightened, beautifully unguarded for only a second or two before caution moved in.

"I figured you'll always be my Angel, even when we're no longer married, so…"

She smiled and thanked him, but the way she clutched the jacket against her chest, like it mattered, spoke the loudest.

"Let's go, biker babe." He slung an arm over her shoulder, and they went to get his bike.

After a quick but thorough lesson in passenger safety, they were on the road.

The engine roared, the wind whipped, but all Zander felt was *Shauna*, warm and solid against his back, her arms wrapped securely around him. She held him tighter around the turns, and before long, he noticed the slight shift in her weight as she allowed herself to trust him even more, leaning with him, following his lead.

He'd never driven slower, never leaned into curves more carefully, never before felt like everything in his life was this fucking perfect.

Chapter Thirty

SHAUNA KNEW THE damage motorcycles could do, the way twisted metal and broken bodies shattered lives. She should be tensing at every bump, bracing for every turn, but she wasn't. Zander had gone over what to expect, and he'd told her to tap his stomach if she wanted to stop. He'd said that tap was like her safe word, which had made her laugh, but it had also made her feel like she had a modicum of control. She hadn't realized she'd needed that control, but she was glad he had. She was still reeling from the gifts he'd given her. She probably should have given him a hard time for giving her a jacket that basically announced she was his property. But the part of her that she hadn't realized existed until he came into her life and treated her like she was special and worth protecting melted every time he called her Angel and liked being *his* Angel.

The soft leather jacket and the shiny helmet fit perfectly, and when she'd wrapped her arms around Zander, feeling his strength and confidence, that had felt perfect, too, and her fears had fallen away with the wind.

It didn't make sense. Nothing about them did, but when they were together, whether they were hanging out at home or knocking around town—or *apparently*, if she was in his arms or on the back of his bike—she felt safer than she ever had. Zander was giving her a lot of *never have I ever* moments. Like this glorious ride. As the world sped by, more vibrant and beautiful than ever, she'd never felt more at peace, or more invincible. That, she knew, wouldn't be possible without that feeling of safety.

She soaked in the views as they drove through one small town after another, reveling in the feel of Zander's muscles flexing against her chest and beneath her hands. The powerful, controlled shift of his weight and the heat blooming in all the places their bodies touched combined with the vibration of the engine in a new kind of foreplay.

This must be the freedom he was talking about, because she couldn't hold on to a single worry right now if she wanted to.

He turned down a rural road. Trees arched overhead and sunlight flashed through the canopies. When the trees gave way to grassy fields and meadows, they rounded a bend, and as they came out of it, they drove beneath an arched metal sign that read WELCOME TO WILDSIDE, and just beyond, a sprawling adventure park came into view. Shauna spotted a roller coaster in the distance, and two tall towers. Excitement bubbled up inside her as they cruised into the parking lot.

Zander parked and cut the engine, but Shauna's body continued vibrating as he pulled off his helmet and climbed off the bike. He raked his hand through his thick dark hair, his entire being radiating new light, as if the ride had rejuvenated him, too. As he locked his helmet to the handlebar, she took off hers and shrugged out of her jacket.

"There's my beautiful wife," he said, helping her off the bike.

Her stomach had been dipping all day at the way *wife* rolled off his tongue so easily. Now it dipped for a whole new reason. With the exception of the day of their wedding, she'd never been called beautiful before, much less *painfully beautiful*, the way Zander had last night, when he'd looked at her in the same way he was looking at her now. Like he truly believed it.

"I hope this is okay," he said. "I thought it would be fun to do some of the things you missed out on as a kid."

Her heart stumbled. "It's better than okay. It's perfect."

"Great." He locked her helmet to the bike and tucked her jacket into the saddlebag. "What's the verdict on the motorcycle ride? Still willing to be my ride or die?"

"That depends. If I say no, are we going to leave without going in there?"

"I'm not that callous." He smirked. "I'll let you have your fun, but I might have to leave you in the woods on the way out."

"How do I drive this thing again?" She started to climb back on the bike.

He laughed and pulled her into his arms, pinning her with a playful gaze. "Spill it, Flores. Did you hate the ride?"

"No. I liked it *too* much."

"Impossible. There's no such thing, and I kind of dig that liking things with me is a recurring theme for you."

"Don't let it go to your head or anything," she teased. "I thought the ride would feel reckless and dangerous, but it didn't. I felt free, like nothing could touch me and anything was possible."

He tilted his handsome face up to the sky and said, *"Yes!"*

She loved seeing him so happy. "But I can see how people could end up driving too fast and get caught up in what's around them instead of focusing on the road."

"It's different when you're the driver. I'm *more* focused on the road and hazards when I'm on my bike than I am when I'm driving a car or truck. And with you on the back, I'm a thousand times more careful than I am when I'm alone."

"Well, since you're my husband now, could you please pay more attention to the road when you're alone?"

"Careful, Angel. Sounds like you're starting to catch feelings for me."

Feeling too seen, she said, "Don't flatter yourself," and stepped out of his arms, seeking safer territory. "I just don't want you to kick off until after you teach me to ride."

"I'll try not to, darlin'." He draped an arm over her. "Let's go have some fun."

Gravel crunched under their feet as they made their way into the park. The scent of popcorn and hot dogs wafted around food stands, while bells and whistles drifted out of an arcade, mingling with the din of the crowd and the whirr of go-karts and other rides. In the distance, people whipped along ziplines from the high towers she'd seen. Her nerves pinged. Not just from the excitement of being there but from the quiet war waging inside her. This trip, and this man and his family and his help, was all so unexpected and over the top, she felt like she was stealing happiness instead of being offered it.

Zander tightened his arm around her shoulder. "You okay, Flores?"

"Yeah. Just thinking."

"Thinking about me can be a dangerous habit."

She smiled. "I never said I was thinking about you."

"You didn't have to." He nodded to the go-karts. "Ready to get your butt whipped?"

"You really are a dreamer. I'm going to blow you away."

"I look forward to it." He winked.

She wrinkled her brow. "You do?"

"Oh, wait, you said *away*, didn't you?" He flashed an arrogant grin.

"Zander!" She swatted his arm, but now that enticing image was stuck in her head.

"What?" He laughed. "I heard you say you wanted to blow me and got a little lost in it." He pulled her closer, speaking gruffly into her ear. "Bet you're thinking about me now."

He was irresistibly wicked, but she'd never tell him that.

They made their way to the track and waited for their turn. When the gate opened, Zander swatted her ass as she walked through it, sending sparks skittering through her. She glowered at him and climbed into a go-kart.

He leaned in, his fingers brushing her arm. "I'm coming for you, wifey."

"Don't you always?" she retorted, earning a sexy laugh and a toe-curling kiss that left her a little dazed as he sauntered off like a proud peacock to his own go-kart.

That dazed feeling was quickly replaced with adrenaline as they raced around the track, egging each other on. Zander flashed that infuriatingly charming, smug grin that dared her to try harder, and she pushed the pedal to the metal, trying to ignore the completely inappropriate and entirely unhelpful butterflies he caused. She blew past him, and her all-seeing butterfly-inducing temporary husband looked at her like he knew what she was battling. She swerved in front of him, and he slipped to the inside lane, slowing to blow her a kiss. *Bastard.*

By the final lap, she was laughing so hard her ribs hurt. When was the last time she'd laughed like that? In the end, they tied, but she had a feeling that was by his design, which only further endeared him to her.

They went from one ride to the next and hit the arcade, talking over the tinny music and the clatter of tokens. She beat him in pinball, and his groan of defeat was sweeter than any prize she could've won. She'd forever remember the faint smell of gasoline and river water when they raced other couples in miniature speedboats, shouting to be heard over the roar of the engines, and cheering when they were first to cross the finish line.

It was a whirlwind day of laughter, stolen kisses, and special moments that felt like treasured secrets. Like when they were waiting for their turn on the zipline. Launching herself off a platform sixty feet in the air wasn't her kind of thrill. Survival was. But as she watched others take the leap, she was buzzing with anticipation and fear, and then Zander's strong arms circled her from behind. His scruff brushed against her cheek, and he said, "Scared?"

"Maybe a little," she admitted. "Is it safe?"

"Yes. I wouldn't have brought you here if I hadn't checked out their safety record first. But if you want to back out, we can walk right back down those steps."

He'd checked out their safety record? She didn't know the man he used to be, the one who didn't think things through, but he definitely wasn't that guy with her. She'd written off risks and adrenaline rushes after getting sober, fearing they might lead to an urge for old habits. But with Zander, what she desired had nothing to do with escaping life. He made her want to live it to the fullest and experience the things people who hadn't spent their childhoods running and hiding had enjoyed. And she wanted to experience them with him.

She put her hands over his, turning her head so she could

see his face, and said, "Okay. I'll do it. You haven't led me astray yet."

"And I never will," he promised, and then he kissed her.

Desperately trying to shore up the walls that had kept her heart safe for so long, she told herself that he took pride in helping others, and that was all this was. A vow to a friend to keep her safe, just like he'd made the night Brian had hurt her.

Much later, as the sun made a slow descent, they found themselves at the ice cream counter. Shauna ordered a scoop of chocolate chip, and Zander told the guy to put it in a waffle cone with chocolate syrup, whipped cream, and rainbow sprinkles. Then he leaned closer to her and said, "I would have made it two scoops, but we have dinner plans," chipping away at those walls once again.

Chapter Thirty-One

THEY STOPPED AT Silver-Stone to return his bike for its transport back to Bayside and picked up the truck. The drive back to the falls was filled with quiet contentment. Shauna liked getting to know, and being part of, these other sides of Zander. She hadn't understood his need to ship his motorcycle out at first, but having seen the joy it brought him and experiencing the thrill firsthand, she was glad he had.

He drove to Goat Island, and as they climbed out of the truck, they were greeted by the sound of the falls and dusky shades of purple and pink painting the sky.

"The sky is so pretty here. It looks like a painting," she said.

"It's pretty everywhere, but you, my sweet wife, rarely slow down enough to notice, like me before the accident."

He took her hand, heading across the parking lot. She saw Top of the Falls Restaurant, but instead of following the other people making their way there, he led her down a walkway. They passed tall trees and beautiful flowers and came to a grassy knoll, where a handful of people were milling about and taking pictures of the falls. Zander led her past them, around a small group of trees, to a picnic spread out in the grass, so beautiful it knocked the air from her lungs. Solar candles flickered around a blue-and-white blanket, with flowers in mason jars and glass-topped platters of cheese, crackers, bread, and fruit, and skewers of meat and vegetables.

"We'll have a great view of the fireworks from here," Zander said, as if he hadn't just turned this public park into something right out of a movie.

Every time she told herself to pull back, he said or did something that drew her deeper into him. She knew she shouldn't get lost in it. That he was just living up to his promise to give her a memorable honeymoon. But she might never feel this way again, and she didn't want to distance herself from the warmth settling inside her. When she turned to him, the softness in his gaze did her in. "This is beautiful, thank you." She went up on her toes and kissed him.

It was just a quick press of her lips, but as she sank down to her heels, noticing other couples watching them with envy and awe, her nerves spiked, and she tried to make light of it. "It's a good thing I never want to get married, because I don't think anyone could ever top this."

"I expect to see that noted in the review."

She was glad for his levity. It eased the tightness in her chest. "Ten gold stars for Zander Wicked, setting the bar high in *and* out of the bedroom."

Dinner was perfectly simple, and conversation came as naturally as it always did. When they were finished, one of the waitstaff from the restaurant came to collect their dishes, leaving them with the blanket, flowers, and candles to take home. Shauna pretended not to notice Zander slipping him a wad of cash.

As the evening wore on, they fell into comfortable silence, surrounded by the sounds of the falls and the din of the people arriving for the fireworks. "It's so quiet, it feels like everyone's holding their breath," she said.

"It's hard to believe there was a time when I couldn't stand the quiet."

"You mean when you first got sober?" he asked, crossing his legs at the ankles as he leaned back on his palms, his shoulder brushing hers.

"Mm-hm. How did you know?"

"You mentioned it the night you moved in. You said you and Brian became gym rats, and you volunteered at the firehouse. I get it. My internal thoughts are loudest when the rest of the world is quiet, too. It used to drive me crazy."

"Really? Your life seems so good. I mean, I was fighting the urge to drink to avoid thinking about all the ways my family let me down and how long I let myself live in a state of only being half aware of everything around me. But you've got an amazing family and great friends, and from what you've said, you've always had women at your beck and call. Most guys would kill to have your life."

He smiled, but there was a shadow in his eyes. "Yeah, well, most guys didn't spend years convinced they were stupid because they couldn't read like everyone else." He sat up, bent one knee, and hooked his arm over it. He looked away, his hand curled into a fist.

Her heart squeezed. "You had trouble reading?"

"Still do." He looked at her then, the vulnerability in his eyes in stark contrast to the pushy, powerful man she knew him to be. "Dyslexia. It's a bitch, and mine's pretty fucking bad. If it weren't for Zeke helping me with every single assignment, I never would've gotten through elementary school, much less graduated from high school."

"Oh, *Zan*." She touched his leg, remembering how he'd asked her to read the list from her phone when they were writing up the prenup. "I don't know much about dyslexia, but I know how hard it is feeling different from other kids. I'm sorry you went through that."

"It sucked, but it's no big deal. I use a text-to-speech app now, so it's all good. I just wanted you to know that I get it, and my life hasn't always been perfect."

She saw how hard this was for him, but she wanted him to know he could trust her and she wouldn't judge him. "I'm glad technology helps, but don't minimize what you went through. You just said you spent years feeling like you were stupid. That's an awful feeling. If you don't want to talk about it, that's okay, but please don't pretend it wasn't hard for my benefit. I understand hard and all the shit that comes with it."

"I wouldn't want to knock down my ten-star rating."

"You couldn't if you tried. I want to know what it was like for you. Did they even know what dyslexia was when you were in elementary school?"

He gave her a wry smile and bumped her with his shoulder. "Are you calling me old, Flores?"

"*No*, but the facts are the facts," she teased, earning a genuine smile.

"They didn't test for it back then, and I had no idea that other kids didn't see letters moving across the page or all mixed up. I thought it was normal and I was just an idiot because I couldn't make sense of it."

"I totally understand that. It's funny the way a little kid's mind works. I didn't realize all parents weren't like mine until fifth or sixth grade, and then I felt ashamed and tried to sink into the background, hoping nobody would notice."

"I did the opposite. I learned to joke around and be outrageously loud to distract people from my inability to read, which made it harder for my teachers and family to realize I had issues that went beyond being a jokester or too lazy to do the work. But that's nothing compared to what you went through. I had support every step of the way, even if it was misguided."

"It's different but just as challenging," she said. "What did your parents do?"

"They tried to get me to settle down and focus, which made me feel even dumber, because I was focusing as hard as I could and still not measuring up. And remember, I had smart older brothers who could figure shit out with one read or by being told things once, so I made it my goal to prove I was as good as or better than them in other ways."

"What other ways?"

"I don't know. Everything from running faster to being funnier. If they got a nod from our old man for mowing the lawn straight, I'd make sure the lines looked like a damn baseball field. If they made a girl smile, I'd..." His brows knitted. "Holy shit." A disbelieving laugh fell from his lips, and he scrubbed a hand down his face.

"What?"

"Women. They started out as part of that competition. My brothers have always been the coolest guys I know. I remember watching them pick up girls when I was thirteen or fourteen and thinking, *I can do that. I'll get the prettiest girls and prove I'm cooler than them.*" He shook his head. "I forgot all about that. What a fool I was."

"You weren't a fool. You wanted to win." She smiled and said, "Besides, a wise man once told me not to knock the practice when you reap the benefits."

"You're a'right, Flores."

"Thanks." She gazed out at the people gathering around the railing. "I guess reading music is different from reading words?"

"No. It's all the same. I tried learning to read music, but it was too frustrating. Mads saw me struggling and taught herself to play the guitar when she was twelve so she could teach me to play by ear."

"Wow. That's amazing." She lifted his hand and touched the tattoo on his middle finger. "Now this musical note makes sense. It represents you, doesn't it? Trapped by your dyslexia? The barbed wire?"

He tilted his head. "You know what a sforzando is?"

"You have a tattoo of my initials on your finger. Did you think I wouldn't google it to see if it was really a musical abbreviation or if I'd married a psycho stalker?"

He almost smiled, but he glanced at the tattoo, his expression serious. When he finally said, "Yeah, it's me," it came out raw.

A distant boom drew their attention, the telltale hiss of fireworks nearly drowned out by the roaring falls. An explosion of red burst into dazzling streaks of light as sounds of excited awe rose from the crowds around them. She and Zander lowered themselves to their backs on the blanket to watch the show. But as fireworks bloomed against the night sky, she couldn't stop thinking about the magnitude of what he'd shared.

She wanted to share something with him, too. "You know that beach party you drove me home from on my twentieth birthday? The whole reason I was there was for the sparklers. When I was little, all the other kids were allowed to hold them on the Fourth, but my parents wouldn't let me. They said they didn't want me to get hurt, but I think it was really because they didn't want me to feel like the other kids. They didn't want me to be as happy as they were, because then I might notice the difference in our families. How unhappy mine was compared to theirs. I really don't think my parents knew I felt that difference every minute of every day."

Zander's fingers curled around hers. "I'm sorry, darlin'."

"Me too. Brian had heard that the people who threw the party on the beach handed out sparklers. That's why we went. But we never got that far. We hooked up with kids we knew and got rip-roaring drunk and high before heading to the beach. I was my own worst enemy."

"You were a frightened girl trying to make it in a world you were never taught to navigate. My parents host that beach bash on the Fourth every year. We'll go this year and celebrate your birthday."

She longed to celebrate with him and his family, but she had to work, and nobody liked to swap shifts on holidays. It wasn't like she was used to birthday celebrations anyway. Birthdays had never been a big deal when she was growing up. Her parents would give her a small gift and present her with a store-bought cake, both of which had felt like obligations. They'd gone to see fireworks a few times when she was a kid, but not often. Brian gave her a card every year, and she'd miss that this year as much as she missed him.

"I wish I could, but I have to work."

"You're doing good work, Angel." He squeezed her hand again, and they went back to watching the fireworks. The air crackled with excitement as thunderous booms rang out, showering them with a visual feast of vibrant colors. When he laced his fingers with hers, she glanced at him. His jaw was tight, and he was staring absently at the sky. She wondered what he was thinking and pressed a kiss to his shoulder, then rested her head there.

A few minutes later, he said, "Hey, darlin'."

"Yeah?"

"Nobody else knows what that tattoo means."

The heady emotions in his voice stirred something in her chest, as hot and bright as the fireworks. "Your secret is safe with me." Not wanting him to worry about her breaking that promise after their obligation was over, she added, "Always."

His chest rose and fell with a long exhalation, as if he had been holding his breath. He held her a little tighter and pressed a kiss to her forehead, murmuring, "Yours, too."

THE LAST SHIMMER of fireworks faded into the night, leaving only the roar of the falls and the murmur of the dispersing crowd. The fireworks were incredible, but it was the way Zander held her, the closeness she felt once she fully let her guard down, that had her wishing it could continue all night.

She started to get up, but Zander kept her close and said, "Let the crowd go first."

In no rush for their night to end, she smiled against his chest, drenched in happiness.

They stayed that way for a long while, eventually making their way back to the hotel. The night replayed in her mind as they walked into the suite for the last night of their honeymoon. The sight of separate bedrooms made her nerves prickle. Would it be wrong to ask him if they could stay in the same room again? Should she expect they would? She looked from the bedrooms to him, at a loss for words, and blurted out, "I'm going to take a quick shower before bed."

He stepped forward, sliding his strong arms around her waist, heat rising in his eyes. "Then do I get to fuck my wife again?"

Yes, yes, yes! "Is that *all* I get? Just a fuck? That's a little disappointing after last night." Feeling saucy, she pushed from his arms and said, "Why don't you make a better plan while I rinse off?" She turned on her heel and sauntered toward her bedroom.

He scooped her up, and she laughed as he charged through the bedroom door.

"*What* are you doing?" she asked through her laughter.

"I made a better plan. We're showering together."

Through laughter and kisses, they stripped off their clothes and ducked into the shower, locking lips as the warm water rained down on them. His kisses always turned her inside out, but with water seeping between their lips and his rigid cock sliding against her belly, it felt sinful and erotic. They groped and caressed, his every touch taking her higher, until she felt like she was going to burst. She reached for his cock at the same time he pushed a hand between her legs.

Yes...

They moaned into fervent kisses. She stroked as he teased, their hips thrusting and rocking. She was on fire, and she wanted *more*. She wanted to feel his hard length in her mouth, taste his salty skin, and see him lose his mind for her.

"You fucking kill me," he growled against her lips, then crushed his mouth to hers, backing her up against the cold tiles. His fingers worked their magic, taking her up onto her toes as she stroked his hard length. "Do you know how badly I wanted to get my hands on you today?"

"You should've done it."

His eyes drilled into her. "You would've been cool with me pulling off the road to bend you over my bike and fuck you into next week?"

Her body flamed, and "Uh-huh" fell desperately from her lips, surprising her. But she knew she would not only have let him do it, but she would have loved it. "As long as no one could see us."

"Fuck." He took her in another brutal kiss, expertly teasing her nipples until they throbbed. Then he blazed a path down her body with his strong hands and talented mouth and pushed her legs apart, growling, "Eyes on me. I want to see the pleasure in them when you scream my name."

She gladly obliged, watching as he used the tip of his tongue to taunt her most sensitive nerves and slid two fingers inside her, fucking her with them as his mouth wreaked havoc with her senses. He stopped finger fucking her, zeroing in on that magical spot inside her that sent pins and needles racing through her core. He took her clit between his teeth, and the breath rushed from her lungs. She went up on her toes, digging her fingernails into his shoulders as he did something that sent waves of pleasure crashing over her. *"Zan—"* flew from her lips, her body quaking and bucking.

He stayed with her, drawing out her pleasure, and as she came down from the high, he sent her reeling again. She grasped at his head, his hair, his shoulders, anything to combat her weakening legs as she surrendered to another earth-shattering orgasm.

He kissed his way up her body, every touch of his lips igniting sparks against her skin. He was so damn sexy with the water raining down on him, she put her hands on his chest and said, "My turn."

She pushed him back against the wall, and he laughed in surprise. But that laughter quickly turned to gritted-out curses and rough praise as she explored his magnificent body, kissing and touching him, from his powerful shoulders, hard pecs, and rippled abs to his thick thighs and, finally—*God, finally*—she wrapped her hand around his thick, hard cock, earning the darkest look she'd ever seen. She was no expert at this, having done it only a few times, but the way he was looking at her made her feel empowered, like she could do no wrong, and she clung to that confidence like a lifeline.

The shower rained down on her as she licked him from base to tip, earning a guttural moan. She stroked him as she swirled her tongue around the broad head, then slicked her tongue again down the length and teased his balls. "*Fuck*, Angel."

He fisted his hands in her hair, sending shocks of pain and pleasure down her body. As she took him in her mouth, his hands tightened in her hair, his eyes boring into her as his cock hit the back of her throat. He growled. Wanting to hear more of *that*, she stroked and sucked, loving the way he watched her, the way he gave her total control of their pace, but held tight enough to send scintillating sensations scorching through her. When she worked him faster and tighter, he made more of those gruff growls, spurring her on.

"*Fuck, Angel. I'm gonna blow.*"

It was a warning she had no interest in heeding. She took him deeper, stroking faster. His entire body flexed, and his hips thrust so hard, she had to grab his leg to keep her balance as "*Shauna—*" tore from his lungs like a bullet, and salty jets spilled down her throat. Gratification, pride, and immense pleasure swamped her as she stroked and sucked, taking everything he had to give until he sank back against the wall, his body jerking with aftershocks.

"Jesus, Angel." Hands still tangled in her hair, he tugged her up to her feet, searching her eyes. His warm hands slipped from her hair to her jaw, rubbing it tenderly. He didn't say a word as one arm circled her waist, drawing her into a blistering kiss. It wasn't urgent or feverish, but even more confident and possessive than ever.

The kind of kiss that said things were different now.

When they stepped from the shower, he dried her off and led her into the bedroom, where they fell ravenously into each other's arms again, and as their bodies came together, *different* was exactly how she felt.

Chapter Thirty-Two

SHAUNA WAS EXCITED and nervous as she stepped onto the upper deck of the Salty Hog, where she was meeting Madigan and the other girls for lunch. She'd gotten to know them pretty well the night of the wedding, and even better through group texts, but that didn't mean getting together for the first time was going to be easy breezy. Nothing in her life was easy breezy, but she'd settle for comfortable enough that her stomach didn't hurt.

She spotted Madigan standing by their table holding Marybelle, who looked adorable with a sprig of a hair gathered in a water fountain on the top of her head tied with a pink bow. Emerson was holding Brennan on her lap, his dark hair as spiky as the last time she'd seen him. Having grown up with shit parents, Shauna had a special place in her heart for children.

The girls saw her heading their way and they all waved, flashing welcoming smiles that helped ease Shauna's nerves.

"Sorry I'm late," she said. "I forgot I had to stop for gas."

"Sha Sha!" Marybelle reached for her.

"I see where I rank," Madigan said as she handed Marybelle over in her little yellow dress with happy animal faces on it. Marybelle immediately grabbed Shauna's cheeks, pulling her closer to rub noses.

Shauna melted a little inside. "I missed you, too, cutie."

"I'm glad you made it," Madigan said, and hugged her around Marybelle. All the girls echoed her enthusiasm. "Marly and Evie couldn't make it, but you'll meet them at the book club meeting if not before."

"I look forward to it." Through their group texts, Shauna had gotten to know Marly, a close friend of the Wickeds, who was engaged to Dante Dubois, a musician, and Evie, Baz's bestie, who'd recently gotten engaged to the other veterinarian in Baz's office, Quinton Anthony.

"Shauna, you look amazing," Chloe said as Shauna sat down and settled Marybelle on her lap.

"I do?" She looked down at her jeans and loose blue tank top.

"You really do," Leah said. "You look refreshed."

"Thanks," Shauna said. "You all look great, too. Where's Leo today?"

"With Papa Tank, having a Daddy-son day," Leah said as Ginger and Conroy sidled up to the table.

Ginger placed a hand on Madigan's and Leah's shoulders and said, "It's so nice to see all our girls together."

"G'ma! Pawpaw!" Brennan exclaimed, his little arms shooting up.

As Ginger reached for Brennan, Marybelle exclaimed, "Gampa!" and scrambled off Shauna's lap.

"Come here, Princess." Conroy scooped Marybelle up, nuzzling her cheek, while Ginger tickled Brennan's belly, and adorable giggles filled the air.

"It's such a shame they're not happy to see you," Shauna teased, and everyone laughed.

"We're lucky." Ginger turned a warm smile on her and said, "How was your honeymoon, sweetheart?"

It had been a week and a half since they'd gotten back from the honeymoon. A week and a half since they'd walked into his cottage and Zander had said, *Should I just put your stuff in my room? You know you're going to end up in there anyway. Sure* had rolled out of Shauna like a foregone conclusion. Ten glorious days of good-morning kisses and coffee by the ocean, sexy showers, flirty, dirty texts, fun renovation projects, and with the exception of the nights she'd worked, enjoying the steamiest sex of her life. The massage oil he'd gotten her was the best present *ever*.

But Shauna couldn't tell them any of that, so she went with what she'd told the girls when they'd texted about it last week. "It was great. Zander is always fun to be with, and he shocked the heck out of me with that trip. He's going above and beyond to make our arrangement believable, which I appreciate."

"He sure is," Ginger said. "I'm glad you had a good time."

"He's not being too pushy, is he?" Conroy asked. "At church last week he said he wrangled you into helping him renovate his cottage."

"Zander is always pushy," Madigan chimed in.

"That's part of his charm," Shauna said. "And he did wrangle me into helping him renovate, but it's the least I can do with everything he's doing for me and Brian."

"Leave it to Zander to put his wife to work," Sid said. "Does he force you to cook, too?"

"*No.* He knows I can't cook, and I've got to tell you, Reba is amazing. She left us dinner in the fridge for the night we got home from the trip. All we had to do was heat it up, *and* she put about two weeks' worth of food in the freezer."

"Food is one of our mama love languages," Ginger said. "Reba and I keep everyone's freezers stocked up from time to time."

"And we greatly appreciate it," Emerson said, and the other girls concurred.

"We all do, but more importantly, Shauna, don't let my brother take advantage of you. You don't have to help him renovate," Madigan said. "It's not like you're not paying him back for helping Brian."

"He's not forcing me to help. I enjoy it, and I'm learning a lot from him." *Like how fun it is to be bent over the counter and to ride him when he's sitting on a kitchen chair.* She was also learning a lot about renovating and was thoroughly enjoying that, too. "You should see the kitchen. It's beautiful. The cabinets are finished, and this week we're choosing the crown molding. Once that's done, we'll paint and then conquer the living room."

"There's nothing wrong with getting your hands dirty," Ginger said.

"I was surprised at how satisfying it is," Shauna said.

"That's what he said," Sid chimed in, making everyone laugh.

"Let's not go down that road," Conroy warned. "We have a surprise for Shauna and our very special mama-to-be, Emerson." He pulled a stack of long, narrow, laminated menus from his back pocket and handed them to the girls. "Our new mocktail menu."

"Yum!" Reese said.

"That's so nice of you." Emerson got up to hug them.

Surprised and touched that they'd included Shauna, she said, "Thank you for thinking of me."

"You're family, darlin'," Conroy said. "We'll always think of you."

"I told Zander we're keeping her after the divorce," Madigan said proudly, and the others nodded and murmured in agreement.

Shauna's chest felt full as they looked over the menu of virgin daiquiris and other mocktails with cute names like Pineapple Punch, Blueberry Mockito, Wicked Watermelon-Basil Fizz, and Chocolate Mocktini. They really made her feel like one of them, and she wondered if it was possible to fall for an entire family.

"A Blueberry Mockito sounds perfect to me," Leah said.

They all placed their drink orders, and when Emerson reached for Brennan, Ginger said, "Don't even think about it. You enjoy lunch with the ladies, and I'll enjoy my grandson."

"Con?" Chloe stood up to get Marybelle.

Conroy rubbed noses with Marybelle and said, "Your mama is so silly. We have work to do. We need to call Grandpa Preacher and make him jealous."

Shauna and the girls laughed as Conroy and Ginger walked away with the kids.

"All right, *Sha Sha*, spill it," Madigan said. "What's happening with you and Zander?"

Caught off guard, Shauna reached for her water and said, "What do you mean?"

"We never got the juicy honeymoon details," Chloe added.

"I don't need *all* the juicy details. He is my brother," Madigan said. "But is there any chance of a surprise pregnancy?"

Shauna nearly choked on her water.

"*Mads,*" Sid chided. "Not everyone wants to talk about their sex lives."

"You cannot tell me that you're not all dying to know," Madigan said.

"Shauna, you do not need to disclose that information," Reese said.

Shauna didn't want to share the juiciest details of their relationship, but she was so happy, she wanted to tell them how wonderful Zander was. He deserved the accolades, and she had no one else to gush about her husband to. She was bursting at the seams to say something. Choosing her words carefully, she said, "We're having a good time. I mean, how can we not? It's Zander. Everything he says is funny, charming, or inappropriate, and I love that about him. Plus, he's incredibly thoughtful, and I mean, let's face it, he's ridiculously hot. All of which makes him irresistible, and he knows it, so he uses it to his advantage."

"Yay!" Madigan said.

"I don't mean to be nosy, but can you qualify *good time*?" Reese leaned her elbow on the table and rested her chin in her palm, looking at her expectantly.

"She just did," Leah said. "She said he uses it to his advantage."

"I'm a scientist. I don't want to assume," Reese pointed out.

All eyes turned to Shauna.

She lowered her voice and said, "Let's just say we're enjoying the benefits of our temporary marriage, and please don't let that information leave this table."

"Yes!" Madigan exclaimed. "I've been hoping you guys would get together."

Shauna's stomach twisted. "I don't want you to get the wrong impression. We're just having fun for now, Mads." It was a good reminder to herself as much as to them.

"Well, you make a cute couple, even if temporary," Emerson said.

"Thanks," she said as Starr, a tall blonde with long, kinky hair and colorful tattoos, arrived at the table with their mocktails.

As Starr set a Chocolate Mocktini in front of Shauna, she said, "I heard you and Zan went on a honeymoon. How was it?"

Unlike the girls, Starr didn't know about Shauna and Zander's arrangement, so she played it up. "It was amazingly romantic."

"Really?" Starr asked with surprise. "I never would have guessed Zander to be a romantic."

"None of us did," Madigan said, giving Shauna a conspiratorial glance. "But love is a magical thing."

"Speaking of love, Starr," Chloe said. "How are things between you and Justice?"

Leah leaned closer to Shauna and said, "Justice is a Dark Knight."

"He and Starr have little girls around the same age, and they take dance together," Emerson explained.

Starr sighed. "We *were* taking it slow, but that man is a decadent dark-chocolate sundae, and I couldn't resist."

The others cheered and peppered her with questions, asking if things were serious and if their girls knew and offered support by sharing advice like, *When it's real, that's how fast it happens.*

Starr lowered her voice and said, "The girls don't know, but I think we're both falling, and we'll probably tell them soon."

Shauna felt a pang of jealousy as the others gushed about how happy they were for Starr. *Get a grip, Flores. That's the difference between true love and a contractual arrangement.* She tucked away those wayward feelings.

"I need to take your orders and get back to work," Starr said.

"Before you take our orders," Chloe said. "Can everyone make it the last Sunday of the month for the book club meeting? It's going to be at Indian Neck Beach."

Shauna pulled out her phone and checked her schedule, while the others talked excitedly about the Paris-themed meeting. She was glad to see she wasn't scheduled to work that day, and said she'd be there, too.

After placing their orders, they sipped their mocktails, chatting about books, and the girls told her more about the book club. The conversation moved from that to Brennan's upcoming birthday party on Saturday. The girls were thrilled to hear Zander had already asked Shauna to go with him to it.

"And don't forget you're coming to my wedding in November, with or without my brother," Madigan said.

"How could I forget that?" Shauna said, although she didn't want to think about going without Zander. But did she really have to? She and Zander had become incredible friends above all else. They could attend her wedding as friends, couldn't they? It wasn't like after they ended their marriage they'd be on the hunt for long-term partners. She told herself they could, and joined in for the rest of the wedding conversation.

Their lunches came, and as if Zander knew Shauna was thinking about him, her phone chimed with a text. She'd sent him a video of a cat patio earlier and had said Kitty needed one.

Zander: *What does it say about me that you're thinking about my Kitty while I'm thinking about yours?*

A devil emoji popped up.

Shauna's cheeks burned.

"Girl," Madigan said, drawing out the word. "What is in that text?"

"Nothing." Shauna tried to tamp down her smile, failing miserably, and quickly pocketed her phone.

"I love when Tank texts me *nothing*," Leah said, and the girls laughed.

"Seriously," Shauna said. "I sent him a picture of a cat patio that a guy built outside his window. It's caged in, so his cat can get out, and I told Zan that Kitty needed one."

"Don't encourage him," Chloe said.

"Zander is the last guy I would ever think would buy clothes for a pet," Emerson said.

"He loves Kitty," Shauna said.

"I think it's a cute idea," Madigan said.

"It would be a cuter idea if Kitty had a friend to share it with," Sid suggested. "We have some adorable kittens at the rescue."

"Don't get sucked in," Reese warned. "She'll have you adopting six of them before you know it."

The girls laughed.

"Zander would have to build another closet if he gets another cat," Shauna said. "Kitty has a bigger wardrobe than I do."

"That's because he's a great cat dad," Madigan said. "He'd be a great baby dad, too."

"Mads, give her a break," Sid said. "On another note, who's going to Bikes on the Beach this year?"

There was a collective "We are" from Madigan, Chloe, Leah, and Reese.

Shauna hoped the girls didn't notice she hadn't responded. The event was after the end of her and Zander's arrangement, and she didn't want to think about it.

"It's too close to my due date," Emerson said. "But I've heard some wild things about that event."

"You mean that it's a total meat market?" Leah asked.

"Or that women walk around in shorts smaller than Marybelle's?" Chloe asked.

"And guys rev their engines like it's mating season?" Madigan added.

"From what Blaine told me, it *is* mating season for most of the guys," Reese said.

"He's not wrong, but it's still fun," Madigan said.

"They've got two bands lined up this year," Sid said. "And Brandon Owens is playing, which means the music will be good. What about you, Shauna? Are you going?"

"Zander mentioned it, but it's after our agreement ends, and Brian will be home by then, so…"

"Oh, right," Madigan said apologetically. "It might be uncomfortable for you to be around Zander if you're not…you know. How is Brian?"

"I don't know," Shauna said. "He asked me not to visit. Recovery is really hard."

"I can only imagine," Madigan said. "That's a bummer about Bikes on the Beach, but if you decide to go, you hang with us."

"Thanks."

"Shauna, have you and Zander talked about what happens after the end of your arrangement?" Leah asked.

"Is it going to be too weird to be around him after?" Sid asked. "I can see how it would, but I hope you'll still hang out with us."

"Like I said, Zan and I are just having fun," Shauna said more confidently than she felt. "I'd like to keep hanging out with you guys. I'll just have to see what life is like when the time comes."

"Sounds good," Madigan said. "I don't know about you guys, but I'm getting something to wear from Dixie and Jace's Leather and Lace line for the event…"

Shauna listened to them chatting about shopping for the event, and she wanted to be part of it. If only her grandfather had asked for six months instead of two. That was a thought she'd never imagined having. But that wasn't a reasonable thought, either. Once Brian came home, he'd need her more than he ever had, and she wasn't about to let him down.

A bittersweet ache took root in her chest with the realization that once he came home and her arrangement with Zander ended, nothing would ever be quite the same again.

THE PERKY BRUNETTE behind the counter at the gym set Zander's copies of the membership papers in front of him and said, "You're all set. Would you like a tour?"

The out-of-the-way gym Shauna was a member of was smaller than any he'd ever been in. From where he stood, he could see the whole damn thing. Weights and aerobic equipment in a big open room, a sign for locker rooms to the left, and classes to the right.

"No thanks, I'm good, but I do need my…" He saw the familiar plastic-rectangular thing behind the register, but fuck if he could remember the word for it, and the brunette was looking at him like he was her next meal. "My, *uh*…" He gritted his teeth, nodding to the little plastic fucker.

"Oh, sorry. It wouldn't be good if I kept your credit card." She glanced at the card, then smiled flirtatiously as she said, "With a name like Wicked and all those tattoos, I bet you're all *kinds* of trouble."

"I'm the best kind of trouble there is." He snagged his card and cocked a grin. "Just ask my wife." He let that sink in before thanking her for her help and heading for the classrooms.

It was easy to find Shauna's pole class. All Zander had to do was follow the glances of the guys checking out the women between sets and the thumping beat of the music coming from the classroom.

He spotted Shauna standing beside a pole, gripping it with both hands just above her head. Her face was a mask of deep concentration as she pulled her legs up, toes pointed away from the pole, lifting them straight and high, then lowered them over her shoulders as she did some kind of upside-down spin that made his brain stall. She hooked an ankle around the pole in a slow, controlled twist, her gorgeous muscles flexing. Her ponytail nearly brushed the floor before she flipped upright and spun, arching with the movement like she'd been born to do it. Zander was mesmerized by her fluidity, the arch of her back, and the sheer strength of the woman he was lucky enough to have in his life, and in his bed.

At least for now.

She caught sight of him as her feet met the floor, and a flicker of confusion clouded her eyes, but it quickly morphed to relay, *What the hell are you doing here?*

Damn, he liked that scowl. He lifted his chin, grinning. *Don't give me rules, darlin', because I'll just break 'em.*

It was Wednesday night, and he had church in half an hour, but he'd timed it perfectly. The class ended, and there was a flurry of activity in the room as women gathered their belongings and checked him out through the glass. Shauna rolled her eyes. She stalked out of the classroom with three other women, who eyed him with interest.

"Ladies," he said, earning smiles, and reached for Shauna's hand. "Hey, Angel. You looked great in there." He pulled her into a kiss, staking claim for the dudes checking her out.

"What are you doing here?" Her voice was edged with disbelief, but her lips twitched like she was holding back a smile.

"I just joined the gym." He held up the membership papers.

Her eyes widened. "You joined *this* gym?"

"Yup. We said we were going to work out together." He folded the papers and put them in his back pocket.

"Right, but don't you have church tonight?"

"Yes, but I wanted to bring you this before I went." He reached into his front pocket and pulled out a small canvas pouch. Curiosity rose in her eyes as he handed it to her.

She opened the pouch and turned it over. The delicate gold bracelet with the triangular charm slid into her hand, and her breath caught. "Is this…?" Voice full of hope, she turned the charm over, her dark eyes glassing over at the sight of Cap's inscription. *"Zander,"* she whispered. "How did you find it?"

"I called every pawn shop on the Cape." He took the bracelet from her palm, and as he secured it around her wrist, he said, "I thought I was too late. But this morning I remembered you and Brian had lived in Wareham. I figured if he knew a drug dealer there, it was worth a shot calling local pawn shops, and that's where I found it."

She threw her arms around him, hugging him tight. "You have no idea how much this means to me."

He'd carried a knot in his chest ever since she'd told him about her missing bracelet, and it hadn't loosened until he'd had it in his hand. "I think I do."

Chapter Thirty-Three

THE SOUND OF the ocean floated in through the open windows as Shauna spread a tarp over the kitchen island, singing along to Tate McRae's "Greedy." It turned out that she was wrong a few weeks ago when she had lunch with the girls. The kitchen hadn't been almost ready to paint. The following weekend, she and Zander had decided to open the ceiling and stain the rafters. It was a huge, messy job, but it was finally done, and their hard work had paid off. The cathedral ceiling changed the feel of the entire cottage. They'd looked beyond the surface and found a hidden treasure. She'd found the same in Zander. A bestie that always had her back, a lover who made her feel impossibly sexy, and a confidant who listened without judgment when missing Brian got too heavy or the skeletons of her past rattled her chains.

She carried the kitchen stools into the living room, excited to paint with Zander when he got home from the store. Kitty was sunning herself in the miniature screened-in porch they'd built her off a window in the living room. The patio idea hadn't worked, since the windows were above ground level. Zander promised he'd outfit Kitty's porch with removable glass for the winter. Shauna felt a pang of sadness knowing she'd no longer be living there in the winter, but she refused to let herself get lost in that. They were almost halfway through their time together, which meant they still had several more weeks.

A knock at the front door drew her from her thoughts.

She glanced out the front window and saw Reba's car. Happiness bubbled up inside her, and she hurried to the door. She'd seen Reba and the rest of Zander's family at Brennan's birthday party a few weeks ago, and they'd had brunch with the family last weekend.

"Hi, Reba."

Reba flashed a warm smile. Her floral perfume drifting in with the breeze had already become comfortingly familiar. "Hi, sweetheart." She held up a large tote bag. "Preacher had a hankering for shepherd's pie, so naturally I made extras for all of our kiddos."

"Lucky us. Come in."

As Reba stepped inside, her gaze swept over the living room and dining room, and her eyes lit in surprise. "You have drywall in the dining room."

"I know. Can you believe it? Zander put it up in the evenings while I was at work." She'd been shocked to come home the mornings after her shifts and see how much he'd done. The dining room drywall wasn't finished, the living room was still only framed in, and they hadn't yet decided what to do about the fireplace, but the cottage felt a lot homier.

"My son has lived with framing for so long, I was beginning to wonder if he'd ever get around to working on it." Reba looked across the room, and her brows knitted. "Tell me Zander didn't build a screened-in porch for his cat."

"Okay, I won't tell you," Shauna said carefully.

Reba laughed. "Where did he get that crazy idea?"

"That would be my fault. I saw a cat patio and thought Kitty would like it. We couldn't make the catio work, so we built the screened-in porch. I know it seems silly, but look how happy she is lying in the sun and fresh air."

"You and Zan are two peas in a pod. She does look happy, and so does Zander lately, which makes this mama's heart very happy. Where is my boy?"

"He went to the paint store. We started painting the kitchen last night and got halfway through one wall when we realized we chose the wrong color. Light gray didn't go well. We thought it might look better once it dried, but this morning we both hated it." Shauna was proud of the work they'd done in the kitchen. "Come on, I'll show you."

As they walked further into the living room, the kitchen came into view, and Reba gasped. "You opened the ceiling."

"Isn't it beautiful? The morning after Brennan's birthday party, we were having breakfast and looking through pictures for inspiration for the fireplace, and one of the pictures had exposed rafters and a slanted ceiling like Zander's. We looked at each other, then we both looked up at the ceiling and said, *Let's do it.* It was a hard, messy job. We tore off the sheetrock, and we had to fill in the screw holes and fix a few things before staining the rafters, but it was worth it. Although I think the stain is what threw off the paint color."

Reba set the canvas bag on the counter, studying her. "And you helped him do all of that?"

"Mm-hm. Like I said, it wasn't easy, but it was fun." *As were the massages and sexy times we enjoyed afterward.*

"I think your idea of fun is a little different from mine." Reba laughed softly and motioned to the partially painted wall. "That color would've looked great with the tiles and the cabinets, but you're right. It clashes with the rafters. What color did you decide to go with?"

"A light taupe. It's really pretty—look." Shauna grabbed her phone and showed Reba the color they'd chosen.

"That's going to be perfect." As Reba put the shepherd's pie in the fridge, she said, "I'm glad Zander's out. I've been hoping to get a minute alone with you, but whenever the family is together, the girls and Zander don't give you a minute alone."

Shauna got a little nervous. "I'm sorry. I wish you'd said something. I would've made time to talk."

"Oh, no, honey. I'm glad you have them, and I didn't want to push myself on you. I figured we'd catch up at some point."

"What did you want to talk about?"

"I just wanted to check in with you to see how you're holding up. It's been about six weeks since Brian went into rehab, and your life has changed a lot since then. It has to be hard being away from him and suddenly being married and thrown into a big family like ours."

Shauna was touched by her concern. "My life has definitely taken some unexpected turns. It is hard being away from Brian this long. In fact, Zander and I were talking about that the other night when I was really missing Brian."

"Have you visited him?"

"No. When he went into rehab, he asked me not to."

"Oh, sweetheart, I'm so sorry. That had to hurt."

"It did. It's hard not knowing how he's doing, but you go through so many emotions in recovery. I don't want to make it harder for him by pushing to see him. Talking with Zander helps, and Brian and I have been joined at the hip forever. This time apart has been good for me, even if it's hard sometimes. I didn't realize how much I needed the breathing space. I'm learning a lot about who I am and the things I enjoy doing, and even about friendships. Mads and the girls have been amazing."

"I'm glad to hear that, and it's nice to hear Zander is helping you through the hard times. How are things between you two?" Reba asked carefully. "Every time I see you together, you seem to get along well, but looks can be deceiving, and I know how it is to be around family. You want everyone to see the good."

If there was a problem area, that was it. She and Zander had fallen into a rhythm that felt *too* good. They talked, joked, argued, and fooled around like a real couple. They'd spent the last few weeks hanging out with his friends and family, working out together, renovating, and going on motorcycle rides with some of the guys and their significant others. Working out together was fun but complicated. Some of the girls in her pole class worked out when they did, and whenever Zander thought a guy was checking her out, he'd give her a kiss or smack her ass. She didn't hate that, but she gave him hell for it, because once their agreement was over, she'd have to explain the divorce to the girls from her class. She and Zander hadn't talked about how they were going to end their relationship or what they'd tell people, and she wasn't looking forward to explaining it to anyone, especially the guys at work. They'd bonded with Zander, too. He showed up once a week with dinner, and he'd hang out until they got a call.

"I don't feel pressure to get along in front of your family. We just do."

"Well, that is good to hear," Reba said. "Zander has never shared a house with anyone but family. I hope he isn't leaving his dirty laundry around or driving you crazy in other ways."

"He's not sloppy, and he does drive me crazy sometimes,

but I'm sure I drive him crazy, too. He's a big planner, and I'm not."

"You sure we're talking about the same guy? Zander has been winging his way through life since he was a little boy."

"Everyone says that, including him, but I don't see it," Shauna said. "I mean, Zan is spontaneous, but when all that stuff went down with Brian, I would've been lost if not for him. When he found out Brian had grabbed me, he formed a plan on the spot to keep me safe, and when Brian showed up here in the middle of the night, Zander came up with another plan in an instant that involved his brothers and cousins helping us."

"Really?" Reba looked shocked.

"Yes, and it didn't stop there. When we decided to get married so I could get my inheritance and Brian could go to rehab, Zander found out what we needed to get married at the courthouse, and all the things we'd need to do to get him into rehab. Then he came up with another plan to take me shopping and get wedding rings and the outfit I wore."

"Zander did all of that?" she asked incredulously.

"*Yes.* He's always planning. Look at our honeymoon. We didn't even need to go on one. He did it so people would believe our relationship was real. I never would have thought of that, and he went to the trouble of planning every minute of our trip and making it romantic since it's the only honeymoon I'll probably ever have. I mean, to ship his bike to Niagara because no self-respecting biker would ever put their wife on the back of someone else's bike? That's not something he could do at the last minute. And look at today. I really wanted to help him paint, but I'm meeting the girls for the book club meeting later, so he set an alarm to get up early to make sure we'd have time to paint before I have to leave."

Reba was looking at her with a mixture of disbelief and shock.

Shauna realized she'd spoken so fast, it probably came across as a rant. "I'm sorry. I get a little protective of Zander. The guys make jokes all the time about how he's the troublemaker of the group, but he's not that way with me. He's more of a…I don't know. A leader? A protector? Not that I need leading or protecting. Those aren't the right words. He's not controlling or aggressive."

"They're not the wrong words, either, honey," Reba said gently. "Zander doesn't bulldoze, like Blaine, but he is a strong leader and a fierce protector. He just has a gentler, more charming way about him."

"He does ooze charm, but he's solid, you know? I've always been the one to hold the reins, and there's this part of me that has always been afraid that if I didn't clutch them to my chest, things would fall apart. But I don't feel that pressure around Zander." Even when Brian was sober and not doing drugs, she'd never felt like she could drop the reins and he'd be there to pick them up. Not in the way she *knew* Zander would.

"I think the word you're looking for is *partner*," Reba said. "Someone you can count on to always have your back and watch out for your best interests."

"*Yes.* Exactly. That's actually a perfect word, given the reason we're married. He's my partner in crime."

"Not in crime, sweetheart. You're partners in hope. The two of you are giving Brian a second chance. I guess Preacher and I did something right."

Partners in hope. She liked that. "You did everything right."

The front door opened, and Zander walked in carrying a paper bag and two gallons of paint.

"Hey, Mom. What are you doing here?"

"Hi, honey. I brought you and Shauna a shepherd's pie."

"Awesome. Thank you." He set the paint on the counter.

"I think you're going to need more paint than that," his mother said.

"It's in the truck." He touched Shauna's hip and said, "I got you something, Angel." He reached into the bag and handed her a beautiful steel-blue wooden frame. "It's for that picture of you and Brian that fell off the wall at your place. I thought it might help you feel better if you put it up where you can see it every day. Maybe on the end table in the living room?"

Her heart swelled. "I'd like that. Thank you." She hugged him.

"That was sweet of you, honey, and this?" Reba motioned around the kitchen. "I love what you've done to the place. I guess what your father says about contractors is really true."

"What does he say?" Shauna asked, looking at Zander.

"A contractor can build a thousand houses and work on a thousand projects, but until he finds the one that speaks to his heart, you'll never truly know what he's capable of," Zander said.

Reba's gaze lingered on Shauna for a long moment before shifting to Zander as she said, "I'm glad you finally found the one that speaks to your heart. I have to go. We're riding with Ginger and Conroy up to Plymouth today. Love you both."

She hugged them and headed out the front door, leaving Shauna to wonder if Reba thought it was the house or Shauna that spoke to Zander's heart.

ZANDER PUSHED THE roller in the paint tray and glanced across the kitchen at Shauna, humming to the music as she rolled paint on another wall. Her hair, like the tarp beneath her feet, was speckled with paint, and there were smudges of paint on her cheek. She'd managed to get almost as much paint on her clothes as she did the wall. She was about as good at painting as she was at cooking. There were drips and streaks everywhere, but he didn't give a damn. He couldn't get enough of the way she threw herself into everything she did, messily and wholeheartedly.

He rolled paint on the opposite wall and said, "I might have to buy more paint if you're going to redecorate yourself and the floor."

"I might have to get a new husband if you're going to criticize my painting," she shot back, tossing him a cheesy grin.

"Darlin', I have no issues with your painting, but when you're out there searching for a new man, you might want to stay away from artists," he teased. "They may not be as kind."

"Well, *my* wall is done, and I'm ready to edge in the next one. I can't say the same for yours." She stepped back, holding the roller like a prize, assessing her work. "What's wrong with my painting? It looks good to me."

"Nothing I can't fix. Just a few streaks."

"They're not streaks. That's texture. I did it on purpose."

He barked out a laugh. "Texture? You're painting a wall, not a—" *Fuck.* The word slipped out of reach. He could see the damn thing in his head, could feel what it meant, *pictures on the wall.*

Her roller stopped midswipe. *"Not a…?"* She looked over, her eyes narrowing. Not in annoyance, but in the way they did when she was trying to figure something out.

"Doesn't matter," he gritted out, and went back to painting. The heat of her stare burned through him as the lost word—*canvas*—appeared in his mind like a fucking bully.

"Zander."

His name felt like a spotlight. "Yeah?" He continued painting to avoid looking into her caring eyes.

"You forgot the word, didn't you?" she asked too damn carefully.

"No," he said with a half laugh, trying to brush it off. "I'm just keeping you on your toes."

"This isn't the first time I noticed it," she said more firmly.

He felt the walls closing in on him and gritted his teeth.

"Zan, please look at me."

Fuck. He turned, and the worry in her eyes slayed him, but he didn't want to be another guy she needed to worry about. It took everything he had to muster a little white lie. "It's nothing, Angel."

"Bullshit." She dropped the roller on the tarp and went to him, her eyes imploring. "Why won't you talk to me?"

Gripping his roller tighter, he forced the grin that had gotten him through life and reached for her with his other hand. "Because I'd much rather kiss you."

She stepped back and crossed her arms. "Don't do that."

"What? Kiss you?"

"No. Don't play that game with me and joke your way out of this. I'm a frigging EMT, remember? I know what can happen from a head injury, and I want to know what's going on with you."

"Fine," he gritted out. "You want to know what's going on?" He tossed his roller into the tray. "Ever since the accident, words sometimes get lost in my head. It's like they're *right there*,

but I can't reach them. I thought it would be better by now. It's better than it was, but it's just one more thing my fucked-up brain can't handle. Okay? Are you happy now?"

She pressed her lips together, her brows furrowed, and shook her head. "No, I'm not happy, but I appreciate you telling me." She stepped closer. "You don't have a fucked-up brain. It's not abnormal after a head injury to have trouble finding words. Brains take time to heal. What does your doctor say about it?"

"I never told him."

Her eyes widened. "Why not?"

"Because I didn't tell anyone."

"Nobody? Not even your family?"

"Fuck no." He paced. "You think I want anyone looking at me the way you are right now?"

"You mean like I *care* about you?" Her tone was sharp, cutting through the bullshit straight to his heart. "Zander, don't you know how lucky you are to have people who care about you?"

Great. Now he looked like a selfish dick. He had plenty of people who cared about him, but he'd never had *this*, and he probably didn't deserve it. "Yes, I *do*. That's *why* I haven't told anyone. I'm sick of being the guy everyone worries about. I appreciate them, and I appreciate you, but none of you need to carry my shit."

"So you'd rather suffer in silence and pretend it isn't happening?"

"I'm not *suffering*. It's not like I can't remember how to drive or do my job. They're just stupid words, and it's not all the time."

"What if it gets worse and it could have been prevented?

What will you tell your family? Because I'm standing here right now as your friend and your wife, and my heart hurts just thinking about it. Your family trusts you, Zander. It would break their hearts to think you didn't trust them enough to tell them the truth. You're doing exactly what I did with Brian. I didn't want to face the issue, so I pretended it wasn't happening until it was too late. Is that really what you want?"

Everything she said had him hitting the brakes, and the look of stubborn determination laced with worry on her beautiful face cut him to his core. "Why would it get worse? You just said it's not abnormal to forget shit after a head injury."

"It's not, but I'm not a doctor, and every head injury is different. You need to tell your doctor and let him check you out. Then we'll know what you're dealing with. I know it's scary, but you don't have to do it alone. I'll go with you."

He scoffed. "I'm not scared. I'll make an appointment, but you don't have to go with me."

"Nice try, but you can't ditch me that easily." She lifted her left hand and wiggled her fingers, her rings glittering under the lights. "You put these rings on my finger, and there are several weeks left on our contract. If you think I'm letting some sexy nurse bat her lashes at you while you're sitting alone in a waiting room, you've lost your freaking mind. I've got a wifely reputation to uphold. Waiting-room hand-holding is nonnegotiable."

He hadn't gone into this arrangement looking for anything, but here he was, standing in his kitchen, heart raw, chest burning, because she gave a damn.

Swamped by emotions he shouldn't have, he did what he knew best and set out on a mission to outrun them. "Careful, wifey. You start demanding waiting-room hand-holding and I'm going to assume exam-room quickies are part of a package deal."

He reached for her, but she stepped back, heat and mischief dancing in her eyes. "Maybe they are. It depends how hot the doctor is."

"*You—*" He lunged, grateful for the reprieve, and she squealed, darting across the kitchen. Laughter rang out as he chased her. "If anyone's defiling you in an exam room, it's *me*," he growled.

"You're not the boss of me!"

He snagged her wrist, but she shrieked and yanked her arm free. Scurrying away, she stepped on the paint tray, sending paint flying. She slipped on the tarp, knocking over the paint can just as he grabbed her from behind, and they tumbled to the paint-soaked tarp in a heap of carefree laughter. Spilled paint be damned, he rolled her beneath him, and *man*, what a sight she was, covered in paint, bright-eyed and dimple-cheeked. But as always happened when they were close, the air heated, pulsing with urgency, their bodies burning every place they touched, and in the next breath, their laughter was silenced by the crush of their lips.

The world disappeared, and they rolled around, kissing, groping, and stripping off their clothes. Finally naked, he took her in a punishingly intense kiss, leaving her whimpering for more as he perched above her. He teased her pussy with one hand, her nipple with the other, and the air rushed from her lungs, desire burning in her eyes.

"You're so fucking beautiful, covered in paint, your pussy dripping for me, and those lips. *Jesus,* those fucking lips taunt me every damn second of the day." He wanted to kiss them, fuck them, and hear his name fly from them all at once. "Looks like I'm the boss now, Angel."

Her eyes narrowed with challenge. "Bosses don't get on their knees."

"You're right, but wives do."

"Gladly." She reached for his cock, stroking him as he fucked her with his fingers.

He used his thumb on her clit, earning more of those sexy sounds, and as she sat up, he knew her mouth on him wouldn't be enough to satiate the primal need burning through him. "I want to fuck your mouth while you come on mine."

As he lowered himself to his back, she said, "The paint—"

"Don't care," he growled, and reached for her. "Smother me with your pussy while you suck my cock." He guided her into position, holding her sex tight against his mouth as she lowered hers over his cock, taking him in deep. He groaned against her pussy, clutching her ass with one hand while he used the other on those oversensitive nerves, making her squirm.

She sucked and stroked as he licked, sucked, and fucked her, using teeth and tongue. She rocked against his mouth, moaning. The sound vibrated around his dick, heightening the sensations, taking him to the brink of release as she cried out, her arousal spreading over his tongue. He held her hips, feasting on her, feeling her muscles spasm, then finally ease as she came down from the high. Her fist circled his cock again, but before she could take him in her mouth, he sent another orgasm crashing over her.

This time as she came down from the high, he needed *more*.

"I need to be inside you. Ride me, Angel."

She moved swiftly, lust flaming in her eyes as she pulled the tether from her hair, sending her paint-streaked locks tumbling over her breasts as she straddled him. As she sank down, her arousal coating the head of his cock, he grabbed her hips, stopping her, and bit out, "*Fuck.* I need to grab a condom."

"No, you don't," she said, feverishly peeling his hands off her hips. "I'm on birth control." She sank down, taking in every aching inch of him. A moan rushed from her lips, and *"Fuuck"* fell from his. She was so tight and hot, bolts of pleasure shot through him, shattering his control. They thrust and gyrated with everything they had. The pleasure was so intense, he sat up, needing his mouth on her, and sucked her nipple to the roof of it.

She arched against him, fingernails digging into his flesh, riding him faster and harder. *"Ohgodohgodohgod. Zan—"*

Her pussy clenched like a vise around his cock. Heat seared down his spine, his muscles cording tight as he gritted his teeth, refusing to come as he pounded into her, taking her right back up to the crest of another orgasm. Her eyes slammed shut, her hips bucking and grinding, and she cried out, catapulting him into a maelstrom of ecstasy so all-consuming, everything else failed to exist.

When she went soft in his arms, he rained kisses over her shoulder and neck. Her skin smelled like paint and sex and *her*, and he wanted to drown in it.

As the world came back into focus, she let out a soft moan and lifted her head from his shoulder. Her cheeks flushed, her eyes at half-mast, she flashed those dimples. "You made a mess of your kitchen."

She was snarky, stubborn, and messy, and he'd never known anyone so intriguing. "I'm pretty sure that's your fault."

She flashed a sweet smile, the softness in her eyes tugging at him, making him want to lay her down, get her hot and bothered again, and spend the rest of the day lost in her. That was the problem with this arrangement. She was too damn easy to get lost in.

He patted her ass. "Come on, sexy girl. Shower time."

"We should have had sex against the wall," she said as they pushed to their feet. "Butt prints would be a great conversation starter."

He laughed. "Has anyone ever told you that you're trouble?"

"Nope." She tapped his chest and said, "I'm pretty sure that's your fault," and headed for the living room, leaving painted footprints.

Jesus Christ. She was impossible.

He hauled her over his shoulder like a sack of potatoes.

"Hey!" She laughed and smacked his ass as he carried her into the bathroom.

"Careful, Flores, you might reawaken the Loch Ness monster."

Laughing, she played his fucking ass like a drum.

When he set her down under the warm spray, steam rose around them, blurring the edges of the world again. She tipped her head back, rinsing the paint from her hair. Paint circled the drain like his thoughts always seemed to circle her. He poured body wash into his palm, telling himself to wash up quickly and get the hell out of there. He needed to get his head on straight and clean up the paint in the kitchen before it dried.

But one smile from his beautiful girl, and he had no fucks left for paint.

As his hands caressed her curves, her arms circled him, and their mouths came together, eager and easy, as if they were two halves always meant to be one.

Chapter Thirty-Four

ZANDER HADN'T REALIZED how much his memory issues had been weighing on him until he'd agreed to go to see a doctor. The last week and a half, while he'd waited for his appointment, had been stressful, worrying about what the doctor would say. He'd done his best not to let Shauna see his anxiety or let it hinder their fun. Last weekend they'd gone to see Madigan play a musical storytelling gig with Tobias, Gunner, Sid, Zeke, and Aria, a beautiful, sweet, though quiet, blonde with colorful tattoos, and the other night they'd had dinner with Maverick, Chloe, Baz, and Emerson. But as he walked out of the doctor's office with the reassurance that what he was experiencing wasn't abnormal, he was overcome with relief. For the first time since the accident, he felt like he wasn't standing on a trapdoor, and he had Shauna to thank for it.

He walked into the waiting room, and his Angel jumped to her feet, heading straight for him. "How'd it go?" she asked anxiously. "What did he say?"

"It turns out my brain is only half-broken." Taking her hand, he headed out the door. "The doc said it's normal to have trouble finding some words after a head injury, and it was progressing as is to be expected. He said it should get better with time."

"That's great!" She threw her arms around him, and as she stepped back, flashing the killer smile that always knocked him a little off-kilter, she said, "And your brain is *not* half-broken. You're just healing."

"Thanks for pushing me to go to the doctor, Angel, and for coming with me," he said as they came to his truck. "I uh…" He looked away for a second, his emotions too raw. "The last week and a half, while we were waiting to see the doctor, I was…I'm glad you were with me. Thank you."

Her gaze softened, and for a second he thought she might say something to reveal feelings similar to his, something to negate their arrangement and make it real. But she reached for the passenger door and said, "Hand-holding clause. It's mandatory, remember? I expect the same if something happens to me."

"You know I will." He helped her into the truck and went around to the driver's side. As he drove away from the medical building, he said, "We should go celebrate. How does ice cream for dinner sound?"

"Great. After we tell your parents."

"Yeah, about that." He wasn't looking forward to admitting he'd lied to them. "I'm fine, so there's no reason to tell them."

"Alexander Wicked, your family would go to the moon and back for you, no questions asked. You need to come clean with them. It's the right thing to do. You shouldn't carry this alone when you have such a great support system."

"I'm not." He cocked a grin. "I've got you, bestie."

She gave him a deadpan look.

"I'll tell them another time, okay? I know you want your sundae."

She reached across the cab and touched his arm. "Please? Your family planned a wedding for you and your temporary wife, a woman they didn't even know, and they've welcomed me into their lives with open arms ever since. Don't you feel even the slightest need to be honest with them?"

Fuck. Yeah, he felt the need, but it wasn't going to be easy.

"Fine. Let's get it over with." He glanced at the clock on the dash. *5:30.* "By the time we get back, they should be home."

ZANDER WAS HOPING his parents had gone out to dinner or decided to work late. Anything other than being home when they got there. But no such luck. He pulled open the kitchen door, and his parents' dogs barreled out, their tails wagging. He and Shauna loved them up on the way in.

They were greeted with the savory scents of something roasting in the oven, bringing back warm memories of loud family dinners and late-night leftovers. But that didn't keep his gut from fisting as his mother breezed into the kitchen, her face lighting up at the sight of them.

"Zander, you didn't tell me you and Shauna were coming by. What a nice surprise." She hugged Shauna. "Hi, sweetheart. How are you?"

"I'm doing really well tonight, thanks," Shauna said.

"Mom, I wanted to talk to you and Dad. Is he around?" Zander was surprised to hear himself say Dad and not Preacher, but it made sense. He felt like he was twelve years old again, about to tell his parents he'd busted his bicycle tire riding in the quarry they'd told him to stay away from a hundred times.

"He's out back with your grandfather, building a kiddie-size picnic table for the yard." Her brows knitted. "Is everything okay?"

He hadn't planned on telling his grandfather. This ought to be fun. "Yeah, fine. Mind if we go talk to him?"

They headed outside with his mother and the dogs. His father was bent over a sawhorse by the shed, circular saw whining as it ripped through a piece of lumber. His grandfather stood off to the side, his arms crossed and his face pinched as the saw wound down.

"Too short," his grandfather barked.

His father set the board aside, scowling. "It's perfect."

"Perfect, my ass," his grandfather muttered. "You cut it half an inch shy. Didn't I teach you anything? Measure twice, cut once. Think you'd've learned by now."

His father reached for the measuring tape, lifting his gaze to Zander, and said, "If I ever do this to you, feel free to kick my ass."

"Well, well, if it isn't the honeymooners," his grandfather said. "I didn't know you were coming over tonight. I would've asked you to bring some cookies."

"Sorry, Gramps. It was kind of spur of the moment."

His father finished measuring the lumber, said, "Perfect," and set down the measuring tape, which his grandfather snagged to remeasure the wood. His father shook his head. "Shauna, it's nice to see you, darlin'."

"It's nice to see you, too."

His father lifted his chin in Zander's direction. "Something going on, or did you come to scarf dinner?"

Zander's heart hammered against his ribs. "I went to see the doctor today."

"I thought he cleared you at your last visit," his father said.

"He did," Zander said, his throat tight. "But I wasn't exactly honest about how I was doing."

"Are you okay?" his mother asked.

"He'd better be, or that doctor and I are going to have a talk that won't end well for him," his grandfather said.

His father looked like he was holding his breath, his worried eyes trained on Zander, but he didn't say a word.

"I'm fine, mostly. I…uh…" He swallowed hard. Shauna hooked her index finger around his pinkie, a quiet show of support he didn't like her knowing he needed, but he appreciated the hell out of it just the same. Any other time, her reassuring smile might have undone him, but tonight it gave him the push he needed to stand up and take his due. "Sometimes I forget the names for things, but the doctor said it's normal and should go away with time."

"Oh, honey." His mother stepped closer. "That must be so scary. I wish you'd said something. Is he sure you're okay? Does he have any idea how long it will last?"

"He's sure, and there's no timeline. Everyone's different. Apparently I'm lucky. People who have cognitive difficulties of any kind, including dyslexia, prior to a TBI typically have a harder time than people who don't. He said many of his patients in my situation need more time to collect their thoughts and often become much quieter to avoid conversation."

Shauna looked at him with a question in her eyes.

"I didn't mean to leave that part out with you, Angel. I was just caught up in the relief of it all."

She smiled. "It's okay."

"Why would you lie to us about something that important?"

his father asked sharply.

Zander drew his shoulders back and stepped forward, unlinking his and Shauna's fingers. "Because I knew you would keep treating me like I couldn't do my job, and everyone else would be watching me like a hawk, looking for more deficits. Do you have any idea what it's like to be the one who's on everyone's radar all the damn time?"

"You brought that on yourself, Zan," his father said. "They watch out for you, because before the accident you were reckless, and you never watched out for yourself."

"Yeah, I was reckless sometimes. I'll give you that. But we both know that's not why they watched over me. They did it because before we found out I had dyslexia, when I was struggling in school to be half as good as they were naturally, everyone thought I was stupid—"

"*What?*" his father fumed. "No one has *ever* thought that. If anything, you were too smart for your own damn good. You were the cleverest of them all. You were always outsmarting us."

Zander scoffed. "Yeah, right."

"He's telling you the truth, honey," his mother said. "You always knew how to fly under our radar and make us think the things you did were our ideas. By the time we realized what was happening, you were off doing whatever it was, and doing it with our unintended blessings. We had no choice but to ask everyone to keep an eye on you."

Her words hit hard, but he didn't fully believe them. "You're just saying that because I was trouble."

"Now you listen to me, son," his grandfather said, stepping forward. "I've got no dog in this fight, but I'm not going to listen to you dismiss the truth. I'm thinkin' you don't remember the night we all thought you were abducted."

"Abducted?" He did not remember that. "What are you talking about?"

"You were eight years old and mad at your parents for one thing or another, and you told them you were going to live with me and your grandmother. Well, your father said you weren't going anywhere but to bed. So you, the kid who was always six steps ahead of the rest of us, asked when you *could* live with us. Your old man said, *Sunday*, thinking you'd forget by then, since it was only Monday. Well, Saturday night at midnight, you packed your backpack, snuck out your window, and took the shortcut by the creek to our place. When your father let the dogs out at three in the morning, he checked on all the kids. Your bed was empty and your window was open. They called out the troops, and everyone went looking for you. They found your sneakers by the creek. Turned out you took them off so your parents wouldn't get mad that you got them wet, and you forgot to pick them up. You got our hidden key out from under the rock, went into the guest room, and went to sleep."

"That was a terrifying night," his mother said, the emotion in her voice making Zander's stomach twist. "We had everyone looking for you. Family, police, the club, neighbors."

"Didn't anyone look at Grandpa's house?" Zander asked.

"No," his father answered. "You and I'd had fifteen other disagreements by then. Plus, I'd had fifty others with your brothers and sister. The only thing I was thinking about was that someone had stolen our boy. That was one of the worst nights of my life."

Zander's throat thickened.

"Of all our lives," his grandfather said. "Hours later, when your grandmother and I finally went home, we were beside ourselves with grief, and there you were, sitting on the living room couch watching television, elbow-deep in a box of cereal. Your grandmother dropped to her knees in tears, and you thought it was because your dad said you could live with us and she didn't want you." His grandfather shook his head. "It was a mess."

Silence fell around them.

Zander scrubbed a hand down his face, trying to ward off the emotions gnawing at him, and said, "I'm sorry I did that. It sounds awful."

"It was," his mother said softly. "But don't you see, honey? You've always been smart. You didn't just run away. You got permission, and while leaving in the middle of the night was wrong, you taught us a valuable lesson to always say what we mean."

"And to listen closer to what you and the other kids said at all times," his father added. "I'm sorry you ever felt like you were anything less than perfect in any of our eyes. Mischievous? *Sure.* Reckless? *Absolutely.* But never stupid. Dyslexia is just another thing our family dealt with. Like Blaine being so controlling he was suffocating everyone, and Zeke being so anal about every lesson, he drove his teachers crazy."

Overcome with emotion, Zander cleared his throat and said, "I know I'm not stupid, and I know none of you think I am now, but it's how I felt as a kid, and the issues I've had since the accident brought it all back. I'm trying to prove I don't need extra sets of eyes on me, and lying to you wasn't the right way to go about it. I'm sorry."

"We're sorry, too, honey." His mother hugged him. "I know you're an adult, and you don't have to tell us anything, but I'd like to think that when it comes to something as important as your health, we'd be able to trust your word."

"I get that now." Zander turned to Shauna, earning another supportive smile, and said, "Someone reminded me how lucky I am to have people who care about me. Shauna is the reason I went to the doctor, and she's the reason I'm telling you the truth." He reached for Shauna's hand. "The truth is, it's been scary not knowing if it would get worse. But now we know it should get better, and honestly, it's not that bad. Nobody even noticed, except Shauna."

"I'm grateful she sees past the smoke and mirrors you throw up for the rest of us," his father said.

"Yeah, I am, too."

"Well, I don't know about you, but with all that worrying, I've worked up my appetite," his mother said. "Can you stay for dinner?"

"I don't know. I promised Shauna ice cream for dinner." Zander arched a brow at her. "What do you think, darlin'?"

"Stick around for dinner," his grandfather encouraged. "You can save Preacher a drive later and take me home."

"Sounds like a plan," Shauna said.

"Wonderful." His mother sidled up to her and said, "I'm looking forward to cooking with you and the girls this weekend."

"I'm excited to learn how to do something other than burn water," Shauna said, and smiled at Zander.

His brothers and Tobias were coming over to help him finish the living room on Saturday. He was glad Shauna would be having fun with the girls. He gave her hand a squeeze, mouthing *Thank you*, before letting go so she and his mother could continue their conversation on their way inside.

Zander helped his father and grandfather put their tools away.

"That girl sees you clear as day, Zander," his father said.

"Maybe clearer than you want to be seen, given your situation," his grandfather said.

She did see him clearer than he wanted, since he'd never wanted to be seen in the first place. He liked skating by, grinning and dodging, keeping all his faults and imperfections out of sight. That was safer for everyone. But he couldn't deny how badly he wanted Shauna to keep looking.

His grandfather nudged him, speaking quietly as the three men headed inside. "We'll hit the ice cream shop on the way home, get your pretty little lady whatever she wants for getting you to smarten up."

Zander chuckled. "Sounds good, Gramps." He made a mental note to go to the ice cream shop that offered sugar-free treats and looked forward to thanking his beautiful wife properly later.

Chapter Thirty-Five

"DUDE, HOLD IT still," Tobias said.

It was Saturday afternoon, tunes were blaring, and Zander's cottage looked like a construction zone. The guys were helping him finish the living room. They'd been giving each other a hard time for hours as he, Tobias, and Zeke hung and taped drywall and Blaine and Maverick did the stonework around the fireplace.

"I'm holding it as still as fucking stone," Zander said, holding the drywall in place for Tobias.

"Still, my ass. You're twitchy as shit," Tobias said.

Zander glared at him. "I'll give you twitchy."

"Shut up and hold still so I can screw the damn thing," Tobias barked.

"That's what she…*Fuck*," Blaine uttered. "Never mind. That's our sister."

The guys laughed.

As Tobias screwed in the drywall, Zeke looked down from the ladder he was standing on and said, "Hate to tell you this, but that drywall doesn't look straight."

"My ass it's not straight," Tobias grumbled, and stepped back to assess it. "Damn it."

"Are you kidding me?" Zander eyeballed it. "It looks better than Zeke's dating life."

The guys laughed, and Zander and Tobias fixed their mistake.

"Speaking of Zeke's dating life," Maverick said as he set a stone in place. "How'd your date go last night?"

Zeke shrugged. "We had a good time, but we didn't have much in common."

"Isn't that the chick you met when you were hiking last week?" Blaine asked.

"Yeah, so?" Zeke said as he taped a seam.

"Sounds like you have hiking in common," Maverick said.

"Maybe she didn't like his tiny pierced dick," Zander teased.

The guys laughed.

Getting no reaction out of Zeke, Zander said, "Come on, man. Every time you take a woman out, you find something wrong with her. She's too talkative, not interesting enough—"

"Not smart enough or too judgmental," Blaine added as he chose another stone for the fireplace.

"Mads thinks it's because they're not Aria," Tobias said.

Zeke scoffed.

"I was trying not to go there," Zander said carefully. "But now that we have, Zeke, you've had a bug up your ass about Aria acting squirrely. Did you ever get to the bottom of that?"

Zeke climbed down from the ladder, his jaw tight. "This isn't about Aria. I just have standards."

"Hate to tell you this, bro, but you've been saying the same shit for years," Blaine pointed out. "One of these days those standards are going to strangle you."

"And you think marriage won't?" Zeke moved the ladder.

"Hey, even if that's the case, then I'm a willing victim,"

Tobias said. "I'd do anything for Mads. *November, baby.* I expect you all to cry at our wedding." He and Madigan were getting married in November at the Salty Hog, where they'd first met.

Zander laughed. "That ain't happening."

"Nobody's going to be crying at my wedding," Blaine said.

The room went silent, all eyes turning on Blaine.

"*Your* wedding?" Maverick asked, his brow arched.

"You finally going to make an honest woman out of Reese?" Zeke asked.

"She's been an honest woman her whole damn life," Blaine said. "I'm just making her my wife."

"You going to tell us when this wedding is, or are we supposed to guess?" Zander asked.

"Next spring, when Lettie is on school break." Blaine secured the stone in place. "We're going to Santorini, Greece, for our honeymoon."

"Are you taking Lettie with you?" Maverick asked.

"No," Blaine said. "I offered, but I let Reese decide. She struggled with the decision, but I'm happy with her choice. I love Lettie, but I'm glad I'll get to have Reese all to myself and spoil the hell out of her."

"You spoil both of them every day," Maverick said.

"Like you don't spoil Chloe and Marybelle?" Tobias pointed out.

Zander listened to their banter, and finally he got it, because nothing made him happier than doing things for Shauna. He was all about her pleasure, but it was so much bigger than that. He never realized making someone coffee every morning just the way she liked it, or sneaking notes into the duffel bag she took to work or leaving them on her windshield with wildflowers could make him feel so good.

"Hey, bro." Maverick stepped into Zander's line of sight, pulling him from his thoughts.

"What?" Zander snapped.

"Chill. You were daydreaming or something. I said your name three times." Maverick pointed his trowel into the dining room. "What is that? In the corner."

They all looked at the shiny pole leaning against the dining room wall.

"It sure doesn't look like a scratching post for Kitty," Tobias said.

"It's a pole for Shauna, and you're going to help me put it up."

"Are you kidding?" Blaine asked.

"Guess we know how she's paying him back for that loan," Zeke said.

"Shut the hell up," Zander said, stifling a laugh. "She takes classes. It's exercise."

Tobias smirked. "Is that what the kids are calling it now? Exercise?"

Blaine's expression hardened. "Dude, is there something you're not telling us about you and Shauna? We've all seen how close you've gotten. We assume you're hooking up, but is this still temporary, or have things gotten serious between you two?"

Fuck.

"And don't tell us you're not sleeping with her, because we're not that stupid," Maverick said.

"I've got no reason to lie about that," Zander said. "Shauna is the coolest woman I've ever met. I like spending time with her, and I love having her in my bed every night. But we're still temporary. It was never supposed to be anything else. We're just having a good time. You know I'm not built for long term. I'll get bored eventually, and she's got a life to go back to and a guy who's going through rehab because she's his world." He fucking hated saying any of that out loud, but he needed to hear it as much as they did. Most of the time when he was with Shauna, it was too easy to forget Brian even existed.

"How's that going? How's he doing in rehab?" Blaine asked.

Zander shrugged. "I can only assume it's going okay since he's still there."

"And the whole inheritance thing?" Maverick asked. "Has that attorney checked up on you two? When does she get the money?"

"She told him we got married, but the attorney hasn't done shit as far as I know. She's going to request the money after the Fourth. We thought it would look suspicious if she requested it right after the sixty days were up. But if all goes well, she should have the money by the time Brian comes home next month."

"Isn't that when your arrangement ends?" Zeke asked.

Zander's jaw clenched. He hated talking about this. "Yeah."

"Then why put up a pole for such a short time?" Zeke asked.

"I'm just being a supportive husband. Don't you think she deserves that? She's doing all of this for Brian. She's like me. She never wanted to get married. It wasn't even on her radar."

"I get being supportive," Blaine said skeptically. "But it's going to cost you a pretty penny to replace the floors and patch the ceiling when you tear it out."

He didn't care what it cost, and he'd had enough of this conversation. He cocked an arrogant grin. "Who says I'm getting rid of it? We don't need a marriage certificate for her to come back and give me private performances."

The guys erupted in laughter and joked about how Zander would never change, leaving him to wonder how he could feel like he'd already changed so much that he'd never be the same again, when nobody else saw it.

SHAUNA AND MADIGAN bumped the car doors shut with their hips, balancing casserole dishes and bags of side dishes they'd made with Reba, Ginger, and the other girls while the guys were renovating. Shauna had tried to absorb the cooking lessons, but she was having so much fun, she wasn't sure she'd remember much of them. Leah had brought Junie and Rosie, and Chloe had brought Marybelle. The little girls had been right in the thick of it, helping with every step. Shauna loved how Reba and Ginger hadn't treated them like they were babies or in the way. They'd given them jobs just like they had Shauna and the others. She was glad those little girls would never know what it was like to feel unwanted.

"What do you think they're up to in there?" Madigan asked as Shauna came around the front of the car. "Talking about tomorrow's ride while they pretend to work, or kicking back watching the waves roll in?"

Shauna and Zander had gone riding with Madigan and Tobias and some of the others last weekend, and she'd loved it. She wished she could go tomorrow, but she had to work. "Zan and I watch the waves roll in first thing in the morning while we have our coffee, but I can't see him doing it at this time of day. He's always doing something." Mornings had become one of her favorite times of the day, when it was just the two of them, before real life stepped in.

"He's never been good at sitting still," Madigan said.

"I believe it. He's been working his butt off on this place, so if they are kicking back, good for them. As long as nobody complains about the burned ziti casserole, I don't care what they do."

"The way they wolf food down, they won't even notice," Madigan said as they climbed the porch steps. "Besides, you didn't burn it. It's just a little brown."

They headed inside, and Shauna couldn't believe her eyes. When she and Madigan had left earlier, they'd had tarps sealing off the living room from the rest of the cottage to keep the drywall dust confined, and the living room had been stockpiled with stones and tools and tarps. All the tarps and tools were cleaned up, except the tarp between the living room and dining room. The entire living room was drywalled and taped, and gorgeous stonework surrounded the fireplace, climbing all the way up to the ceiling.

She and Zander had spent forever choosing stone, and it was even more beautiful than she'd imagined it would be. Music was blaring, Tobias was coiling an extension cord, joking with Zeke as he put something in a box, and Blaine was wiping down tools. Maverick dried his hands on a rag, then snapped Blaine with it, and in the middle of the room was Zander, dusty from head to boots, pushing a shop vac across the floor. Shauna watched his muscles flexing, remembering how good they'd felt against her last night. He turned, catching her staring, and winked, sending a shiver of heat through her.

"*Wow*. This place looks amazing!" Madigan exclaimed, startling Shauna from her trance.

Zander chuckled as he turned off the vacuum. The brat

never missed a thing, and he was closing the distance between them with a cocky swagger that told her he knew it.

"Hey, Blue Eyes," Tobias called to Madigan as he set the extension cord down.

Zeke turned off the music and said, "Hope that food is for us. I'm starved."

As Madigan and the guys talked about food, Zander slid a hand to Shauna's back and said, "What do you think, Angel? We still have to put in the mantel and do a few coats of mud and sanding, but it should be ready to paint by next weekend."

"It's gorgeous. I can't believe this is the same cottage I walked into and wondered if you were really a serial killer who might bury my body at sea."

He laughed.

"He'd never risk getting blood on his boat," Blaine said.

"That's true," Maverick hollered.

"Well, it looks incredible," Shauna said. "You guys must be hungry from all that hard work."

"Hold on, Angel. Before we eat, I've got one more thing to show you." He walked over to the tarp hanging in front of the dining room.

"Did you paint the dining room?" she asked excitedly. They'd chosen a color a few days ago.

He didn't answer as he unhooked one side of the tarp and Zeke unhooked the other and yanked it to his side of the entryway.

Shauna's jaw dropped, the casserole dish wobbling in her hands. "Zan. Is that a *pole*?" Her cheeks burned, but her heart thudded faster.

"It's a unique dining room showpiece, don't you think?" Maverick said, taking the casserole dish and the bag from her.

Shauna couldn't think at the moment. She could do little more than stare at Zander.

"He said it was for *exercise*," Tobias chimed in.

"I bet it is," Madigan teased, earning a round of laughter.

Zander shrugged, like he hadn't just shocked the hell out of her. "I thought you might want to have one of your own to practice on. It's not like Kitty needs the whole dining room for her toys."

Shauna walked into the dining room and touched the pole as she circled it. "You really are crazy."

The guys laughed.

"So I've heard," Zander said.

"This is as amazing as the living room." She couldn't stop smiling. "I don't know what to say."

"Say you'll give us a demo," Zeke said coolly. "I've got a few twenties."

"Hey, that's my wife you're talking about." Zander shot him a narrow-eyed glare. "She doesn't *work the pole*, asshole."

"That explains why you've been so grouchy," Zeke quipped, and the guys howled with laughter.

Shauna strutted into the living room, eyeing Zeke, and said, "I think what Zan meant to say was that I don't give demos to anyone who didn't give me a ring and a vow."

"Oh, man," Maverick said.

The guys broke into laughter and jeers, and Madigan said, "Way to shut him down, Shauna."

Zander squared his shoulders like he'd won a prize, and that had Shauna's heart doing somersaults.

Blaine and Maverick went home to eat with their families, but Shauna and Zander had a great time with Tobias, Madigan, and Zeke. The guys raved about the meal, and afterward, they helped clean up, which she knew was a Wicked thing. Eventually they made their way to the door and said their goodbyes.

"Have fun *exercising* tonight," Madigan said as she and Tobias headed out.

"Zan, you'd better hydrate before she practices with that pole so you don't overheat," Zeke chimed in before climbing into his truck.

As Zander closed the door behind them, Shauna admired the living room, the echo of family lingering like a smile. Zander's arms slid around her middle, his scruffy cheek tickling her skin. "Did you miss me today?"

"Like a sore thumb." She turned around, soaking in his grin.

"Did you have fun with the girls?"

"It was a blast. Lettie wasn't kidding about gossip. I learned a lot today."

"Care to share?"

"Nope. Girl code. I'm sworn to secrecy, but I can tell you that your cousins and brothers and Tobias are very well loved. Chloe and Leah brought their girls, and they were so freaking cute. I picture you and Zeke when you were younger to be like Rosie and Junie."

His brows slanted. "What do you mean?"

"You said Zeke always watched out for you, and that's what Junie does for Rosie. I can see how it could be too much as they get older, but it's really special how much Junie loves her little sister."

He was quiet for a beat before responding. "Yeah, it is."

Shauna glanced into the dining room at the pole, and happiness filled her up anew. "Thank you for the pole. I still can't believe you put one up."

"I'm glad you like it. I know how much you enjoy your classes, and I thought you might want to practice without driving across town. No big deal."

Like it? She loved it, and she loved that he'd thought about what made her happy and went to the trouble of putting up the pole. Maybe that level of generosity was just the kind of thing that these big-hearted Wicked men did, but to her it was a very big deal.

She dragged her finger down his chest and sauntered into the dining room, where she brushed her fingers along the cool metal as she circled the pole. "So, do you want that demo my brother-in-law asked for?"

Heat flared in his eyes. "Is that a trick question?"

"I'm not into trickery, so I'll take that as a yes." Her pulse quickened as she toed off her sneakers and tugged off her socks. "It'll be hard to do with all these clothes on."

Those piercing blue eyes were trained on her as she stripped off her shorts and tank top. His jaw clenched, his lips curving in a devilish grin as she stood in her underwear and bra, navigating to "Pour Some Sugar on Me" on her pole playlist. She hit play and set her phone down.

Keeping her back to Zander, she wrapped one hand around the pole, went up on her toes, and rocked her hips to the beat. Bending at the waist, she ran her hand down one straight leg, flipped her hair forward, then back, and tossed him a seductive glance over her shoulder as she ran her hand back up her leg, starting the sexy dance she'd been imagining doing just for him.

Strutting around the pole, she reached up, curled both hands around it, and propelled into a spin, knees bent, back arched, eyes on him. She lowered her feet to the floor for only a second before lifting straight legs up and over each shoulder, knowing the view of her ass would drive him wild.

"You're so fucking sexy," he growled as her toes touched the floor and she twirled around the pole.

She threw in hip dips, then hooked one leg behind the pole, launching into a back-hook spin, momentum carrying her around the pole in a graceful sweep. It wasn't flawless as her feet touched the floor, but the look on Zander's face told her it didn't matter one damn bit. She sank down on her knees, facing him, then grabbed the bar behind her and went up on her toes, bringing her body parallel to the floor, and undulated her hips.

Fuuck." He grabbed his groin, adjusting himself. His gaze was volcanic, his body wound tight, like she was fire and one more move might set him ablaze.

Burn, baby, burn. She rose to her feet, one hand on the pole, and wound her legs like a clock in a fan kick. Her hair whipped over her shoulder as she twirled around the pole again, hooked one knee around it, and leaned back, arching as her hand traced the line of her own thigh, then pulled herself upright with a twist that brought her face-to-face with his hungry stare. Heat rushed through her, and he charged forward, lifting her into his arms like a Neanderthal claiming his prey.

She laughed. "I was just warming up."

"You get any hotter and the whole fucking house will go up in flames." He headed down the hall to their bedroom.

"But I didn't get to finish."

"You'll finish all right. *Several* times."

Chapter Thirty-Six

WAKEFULNESS DRIFTED IN as soft and welcoming as the ocean breeze shifting the curtains and the sunlight sprinkling through them. Shauna inhaled the sea air and stretched across the empty bed, curling her arm around Kitty, who was fast asleep on Zander's pillow, and nuzzled in. "Good morning, baby girl. Looks like your daddy slipped out earlier than usual." She closed her eyes, homing in on the faint sounds coming from the kitchen, and smiled. It was July fourth, her twenty-fifth birthday, and her heart was happy.

There was a time when she hadn't been sure she'd make it to eighteen, much less twenty-five. When she and Brian had run away with nothing but fear and the promise of freedom ahead of them, she'd had big dreams of a better life. But there were so many times she'd questioned their ability to keep themselves safe. Years of blurry days and incoherent nights when she'd held Brian up or had nearly drowned herself right alongside him.

But she'd made it to twenty-five, sober, happy, with a job she loved, a temporary husband she was trying not to fall for, and more friends than she'd ever dreamed of having.

As she rolled onto her back, the bracelet Cap had given her slid down her wrist. She touched the charm, and her heart squeezed. She'd been devastated when she'd thought it was gone forever, swallowed by the riptide of her life.

Zander had saved her from that riptide, just as he'd unknowingly given her a lifeline on this very day, five years ago. She'd like to believe she'd given him a lifeline, too, the day she'd pulled him from his burning car. She knew it wasn't the same. He'd given her a home, a family, friends. He'd made space for her without any limitations or expectations. He made her laugh when she thought she'd forgotten how. And God help her, she loved falling asleep in his strong arms, his heart beating sure and steady against her cheek. She loved the way he smelled, the way he touched her, the way he could go from joking to lustful or serious in the blink of an eye. But the biggest thing he'd given her was the safety to trust. She'd kept her circle small because trust had always felt like a weakness, a crack someone could pry open and use against her. She'd been thinking about that a lot lately. Her parents had never trusted anyone. That was part of addiction, hiding their secrets. She'd learned to hide hers and had lived in that tiny, untrusting world she'd created even after she'd clawed her way to sobriety. Then Zander came into her life again and showed her that trust could be a strength, and allowing people in could enrich her life, not upend it.

But this magical world he'd brought her into, this pretend life they were creating together, was coming to an end. In two short weeks Brian would be home, and she'd move back to their cottage. She missed him like crazy, and she couldn't wait to see him, but she was also nervous. They had a long road ahead, and she knew they'd make it through. Brian was her *real* family, her first best friend, and for most of her life, her only anchor. Now she wondered if a person could have two anchors. Two very different best friends? Brian owned a big part of her heart, but she feared the rest of it was no longer hers alone. She'd tried to keep some semblance of walls around herself these past few months, but Zander had been chipping away at them without even trying, and in doing so, he'd not only claimed a big part of her heart, but he'd also helped her find herself.

They may not be meant for forever, but she'd always have the stronger, happier woman she'd become with him. Hopefully that would be enough to start shoring up her walls again, because if she fell any harder for Zander, she'd never be able to walk away.

She heard the floor creak and glanced toward the open bedroom door, picking up the faint smell of paint. They'd finished painting the living room two weeks ago, but once it was done, the hallway had looked dingy, so they'd painted that. She smiled, remembering the chaos of rollers and laughter, of Zander stripping her naked and pinning her against the wall, leaving butt prints that he refused to let her smooth over. *Conversation starters.* Since then, he'd thrown himself into a big renovation project at work. He'd been working later in the evenings, and she'd taken a stab at cooking and having dinner ready a few times, thanks to her cooking lessons with Reba and the girls over the past few weeks. Zander was always appreciative, even on the nights she'd burned their meals.

His voice floated in from the hallway as he sang, *"Happy birthday to my Angel. Happy birthday to my wife."* He appeared in the doorway wearing a sexy grin, black boxer briefs, and a tool belt with a can of whipped cream in the hammer holder, utensils and napkins in one pocket, and a jar of maple syrup in another, and carrying a plate of pancakes and a steaming mug of coffee. *"Happy birthday, you sexy thing. Thanks for letting me share your life."*

So much for shoring up those walls. She melted like chocolate in the sun as he set down the plate and mug, then leaned down and kissed her, sending Kitty scampering to the floor.

"Happy twenty-fifth, darlin'."

He was hands-down the swooniest man on the planet. "This looks amazing. Thank you. I've never had breakfast in bed."

He smirked. "We both know that's not true."

"I meant *food*," she said with a laugh.

She leaned forward to snag the whipped cream from his tool belt, but he grabbed it first with a devilish spark in his eyes and said, "Back off, birthday girl." He emptied the tool belt onto the nightstand, put a dollop of whipped cream on her pancakes, and unhooked his tool belt, dropping it to the floor. "The rest is for the other half of your birthday present, and *my* breakfast."

He threw the covers back, and she laughed. "That pretty little tank top has to go." He waved the can of whipped cream. "Go on, now. Take it off."

"Bossy." She took it off and threw it at him.

He caught it and said, "This'll do nicely."

"Do…?"

A slow grin slid into place as he straddled her. He set the can of whipped cream beside them on the mattress, still holding her tank top, and said, "Give me your wrists, darlin'."

Her nerves caught fire with his titillating request, but she wanted to explore with him. She held out her wrists. He took her left hand in his, holding her gaze as he pressed a kiss over her wedding ring, then proceeded to wrap the tank top around her wrists. She swallowed hard as he secured it with a knot.

"Trust looks beautiful on you."

His words slid beneath her skin, gentle, thrilling, *emboldening*, as he guided her arms over her head and came down over her. He brushed his scruff along her cheek, sending prickles of heat down her chest, and rasped, "Open your mouth, darlin'."

Those prickles of heat were nothing compared to the scorching anticipation of his gruff request. Her thoughts ran through possibilities of what he might do as she complied.

He sprayed whipped cream on her tongue, then sealed his mouth over hers in a domineering act of passion, like he was trying to erase any space between them. She opened her mouth wider, willingly handing him that space. He took the kiss deeper, the taste of sweet cream and *him* colliding in an electrifying combination, and she was there for it. She bowed beneath him, meeting every inch of his hard, hot body, desperate for more even as the force of their kisses threatened to shatter her.

He tore his mouth away, leaving her breathless, bound, and utterly lost in his ruining. His grin was dark and *gratified* as he picked up the can of whipped cream and shook it, his eyes trained on her as if daring her to protest.

Protest against something that would lead to his mouth on her? *Never.*

When the cold whipped cream landed on her nipple, she gasped. His lips curved up as he sprayed it on her other nipple and then dragged that nozzle straight down the center of her body, those hungry eyes following all the way down to the edge of her underwear, like he was mapping a trail only *he* was allowed to travel. Setting down the can, he dragged his tongue around one nipple, then lowered his mouth over it, sucking it to the roof of his mouth. Lightning sparked in her core, a desperate sound shooting from her lips. He gave her other nipple the same excruciating attention.

"Who needs coffee when I've got you to get me going?" she

panted out.

A rough laugh fell from his lips, and then that talented mouth was on her again, slowly and deliberately making its way down the trail of whipped cream. "Sweet and messy. Just the way I like you."

Her laugh broke on a shiver as he slicked his tongue down her stomach. He continued licking, sucking, and nipping his way south, groping and caressing, making gruff, appreciative sounds as she writhed and pleaded, her wrists fighting against their tether. By the time he reached her underwear, she was trembling with anticipation. He wasted no time stripping off the thin cotton and snagged the can of whipped cream, his eyes gleaming with wicked intent. "Time for my favorite breakfast."

"Get busy, or I'm charging for room service."

His laugh was sinful as he covered her neediest parts in whipped cream. Tossing the can to the floor, he buried that sinful mouth between her legs in a fierce devouring, stealing the breath from her lungs. Every slick of his tongue and graze of his teeth, every greedy suck and kiss, drove her ache deeper. When he brought his hands into play, she shattered like glass, sharp and loud against his masterful ministrations.

Just as she started to catch her breath and sink to the mattress, he quickened his efforts, reaching up with one hand to squeeze her nipple, catapulting her into oblivion. *"Zander—"* shot from her lungs, and she threw her bound wrists forward, grabbing his hair. "I want *you*."

In the space of a few heart-thrumming seconds, he was naked and driving into her. They both cried out as their bodies took over, thrusting and grinding. "Need your hands on me," he growled, and tore the binding from her wrists. She clung to him as their mouths fused like molten metal in a savage kiss, all heat and teeth and hunger, unraveling her more by the second. Their every move, every touch, was like fire, blazing and building, and he was burning and climbing with her. His muscles flexed and his powerful hips thrusted harder and faster, unleashing a tidal wave of sensations that tore through her at the same moment he growled her name, rough and unguarded, as if she'd wrung it from his soul.

They rode out their storm of passion until all that was left were aftershocks and gasps, clinging to one another like survivors of something earth-shattering. Something bigger than the two of them. Something Shauna couldn't afford to think about, and never wanted to escape.

Chapter Thirty-Seven

SHAUNA WAS THINKING about her and Zander's whipped-cream sexcapade while she finished restocking the ambulance later that morning, when her phone chimed with a group text from the girls. She'd already received texts from Preacher and Reba.

Madigan: *Happy birthday Sha Sha! I can't believe we had to find out it was your birthday from Zander. We could have planned a party!*

Shauna hadn't even thought to mention it to them, but she wasn't surprised Zander had. He was so thoughtful, and he knew how much she loved the girls and appreciated their friendships. Before she could respond, more texts rolled in.

Chloe: *Happiest of birthdays, Shauna! We'll miss you at the fireworks tonight, but let's plan a time to celebrate. You only turn 25 once!*

Emerson: *I'm baking you birthday cookies! I can't believe your birthday is July 4th!*

Sid: *Happy birthday! A cat makes a great gift. The rescue is open tomorrow. Come pick one out.*

Reese: *We should def plan a party. Happy birthday!*

Leah: *The kids are making you birthday cards, and next time I see you, I'm giving you a big birthday hug. Happy 25th!*

Shauna's throat thickened as she thumbed out a response.

Shauna: *Thank you! I'd love to get together, but I'll pass on picking out a cat until—*her thumbs stilled over the buttons, the rest of the thought, *until she moved out of Zander's,* stopping her cold.

Howie came out the firehouse door and called over to her, "Hey, Flores, Cap wants you in the dayroom."

"One sec," she called out, and with her heart in her throat, she quickly finished typing the message—*I move out of Zander's. I'll miss cuddling—*with him and—*with Kitty. I've got to run. Cap needs me, but thank you again for the birthday wishes!*

Madigan: *Tell Cap we said hi!*

Shauna sent a thumbs-up emoji and pocketed her phone as she headed into the station. She heard the guys talking as she came down the hall. The second she stepped into the dayroom, a sharp click overhead made her flinch, and a burst of confetti rained down on her in a blinding paper storm. Colorful strips clung to her hair, her lashes, and even her mouth as she sputtered, half-startled, half-laughing. The guys cheered, "Happy birthday!" as they popped out from various hiding places and drenched her with Super Soakers.

She shouted, "Seriously?" trying to dodge the streams as she ran to the other side of the room, laughing.

"Got you!" Mike shouted as he pelted her back with his Super Soaker.

She spun around, confetti sticking to her wet clothes, and Cap sprinted past, spraying her. "You too?"

"Couldn't let the boys have all the fun," Cap said with a grin.

She rolled her eyes, but her cheeks hurt from smiling so hard.

"And we couldn't let your birthday pass without getting you something," Lance said.

She plucked a piece of wet confetti from her cheek. "Just what I always wanted, a confetti shower."

"Nah, we got you something better than that," Paul chimed in.

"I'll get it!" Mike tossed his Super Soaker onto the table and ran to the kitchen. He reappeared with a pink-frosted cake covered in strawberries.

Shauna laughed. "You got me your favorite cake?"

"Hey, it's a classic!" Mike said.

Howie cuffed him on the back of the head. "Dude, I told you to get her something *she'd* like."

Warmth bloomed in her chest as they gave Mike a hard time. They were rowdy and could be annoying, but they were her family, too, and she loved them.

"Sorry, Flores," Mike said.

"It's perfect," she said, just like today was, with the exception of not seeing Brian.

"What'd loverboy get you?" Lance asked.

Her traitorous heart warmed with the memory of their sexcapade and how much she'd enjoyed having her wrists bound.

"That look screams X-rated gift to me," Paul said, and the guys howled with laughter, like they were in on her secret.

"All gifts should be X-rated when you're newlyweds," Howie added.

"No wonder she was glowing this morning," Lance said.

"Our little girl is finally getting some," Mike said.

Shauna laughed despite herself. The arrangement might be fake, but she liked living in this very real bubble of happiness.

LATER THAT AFTERNOON, Shauna stretched her shoulders as she headed to the ambulance in front of their latest call site. Thankfully it had gone smoothly, just a small kitchen fire and a panic attack.

Cap was leaning against the fire truck, his arms crossed and his eyes on her in that quiet, steady way of his. "Sorry about the water guns."

"No, you're not. It was fun." She leaned beside him, exhaling. "I'm glad this wasn't worse."

"You and me, both." He looked over at the firefighters talking to the homeowners for a minute before turning back to Shauna. "How're things with Zander? Still think you made the right decision?"

Cap had checked in with her a couple of times, and she appreciated it. "Things are good, and yes. I know I made the right decision."

"Good. And when it ends?" He cocked a brow.

She forced a laugh. "Then it ends. No big deal."

He lifted his brows knowingly.

"Ugh. *Fine.* It's not no big deal, exactly. I mean, he's really good at playing the part, and sometimes it feels real. Like we're an *us*, you know?"

He nodded slowly. "Yeah. I do. That's why I'm asking. I don't know if it's Zander, or Brian going to rehab, or both, but you've changed. You seem lighter, happier."

"Thanks. I think it's both, and his family and the friends I've made through them," she said honestly. Then she forced those squishy feelings down deep, forcing steel into her spine, for the reality bearing down on her. "But you don't have to worry about me, Cap. After this arrangement is over, I'm not going to fall off the wagon. I'll snap back to my grumpier self and help Brian through his recovery."

He smiled. "Shauna, you're never grumpy. Closed off and tough, maybe. But not grumpy. Are you ready for Brian to come home?"

His coming home felt like a double-edged sword. "Yeah. I'm looking forward to seeing him."

"Promise me you will not try to shoulder it alone this time," he cautioned gently.

"I give you my word." She met his gaze. "I've learned my lesson, and I'll never try to cover up for him again."

"Good. You know if you need me, I'm here for any and all of it."

Warmth curled in her chest, but before she could respond, Howie shouted, "Hey, birthday girl. You leaving me with all the paperwork?"

Shauna turned back to Cap, but he'd already walked away, leaving her with the weight of his words and an ache she couldn't quite shake.

ZANDER SAT IN his truck in the firehouse parking lot watching the rigs roll into the garage, hoping Shauna hadn't spotted him. He noted the time, starting the twenty-minute countdown for Shauna to complete her post-call procedures of restocking, sanitizing, and whatever else needed to be done before he could bother her. Cap had told him it usually took about that long and had suggested asking Howie to do the post-call procedures for her, but Zander knew his girl too well. She hated shirking her responsibilities.

If the gods were on his side, she wouldn't get another call right away, and he'd get to spend some time with her. He'd missed her today. Hell, he missed her whenever they were apart.

He zipped off a text, climbed out of the truck, and got to work laying out a nest of pillows and blankets in the truck bed, then set up the hibachi and cooler near the tailgate. He put out plates and silverware, glasses and drinks, and grabbed a few wildflowers from the field, tucking them into the string lights he'd hung around the frame of the truck bed.

After twenty minutes he made his way into the garage and spotted Shauna heading for the firehouse door with Howie. She looked tired, but so fucking beautiful, she was the best damn sight he'd ever seen.

"Shauna," he called out.

She turned, startled, and her whole face brightened as he closed the distance between them. "Zan. What are you doing here?"

"Having dinner with my wife on her birthday." He lifted his chin to Howie. "How's it going, man?"

"Great, but you keep this up, and you're going to give the rest of us husbands a bad rep."

Zander laughed. "Better up your game if you want to keep your woman."

Howie shook his head and headed inside.

With a hand on Shauna's back, he said, "Can you sit outside for a bit?"

"Sure." As they headed out of the garage, she said, "I thought you were having dinner with your family at the beach and then watching the fireworks."

"And let my girl spend the anniversary of the day we met alone? I don't think so."

She looked at him like he'd hung the moon. "We have an anniversary," she said softly, as if it were the first time she realized the day they'd met could be called that.

"Yes, we do. Technically we have several. The day we met, the day you saved my life, the day I proposed, the day we got married, the first time you stuck your tongue down my throat." He pulled her closer and said, "The first time you seduced me."

She laughed as he led her around his truck, and those dimples appeared, deep and devastating, when she saw what he'd done. She leaned into him and said, "You really do put other husbands to shame."

"Only for you, Angel."

Her glorious smile faltered. "This is incredible, Zan, but you know I could get a call at any time, and you went to so much trouble."

"Don't you think I thought about that?" He lit the hibachi. "Tonight is yours, darlin'. If you get called away, I'll be here waiting when you get back."

"*No.* Don't waste your time waiting for me. Calls can take forever if they're bad. Especially on holidays."

"Save your breath, Flores," he teased. "I'm a big boy. I can entertain myself until you get back." His phone rang. *Right on time.* He pulled it from his pocket, seeing Brian's name on the incoming video call. He brushed his thumb over the edge of the phone. He'd planned this moment for her. He *wanted* this moment for her, but that didn't ease the tightness in his chest as he hit the green icon and said, "It's for you, darlin'," and handed her the phone.

Confusion riddled her brow as she took it, and gasped when she saw Brian's face on the screen. Her gaze flicked to Zander with disbelief, then back to the screen. *"Brian."* Her voice cracked.

"Happy birthday, Shauna." Brian's voice was rough but happy, his eyes clear and sharp. "You staying out of trouble?"

Zander stepped away, struggling against the tug in his chest. She'd lit up in a different way at the sight of Brian than she did with Zander. He'd wondered if she would. Or maybe he'd known she would. It was Brian, after all. Her comrade in arms. The one she'd run away with, sacrificed for, and loved with a piece of herself Zander could never touch. He'd known that from the start, but he hadn't expected to feel so much, and it gutted him.

He stuck by the hibachi, trying not to eavesdrop, but Shauna remained too close for him not to hear their conversation. They asked after each other, and Brian told her how well he was doing and how much he missed her. She did the same, omitting how close she and Zander had gotten and their honeymoon, with a simple, *He's been great.* Zander tried to ignore the way that stung, but he knew she didn't want Brian knowing they'd had to get married.

"I wish I was there with you," Brian said.

"Me too, but you're doing what you need to, and I'm so proud of you."

"You sure you're okay?" Brian asked, his tone somber.

"Yes. I'm great, but I'll be even better when you come home."

"The next two weeks can't go fast enough. You're still picking me up?"

"I wouldn't miss it for the world."

Someone called to Brian from off-screen, and he said, "I've got to go. I love you."

Zander looked over just in time to see Shauna's smile tremble as she said, "I love you, too," and ended the call. She closed her eyes, holding the phone to her chest, and inhaled deeply before turning to Zander, her shaky smile lingering as she handed him the phone. "Thank you."

He pocketed his phone. "You okay?"

"Yeah." She swiped at her tears.

"Would you like to talk about it?"

She shook her head. "No, I'm okay, really. But I am curious, did you arrange that call, or did Brian reach out to you?"

"I arranged it," he admitted. "I figured you needed to see that he was okay, and I thought the way he left things with you, he might appreciate an olive branch and need to see you, too."

"I think we both needed it, thank you for thinking of us," she said unevenly.

"Always. Listen, I know you will be there for Brian as much as you can, but you can't be his only support."

"I know. I've already looked into meetings, and I'm going to take him to one after he's settled in back home. It could take a while to find him a sponsor, so for now, I'm the only one he's got."

"He's got me, too, and my family."

"I'd never do that to you," she said vehemently.

"You're not doing anything to me. I was there when things went bad, and I'm not going to let him flounder or let you shoulder it all by yourself. You're scheduled to work the day after he comes home. He's going to need someone to be there, to go to meetings with him, and tell him how great he's doing. I'll be there."

Her brows knitted, and she pressed her lips together. "You're serious?"

"Dead serious. I talked with Preacher and the guys, and they're all on board. Preacher brought it up at church this week, and a few of our members are sponsors. They're willing to take Brian on if he's comfortable with any of them, and if he's not, then we'll reach out to others until we find someone he is comfortable with."

She looked up at the sky, blinking at tears, and shaking her head.

"Don't shake your head at me, darlin'. I told you that first night, once you're in our world, we'll always have your back." He was about to reach for her when she cleared her throat and drew her shoulders back in the show of strength he knew so well.

"Well, Mr. Wicked, your review just shot up to twelve stars, and that call is at the top of my Best Birthday Gift list right alongside breakfast in bed."

She looked at him with as much strength as deeper emotion, and as much as he wanted to pull her closer, he knew she needed the space, and granted it.

They grilled burgers and sat on the nest of blankets and pillows, talking about their day while they ate. When they finished eating, he pushed to his feet in the bed of the truck and reached for her hand, pulling her up to her feet. "Time to get out of the truck for dessert." He pulled her up to her feet.

"That sounds questionable," she said as they climbed down.

"As much as I'd like to do dirty things to you in this field, I think Cap would have my ass in a sling if I tried." He pulled her in for a kiss, then smacked her ass and said, "Turn around, darlin'."

"What are you up to?" she asked as she turned around.

"You'll see." He took the chocolate-frosted cupcake with rainbow sprinkles out of the cooler and put it on a plate, then stuck a sparkler in the center of it and lit it. "Happy birthday, Angel."

She turned around, and her face lit up brighter than the sun as sparks flew. "A sparkler! I *love* it! Can I…?" She reached for it.

"Go for it. I brought a whole box of them."

She snagged the sparkler and let out a little squeal as she ran across the grass drawing shapes in the air with it. "Look! Zan!"

The truth he'd been trying to deny hit him like a punch to the gut. He wanted more of this. More of *her*. He didn't just want to *see* her smile or hear her laugh as she experienced the shock and delight of discovering new things. He wanted to be the man who brought her those experiences and earned those stunning reactions. He wanted to be the man who made her coffee and ate her burned casseroles, and he wanted it every day of their lives.

He wasn't sure what to do with those feelings, given everything between Shauna and Brian, and the end of their arrangement closing in on them, so he shoved them down deep to deal with another time, and pulled out his phone, taking pictures and a video of his excited girl. He may not have forever figured out, but she was his wife for now, and he wasn't going to let anything ruin it.

"Light two more!" she called out. "One for each of us!"

He did, and for a little while, Zander set everything else aside and became a kid again with her, dueling with sparkler swords, drawing pictures in the air, and laughing like his heart wasn't growing too big for his chest.

When she'd had her fill, they headed back to the truck. "That was so fun!" she exclaimed. "What a perfect birthday."

"I have one more present for you, Angel."

"Another one? You've already spoiled me rotten."

"Hardly." He opened the back door of his truck and grabbed the large gift box with a red ribbon tied around it.

Her eyes widened. "That's *huge*."

He smirked.

"You have such a dirty mind." She whispered, "I like it!" as she took the box and set it on the tailgate to untie the ribbon.

She lifted the top, and her breath caught, those pretty eyes moving over the fabric cover of the memory album with SHAUNA AND ZANDER'S EXCELLENT ADVENTURE embroidered on another piece of striped fabric with rough edges made to look like a torn piece of paper. A shaky laugh fell from her lips, and "*Zander...?*" followed, an incredulous whisper. Her gaze flicked to him as she lifted the thick memory book out of the box.

"You know all those nights I said I was working on a project?"

"Yeah."

"This was the project. I was at Maverick and Chloe's. She helped me put it together. I'm sorry I lied to you, but I didn't want to order a memory book online or let Chloe make it on her own. I wanted to decide what went on the pages, and all the rest."

Her eyes went glassy. "I love that you did that."

She opened the album, running her fingers around the pictures, four on each page, decorated with items from each event. They weren't posed photos, but real-life candid shots of Shauna cuddling Kitty when she'd first moved in, already looking like she belonged with them, and of her sitting on the counter tiling the backsplash, which he'd taken when she wasn't looking. She lingered on a picture he'd taken of them lying on a lounge chair in the early-morning light, Shauna's cheek resting on his bare chest beside the number four charm around his neck. Above the picture he'd written OUR LUCKY CHARMS. On one side of the page, he'd written YOURS with an arrow pointing to the necklace, and on the other side of the page he'd written MINE with an arrow pointing to her. On the same page was a picture of his hand covering hers, the tattoo of her initials on his finger and the tattooed number four on her hand, as clear as day.

There were pictures of glitter between couch cushions taken weeks after the Kitty debacle, and of the two of them having ice cream the day they'd bought their wedding rings. He'd glued the napkin that she'd written PRENUP on to the page, which made her laugh.

Her fingers trailed over pictures of their wedding—Shauna walking down the aisle with Cap, looking nervous in one picture, and in the next, the two of them standing before Preacher with something akin to hope in their eyes. Zander's chest burned when she touched the picture of them kissing. *Man, that kiss.* He felt the same burn in his chest as he'd felt then.

She lingered over candid shots of her rubbing noses with Marybelle, one of his favorites, and laughing with the girls. There were pictures of her with his parents and his grandfather, and pictures of her and Zander talking with his brothers and cousins, his arm slung over her shoulder and so much pride in his eyes, he wondered if she could feel it.

She admired page after page of memories he'd never forget. Shauna drenched and gorgeous on the boat by the falls only moments before they'd given in to the unrelenting heat between them. She smiled at the pictures of their suite, one room messy with their belongings, the other untouched, and the basket on the table with sparkling cider instead of champagne, which she'd found out Zander had requested. Above the pictures he'd written *Your room or mine?* He'd taken a picture of their suite number, which she hadn't noticed until he'd pointed it out. *404.* Shauna laughed at a picture of a pile of empty French vanilla creamer cups stacked like trophies on the table in the café where they'd had breakfast on their honeymoon.

When she came to pictures from the amusement park, she pointed to one of her behind the wheel of the go-kart, grinning like she was queen of the track, and said, "I don't remember you taking this."

"That was the point."

She shook her head at the picture of her flying through the air on the zipline. "I was so scared."

"But you did it anyway, because nothing can hold Shauna Flores down."

There were dozens of selfies of the two of them smiling, scowling, laughing, and making funny faces, with paint-smeared cheeks, holding ice cream cones, sitting by the ocean, holding coffee cups, and with Kitty in her cut and other outfits. There were pictures of them at the gym and of Shauna practicing on the pole in the dining room, and a montage of Shauna in a towel after a shower, hand on her hip, giving him grief for taking the picture, and of her brushing her teeth, putting up her hair, and another of her curled up in his bed wearing one of his Dark Knights T-shirts with Kitty tucked against her stomach, the two of them fast asleep.

When she turned the last page, taking in the picture he'd

taken on their honeymoon right before they'd gone for their first motorcycle ride, she studied it. She was sitting behind him on the bike, wearing her shiny new helmet and leather jacket, her arms wrapped around his middle and her chin resting on his shoulder. She couldn't know that behind his helmet, he was grinning so hard, his cheeks hurt with the memory. Above the picture he'd scrawled THANKS FOR GETTING SWEPT AWAY WITH ME, ANGEL, and under the picture, he'd signed it LOVE, ZANDER, YOUR IRRESISTIBLY WICKED BEST FRIEND, and included ten gold stars beneath it.

It was all there, their friendship and temporary marriage laid bare, looking realer than he'd ever admit out loud, and the thought of losing it carved an ache too deep to name.

"Zan, this is…" Her voice trailed off as she closed the album, her glassy eyes still trained on it.

"I'm glad you like it. Our marriage may be temporary, but our memories are forever."

"You've given me everything I could have asked for and more." She lifted her gaze to his, a thousand emotions flickering in her eyes. She hugged the album to her chest, her lips parting like she might say more, but then she looked away.

He felt her walls going up again.

She turned back to him with just enough distance for him to feel the difference and said, "I can't believe how fast the time went." She reached for the box the album had come in and said, "Hopefully when I call the attorney, it'll get things moving quickly."

He watched the woman he wanted more than anything in the world tuck their memories into a box like she could put the lid on it and they wouldn't bleed through. She had given him her trust, had shared her body and her heart—and she just reminded him that they weren't his to keep.

Chapter Thirty-Eight

THIS IS IT. The beginning of the end echoed painfully in Shauna's mind as she padded into the living room wearing one of Zander's T-shirts she'd claimed as her own. She was picking up Brian from rehab today. She'd spent the last two weeks standing on a double-edged sword, but today it felt sharper than ever. She was elated that he'd worked hard, had stuck it out, and was getting a second chance at a sober life. It would be a fresh start for them, but it came at a price she hadn't fully expected to hit so hard.

Kitty meowed at her feet, sharpening that sword a little more.

Shauna picked her up and looked around the beautiful home she'd been part of bringing to life, memories dancing in every corner. From the pole in the dining room where practicing always led to Zander chasing her, tackling her on the couch in a fit of giggles and kisses, or hauling her over his shoulder and throwing her onto his bed, and the picture of them on the *Maid of the Mist*, hair drenched, smiling down from the mantel among photos of his family and the picture of her and Brian. When she'd walked into the shell of a cottage a few months ago, she never would have imagined falling in love with it or with the wonderful man standing on the beach out back, looking like she'd seen him nearly every morning for the past three months. He was shirtless, his jeans hanging low on his hips as he gazed out at the water, coffee mug in hand, the ink on his back now achingly familiar.

She pressed a kiss to Kitty's head, a lump forming in her throat as she whispered, "I'm going to miss this." *All of it. You, him, and our quiet mornings. Our busy days with a million texts and our sexy nights. And this peaceful, happy feeling of belonging, and wanting and being wanted, and not walking through life clutching the reins.*

But falling in love with Zander wasn't part of the agreement, and if ever there was a day for her to pull up her big-girl panties and do what she needed to, it was today. The attorney said the money would be in her account today, and once she had it, she'd pay Zander back, they'd sign the divorce papers, and that would be the end of it. Then she could focus on Brian. She and Brian had a long road ahead of them, and Brian didn't need to see the fissures forming in her heart. He needed, and deserved, her strength and support delivered with all of the pride and happiness she felt for what he'd accomplished and what she knew he'd achieve moving forward.

With that resolve in place, she gave Kitty another kiss and set her down as she headed out to the patio door. She was greeted with the warmth of the sun and the sounds of the waves kissing the shore. She'd miss that, too.

Zander turned, the sun catching the gold charm resting against his chest. His gaze drifted down the length of her, his lips curved up in that lazy, sexy smile she'd come to adore. "Morning, Angel."

"Morning."

He reached for her, like he did every morning, drawing her against his warm skin, and kissed her soft and sweet. "Did you sleep okay?"

"Mm-hm." She hadn't expected to, with so many changes coming up, but in Zander's arms, she'd gone out like a light.

He sat down on the lounge chair and widened his legs for her to sit between them. As she settled her back against his chest, she saw her coffee mug on the table beside them. He put his mug beside it and wound his arms around her. Brushing his scruff against her cheek—another thing she'd miss—he said, "I see you eyeing your coffee, but I don't have many mornings left to do this, so give me a minute."

She crossed her arms over his, holding on to the longing in his voice, and at the same time, not allowing herself to get lost in it. "Careful, Wicked, or I'm going to think you'll miss me." He tensed up a little, and she wondered if he *wasn't* going to miss her.

"I'll miss your sexy ass in my bed." He nipped at her shoulder, sending heat prickling through her. "And my private pole dances." He kissed the spot he'd bitten. "And I'll probably miss a few other things, like those adorable dimples and the way you call Kitty up onto the bed as soon as you think I'm asleep."

"You knew I did that?"

"Every damn night."

She heard the smile in his voice.

"I'll miss you, Flores. We're good together, and I know you'll miss me."

More than you can imagine. She leaned her head back and closed her eyes, releasing a tease to keep her own emotions at bay. "I'll miss your incredibly generous barista skills."

"That's it?" He grabbed her ribs.

She startled out a laugh. "*Okay, okay.* I'll miss your Loch Ness monster."

"That's a given," he said arrogantly, and hugged her tight.

She took a deep breath, gathering her courage, "The truth is, I'll miss you a lot."

"Yeah, me, too." He kissed her shoulder. "Are you nervous about picking up Brian?"

"Yes, but I'm also excited to see him. It feels like it's been forever since we were in the same room, and we have a lot to talk about."

"My offer still stands to go with you."

He'd offered every time they'd talked about it, but as much as she wanted him to be there for her, she had to put Brian first. "I appreciate that, but I think it'll be easier for him if it's just the two of us."

"Did you decide if you're going to tell him about the marriage?"

She'd spent the last two weeks mulling that over, and it was one of the hardest decisions she'd had to make. "I'm not going to. I hate keeping secrets from him, but I don't want to do or say anything that might set him back. I'll tell him eventually, when I feel like he's in a good enough place. We have so much to do once he's home. He needs a sponsor and a job, and I don't know how well his car will hold up, so he may need to find a job on the bus line, and we need to heal our relationship."

Zander hugged her tight again, but he was quiet, leaving only the sounds of the waves to buffer the worries in her head.

"He doesn't have to worry about transportation," he finally said. "We cleaned out Brian's car to make sure there was no hidden drug paraphernalia, and Tobias used to be a mechanic, so I had him fix it, to be sure it's safe. I've also been taking it out once a week to keep it running. Cars shouldn't sit idle."

Shocked, and a little annoyed, she leaned to the side, looking up at him over her shoulder, and said, "Zander, you didn't have to do that. Brian and I would have figured it out."

"I have no doubt, but like you said, rehab is just the beginning. He's got a long, hard road ahead of him, and so do you. From what I know about addiction, every minute of the day can be a struggle. I'm sure the urge to go back to old habits when things get hard is a torturous battle. I just wanted to give him a leg up. A fighting chance."

How could she be irritated at that? "Thank you. I appreciate that. I really do, but I wish you'd said something about it before doing it. Part of recovery is making amends for your past mistakes. I'll make sure Brian pays Tobias for the work he did."

"If you think he needs to for his recovery, that's fine, but it's not necessary."

"I know, but he needs it. Trust me, he'll want to do it." She settled against his chest again. "Are you sure you want to see him tomorrow?"

"Yes."

"Why? I know you were raised to help people, but why put yourself in that position?"

"Because you were his before you were mine, and you turned your life inside out for him. That tells me he's worth fighting for, and just because our contract is ending doesn't mean you're on your own. It's not just you and Brian anymore. You have a support system, and so does he. We've all got your backs, and we always will."

Her eyes teared up. She was glad he couldn't see her face as she tried to blink them dry.

"I bet you wish you'd bought those baggy sweatpants and a mask now, don't you?" he asked, and kissed her shoulder.

A nervous laugh tumbled out, and she stretched her arms, arching away from his chest so he wouldn't feel the tremble tiptoeing through her. "*No*, but I bet you do."

"Fuck yeah, I do." He handed her the warm mug of coffee and said, "You're the best friend I've ever had, and those benefits?" He whistled. "You know I'm going to have withdrawals."

This was a lot harder than she'd thought it would be. "I'm sure there are plenty of willing women who'd love a turn as the fake Mrs. Wicked. At least you'll know they're not just repaying a debt."

"Don't try to pretend that's why you slept with me," he said with a biting tone.

"*If you say so,*" she said sarcastically.

He shifted to the side, glowering at her. "You did not."

"Whatever you need to believe," she teased.

"You're a wicked woman, Flores."

Don't I wish. Wicked with a capital W, that is.

THE SUN BEAT down on Zander's shoulders, the sand giving way beneath his feet with every step as he ran down the beach. He was dripping with sweat, the music blasting in his ears not doing a damn thing to drown out his agonizing thoughts. He pushed himself harder, his lungs burning. The cottage had been too quiet after Shauna had left to get Brian. He'd thought a four-mile run would do the trick, but as his cottage came into view in the distance, he knew he was supremely fucked.

There was no outrunning the emptiness he felt closing in on him.

He slowed to a walk, squinting against the sun as he made his way down the beach, hoping Shauna had gotten to the rehab center safely and things were going smoothly for her and Brian. He knew how well Brian was doing. When he'd reached out to the rehab center to get a message to him, he hadn't even been sure Brian would call back. But when Brian did, he'd sounded sharp and clear-headed, and it was obvious he'd do anything to talk to Shauna. He'd been appropriately apologetic and grateful. Zander hoped to hell Brian could fight his demons because if he laid a hand on Shauna again, now or a decade from now, he'd have Zander to deal with.

He picked up a rock and threw it into the ocean. Sweat dripped into his eyes. He dragged his forearm across his brow and headed up the incline toward the cottage, spotting Zeke and Maverick standing out back and Blaine coming from the side yard. He was in no mood to dick around.

"Hey, man," Zeke said. "How you doin'?"

"Fucking fantastic," he gritted out. "What are you all doing here?"

"Getting your ugly ass away from this place," Maverick said.

"No thanks."

"It's not a request," Blaine shot back. "We know today sucks, but it doesn't have to suck alone."

"I'm *fine*," Zander gritted out.

"Yeah, we know you are," Zeke said. "But we're not fine knowing Shauna's with Brian and you're overthinking it six ways to sundown."

Zander scoffed. "I—"

"Save it, Zan. The guys are waiting," Blaine said.

"What guys?" Zander asked with irritation.

They didn't answer, just lifted their chins toward the front of the house and headed in that direction, leaving him to follow. When they came around the corner of the cottage, he stopped short. Preacher, Conroy, and his cousins stood by their bikes. Behind them, half the club lined the road, chrome glinting in the sun, leather vests proudly displaying Dark Knights' patches.

Preacher stepped forward, his expression as solemn as a sermon. "Better get some clothes on, son."

A ripple of laughter rose from around him.

Confused, Zander said, "I didn't know we were riding today."

Preacher looked at Conroy. "Hear that, Con? He didn't *know*."

"I heard it, but I don't believe it." Conroy shook his head. "He knows damn well no one battles demons alone in this family, which can only mean one thing."

"Damn fool went and fell in love with his temporary wife," Blaine said.

"Sounds like a permanent problem to me," Zeke added.

Maverick clapped a hand on Zander's shoulder and said, "Happens to the best of us."

Zander gritted his teeth, but as the guys started ribbing him, their jeers and laughter carrying in the breeze, the knot in his chest loosened.

Damn it to hell. He hated how much he needed this.

Chapter Thirty-Nine

THE DRIVE BACK from the rehab center was quiet, both Shauna and Brian lost in their own thoughts. The silence was heavier than it used to be. It wasn't hostile or awkward, just *different*. A new energy between them, shaped by everything rehab had changed and everything it hadn't. Change was a running theme in her life these last few months, and the long drive to and from the center had given her time to think about those changes and what they meant for her and Brian.

"Home sweet home," Shauna said as she parked in front of their rental cottage, although it didn't feel like her home anymore. She reached over to grab the subs and chips they'd bought on the way home and, for the millionth time today, felt the absence of her rings, which she'd left at Zander's so Brian wouldn't ask about them.

She climbed out of the car, and as she pressed the button on the key fob, opening the trunk for Brian to grab his bag, she noticed he'd stopped short and was staring at his car parked out front.

He blinked hard, like he didn't trust what he was seeing. "You fixed my car?" His voice was equal parts disbelief and awe.

Shauna followed his gaze. The front of his car was no longer mangled, but smooth and whole. Her chest tightened. *Not me. Zander.* She wasn't ready to open that can of worms yet, so she said, "Zander's brother-in-law, Tobias, fixed it."

Brian dragged a hand over his chin, still staring at the car. "I'm paying him back. Every penny."

"I know you will," she said, glad he was taking responsibility for his actions. "Come on. Let's get your stuff inside."

The cottage felt foreign, like something from a past life. As Brian's gaze swept over the living room and kitchen, she could tell he felt it too. She saw relief, like it was good to be back, but nothing could hide the shadow in his eyes. The cottage wasn't merely his home. It was a journal of shame and heartache, holding the secrets of everything that had happened. The couch he'd passed out on, the worn floors he'd littered, the empty spot where the TV once sat. She didn't want to think about the pain the bedroom would bring, but this was all part of the process. She'd lived with that bone-deep shame for a long time after she'd dragged herself out of the dredges of addiction. They both had, but she wouldn't let this pull him under again. A lot might have changed, but they would always have each other's backs.

Zander's voice whispered through her mind. *It's not just you and Brian anymore. You have a support system, and so does he. We've all got your backs, and we always will.* At some point she needed to convey that to Brian, but right now she needed to help him get settled in.

"Hey," she said softly, drawing his attention. "I know it feels heavy, but these walls don't hold your secrets."

"I blew that cover in the worst way, didn't I?"

"You definitely upended our worlds, but I can think of worse ways it could have ended." She smiled and put the subs and chips on the coffee table. "We've had tons of great times in this place, too, haven't we?"

That earned a smile. "Yeah, we did."

"The walls remember those, too. Come on. Let's get your stuff put away. Then we can talk and eat and make a plan."

"There's a meeting at three I want to go to, and another at seven," he said on their way down the hall.

She was beyond happy that he'd already looked into meetings. "Great. I could use a meeting."

He touched her arm, his eyes serious. "You okay?"

"*Yes.* I just haven't been to one in a while. Come on. Let's unpack your stuff. I'm starved."

"You're always hungry," he teased, but when he walked into his room, the amusement drained from his features. His jaw tightened, and he started emptying his bag. He set his toiletries on the dresser and went through the motions of putting his clothes away.

Shauna could tell he was angry with himself by his stiffness, probably battling shame and disappointment, too. They were all valid feelings, which was why she didn't try to soothe that pain, even though she was aching to. He needed to feel them, to accept them, and to deal with them at his own pace.

He tossed his empty bag in the closet and sat on the edge of the bed. He leaned forward, resting his elbows on his knees, his eyes trained on the floor, and worried his hands.

Shauna sat beside him. "I'm proud of you. I know this is hard, but we'll get through it."

"It should never have been your problem to deal with in the first place." He looked at her, regret brimming in his eyes. "I'm sorry, Shauna, and I'm so fucking thankful you stuck by me and convinced me to go to rehab. I learned a lot about myself in therapy and in group. There was so much stuff about how we grew up that I didn't want to face, but I needed to. We were so young when we set out on our own. It's a wonder we survived."

"We were strong," she said.

"Yeah, and stupid. I carried so much anger toward my parents and toward yours. I've learned a lot about why I got back into drugs and ways to handle stress better in the future. Now I understand why Cap kept pushing for me to go to rehab when I was first trying to get sober. I should have listened to you back then and let him help. I never should have made you feel responsible for my well-being. It wasn't fair or right, and I am so sorry."

"Brian—"

"No, let me finish, please." His voice cracked. "I know I put you through hell. I pawned your TV and your bracelet from Cap. God, Shauna, I'm so sorry. I'm sorry for the lies and the shit I said and did, and…" His jaw clenched and his gaze trailed away, but it came right back to her, wet with tears. "I can't believe I put my hands on you." He swiped at the tears. "There's no excuse for that, and there's nothing worse. I hope you'll forgive me, but I'll understand if you can't. I'm so damn sorry."

Her heart was taking a beating, but she had to stand her ground, for both their sakes. "All those things really hurt me." Wiping her own tears, her throat burning, she said, "I forgive you, but I'll *never* put up with that again, Brian. I can't. I love you, and I love myself, too much."

Shame, relief, and determination collided in his eyes. "I swear to God, Shauna, I will do everything within my power to make sure it doesn't happen again."

Too choked up to speak, she nodded and threw her arms around her first best friend. They clung to each other, Brian saying he was sorry, both saying *I love you*, and crying the tears they'd held in for too many years. Shauna cried for the mistreated children they'd been, for the survivors they'd been forced to become, and for the friendship that would be forever changed by their latest turn of events.

They held each other until they had no tears left to cry.

Brian cleared his throat and got up to look out the window. "You saved my life, Shauna." He turned to look at her. "I know rehab wasn't cheap. How did you pay for it?"

"I got an inheritance from my grandfather. The letter from the attorney came a few weeks before I found you in here using."

His brows knitted. "I didn't know the old bastard died. Are you okay?"

"Yeah. I mean, the money saved you, so it's all good."

"I'm paying you back," he said vehemently.

"You don't have to. It's a ton of money, and it's not like I was counting on it for anything. It came out of the blue."

He lifted his chin stubbornly. "Doesn't matter. I don't care how long it takes. Ten years, twenty. I'm paying you back. I need to do it for my own peace of mind."

"Okay." She pushed to her feet.

He grabbed his toiletries. "Let me put this stuff away, and then we can go eat." He headed into the bathroom.

She took a deep, calming breath.

"Shauna?"

"Yeah?" She met him in the hallway. He was frowning. "What's wrong?"

"Where's your stuff? Your toothbrush, all your lotions?" He shot a glance into her bedroom, his brows furrowing. "Did you move out?"

Shauna's gut twisted. "Yes. Zander didn't like the idea of me staying here alone in case any drug dealers came by, and honestly, I was wrecked after everything that happened."

Brian's face crumpled. "Shauna—"

"I'm not trying to make you feel bad. I just don't want to lie about it." She headed into the living room. "I was exhausted and overwhelmed. I felt guilty for not realizing earlier that you were having trouble and for not asking Cap or your old sponsor for help once I realized what was going on, but I was too embarrassed and hurt and scared. I didn't want to believe it was happening."

"Fuck." His brows knitted. "I really screwed you up."

"No. I screwed myself up. I knew better than to enable you. You know I did, but I'm in a really good place now. I promise, and you know I've learned my lesson, because I told you I won't allow myself to be in that situation again, and I meant it."

"I believe you, and I'm glad, but I'm sorry I put us in that situation. Where are you living?"

"I've been staying at Zander's. His family, the Wickeds, have been incredibly supportive. I don't know if you remember, but his brothers Zeke and Blaine were the ones who stayed with you right before you went to rehab. His family helped me find my footing again, and I've got girlfriends now, believe it or not. They're good people, Brian, and they want to be here for you, too, if you'll let them."

His mouth twisted. "Are you and Zander *together*?"

She'd been dreading the question, and although she'd planned a safe answer, she couldn't lie to him after everything they'd been through. Everything *he'd* been through. The truth was, whatever she and Zander had together was over, and she needed to face that.

"Zander has been there for me more than I expected," she said honestly. "I couldn't get the inheritance unless I was married, so we got married and faked it for everyone. Well, not everyone. Cap and Zander's family know it isn't real, but nobody else knows because we didn't want the attorney to find out. Anyway, Zander and I got close, but it's not like we're a couple or anything. Once we sign divorce papers, it's a done deal."

Pain and confusion moved over Brian's face. "Jesus, Shauna. You hate the very idea of marriage. You did that for me?"

"It was the only way to make sure you got the help you needed."

"And he agreed to it?"

"Yeah. He's the guy I pulled from that wreck on New Year's Eve. I saved him, and he wanted to help me help you in return. He was all for the ruse even before I was, but the night you showed up at his house, I knew I had to do something fast."

Brian sank down to the couch. "So where does that leave us? Are you moving back in?"

"Yes, on Monday, since I have to work tomorrow." She sat beside him, carefully choosing her words. "But I want to talk to you about that, too. One thing this time apart has taught me is that we need to widen our circle. We've been each other's lifelines since we were little kids, and I don't want that to change, but I'm worried we've become too closed off from the rest of the world. Maybe a little codependent."

He leaned forward again, his elbows on his knees. "The therapist at rehab said the same thing."

Relief washed through her. "They did? That makes me feel better. I was thinking that since our lease is up at the end of September, it might be a good thing if we find separate apartments. That's assuming you've got a sponsor and a job and you feel ready for it by then. But I don't want to set you back on your recovery, and I still want to go to meetings with you and hang out when we can. I just think we both need a little breathing space and room to meet new people and build healthier lives. We've never really had friends outside of work, and now that I do, I want that for you. It changes everything, Brian. Life feels fuller and happier, and I know with the right people, it will for you, too."

"The therapist suggested the same thing. Not right away, of course, but once I've got my feet under me," he said.

She did not expect that. "That's good, but how do *you* feel about it?"

"Scared." His voice was strained, but he let out a half laugh. "I'm not exactly sought-after friend material. I'm fresh out of rehab. A walking red flag to most people. But I know it's the right thing to do if I can afford it by then. I can't keep holding you back, and it's time to grow up. It'll be a fresh start for both of us."

The relief she felt was bittersweet. She knew she wasn't losing him, but easing the reins of their friendship was scary for her, too. Almost as scary as letting go of her marriage to Zander was painful. But she kept that to herself and focused on Brian.

"I'm in recovery too, you know, so we both might be a red flag to some people. But to me, you're a pillar of strength. You're conquering your addiction, and we both know that's no easy feat." She let that sink in before adding, "And I've learned that not everyone sees us as red flags. There are good people in the world, Brian. People who don't judge and who see beyond our addictions. People who will love all the things about you that I do."

"You're talking about Zander and his family, aren't you?"

"Maybe," she said with a smile. "I know if you get to know them, you're going to feel incredibly loved and supported, because that's how they've made me feel since the first time I met them."

"I don't want their pity," he said with an edge.

"I was worried about the same thing. But they don't pity me, and I know they won't pity you. They're real people who have lived through horrible things. They get it." She told him about Ashley and about the loss of Leah's brother and what Reese and Lettie had been through. And then she told him about the friendships she'd developed and how Zander's family had come around for him, and for her, despite not having ever met her. "Zander says helping people is in their blood, and I'm not sure he's wrong. His father and uncle founded the Bayside chapter of the Dark Knights, and they're involved with anti-drug programs in schools and suicide prevention, and some of the Dark Knights are sponsors around the Cape. They offered to meet with you, and Zander said he'll come by tomorrow and go with you to a meeting while I'm at work."

"Fuck," Brian said with a heavy sigh. "I hate needing people."

"Yeah, me too. But I've learned it's okay to need others. That's what friends are for. The girls and I text all the time about books and work and stupid stuff. It's nice, Brian. And you'll love Zan and the rest of the guys. They're totally down to earth, and they give each other crap all the time, like we do. Imagine having more friends like me."

"Imagine? I have nightmares about it."

"Hey!" She gave him a playful shove.

"I'm kidding. I know what you mean about friends. I made

a few in rehab, and it was nice having people to talk to. But, Shauna, I hope you know how much I appreciate you. I want you to know that I'm not taking any of this for granted. I know how lucky I am that you're sitting here with me right now and that you're even willing to share your friends with me."

"I know."

"Good, then hopefully you'll understand this. Last time I got sober, I think I did it for you more than me. This time I went into rehab because I was afraid of losing you, but I could have checked out at any time, and I didn't. I stayed for myself. I want this. I want to live a drug-free life, and have friends, and be a better person than my parents were."

"I want that for you, too."

"I know you do. I just needed you to know I'm doing it for the right reasons this time, and as much as I don't want to *need* other people's help, I wouldn't have this chance without it. If Zander is willing to come by tomorrow when you're working, I'd really appreciate it, and I've got to say, it sounds like you found your people with these new friends."

"You're my people, and you always will be. *Still waters or reckless tides.*"

"Anchors forever, side by side," he said with a smile. "Hopefully we've got still waters ahead."

"I have faith that we will. I'm so happy you're home, and I hope in time the Wickeds can become *our* people."

"Whether or not they do, I'm happy you have them." He grabbed the subs and set one in front of her. "But you should be sure before you introduce me to them."

"Why?"

"Because they may end up liking me more than they like you, and then you'll get pissed, and that'll just turn ugly."

She smiled, glad to hear him joking. "Because you're easier with new people than I am?"

"No, because I'm cuter," he teased.

"That's debatable."

They fell into easy banter, as if it had been lying in wait. It wasn't the same as it had been before, but they weren't, either, and she looked forward to finding their new normal.

THE HOUSE WAS dark, save for streaks of moonlight coming through the windows. Zander sat on the couch in a pair of sweats, staring absently at the fireplace, feeling hollowed out. It was after midnight, and Shauna never came home.

Back. She never came back.

As much as he felt like his cottage had become her home, he couldn't fool himself any longer. He knew better. She didn't come back because she was *home* with Brian. Brian would get to hear her singing with her earbuds in while she did word searches and humming Avril Lavigne when she was pushing herself at the gym. The thought grated like sandpaper. He rested his head back and closed his eyes, telling himself to get a fucking grip.

Kitty jumped onto the couch carrying the shirt they'd gotten her in Niagara Falls in her mouth, and climbed onto his lap.

"Hi, baby girl." He took the shirt, hit with the memory of Shauna's scowl when he suggested he get her one with BIKER DADDY'S RIDE OR DIE on it. "You missing her, too, or just feelin' pretty?" he asked as he put the shirt on Kitty.

Kitty curled up in his lap and purred.

He was jealous that his cat could find comfort so easily

when he was drowning in jealousy.

He rested his head back again and closed his eyes. The lock on the front door clicked, and his fucking heart jumped as the door eased open and Shauna stepped quietly inside. She closed the door carefully, and as she toed off her sneakers, he said, "Hey, Angel."

She startled, her gaze sweeping toward him. She smiled, but even in the dimly lit room he could tell it was a tentative one. "You scared me," she said, making her way over to him.

"I didn't know if you were coming back tonight."

"My uniform is here. Sorry to show up so late. I should have texted."

"No, it's fine. How'd it go?" He patted the cushion next to him.

"Great," she said, sitting beside him, but she sounded tired. "I didn't realize how much I missed him until I picked him up. I swear we hugged for ten minutes straight."

"Is he glad to be home?"

"Yeah. It's hard for him. There are a lot of tough memories. But we knew it would be. We talked a lot, and we went to two meetings. I told him you'd come by tomorrow and I'll move my stuff in Monday after my shift ends. Our lease is over at the end of September, so once he's settled with a sponsor and a job, we're going to look around at apartments for a fresh start."

He'd known this was coming. If he were honest with himself, he'd been bracing for it since the day they'd said *I do*. But knowing it and hearing her say it were two very different things. There was no bracing for the pain of the fault line ripping open inside him. He tried to convince himself it was relief. This was always the plan, after all. Now he could go back to his life without making extra coffee with too much creamer and packing breakfasts or rushing home to see her after work. He wouldn't have to do twice as much laundry or clean up new toys every other week because Shauna insisted Kitty needed them.

Fuck. He was going to miss all of it.

Her eyes lingered on him, searching, as if she heard the crack he'd felt, but if she did, she didn't acknowledge it. She simply petted Kitty's head and said, "I got the wire transfer today from the attorney, but I'm really tired. Is it okay if I give you a check in the morning?" putting the nail in his coffin.

"I'm not worried about it. I'm heading out early tomorrow to get a ride in before going over to Brian's." It wasn't true, but the thought of pretending through another morning was too much.

She gave a small, tired smile. Silence stretched between them, and she rested her head on his shoulder. "It's been a day," she said with a yawn. "Would you mind holding me? Just for a little while?"

The qualifier, *just for a little while*, burned.

"Sure" came out as ragged as he felt. "Let's lie down."

Shauna stood, and Kitty jumped down from the couch, ready to follow as she turned toward the bedroom, but Zander couldn't take her into his bed without wanting to be as close as possible and love her with everything he had.

He reached for her hand, pulling her down to lie on the couch. Instead of spooning like he'd expected, she buried her face in his neck, her arm around him. She lifted her face only long enough to call Kitty. Kitty jumped up to the armrest, and as if she knew Zander needed her, too, she padded over and lay on him, her head resting on Shauna.

Zander closed his eyes, breathing Shauna in, memorizing the feel of her against him, the cadence of her warm breath on his neck, giving her the comfort she needed as his own heart shattered.

If this was the last time he'd get to hold her, he'd let it break him a thousand times over.

Chapter Forty

SHAUNA AWOKE IN a fog, registering the warmth of Kitty curled against her stomach and the scent of Zander beneath her cheek. She forced her eyes open, squinting against the sting of too little sleep. She expected the familiar smell of coffee to greet her, the sight of Zander standing outside the patio doors, but that brief blissful bubble popped when she remembered he'd gone riding. She vaguely recalled feeling him brush a kiss to her forehead when he'd gotten up, but she and Brian had talked for hours last night. He'd told her about rehab, and she'd told him about her life, including how Zander had found her bracelet. They'd run the gamut of emotions, and by the time she'd gotten to Zander's, she'd been bone-tired and hadn't been able to muster the energy to wake up and say goodbye this morning.

She gave Kitty some love and sat up, her attention drawn to the photos on the mantel. She'd never forget the day Zander had come home with the frame for the picture of her and Brian, or when she'd come from a grueling shift to find that picture, along with one from her and Zander's honeymoon, up there on the mantel with his family photos. She knew they were contractually bound, but they didn't feel like just an obligation. Or at least they hadn't, until they'd acknowledged the end of their relationship yesterday morning, and then confirmed last night that she was going to be moving out.

Could she have romanticized her feelings?

She was too grounded for that, wasn't she?

She got up to take a closer look and took the photo of them down from the mantel to study it. There was joy in Zander's piercing blue eyes. He couldn't fake that, could he? She thought about the day he'd dropped to his knees and presented her with that outrageously beautiful ring. *What do you say, Shauna? Will you marry me and show the world we're not just great looking, but we're also the best damn actors around?*

Fucking actors.

She swallowed hard with that reality. The strange thing was, she felt like she was acting every day of her damn life, trying to fit in, pretending she wasn't lonely or worried about one thing or another. The only time she *wasn't* acting was when she was with Zander.

But he was.

She set the picture back on the mantel and tried to shake off the weight of the truth as she made her way down the hall to get ready for work.

Her stupid legs stopped working by the butt prints on the wall, the memory of making them slamming into her. *The paint!* she'd squealed. He'd flashed that devilish grin and said, *Conversation starters*, and then he'd fucked her senseless.

With a tremor in her chest, she headed into the bathroom.

She took a long, hot shower, trying to scrub the ache away, to no avail. She pinned up her hair, dressed for work, and packed her duffel with an extra uniform and a change of clothes for tomorrow. She put her bag by the front door, then headed into the kitchen for coffee. She glanced at a stack of papers on the island as she walked past and froze, her mind tripping over the words DIVORCE AGREEMENT. Her knees wobbled, her feet rooted to the floor. She couldn't breathe, could barely see through a rush of tears.

"Nonono." Not now. Not yet.

Her hand trembled as she frantically shoved each page to the side. In her haste to get to the last one, papers sailed off the island, and she stood numb, the sight of Zander's signature slicing through her as brutally as a knife.

She stumbled backward, trying to drag air into her lungs. She thought she could handle this. Thought she was prepared for the inevitable end of their agreement. But he wasn't supposed to mean so much, and *God*, she wasn't supposed to feel so much. She hadn't even known she was capable of it. She grabbed the counter to combat her weak knees.

Breathe. Just breathe. You save lives. You saved your own life. You can do this.

Shoring up the walls she no longer wanted, she fumbled with the junk drawer and grabbed a pen. It felt wrong in her hand as she signed her name. Kitty wound around her feet in her tiny pink shirt, but Shauna didn't trust herself to pick her up without breaking down, and she couldn't afford to break down. She had to get to work, had to be on top of her game to do her job, so she blew out a breath, drew her shoulders back, and started making a game plan.

Heading back down the hall to the bedroom she hadn't used since the honeymoon, she found her checkbook. She wrote a check to Zander to repay him for Brian's rehab; then she headed into his bedroom, trying to ignore that ache it brought to see the bed they shared, the dresser that held their clothes, and focused on the jewelry box. She wanted to pack all her stuff, but she had to get to work. Zander would be at work when she came back Monday morning to get her things, so she put on blinders, grabbed her engagement and wedding rings, and made a beeline for the kitchen.

Quickly picking up the papers from the floor, she piled them on the counter and put the rings and the check on top of them. It only took ninety days for her to fall madly in love with Zander Wicked, but as she strode out of the kitchen, trying not to look at the cat she loved or the home they'd built, she had a feeling it would take a lifetime to get over him.

Chapter Forty-One

ZANDER SPED DOWN the highway, his helmet shutting out the world. No wind on his face, no distractions. Only miles of open road and the familiar roar of his motorcycle. Riding was supposed to clear his head, but he'd been riding since before dawn, and it only made the noise louder.

He'd woken to Shauna sprawled over him on the couch, her hair spread across his chest. He hadn't wanted to move, much less leave her, but he'd needed to so he didn't fuck up her life. Signing the divorce papers with Justice yesterday and having them notarized had felt like he was ripping out his own damn ribs, but leaving the papers for Shauna to find? Christ, that was worse.

So he rode.

For hours.

But *fuck*, he couldn't do this alone, and that pissed him off.

The sun burned high in the sky, sadness clinging to him like baked-in sweat as he pulled off the highway, slowing to merge onto the main drag, and headed for the only place that made sense. To the only person who knew how to talk him off a ledge. The one he gave shit to for having his back when he didn't want it. Now here he was, winding through backroads, hoping like hell his brother could help him one last time and that he still had enough fight left to listen.

He parked in the dusty drive and stalked up the porch steps. His heart hammering and his mind whirling, he pounded on the door. Too restless to wait, he threw the door open and stormed in, hollering, "Zeke! Where the hell are you?"

He heard Zeke curse up in the loft and headed over to the stairs.

"Zander, do *not* come up here." Zeke's warning split the air, deep and serious.

"Fuck," Zander bit out, and paced the living room. He heard Zeke talking to someone, heard the clinking of metal. There were reasons he didn't make a habit of showing up at his brothers' houses without texting first. But nothing was normal right now.

Zeke stalked down the stairs buttoning his jeans, his jaw tight. "You okay?"

"*No*, I'm not fucking okay. I've been riding around for hours trying to get my head on straight, and I can't," Zander gritted out, taking in the scratches on his brother's shoulders and feeling like a dick for interrupting. "Sorry about..." He nodded toward the loft, still wearing a path in the hardwood floor.

Ignoring the comment, Zeke crossed his arms, watching Zander pace. "What happened?"

"I left the divorce papers for Shauna this morning and took off before she got up, and *fuck*, Zeke. I feel like my heart is being ripped to shreds."

"Why the hell did you leave them for her instead of handing them to her?"

"Because I fucking *couldn't*," Zander seethed. "You have no idea how hard this is."

"So go get the papers. Take them back."

"I can't do that. She doesn't *want* that." No matter how many times he said it, it still didn't feel true or possible that he was alone in what they had. He'd *felt* her love, had lived in it. Hell, they'd built a whole damn cottage around it. Those were the thoughts that had him feeling like he was losing his mind, so he wrestled them down deep and said, "She's moving back in with Brian tomorrow and going back to her life. That was the agreement. Brian needs her. She loves him. They're making future plans, and I'm not about to fuck that up for her. I just need help getting my head on straight."

A tall brunette walked out of the loft and headed down the stairs in a short, fitted dress and heels that reeked of money. With her head held high and her tousled hair cascading down her back, she glanced at Zander when she reached the landing, giving him a keen-eyed once-over, her lips curving up like she knew something he didn't. Turning a confident smile on Zeke, she said, "I called a car, and it's almost here. I'll catch up with you next time I'm in town."

Zeke nodded and graced her with the coy smile that held a mix of flirtatiousness and mystery and had been mesmerizing women for as long as Zander could remember, despite the crap he and his brothers gave Zeke.

After she was out the door, Zander said, "Dude, is she an escort?"

"No, you idiot. That's Genevieve—*Gigi*—Nice. She owns an elite gentleman's club in New York."

"How the hell…? Never mind. Hope she wasn't too *nice*," Zander bit out, pacing again, too irritated at his own situation to deal with the one he'd caused for Zeke. "I need you to talk me off the ledge. I don't know what to do with all these feelings. It's not supposed to hurt this much."

"Yes, it *is*," Zeke said evenly. "You were catching feelings for her before you even got married."

Zander glowered at him. "You're not helping."

"What do you need me to say?"

"Tell me I'm doing the right thing," Zander barked.

"I can't tell you that," Zeke snapped back. "This is about feelings, not buying a new bike or what tool to use. Only you know the answer to that question."

"What the fuck, Zeke?" Zander seethed. "You stick your nose in my business twenty-four-seven, and the *one* time I really need you, you've got nothing to say? Forget I said anything. I've got to go see Brian." He headed for the door, feeling like a prick for blaming his brother when, like always, Zeke was fucking right.

Zeke grabbed his arm. "You are *not* taking this out on Brian. He just got out of rehab."

"No shit." He yanked his arm away. "I'm not a total asshole. Shauna's working today. I told her I'd check in on him. I don't want that guy floundering after all the hard work he's done."

"Let me take a quick shower, and I'll go with you." Zeke headed for the stairs.

Zeke's offer after Zander had barged in and screwed up his morning had Zander biting back the knee-jerk reaction to bark at him and storm out the door. He forced himself to calm down enough to give his brother the respect he deserved.

"Thanks, man, but I've got this. I'm not going to scare the guy. I'm pulling for him, and I'm sorry for barging in here and fucking things up with that woman."

Zeke lifted his chin. "It's all right."

"*No*, it's not. I shouldn't have barged in and expected you to talk me off the ledge. This is why you've always felt the need to rein me in, because I do what's in my head without thinking it through, which is exactly why I'm in this situation with Shauna *right now*."

"I can't dispute that," Zeke said earnestly. "But today it's your heart driving the bike, not your dick and not your need for thrills."

Zander let out a breath. "I'm fucked, aren't I?"

"You're definitely not used to dealing with real emotions, but that doesn't mean you're fucked. You need to go with your gut on this, Zan. Are you sure you *want* to go see Brian alone? I'm not asking because I think you'll go off on him. You said you won't, and I believe you. I'm asking because that big-ass heart of yours is torturing you, and while you're giving Brian support, you might need some for yourself."

"Thanks, man, but this is something I've got to do on my own."

Zeke gave a curt nod and pulled him into an embrace, clapping him on the back. "Call if you need me."

"You know I will." Zander couldn't resist asking, "When did you go to New York? Or was that chick really an escort?"

"Jesus, Zan. With everything that you're dealing with, *that's* what's on your mind? I love you, man, but get the fuck out of here."

ZANDER PULLED UP in front of Shauna and Brian's cottage and cut the engine, the rumble of his bike giving way to the rustling of leaves in the warm summer breeze and the torrent of conflicting emotions inside him. He'd told Zeke the truth. He wanted to see Brian succeed. Not solely for Shauna but because Zander truly gave a shit about others, despite his sometimes selfish habits. That didn't mean it was going to be easy facing a man who had loved Shauna's body and had later left it bruised. The man who owned a piece of her that Zander could never touch. He just had to remember that Brian had also been there for Shauna when she'd had nobody else.

He climbed off his bike and headed up to the door, his chest tight, his stride steady. His phone conversation with Brian about Shauna's birthday had been cordial, but short and to the point. He didn't know what to expect from Brian or himself today.

He knocked, standing taller as footsteps sounded on the other side of the door.

The door opened, and when their eyes met, the feeling that this was some sort of minefield fell away. The last time he'd seen Brian in person, he'd been spitting fury through a drugged and drunken haze. Now he was clear-eyed, fresh-faced, and looking at Zander with a mix of apology and gratitude, and so damn nervous the air buzzed with it.

"Brian," he said, his voice even, though his pulse didn't match, and offered his hand.

Brian's brows knitted, and he looked at Zander's hand like it was the last thing he expected, but he shook it, a little awkwardly, and said, "Thanks for coming over."

"No problem."

Brian stepped back. "Want to come in? Sit down?"

"Sure." Zander headed inside. The place was still clean, the faint smell of coffee lingering in the air.

"Want something to drink? I've got water, iced tea, coffee. That's about it."

"Nah, man. I'm good, thanks."

"Do you want to sit down?" Brian motioned to the armchair.

Zander nodded and sat in the chair, while Brian lowered himself to the couch. "You look good. How're you feeling?"

"I'm still trying to figure that out." He smiled. "I mean, overall I feel good. Rehab helped more than I ever thought it would. I see everything differently now. Who I am, how I got here. It's kind of surreal being sober and back home with Shauna, but it's also scarier than hell. I've got a long way to go, and I know it's going to be an uphill battle, but I'm determined to do it right. I've been given a second chance, and I don't want to screw it up, you know?"

"I do know, believe it or not. I came out of my accident feeling that same way. Not that I had the same kind of battle after the accident as you have ahead of you, but I know the feeling of not wanting to fuck up." Thinking of how he'd selfishly blown into Zeke's house that morning, he realized he could still fuck up like that and his life wouldn't spiral the way one drink or one hit of a drug could devastate Brian or Shauna. They carried the weight of their addictions on their shoulders every damn day, and their entire lives hung in the balance.

"Life, man. It's crazy sometimes." Brian leaned his elbows on his knees, worrying with his hand, and tilted his face to look at Zander. "I probably wouldn't be here if not for you and Shauna. I really appreciate everything you did, and I want to apologize for coming to your place and making a mess of your life."

"Like you said, life can get crazy, but all we did was get you into rehab. You're doing the heavy lifting, and you didn't make a mess of my life. You going into rehab and Shauna needing a shoulder to lean on actually helped me pull my shit together."

"Well, I can't thank you enough for being there for Shauna. She didn't deserve any of this, and I'm going to spend the rest of my life showing her how incredible she is and making sure she never has to face it again."

How could something so right feel like a sucker punch?

"I'm sure she appreciates that," Zander finally said. "Shauna said she mentioned to you that a couple of the guys in my club are sponsors."

"Yeah. I'd like to meet them, if that offer still stands."

"Absolutely. Saint will be at an NA meeting in Brewster at noon, and Sarge will be at an AA meeting in Eastham at four. If you're up for it, I'm happy to go to both and introduce you. If you don't feel comfortable with either of them, there's another guy who lives down in Dennis."

"I'm definitely up for the meetings, and I'd appreciate the introductions."

"What about work? Have you thought about what you might want to do?"

"Yeah, I've been thinking about it for weeks," Brian said. "I know it's going to be hard to get someone to trust me, so I figure I'll take what I can get."

"Shauna said you were a driver. Do you have other skills?"

He sat up. "I've done a little of everything, driving, landscape, construction."

"What do you want to do?" Zander asked.

"No idea." He took a deep breath. "I just want something stable, where I can prove myself. Something physical. I'm not built to sit behind a desk or stand behind a counter all day.

Driving was okay, but I think the confinement made me edgy."

"Yeah, I get that. My brothers Blaine and Maverick own a masonry business. They're always looking for help, but it's backbreaking work."

"I appreciate that, but you've done enough already." Brian shook his head. "You gave me my life back, you had your brother-in-law fix my car, and you watched over the one person I have in this world. I already owe you more than I can ever pay back."

"Bullshit," Zander said. "There's no debt when it comes to helping people. If you need to repay Tobias for fixing your car to make amends for your program, that's fine, but you don't owe me anything. Continuing to fight for your own well-being and being good to Shauna is all I need."

Brian looked away, his jaw tight.

"I know it's only ever been you and Shauna, but you've got a lot of people pulling for you right now, Brian. People you don't know yet, but one day, when you're ready and if you want to, you can get to know them all."

"You can't imagine how it feels to hear that as a man who has only ever had one person on his side." His voice was raw, but his eyes showed a deeper vulnerability.

"I'll never know what it's like to be as alone as you and Shauna were for so long, but at one point or another, I think we've all felt like we were standing alone on an island, even when we were surrounded by people."

He nodded. "Yeah, the therapist at rehab said something similar."

"That's another thing. If you work with Blaine and Maverick, you'll get health insurance, and you can continue therapy if that's something you're looking for."

"Really?" His eyes lit up.

"Yeah. And no pressure or anything, but you'd be doing Blaine and Maverick a favor. They need the help. They'll work you hard, and they've got high standards, but they'll also teach you to be one hell of a stonemason."

"That sounds better than you can imagine. I always felt like I was floundering. Even with driving, it didn't feel like I had a purpose. It would be good to create things and see finished products."

"Then let's make a—" *Fuck.* The word evaded him. "Shit. Sorry. Let's..." *What the hell is the word?* Brian was looking at him expectantly. Zander could make up anything, but Brian had been through so much shit, he wasn't about to pretend like he had a perfect life. That's not what Brian or Zander needed. "Sorry, man. I forget words sometimes. It's from the head injury, from the accident." The word he'd been looking for flashed in his mind. "*Plan.* That's it. Let's make a fucking plan. *Jesus. Finally.*"

"Man, that's got to suck," Brian said empathetically. "Sorry you're going through that."

"It is what it is. I can't read worth shit, either, so there's that." Zander shrugged, trying to make light of it.

"I know how to read, so if you need help, it's the least I can do, and we could have some fun with the forgetting-words thing."

Zander looked at him curiously. "How's that?"

"If you lose a word when we're around other people, I'll fill it in for you. If you say *let's make a...*I'll say, *sundae* or *sand castle*, and confuse the hell out of them."

Zander laughed, and damn, he needed that.

"You're going to fit in great with the guys. So, what do you say we grab a couple of sandwiches, my treat, hit the noon meeting, then go see my brothers? After that we'll hit the four o'clock meeting and see what comes of it."

"You've got all day free?"

"Nah, man. It's booked with you. Let's go. But you've got to drive. I've got my bike."

They pushed to their feet, and as they headed out the door, Brian said, "I can't believe you're willing to do all this for me."

"Might as well get used to it. I don't know what Shauna told you, but my family is like mosquitoes you can't swat. We just keep coming back."

"You say that like it's a bad thing."

Zander chuckled. "Give me time. I'll get under your skin."

As they climbed into the car, Zander thought about Shauna and how she'd fought tooth and nail for Brian, refusing to give up on him when so many others might have walked away. That loyal, loving heart was what he loved most about her. He had no fucking clue how to reconcile the love she'd poured into him with the fresh start she'd chosen with Brian, when in his heart and soul she was *his* and he would forever be hers.

Chapter Forty-Two

THE DAY HAD gone better than Zander had dared to hope it would.

Brian hadn't just sat through the substance abuse meetings. He'd been present, honest, and unguarded. He'd shared his story and listened thoughtfully to others. He'd met Saint and Sarge, had been respectful, and asked insightful questions. When he'd talked with Blaine and Maverick about the stone work, he'd done the same, and he didn't flinch when they told him exactly what they'd expect and how hard the job would be.

Zander didn't know Brian well, but he knew what a man looked like when he was trying. And today that's what he witnessed. When he'd left Brian tonight, with the offer to come back if he needed anything at all, Brian had sounded not only determined to do well and grateful for everyone's help, but excited to have two prospects for sponsors and a new job to look forward to. Shauna had texted Brian while they were out. It had stung like hell that Zander hadn't gotten a single message from her.

He was still stewing over that as he headed into his cottage.

It was too damn quiet. The kind of quiet that crawled under his skin and made him edgy. Kitty meowed at his feet. He tossed his keys on the table by the door and scooped her up.

"You hungry, baby girl?" He kissed her head on his way into the kitchen and flicked on the light, stopping cold at the sight of Shauna's rings shimmering under the bright lights.

The papers were still there, neatly stacked. Leaving them was the biggest mistake of his life.

He stepped closer and saw a check written out to him in the exact amount of Brian's rehab. *Fuck.*

He stared at the papers like they were the enemy, but *he* was the one who'd left them there. *He* was the one who had signed them in front of a notary yesterday. He was the enemy within their home, and he wasn't ready to face her signature on that fucking final line.

Grief coiled tight and painful inside him as he went through the motions of feeding Kitty, trying to ignore the pain and the full-on war raging in his head.

After setting Kitty's bowl on her mat, he turned back to the island, his teeth clenched. He carefully moved the rings, the check, and the fucking pen she must have used to sign the damn things and shifted the papers to the last page, her loopy signature staring back at him. His chest seized, and the room spun, heartache and rage snapping through him like live wires.

"You signed them," he growled. "You fucking signed them."

Of course she did, you idiot. You basically handed her the god- damn pen. What the hell did you expect?

"Fuck!" He slammed his fist against the counter, sending Kitty scampering out of the kitchen.

He sank back against the counter, grief like a weight drag- ging him under, rage like a storm trying to slash its way free, and his fucking heart shattering so painfully, he wanted to put his fist through his chest wall and tear the damn thing out.

"HEY, FLORES," MIKE called out from the open bay. "I'll pull my truck in next."

Shauna looked up as she filled a bucket with soapy water to wash the ambulance and shot him a deadpan look, pretending the sting in her eyes was from the low-hanging sun and not the crushing feeling she'd been carrying around all day. The papers were signed, the debt was paid, and Brian was making headway toward getting settled, but she felt empty, her heart splintered. The iron threads that had held her together since she was too young to realize it were unraveling against her will.

"Dude, leave her alone," Paul said. "She's been crabby all day. She obviously didn't get any last night."

"I told you there was trouble in paradise," Lance said.

She hosed down the ambulance, tuning them out as they debated her life. They had no idea her marriage was supposed to be fake by all means other than the legal contract that bound her and Zander together. She hadn't even thought about how she'd explain the end of it to them. Emotions were never part of the deal, but they'd been there from the start for her, hadn't they? There was something about Zander she'd trusted from the get-go. Something that drew her back to that hospital room day after day, to the man who had called himself Zeke and had pleaded with her not to let him go when he'd been lying on the ground bleeding.

Setting down the hose, she picked up the soapy sponge and began furiously scrubbing the ambulance.

"Don't worry, Flores," Howie called over. "Everyone goes through a honeymoon period, and then real life sets in, and you realize you don't like finding his towel on the floor or his clothes by the hamper instead of in it. But you and Zander will get through this."

The fragile hold she had on herself snapped, and she spun around, spewing the truth. "No, we won't! It wasn't *real.* He was just helping me get my inheritance so I could pay for Brian's rehab. I wasn't supposed to fall for him, but I did, and—"

The roar of a motorcycle drowned out her voice, and they all looked toward the street. The sponge slipped in her hand, her heart tripping up as Zander came barreling down the road and rolled to a stop at the curb, his black bike gleaming. Kitty was strapped to his chest in some kind of carrier with a tiny helmet covering her head. The ridiculous sight should have made her laugh, but as Zander took off Kitty's helmet and then his own, the fury etched into his face made it hard for her to breathe. Why was he angry? She'd kept her end of the deal. Had he wanted her to move out this morning?

She was vaguely aware of one of the guys saying, "Oh shit. He looks pissed," as Zander swung his leg over the bike and stalked up the driveway, his jaw clenched and eyes trained on her like she was the only thing he saw and the last thing he wanted to look at.

Shitshitshit. She didn't think it was possible for her heart to hurt more than it already did, but here she was, feeling the blood draining from her face and stifling the urge to ask what she'd done wrong. But she wouldn't let him see that weakness. Not if she could help it. She'd made this deal, and she owed it to him to hold herself together.

Gathering all the strength she could muster, she straightened her spine, meeting his angry gaze. "What are you doing here?" Her voice was steadier than the panic inside her.

"Is that any way to greet your husband?" he growled.

Her thoughts stumbled, and then she realized he was saying it for the rest of the crew. "You don't have to pretend anymore. I told them the truth, and I signed the papers and left you a check in the kitchen. Didn't you find them?"

"I found them, and I burned them. The check, too. You're not dumping me that easy."

"What are you talking about? *You* left those papers for me, and you had already signed them!"

"Yeah, because I was holding up my end of the bargain," he barked, ragged and rough, like the words were scraped from his chest. "I know you think you belong with Brian. Your whole life has been tied to him, and it always will be, but damn it, Shauna, that doesn't mean you can't have the life you want and the love you deserve."

Her pulse jumped, but her mind lagged behind, her thoughts tangled.

"I'm not going to walk away and pretend all I feel is friendship for the woman I love more than life itself. Not without shooting my shot, which makes me a raving asshole because Brian went through rehab for *you*, but I love you, Angel, and I never believed in regrets, but now I have a list of them. I wish I'd never left you the night I drove you home all those years ago, so I could have been there to help you get sober, and we could have had the years in between together. I wish I'd never hidden my feelings from you, so you would've known how madly and passionately I was falling for you every step of the way."

I love you, too was on the tip of her tongue. She wanted this. She wanted him. Forever. But she didn't know how to let herself have it when it meant Brian might falter again.

Zander stepped closer. "And most of all, I wish I hadn't been with so many women before you, because I know in my heart I was always meant to be yours, and you were always meant to be mine." He took her hand in his and lifted it between them. "This four on your hand is me, and the sforzando on my finger is you. We were bound by ink before we even knew it."

Emotions clogged her throat.

"The ball is in your court, Angel. I love you, and I want to be the man who gives you all your fresh starts. I know I've got a lot of flaws. I say whatever pops into my head, and I can't keep my hands to myself around you."

"That's not exactly a flaw," she managed, earning a smile that burrowed into her heart.

"Good to know. I adore you, darlin', and I think you love me, and I know you love Kitty." He kissed Kitty's head. "If you don't want to be married, that's okay. We don't need that piece of paper. Just give me a chance to love you with everything I have, and then you can decide if I'm the right guy for you."

Tears spilled from Shauna's eyes.

"We both know I am."

She laughed and choked out, "You're so cocky."

"You love that about me."

"I *do* love that about you." Another overwhelmed laugh bubbled out with her tears. "I love you so much, it physically hurts to think about not being with you, but I can't leave Brian to flounder. He needs me now more than ever. I told him I was moving back in, and I need to do that. I have to be there for him. At least until he's on solid ground."

"So I'll date my wife for a while. That could be hot." He waggled his brows. "I want Brian to succeed and have a great life. That's why I introduced him to the sponsors from the club and why I asked Blaine and Maverick to give him a chance at a job. I know they'll help him every step of the way, give him a purpose and a future he can count on if he wants it. I don't want to take you away from him, Shauna. I want to be there to walk that path with you, to help you help him."

"But…you don't want your freedom back?"

"Did you hear a word I said?" A playful grin curved his lips. "You're hung up on my looks and my adorable cat, aren't you? We do make it hard to focus."

God she loved him.

"Shauna Zoe Flores, Angel, darlin', you are my first and only ride or die. The only freedom I want is to call you mine every day for the rest of my life." He pushed his hand into his pocket and withdrew her rings. "What do you say, Angel? Want to get swept away with me and forget the divorce?"

Trusting that this big-hearted, beautiful man would never abandon Brian any more than she would, Shauna let down her walls, released the reins, and allowed herself to have the happily ever after Zander had helped her believe she deserved. Her chest was so full, she feared it would burst as she said, "Yes." Then louder, steadier, for him and every man within earshot to hear, she said, "Hell *yes*."

"Fuck yeah!" Zander cheered, and the second he slid the rings onto her finger, he hauled her against him and Kitty, and his mouth covered hers in a spine-tingling kiss.

Catcalls and cheers erupted behind her, someone whistled, and someone else shouted, "Finally!"

Zander broke the kiss long enough to rasp, "I love your crew, but you're *their* Flores. How would you feel about changing your name and being *my* Wicked wife?"

Her heart skipped, but she couldn't help teasing him. "You mean to show the world I belong to a possessive biker with a jealous streak?"

"If the shoe fits."

Oh, it fit all right, and she loved it. "Can I get you a T-shirt that says PROPERTY OF SHAUNA WICKED?"

"Fuck the T-shirt. I'll proudly ink that shit across my chest."

She laughed.

"You think I'm kidding?"

As he lowered his lips to hers again, Mike shouted, "Wait! So all that stuff you said before about this marriage being fake? That was real?"

Shauna's heart raced, her love growing impossibly stronger as she gazed into Zander's eyes and said, "Every last word of it. Contract or no contract, he's stuck with me, because that's how Wickeds roll."

As the crew whooped around them and Kitty purred between them, Shauna tugged Zander down for another kiss, vowing to never let him go again.

Epilogue

THE BLISTERING HEAT of summer had long since given way to the cool breezes of fall, the change of seasons just one more thing Zander had overlooked before his accident. These days he was counting every blessing. It was mid-November, and they were at the Salty Hog for Madigan and Tobias's wedding. The last four months had been a hell of a ride. *Four months, four seasons.* His and Shauna's signs were everywhere. All he had to do was look in the mirror. He was the fourth child in his family, after all. He hadn't known he could fall so hard, but with Shauna he was in a constant state of freefalling deeper and more passionately in love with her by the moment. Love wasn't something he'd looked for, but now it—*she*—was the one thing he lived for.

He looked around the room for his beautiful wife. The rustic restaurant had been transformed into a bohemian dream for Madigan and Tobias. Strings of twinkling lights decorated the wooden beams like stolen stars. White roses and eucalyptus garland spilled from colorful vases, their scent weaving into the hum of voices and the steady beat of the band. Dark Knights had come from near and far, including his cousins from Colorado, Maryland, and Upstate New York. The sea of leather cuts was a familiar, comforting sight. He might have changed, but he was glad some things never would.

"It's a hell of a wedding, isn't it?" Preacher said as he sidled up to Zander with Zeke and their mother in tow.

"I didn't know Tobias knew how to smile like that," Zeke said.

Zander glanced across the room at their new brother-in-law, who looked sharp in a crisp white shirt, black slacks, and a fitted vest. He was talking with his sister, father, and some of Zander's cousins, and he was grinning from ear to ear. "He looks like a man who feels like a king because he's won his queen." Zander knew that feeling well.

"As he should," his mother agreed. She looked beautiful in a floor-length champagne dress.

"I'm really glad he decided to prospect the club," Preacher said.

"He'd better stay safe. I don't want to deal with Madigan's wrath," Zeke joked.

Zander chuckled. Their sister had complained that Tobias joining the club meant she'd forever be outnumbered, but she'd confided in Zander that she was thrilled with his decision. She'd also laid out a threat to each and every one of them, saying if they put Tobias in a situation where he got hurt, they'd have *her* to deal with.

"Our baby girl turned out to be one tough cookie," Preacher said.

"She had to, to survive the likes of these boys," his mother said. "She looks like a boho princess tonight, doesn't she?"

Zander followed her gaze to Madigan, who did look like a princess in her bridal gown with a corset top, off-the-shoulder sleeves that fell in soft layers, and a gauzy skirt with a slit that climbed too high for their father's liking. The white snakeskin boots peeking out from beneath showed off her rebellious side. She was dancing with Shauna and the other bridesmaids. Zander's pulse ratcheted up, like it always did when he saw his wife. Shauna looked like a dream in wine-colored lace, holding Baz and Emerson's three-month-old baby girl, Ashlyn Lockhart Wicked, named for Ashley, and for Emerson's parents, but given a name all her own to conquer this wild world.

"She sure does," he said. "But my wife outshines everyone in this room."

Shauna had cried the day Madigan had asked her to be a bridesmaid and had shocked the hell out of Zander when she'd gone shopping with the girls and had come home with that killer dress that knocked him on his ass. He couldn't believe she'd bought a dress after the way she'd fought him seven months ago. But his confident wife had stayed true to herself, and she was beyond breathtaking with a swooping neckline, fitted bodice, and lace that trailed all the way to the floor. Beneath the sheer lace skirt were sewn-in thigh-skimming shorts with scalloped trim that he got flashes of as she spun. She was fearless, unapologetic, and sexy as hell.

And she was *his*.

"Shauna looks like she's waited her whole life to hold something as precious as that little girl," his mother said. "She was going gaga with the girls over a picture of Silas." Silas, Bear and Crystal's new baby, had been born last week.

"I think that's a nudge toward having grandbabies, Zan," Zeke said.

Zander's heart beat a little faster every time he saw Shauna with one of his nieces or nephews, but he was in no rush to share her, or to bring more responsibility to the woman who'd already carried more than her fair share. "Maybe one day, but she's never had the luxury of just enjoying life…or *me*."

Zeke barked out a laugh. "In no hurry to give up those private pole dances, huh?"

"Zeke," his mother chided.

"He's not wrong, Mom." Zander laughed. "But honestly, I want nothing more than to give her everything she could ever want, and if or when that turns out to be a kid or a pack of them, then so be it."

"You both got new leases on life this year, and you're not the only ones." Zeke nodded at Brian heading for Shauna as she handed Ashlyn to Emerson.

Shauna hadn't been sure how Brian would react when she told him she and Zander were in love, but Brian had surprised them and said he'd known since her birthday. He'd seen it in her eyes on the video call and claimed to have seen the same in Zander's that first time they spent the day together after he got home from rehab. The transition hadn't been easy. Zander made sure she and Brian got time alone, but he couldn't give up starting each day with his dimpled darlin'. He was on their doorstep every morning, coffee in hand—for him and Shauna, and their plus one. The three of them had carved out a new rhythm and had not only developed a great friendship, but a family of three in its own right.

As Brian swept Shauna into a twirl, Aria stepped away from the rest of the girls, and Zeke said, "I'll catch up with you later," and went after her.

Zander had seen him and Aria in a heated discussion earlier, but when he'd asked about it, Zeke had shrugged it off.

"That boy's head is sharp, but his heart? That's where his fire lives," his mother said.

"That's where all of our fires live," Preacher said, pulling her into a kiss. "Speaking of hearts and fire, Alexander, you did the right thing helping Brian."

Brian was working hard at his recovery, attending several meetings each week, working with Saint as his sponsor, and seeing a therapist, and he was doing a fantastic job for Blaine and Maverick. He joined Zander and Shauna at the gym and for outings and barbecues with friends and family and had made a few new friends on his own, too. Shauna had moved back home with Zander six weeks ago, and Brian had moved into a one-bedroom cottage not far from their place. Some mornings he showed up bright and early on their doorstep, three coffees in hand, and Zander and Shauna welcomed it.

"We never should have doubted you," Preacher said.

"I appreciate that. As much as I hated thinking you didn't believe in me, those early doubts made me stronger. You helped me realize how badly I wanted to be there for Shauna, and in turn, for Brian."

"Brian is such a nice young man. We're really proud of him," his mother said. "He's come a long way."

He's not the only one.

Zander had watched his beautiful wife flourish as he and his family walked alongside her and Brian on his recovery journey. But since she'd moved back home, the pieces of their lives had come together even more connected than before, and she'd roared to life like a bike that had finally found an open road.

He looked across the room at her now, taking in the music, the laughter, and the din of family, so happy Shauna had become a part of it. As he headed for the angel who had saved his life, the woman who had changed his world, "Never Stop" came on, the lyrics so perfect, they could have been torn from his soul just for her.

THE LIVELY CELEBRATION had eased into the comfortable hum of an evening nobody wanted to end. Shauna stood by the dance floor with Zander, Brian, and a handful of others, volleying conversations. Brian was arguing with Sid about the best barbecue in town, while Gunner and Zeke tried to stir the pot by telling them both they were wrong. Chloe was leaning against Maverick's side, shaking her head at them, and Madigan was holding court in her wedding gown like the queen she was, commenting on everything. Aria stood beside Zeke, taking it all in, while stealing glances at Blaine and Reese, and Starr and Justice, who were slow dancing by the band.

Emerson sat a few feet away, nursing baby Ashlyn, while Baz stood beside her with Brennan asleep on his shoulder, chatting with his best friend Evie and her fiancé and two of Zander's cousins from Colorado. There were so many people there, Shauna couldn't keep their names straight.

Across the room, Grandpa Mike hovered near the dessert table like a man on a mission, while Ginger and Reba kept eagle eyes on him, ready to swat his hand away. Rosie was sneaking behind them, hoarding cookies for him. Shauna wasn't about to tell Rosie or Grandpa Mike that Ginger and Reba were one step ahead of them. Every dessert on that table was sugar free. They were simply playing a part, so as not to spoil Grandpa's or Rosie's fun, because Grandpa enjoyed sneaking around and Rosie was delighted to be his coconspirator.

That was only one of the many reasons she adored this

family. They didn't try to change people. They accepted them for who they were and watched out for them in ways that would go unnoticed by many. The way they had welcomed her and Brian into their close-knit group warmed her heart. Brian had been cautious at first. Like Shauna, he'd had to learn how to relate to people who wanted to get to know him for no reason other than genuine friendship. It was harder for Brian, being fresh out of rehab. He'd had to learn to trust himself in order to trust others. His therapist was helping, and Zander was as patient and thoughtful with Brian as he'd always been with her. She was proud of Brian. He was taking responsibility for every aspect of his life and working hard to stay on the right side of sobriety. She couldn't be happier to have her first best friend back.

"You think you can outdance me, Con?" Dare Whiskey, one of Zander's many cousins from Colorado, shouted.

"I don't think. I *know*," Conroy said. He handed the adorable toddler he was holding, Leo, to Preacher, and then strutted toward the dance floor.

"Shit, I'll outdance you both!" another cousin called out.

The room erupted into shouts and challenges, and people rushed to the dance floor as the band started playing "Uptown Funk." Within seconds men and women were stomping and spinning, hips shaking, arms waving, with exaggerated flair. The crowd circled them and cheered them on. Kids came running, giggling as they tried to copy the adults' moves.

Lettie burst through the crowd in a pretty green dress, her hands raised. "Move over, old ones. Let me show you how it's done!" Lucas, a teen relative from Colorado, barreled onto the dance floor after her. Blaine pushed through the dancing crowd, planting himself beside Lettie, and stood there, arms crossed, like a freaking bodyguard.

"Let's go!" Madigan hollered, dragging Tobias toward the dance floor, inciting mayhem.

Amid the flurry of excitement, Aria took a step back, and Zeke put an arm protectively around her.

"Let's go, darlin'!" Zander took Shauna's hand, and they followed Brian and the others to the dance floor.

They all danced in a group, acting silly, wiggling their butts, twirling around, and cracking up. Even Blaine and Tank got in on the fun as one song bled into another. They danced until they were all out of breath, and then they made their way to the refreshment table, laughing and joking.

"That looked like fun," Aria said as she and Zeke joined them.

"You should've come with us," Madigan encouraged, sinking back against Tobias, who wrapped his arms around her from behind.

Aria shook her head. "Too wild for me."

"I don't blame you," Shauna said. "That was total chaos."

"Nah. It's just family, darlin'." Zander pulled her in for a kiss.

"Translation for people like us…This is what *normal* families do," Brian said, holding a plate stacked with pigs in a blanket. "It's like getting used to people showing up at your door at six in the morning."

"Or stealing food off your plate," Gunner said, snatching a snack off Brian's plate.

"Dude," Brian complained, but he was beaming.

"I'm starved." Maverick reached over Brian's shoulder to grab one and popped the whole thing into his mouth.

Gunner high-fived him.

Chloe rolled her eyes. "Men. You give them food and they still act like toddlers."

"Toddlers with better facial hair," Maverick said, planting a kiss on Chloe's cheek. He stole another pig in a blanket off Brian's plate. "Thanks, man."

"Don't thank me. Thank Zander," Brian said. "I would have a plate full of sugar if not for him. He's got me watching my macros and working out harder. I swear this guy's got my brain and my body working better."

Shauna leaned into Zander and said, "He's good at taking care of people."

"I've got to admit, Zan, you've become hella responsible," Zeke said.

Zander scoffed. "Don't spread that rumor. You'll ruin my reputation."

"I didn't think I'd live long enough to see Zander domesticated," Aria said sweetly. "I've got to admit, it suits you."

"Domesticated?" Zander scoffed. "You make me sound like a house cat."

"Well, you are kind of a pussy," Gunner said with a snicker, and bumped fists with Tobias.

Aria's cheeks pinked up, a smile tugging at her lips. "I meant a lion or a tiger."

Shauna laughed. "Lion, tiger, *beast*. It doesn't matter what you call him, he'll always be the king of my jungle."

"My girl likes my claws," Zander said with a proud smirk.

"And you like mine." Shauna glanced at Aria and said, "I know how to make him purr."

The guys hooted and laughed, and Zander pulled her into a scorching kiss.

"A'right, you two. Save it for the bedroom," Sid said.

"Now that you've been caged and I don't have to watch your back, what will I do with all my free time?" Zeke said with a mischievous glint in his eyes.

"Take up knitting," Brian suggested, earning chuckles.

"You've already got that grumpy-old-man vibe going on," Gunner added.

"Don't go counting your chickens just yet, Zeke," Zander said, flashing a sexy smirk.

Zeke held his hands up. "Not my circus anymore. Now it's your wife's job to keep you in line."

"I'll gladly take on that job for my hunka hunka burnin' love, but I happen to like his circus," Shauna said, sliding her arm around Zander's waist.

"You tell 'em, darlin'," Zander said.

"Well, you are her husband," Madigan said.

"Some might say, her *property*," Chloe added.

Zander glanced at Shauna with a silent, knowing taunt and said, "Have you been bragging about your man, Angel?"

She grinned. "I might have told them what you did yesterday."

"Jesus, Zan. What the hell did you do now?" Zeke asked.

Zander flashed the wicked grin that sent heat curling low in Shauna's stomach and said, "Just got some new ink." He unbuttoned his shirt and pulled it open with both hands, revealing PROPERTY OF SHAUNA WICKED in fresh, bold script across his chest.

Everyone roared with laughter. Aria shrank back from the noise, tucking herself against Zeke's side, but she was laughing, too, as jokes rang out, and Zander ate it up. When he'd come home yesterday and had shown Shauna the tattoo, she hadn't known whether to laugh or cry. She'd ended up doing both. He was wildly impulsive, but his love knew no boundaries, and she was the luckiest woman in the world to be claimed so fiercely by him.

"Did you tattoo that on him?" Zeke asked Aria.

Aria shrugged, an unstoppable smile egging him on as she turned and walked away, which made everyone laugh harder.

Much later in the evening, as couples mingled and babies slept, Zander led Shauna onto the dance floor and drew her into his arms, his hot, possessive hands holding her close. He brushed his scruff along her cheek, rasping into her ear. "I cannot wait to see that dress on our floor."

Lust coiled low in her belly. She'd never tire of his naughty side. "Funny, I was thinking the same thing about your clothes." Her pulse skipped at the heat in his eyes, and she lowered her voice. "I have a confession to make."

"If it's that you've been thinking about dragging me into the office so I could bend you over the desk, I'm in."

Yes, please.

"What's the confession, darlin'?"

"Um…I'm still thinking about the office." She laughed softly.

He nipped at her lower lip. "Careful, Angel. I've spent all evening watching you slink around in that sexy dress, thinking about tying your wrists to the pole when we get home, so I can play out all the fantasies I've come up with." His hand slid down her back, holding her tight against him as he rasped, "If I take you into that office, I'm going to make you come so hard and scream so loud, everyone in here will be scarred for life."

Her body ignited.

"Ready to confess your sins, sexy girl?"

She tried to force her thoughts away from the enticing picture he'd just painted. She was a little nervous to reveal her secret, but there was no taking it back. "Uh-huh. You know how I said I had to leave early to meet the girls today?"

His brows slanted. "Yeah."

"I wasn't really getting ready for the wedding with them *all* morning. I was getting a surprise for you, and I can't wait to get home to show it to you."

"That sounds promising. Go on."

As they swayed to the slow song, she said, "I might've gotten a tattoo."

"What kind of tattoo?" he asked, low and gruff.

"One that says *Zan's ride or die* with angel wings around it."

He stopped dead, muscles going rigid against her. The feral look in his eyes made her knees weak and her body hum. "Where?" he demanded.

She went up on her toes and whispered, "Someplace only you get to see it."

In the next breath, he was dragging her off the dance floor.

"Where are we going?"

"Office," he gritted out. "I want to see my tattoo."

A little voice told her sneaking off to do dirty things during a wedding reception was wrong, but as he pulled her through the office door and his hot, loving mouth claimed hers, she knew with every beat of her heart that loving Zander Wicked was the rightest, truest thing she'd ever do.

Ready for More Wickeds?

Fall in love with Zeke and Aria in LOVE ME WICKED

Tattooist Aria Bad has mastered the art of hiding in plain sight. Her art is her only safe place. Crowded rooms make her panic. People's eyes burn too hot. Except *his*. Zeke Wicked has been the steady presence she's leaned on since he tutored her through high school. He's a loyal, protective Dark Knight biker, the kind of man who sees everything and the one man who could unravel her without even trying. Every year he takes her to see her family for the holidays, but this year she's harboring a secret and needs to go alone.

Years ago, Zeke swore to protect, and never touch, Aria, but that didn't stop his heart from staking claim to her. Lately she's been secretive and has been pulling away, and now she's determined to make their annual trip without him, but his instincts won't let her go alone. When a storm strands them, boundaries blur and buried feelings rise to the surface, unearthing a passion neither can deny. But as the storm clears, they discover two dangerous truths—one that ties them together and one that threatens to tear them apart.

Have you met the Bradens at Ridgeport?

Fall in love with the hot, wealthy, fiercely loyal, and wickedly naughty, Bradens at Ridgeport and join these business-savvy, pleasure-oriented New Englanders as they fall head over heels with their forever loves. Loaded with heat, humor, and heart, with breathtaking happily ever afters, each book is written to be enjoyed as a standalone romance or as part of the larger series.

Ready for more Dark Knights?

Take a trip to Redemption Ranch in Hope Valley, Colorado, and get to know the Wickeds' cousins the Whiskeys!

The Whiskeys: Dark Knights at Redemption Ranch are a small-town, big-family series of standalone romance novels featuring fiercely loyal, insanely sexy bikers who give horses—and people—a second chance. Buckle up for a wild ride in Hope Valley, CO, as these big-hearted badasses and their sassy sisters wrangle in their forever loves. No cliffhangers, no cheating, and always a happily ever after.

More Books By Melissa Foster

LOVE IN BLOOM BIG-FAMILY ROMANCE COLLECTION

SNOW SISTERS
Sisters in Love
Sisters in Bloom
Sisters in White

THE BRADENS at Weston
Lovers at Heart, Reimagined
Destined for Love
Friendship on Fire
Sea of Love
Bursting with Love
Hearts at Play

THE BRADENS at Trusty
Taken by Love
Fated for Love
Romancing My Love
Flirting with Love
Dreaming of Love
Crashing into Love

THE BRADENS at Peaceful Harbor
Healed by Love
Surrender My Love
River of Love
Crushing on Love
Whisper of Love
Thrill of Love

THE BRADENS & MONTGOMERYS at Pleasant Hill – Oak Falls
Embracing Her Heart
Anything for Love

Trails of Love
Wild Crazy Hearts
Making You Mine
Searching for Love
Hot for Love
Sweet Sexy Heart
Then Came Love
Rocked by Love
Falling for Mr. Bad

THE BRADENS at Ridgeport
Playing Mr. Perfect
Sincerely, Mr. Braden

THE BRADEN NOVELLAS
Promise My Love
Our New Love
Daring Her Love
Story of Love
Love at Last
A Very Braden Christmas

THE REMINGTONS
Game of Love
Stroke of Love
Flames of Love
Slope of Love
Read, Write, Love
Touched by Love

THE RYDERS
Seized by Love
Claimed by Love
Chased by Love
Rescued by Love
Swept Into Love

SEASIDE SUMMERS

Seaside Dreams
Seaside Hearts
Seaside Sunsets
Seaside Secrets
Seaside Nights
Seaside Embrace
Seaside Lovers
Seaside Whispers
Seaside Serenade

BAYSIDE SUMMERS

Bayside Desires
Bayside Passions
Bayside Heat
Bayside Escape
Bayside Romance
Bayside Fantasies

THE STEELES AT SILVER ISLAND

Tempted by Love
My True Love
Caught by Love
Always Her Love
Wild Island Love
Enticing Her Love

THE SILVERS AT SILVER ISLAND

Flirting with Trouble
The Trouble with Flings

THE WHISKEYS: DARK KNIGHTS AT PEACEFUL HARBOR

Tru Blue
Truly, Madly, Whiskey
Driving Whiskey Wild
Wicked Whiskey Love
Mad About Moon

Taming My Whiskey
The Gritty Truth
In for a Penny
Running on Diesel

THE WHISKEYS: DARK KNIGHTS AT REDEMPTION RANCH
The Trouble with Whiskey
Freeing Sully (Prequel to For the Love of Whiskey)
For the Love of Whiskey
A Taste of Whiskey
Love, Lies, and Whiskey
My Whiskey Redemption

THE WICKEDS: DARK KNIGHTS AT BAYSIDE
A Little Bit Wicked
The Wicked Aftermath
Crazy, Wicked Love
The Wicked Truth
His Wicked Ways
Talk Wicked to Me
Irresistibly Wicked
Love Me Wicked

WILD BOYS AFTER DARK
Logan
Heath
Jackson
Cooper

BAD BOYS AFTER DARK
Mick
Dylan
Carson
Brett

SUGAR LAKE
The Real Thing

Only for You
Love Like Ours
Finding My Girl (Graphic Companion Booklet)

HARMONY POINTE
Call Her Mine
This is Love
She Loves Me

SILVER HARBOR
Maybe We Will
Maybe We Should
Maybe We Won't

STANDALONE ROMANTIC COMEDIES
Hot Mess Summer
The Mr. Right Checklist

HARBORSIDE NIGHTS SERIES
Includes characters from the Love in Bloom series
Catching Cassidy
Discovering Delilah (F/F)
Tempting Tristan (M/M)

More Books by Melissa
Chasing Amanda (mystery/suspense)
Come Back to Me (mystery/suspense)
Have No Shame (historical fiction/romance)
Love, Lies & Mystery (3-book bundle)
Megan's Way (literary fiction)
Traces of Kara (psychological thriller)
Where Petals Fall (suspense)

Acknowledgments

I hope you enjoyed Zander and Shauna's story and are looking forward to reading Zeke and Aria's story, *Love Me Wicked*. It promises to be a wild ride.

I have many people to thank for helping me bring Zander and Shauna's story to life. Loads of gratitude go out to EMT Danielle Kirby, paramedic and fire captain John Streeter, my lovely daughter-in-law, Dr. Aurelia Kucera, and registered cardiac invasive specialist Erin Pettazzoni, each of whom patiently answered my endless questions. Many thanks to Becca Mysoor for her plotting help, Jennifer DeJong for "Zan's Angel," and Meghan Tubbs for "Sha Sha."

I'm blessed to have the support of many friends and family members and cannot name them all, but I am grateful for each of you and for my exemplary editorial team: Kristen, Penina, Elaini, Juliette, Lynn, and Justinn.

I am inspired by readers on a daily basis and enjoy chatting about my writing process and my books. If you'd like to get to know me better and haven't joined my Facebook fan club, I hope you will. We have a lot of fun, and members get special sneak peeks of upcoming publications and exclusive giveaways. I hope you'll join me there! Facebook.com/groups/MelissaFoster Fans

Meet Melissa

MelissaFoster.com

Melissa Foster is a *New York Times*, *Wall Street Journal*, and *USA Today* bestselling and award-winning author. Her books have been recommended by *USA Today*'s book blog, *Hagerstown* magazine, *The Patriot*, and several other print venues.

Visit Melissa's online bookstore for exclusive discounts on ebooks, print books, audiobooks, early releases, bundles, and more. Melissa enjoys discussing her books with book clubs and reader groups and welcomes an invitation to your event. Shop.MelissaFoster.com

Melissa also writes sweet romance under the pen name Addison Cole.

www.ingramcontent.com/pod-product-compliance
Lightning Source LLC
Chambersburg PA
CBHW031238310726
48971CB00004B/1075